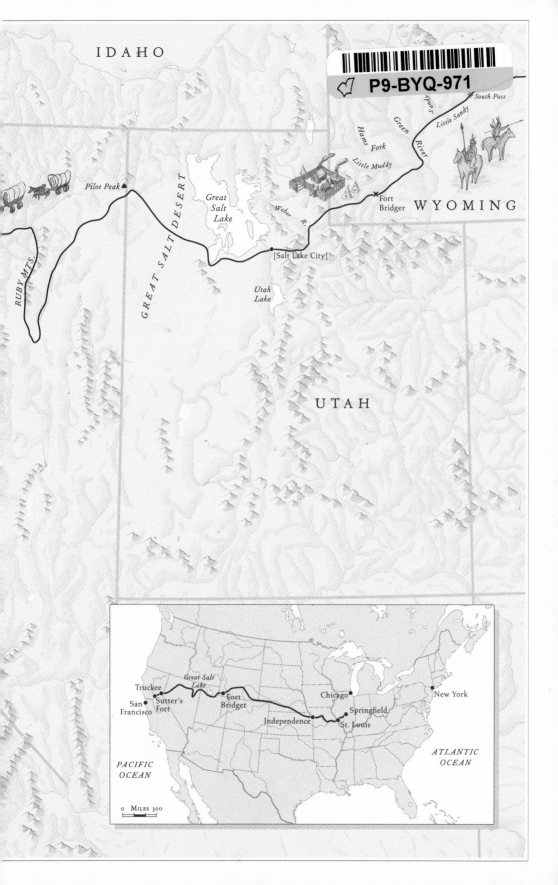

IDAHO

WYOMING

South Pass

Little Sandy

Green River

Hams Fork

Little Muddy

Fort Bridger

Pilot Peak

GREAT SALT DESERT

Great Salt Lake

Weber R.

[Salt Lake City]

RUBY MTS.

Utah Lake

UTAH

P9-BYQ-971

Truckee

San Francisco

Sutter's Fort

Great Salt Lake

Fort Bridger

Chicago

New York

Independence

Springfield

St. Louis

PACIFIC OCEAN

ATLANTIC OCEAN

0   MILES 300

ALSO BY JAMES D. HOUSTON

NONFICTION

Farewell to Manzanar (with Jeanne Wakatsuki Houston) 1973
Three Songs for My Father 1974
Californians 1982
One Can Think About Life After the Fish Is in the Canoe 1985
The Men in My Life 1987
In the Ring of Fire: A Pacific Basin Journey 1997

FICTION

Between Battles 1968
Gig 1969
A Native Son of the Golden West 1971
Continental Drift 1978
Gasoline 1980
Love Life 1985
The Last Paradise 1998

SNOW
MOUNTAIN
PASSAGE

SNOW
MOUNTAIN
PASSAGE

A novel by

James D. Houston

To Bob—
How great to meet again
here in Del Mar—

Jim Houston
May 23, 2001

ALFRED A. KNOPF   NEW YORK   2001

THIS IS A BORZOI BOOK
PUBLISHED BY ALFRED A . KNOPF

Copyright © 2001 by James D. Houston
Endpaper map copyright © 2001 by David Lindroth, Inc.
All rights reserved under International and Pan-American Copyright Conventions.
Published in the United States by Alfred A. Knopf, a division of Random House, Inc.,
New York, and simultaneously in Canada by Random House of Canada Limited, Toronto.
Distributed by Random House, Inc., New York.
www.aaknopf.com

Knopf, Borzoi Books, and the colophon are registered trademarks of Random House, Inc.

Library of Congress Cataloging-in-Publication Data
Houston, James D.
Snow Mountain passage : a novel / by James D. Houston.
p.   cm.
ISBN 0-375-41103-8
1. Donner Party—Fiction.
2. California—History—1846–1850—Fiction.
3. Overland journeys to the Pacific—Fiction.
I. Title.
PS3558.087 S65 2001
813'.54—dc21   00-062009

Manufactured in the United States of America
First Edition

To my father and mother, who brought their dreams to this western shore

Think of America, I told myself this morning. The whole thing. The cities, all the houses, all the people, the coming and going, the coming of children, the going of them, the coming and going of men and death, and life, the movement, the talk, the sound of machinery, the oratory, think of the pain in America and the fear and the deep inward longing of all things alive in America.

—William Saroyan,
in *The Daring Young Man on the Flying Trapeze*

CONTENTS

ACKNOWLEDGMENTS

Remembering Frazier Reed II of San Jose, who generously shared his recollections, and with thanks to the Rockefeller Foundation for a Bellagio residency that made it possible to begin the work

SNOW
MOUNTAIN
PASSAGE

Prologue

from *The Trail Notes of Patty Reed*
Santa Cruz, California
October 1920

Last night I dreamed again about my mother. She was standing in the snow. There were trees with snow-laden branches. She wore a long coat, and her hair hung loose. Her arms reached toward me. She was speaking words I could not hear. I ran through the snow, while her mouth spoke the silent words. I was young, a little girl, and also the age I am now. For a long time I ran toward her with outstretched arms. Finally I was close enough to hear her soft voice say, "You understand that men will always leave you."

I stopped running and in my mind called out to her, "No. It isn't so!"

Her mouth twitched, as if she were about to speak again. She wanted to say, "Listen to me, Patty." She was trying to say it.

I woke up then and spoke aloud. "Women leave you too."

I was speaking right to her, and I waited, expecting to hear her voice in my ear, as if she were close by me in the dark. I whispered, "Don't you remember?"

But she was gone.

I dropped back against my pillow and lay there half the night trying to fall asleep so she would come to me again and speak again. I couldn't sleep. I had started thinking about her life and papa's life and all our lives, about who stays and who leaves who, and when, thinking how a man can be right there next to you and at the same time somehow gone *off by himself, or maybe already gone away forever, how a mother can do that too, thinking then about all of them from those years so long ago, walking in and out of my mind like people in a pageant, ordinary people who did not expect such a crowd to be watching them pass by, papa and mama, my brothers and sister, the teamsters and mule skinners and grizzled husbands on their dried-up wagon seats and their women watching the trail ahead and the Indians who traveled with us from time to time, every kind of Indian you can think of, Sauk and Delaware and Sioux and Shoshone and Paiute and Washo and Miwok, along with all the others we met by accident on the way, though when you look back it seems anything but accidental.*

Now, this morning, from my porch I watch the road that runs beside the lagoon and down to the beach. Between the beach and this lagoon there is a rail line that follows the sand. It's an odd sight. Hundreds of pilings support the track, like a centipede walking from town to town along the shoreline. Beyond the sand the water's edge today is quiet, like a lake. Beyond the beach, beyond the rail line, the Pacific Ocean spreads and spreads.

When I was a girl there were no trains anywhere yet out here. When we came through the mountains there was hardly any trail. Where the train cuts through the Sierra Nevada now, we made that trail. What a long road we have followed. And it has finally brought me here, to yet another house, where I have become another old woman looking out, looking back.

The ocean I see is not what we came searching for. The farthest border of the land was not our goal, but the land itself. I should say, <u>his</u> goal—the farthest land my father could envision, where he would somehow be his own man at last or be a new man in some new way and have a hand in starting something fresh and bigger than himself. I am not saying this is how it turned out. But these were his dreams. He was a dreamer, as they all were then, dreaming and scheming, never content, and we were all drawn along in the wagon behind the dreamer, drawn along in the dusty wake.

When you are eight years old, of course, you worship your father, as I worshipped mine. We trusted him to get us through these situations no one could have prophesied ahead of time. As long as he was riding beside the wagon on his precious mare, we figured nothing could go too far wrong. That's how tall he was in my eyes then.

Seventy years and more go by, and everything looks different. I look at where the dreaming led papa, and led us, and I cannot excuse him as I could when I was eight, or eighteen, or even twenty-eight. Yet neither is it my place to judge him, as others have, or judge the way he contended with the trials of that crossing. Some have blamed him entirely, and blame him even now, after all this time, since he was the one who had organized the journey out of Springfield in the first place. Donner, of course, is the name that stuck, the one they have named the lake for and the route through the mountains and the monument that stands beside the route, with its brave-eyed family cast in bronze atop a pedestal raised as high as the snow that year was deep.

Maybe it has been a blessing, in the end, since the name itself causes a shroud to fall around the one who utters it, having become a synonym for disaster, poor planning, and savage behavior that makes the average person shudder and also salivate for the gruesome details of what went on. I have read stories and articles of what happened during that hateful winter until I am sick to death. Newspaper reporters and photographers still come around here to hound and pester me as if the only thing I ever did my entire life was spend five months in the snow. And yet, with all these books and diaries and endless accounts and semi-truths and outright fantasies that have spread around the world, the story of our family has been only partly told, and the story of my father. I have had a hand in that, I admit. Like a good daughter I have tried through the years to paint him as a hero, even when I knew better. And I do not apologize one bit. Why should I? He did some things almost anyone could call heroic. But now that there's only me and the last few others still alive, there's no harm saying he did other things that gathered enemies to him like an open jar of jam will gather ants and blowflies, and this cannot be denied.

You take his wagon—a good example of what I'm talking about. Did he foresee that it would be the biggest contraption on the western trail? Did he foresee that his children would be envied and pursued by others hoping for the chance to ride along and test the springs in the fancy seats? Did it occur to him that other men would laugh behind his back, calling it ingenious, but also grandiose, while women would resent his wife for traveling as if she were some kind of Arabian princess?

"If they'd have thought of it," I once heard papa say in his own defense, "they'd all be riding along like this."

Prologue

It takes you half a lifetime to figure out what your folks were really up to when you were young. Eventually you come to know them and what they were capable of. You get to be my age, their very natures lurk within your own, as year by year more and more of who they were is revealed to you. Some things I never heard my mother say with her living voice, I hear her saying now, her voice alive somewhere within me. Her face visible somewhere in my face. I look in the mirror. I say, There's mama. There's papa.

Sometimes very early, before it gets light, I will still see him the way he looked the day we left Illinois. In his face I see true pleasure and a boyish gleam that meant his joy of life was running at the full. I see him with his hat tipped back, standing by the wagon he designed himself, the one other travelers would come to call the Palace Car. Everyone else who started west had been content with horses, mules, oxcarts, Conestogas. But not James Frazier Reed. A double-decker Palace Car that took four yoke to pull it, with upholstered seats inside, and a thoroughbred racing mare, and hired hands, and brandy after dinner—that was papa's vision of being a pioneer. At least, when we started out it was. I have to say this for him, his vision was not like anyone else's I have heard of.

PART ONE

CROSSING

Somewhere in Nebraska

June 1846

They have been following the sandy borders of the Platte through level country that changes little from day to day, an undulating sea of grasses broken here and there by clumps of trees along the river. Jim Reed likes it best in late afternoon, the low sun giving texture to the land, giving each hump and ripple its shadow and its shape, while the river turns to gold, a broad molten corridor.

He likes being alone at this time of day, with the mare under him. He wears a wide-brim hat, a loose shirt of brown muslin, a kerchief knotted around his neck. His trousers are stuffed into high leather boots, and his rifle lies across the saddle. He has been scouting ahead, in search of game, and now, as he takes his time returning, his reverie is interrupted by the sight of another rider heading toward the wagons. As the man and horse draw nearer, Reed recognizes him and calls out.

"Mr. Keseberg!"

The German is not going to stop, so Jim overtakes him.

"Keseberg, hold on! What are you carrying there?"

"Something for my wife, to help her sleep a little easier."

Jim rides in closer. Two shaggy hides are heaped across the pommel. "Looks like buffalo."

"Indeed it is."

Jim has not seen a buffalo for several days. Keseberg isn't much of a shot, in any event, nor could he have skinned a creature for its hide, even had he somehow brought one down.

"May I ask where it comes from?"

"This was a gift."

"A gift?"

"From a dead Indian. The best Indian is a dead Indian. Isn't that what you Americans say?"

Keseberg seems to think this is funny. His mouth spreads in a boastful grin.

"Some say that. I do not."

"But surely you will agree that these are fine specimens."

Keseberg is a handsome fellow, with penetrating blue eyes and a full head of blond hair that hangs to his collar. Knowing that he crossed the ocean less than two years ago, Jim is willing to make allowances. He wants to get along with this man, though he does not like him much. They will all need one another sooner or later.

"Have you had much experience with Indians, Keseberg?"

"As little as possible."

"If these robes come from a funeral scaffold, you'd better put them back."

His smile turns insolent. "So you can ride out later and take them for yourself?"

"When I want a buffalo robe I will trade for it, not steal it."

"And in the meantime you would leave these out here to rot in the sun and in the rain."

This remark seems to please Keseberg. His face is set, as if all his honor is at stake and he has just made a telling point. Clearly he has no idea what he has done, nor does he care.

Jim looks off toward the circle of wagons, which are drawn up for the night about a quarter mile away. He does not see himself as a superstitious man. He sees himself as a practical man. Stealing robes from a funeral scaffold is simply foolish for anyone to try, given all they've heard about the Sioux. It nettles him; it riles him. He does not like being snared in another man's foolishness.

Near the wagons he sees animals grazing, children running loose, burning off the day's stored restlessness. Women hunker at the cooking fires. His wife will soon be laying out a tablecloth wherever she can find a patch of grass. "We're going to stay civilized," she will say to someone, once or twice a day, "no matter how far into the wilderness we may wander."

Such a poignant scene it is, and all endangered now by the thoughtless greed of this fellow who pulled up to the rear of the party on just such an evening and asked if he could travel with them. George Donner had met the man briefly in St. Louis before they crossed the Mississippi. At the time Jim had no reason to protest. Keseberg is young and fit, somewhere in his early thirties, and he is not a drifter or a desperado as some of the younger, single riders have turned out to be. He looks prosperous enough. He has two full wagons, one driven by a hired man. He has six yoke of oxen, two children, a pretty wife. She can barely speak English, but Keseberg speaks quite well for one so recently arrived. He is something of a scholar, too, knows four languages in all, or so he claims. The other German travelers have welcomed him, and so has Donner, whose parents come from Germany. Jim has never had any trouble with Germans. But he sees now that he is going to have trouble being civil to Keseberg. Rumors have been circulating that he beats his wife. This is why she wears so many scarves and bonnets, Margaret whispers, even on the warmest days. Jim shrugged this off at first. Now he wonders. Into Keseberg's eyes has come a look that seems to say he is capable of such things. Defiant. Selfish.

"Mr. Keseberg, these robes are not yours to keep."

"Nonsense," he says.

Jim's color rises. "They *have* to be returned!"

With sudden gaiety that could be a form of mockery, Keseberg says, "My God, man! The sun is going down! The day is done! My dinner will be waiting!"

He gallops away toward the wagons, sitting tall, as if he is a show rider in a circus troupe.

By the time Jim catches up to him, Keseberg has dismounted and is holding high one of the long robes for his wife to see, speaking endearments in German as he presents her with this gift, for his sweet one, the companion of his heart, for his dearest Phillipine. In front of her he has turned boyish, a schoolboy bringing something home for his mother, and she is smoothing down her skirt with nervous hands, as if preparing to throw this robe around her shoulders. She wears a bonnet, though the sun has nearly set, and she wears a scarf wrapped around her neck, while above the scarf her cheeks are flushed with happiness.

Half a dozen emigrants from other wagons have stopped whatever they were doing to watch, and you might think a fiddler has just touched bow to string and these two are about to dance the prairie jig wrapped together in a buffalo robe. She is like a girl at a dance. He is laughing a wild, high, adolescent laugh, as Reed climbs off the mare.

"Keseberg, you idiot!"

Turning to the small circle of observers, with his hands thrown wide, Keseberg says, "Why is this man calling me a criminal?"

"You *are* a criminal! Dammit, man. If the Sioux come after us, you and I will be killed, our wives will be taken, our children too!"

He is shouting. His eyes are wide and fierce.

Someone calls out, "Hey Jim, what's got into you?"

"These are burial robes! But Keseberg thinks they belong to him!"

"Better him than the Indians," one fellow says.

"Haw haw," laughs another.

"I don't know," says a third. "Wouldn't mess with them Sioux."

"Me neither," says someone else. "Ain't worth no buffalo skins."

"I wouldn't mind pickin' off a brave or two," the first fellow says. "Whatta we got rifles for?"

"I think Jim is right. Maybe you'd pick off a few, but you wouldn't live to tell the story. Any way you look at it, we'd be outnumbered a hundred to one, and don't you think otherwise. It ain't worth it. I'd get rid a them hides right now."

A dozen more have joined the circle, and the commentary spreads into a noisy debate. Some envy Keseberg's trophies and are content to stand feasting their eyes on his handsome wife, imagining how she will look inside the wagon relaxing on these soft, seductive robes. Others grasp the full weight of this predicament, among them George Donner, an elder in the party, with the look of a patriarch, his face wide, his jaw firm, his hair silver. Though often regarded as a leader, he lacks Jim's eagerness to take command.

Donner listens a while, then looks at Keseberg. Quietly he says, "Jim is right. You ought to do what he says, Lewis, and the sooner the better."

Now Keseberg cannot look at his wife, who has been mystified by all the turmoil, her eyes darting wildly from voice to voice. She understands enough to fear that her new possession will soon be taken from her, and she clutches the robe to her chest. For the German this is very hard medicine, but he respects George Donner. "All right," he says. "All right. I will do it first thing in the morning."

Jim says, "We'd better do it now."

Keseberg puffs out his chest and begins to prance back and forth, slamming a fist into his palm, *pop pop pop,* as if he has been condemned to the firing squad and has now been denied his final request.

"And I'll go with you."

"I said I'd do it!" Keseberg cries. "My word is good!"

Jim says, "You'll need someone to hold your horse."

On the ride out, Keseberg refuses to speak. The sun is setting as they come upon the scaffold, about a mile from the wagons and near the bank of a small creek winding toward the Platte. There are other signs of recent encampment, ashes, close-cropped grass. The scaffold is made of four slender poles stuck into the earth, supporting a platform of woven branches lashed with thong. Laid out upon the platform are the remains of a chief. Feathers fall against his black hair. His shield and lance are with him. On the bare soil beneath the scaffold, bleached buffalo skulls are arranged in a circle.

As the two men sit on horseback regarding the corpse, the wind around them gradually falls off. Across the prairie Jim can see wind moving, but right here the nearest grass is still. The surface of the creek is slick and motionless. The sky is suddenly sprayed with crimson, while underneath its gaudy panorama, the space in front of them seems lit by some separate and brighter column of afterglow. On his arms the hairs rise. Under him he feels the mare tremble.

He instructs Keseberg to wrap the robes across the corpse exactly as he found them, to duplicate the look as closely as he can. As he watches, holding both sets of reins, the horses begin to twitch and rear, as if another animal is nearby. Jim squints toward a grove downstream, sees nothing.

All four are eager to get away from there, the men and the horses. As they lope toward the wagons, Keseberg still won't speak. At last Jim says, "Before we set out tomorrow I'll call a meeting of the council. I'm going to propose that you be expelled from the party."

He waits. When he hears no reply he turns and sees the blue eyes inspecting him with scorn.

"You have put the lives of everyone at risk. But we may be less at risk if you fall back. Do you understand my meaning?"

Keseberg's voice is low and harsh. "I have never been spoken to like this."

"Well, I am speaking to you like this. I know George Donner will support me. You can resist, if you choose, but I assure you that others on the council will agree. In this wagon party you are no longer welcome."

"You are going too far," says Keseberg.

"Maybe you'd rather leave tonight and avoid an embarrassment. It's your choice."

"I believe in discipline, Mr. Reed. But you have gone too far."

In a dramatic burst of horsemanship, Keseberg spurs ahead, kicking up a long plume of dust. Jim gives him plenty of room, lingering in the twilight, to let the dust plume settle, and let his own blood cool down.

A FEW MORE minutes pass. From the deep grass beyond the clearing, a Sioux brave sits up on his haunches and watches them ride away. He wears a buckskin tunic, arrows in a quiver. He creeps close enough to touch the robes and sniff around the edges. There is a faint white smell. Nothing has been cut or marked. He has never seen such a thing. If the Pawnee had stolen these robes, they would never bring them back. They steal for the insult. They scatter the skulls and throw the body down and defile it.

Who are these men? He could have killed them both and taken their scalps, first the one who held the horses, then the bright-haired one whose scalp would be highly prized. He could have gone back with the scalps and reported that he had found the thieves. But now they have returned the robes. Why? It is very strange. What kind of people would do this, take away the buffalo skins, then bring them back?

When he can no longer see the men, he stands for a long time listening. Voices come toward him on the wind, distant sounds of women and children. In the near-dark their fires light the sky. It is a village. A village of tents that move. All day he watched them passing along in their white tents. Between one rising and setting of the sun he has seen four villages of white tents, and many horses and many animals like the buffalo, with sharp horns, and men who drive the animals but do not shoot them, though some carry rifles. Are they warriors? They do not have the look of warriors.

Where do they come from? Where are they going?

Lover, Husband, Father, Son

His hair is thick and black and parted right of center. He wears a black moustache and beard. His skin is very white, from the collar down, from the wrists up, where it isn't burnt by the sun. He has what they call the Black Irish look, meaning features common to the British Isles that have acquired a faintly Hispanic or Slavic line. According to the family legend Jim Reed has Polish in his blood.

"We were nobility in Poland," he has told his children. "It puts fire in the eyes, you know. We had stables filled with horses there, a large estate with gardens, rows of poplar trees. We drank French wines and ate imported cheeses. We came across to Ireland, oh, it's hard to say for certain, some time back, late in the eighteenth century or thereabouts, so I've been told, rather than submit to the tyranny of the Russians, who wanted to take it all away, not only our lands and all our animals, but our dignity too. Be proud of that," he has told them. "Be proud to move when it is time to move."

He barely knew his father. A fever took him when Jim was three. Ever afterward he has had a fear of fevers, and a fascination too. The excessive color that comes into the face to announce that the body is overtaxed, putting up resistance—this is a signal for alarm, and also a sign of life working overtime to declare itself. All her days his mother had a feverish complexion, whether ill or healthy, a brimming color that gave her a look of passionate restraint.

Jim does not remember Ireland at all. But he remembers the Atlantic, the stormy crossing, nights of bitter wind and slashing rain and mountainous seas. His mother, who he thought was indestructible, fell sick and couldn't eat. She was a small Scottish woman with dark hair and dark eyes and a sturdy Presbyterian spine. With her husband gone she had sailed for the States, as half her relatives had already done, to start another life, just her and the son.

On the packet out of Ulster he was surprised to find himself holding her hands, touching her beaded brow, running for buckets. He watched his mother groan in the dim, dingy, claustrophobic bunk, terrified that she too would die and he would be left alone on the lunging ship. She clutched his hand, as if she had the same fear, as if without his hand she would slide overboard. He held her close and said, "When we get to America you'll feel better, ma, I know you will."

IN THOSE DAYS the land that had called them was the youngest nation on earth. Jim Reed grew up as the nation grew, later on he would move as the nation moved. From Boston they traveled to Baltimore, then to Philadelphia, and from there down into Virginia. A lean and restless fellow, he finally struck out on his own and landed in Illinois, where he fell in love with a feverish woman.

She was a recent widow whose husband had lost his life when cholera came creeping up the long, humid Mississippi valley like an invisible cloud. Margaret was her name. She was only twenty. The untimely death left her bedridden for weeks, like a wounded cat lying still, waiting to heal. During the season of her mourning Jim would keep the widow company. He knew her family, had often been a Sunday dinner guest. Next to her he felt a brotherly kinship, sometimes a fatherly kinship. At thirty-four he felt protective. He brought her books to read. They talked about her health and her parents and her brothers and other people in the town and whether or not she would go back to teaching school, which she had done for half a year, until her daughter came along.

As Margaret's strength returned, they would take short walks, and he would carry little Virginia on his shoulders, tickle her ankles and make her laugh. Once they all rode in a carriage out to his land, and he described the house and barns he planned to build. Neither of them would ever be able to say precisely when consoling turned to courtship, when one form of intimacy led to the next. Margaret had large, watchful eyes and walnut hair that hung in curls beside her cheeks. She was lying on her bed in a robe and running a fever on the day he took her hand and asked her to marry him.

"Maybe we should wait," she said, "until I am entirely back on my feet." Her face was glowing, pink and moist and vulnerable.

"No," he said, his eyes wide with eagerness and desire. "We mustn't wait. I want to marry as soon as we possibly can."

He leaned to kiss her, and she turned aside, as if to say, *Whatever has afflicted me might be contagious.* He touched her chin and brought her face around and placed his lips upon hers, as if to say, *I have no fear of it, my love is so much larger than my fear.* She allowed it then, she allowed the kiss. She allowed his eager hand to touch her neck, to slide across her shoulder and push the cotton robe aside, to roam the pale and lustrous flesh. Her eyes opened as if for the first time, as if she were new on earth, and regarded him as if he were the first creature she had seen. He had never observed eyes at such close range. Threads of light glinted around the small, dark centers. Her arms opened. Falling back against the pillow she drew him into her circle of heat. She whispered his name and seemed to swoon, with a little moan, barely audible. Jim swooned too, as her lips melted into his, as she surrendered her mouth and the sweet tips of moisture all around her mouth.

IN TIME HER fever subsided. But other ailments followed, one upon the next. While she ran her household wisely, neighbor women called her "frail." Ten years and three children later, when she and Jim began to dream of moving farther west, she suffered from headaches that could cripple her once or twice a month. Whether the cause was a lingering grief, or the stresses of childbirth, or some irritant rising from the soil or drifting down from the trees or from the spore-generating coats of animals, no one could tell. Her headaches became a mystery often wondered at, never solved.

On the days of her confinement, after the worst had passed, he would read aloud from books and articles he had collected about the distant shoreline and the western trail. She would lie back and listen, as if to folktales of ancient and improbable events. He read from Thomas Farnham, from John Bidwell's diary, from the accounts of Captain Fremont's second expedition. He read from *The Emigrants' Guide,* by Lansford Hastings.

"Close your eyes," he said to Margaret, turning down the corner of a page so he could come back to these lines and study them. "Just close your eyes and picture this."

The purity of the atmosphere is most extraordinary and almost incredible. So pure it is that flesh of any kind can be hung for weeks together, in the open air, and that, too, in the summer season, without undergoing putrefaction. The Californians prepare their meat for food, as a general thing, in this manner; in doing so, no salt is required, yet it is sometimes used, as a matter of preference. The best evidence, however, of the superior health of this country is the fact that disease of any kind is very seldom known. Cases of fever of any kind have seldom been known anywhere on the coast. . . .
All foreigners with whom I have conversed upon this subject, and who reside in that country, are unanimous and confident in the expression of the belief that it is one of the most healthy portions of the world.

He looked up from the page and saw that this passage had revived her. She was gazing at him with amusement. In her eyes he saw a playful doubt. "Can there really be such a place? Do you think it's possible?"

"This Hastings is no fly-by-night. He's a lawyer from Ohio. His book was published in Cincinnati."

She laughed like a child delighted by a nonsense rhyme. "People say outlandish things in books, James."

"But he has been there. He has been there twice. He led one of the first emigrant parties. He has visited all the principal towns. Think what it could mean! A place without fevers. Without mosquitoes. Or malaria. In our county alone, how many have died of malaria since the last rains?"

"It's something to think about, all right."

Now he sounded like an attorney arguing a case. "I can't see that he makes any claim for himself. He isn't trying to persuade us to invest money in some far-fetched scheme. He describes what he has seen. Why would anyone lie about matters of health and well-being?"

"Well, yes," said Margaret, sitting up on the couch. "And when you think of it, what would be the point?"

"There you have it! There wouldn't *be* any point. You see what I am trying to say? Suppose we could travel to a place where you would never have another headache? Isn't that worth considering? I am just thinking out loud. . . ."

"What else does it say, James? What does it say about the towns?"

He read some more. He read accounts of places called Sonoma, Yerba Buena, San Jose de Guadalupe, Santa Barbara—all free of pestilence, surrounded with pasturelands and sunny valleys where anything would grow. There were harbors and vineyards and limitless supplies of water, and this was not ancient history or some half-cocked brand of wishful yearning. Weren't these things Lansford Hastings had seen within the past three years? Jim read some more:

A great variety of wild fruits also abound, among which are crab-apples, thorn-apples, plums, grapes, strawberries, cranberries, whortle-berries, and a variety of cherries. The strawberries are extremely abundant, and they are the largest and most delicious that I have ever seen, much larger than the largest which we see in the States.

It sounded too good to be true. But Jim and Margaret wanted it to be true. They wanted to believe such a place could exist somewhere on Earth. They told themselves that of course getting there would take a bit of work. If getting there were easy, well, wouldn't such a place have long ago been overrun?

And so they talked themselves into it, little by little, though Jim did most of the talking. He had a rising lust for this journey, this pilgrimage, while Margaret could not suppress the hundred doubts that soon sprang up to hover around the plan. What about the house? What about the furniture? The children? Their schooling? What about the many friends and relatives we leave behind? What if we need a physician out there?

Jim listened. He made promises. He made lists. He collected maps and articles from newspapers in St. Louis. He wrote to merchants for advice on what to bring and what to buy en route. He conferred with George and Jacob Donner, farmers in Springfield, prosperous men, like him, and past the time in life when you set out to make a new mark in the world. They had no real reason to leave their fields and holdings, yet they too were willing to make the leap. High risk was in the air. High stakes. High promises. Jacob Donner, in poor health and pushing sixty, was ready to gamble on the outside chance that he could find a land free of arthritis, kidney stones, and hot sweats in the middle of the night. His brother, George, liked to pontificate about "larger opportunities," quoting James Polk, who had said in his inaugural address that our dominant place in the Far West was only a matter of time. Britain was about ready to let go of the Oregon Territory and cede it to the United States. California surely would be next, according to the president, who had advised Mexico, for its own good, to get out of the way.

These Illinois men felt history gathering like a wind, like a river current that could not be resisted, and upon it they would be borne west like gamblers on a riverboat—though they would not be traveling as so many gamblers before them had, in the singular, as men alone.

Jim Reed knew all the famous tales of trappers and explorers setting out for the farther shore. Meriwether Lewis. Kit Carson. Lansford Hastings. Jedediah Smith. As a younger man he had known that kind of itch. The Mississippi was about as far west as he could have imagined at the time, the last frontier, they said, before you stepped off into Indian Territory. He had crossed the Alleghenies to the Ohio and worked barges to the mouth, then started up the valley of the Mississippi, talking to settlers, getting the lay of the fertile land, on past St. Louis, where they still spoke French, until he reached Illinois and found a job in the lead mines. It was dirty and dangerous. Every day or so a man passed out from poisons in the air. But Jim lasted long enough to get some money ahead, and he moved again, to Springfield, in the middle of the state, where the land was richer, where he leased himself a farm and found a wife.

He was feeling it again, that itch, that hunger to move, but it was not a young man's hunger now. He did not imagine setting out alone, to push ahead and stake a claim. He was a husband and a householder. He saw them all together on the long trail west. It was a husband's dream. A father's dream. He imagined them arriving in California together, as a clan. Already he saw the house, the rolling acreage, his sons and daughters galloping home in time for dinner.

One by one he took them aside, to explain the plan and where they would be going. The man who had never known his father had become the father of four. He spoke first to the boys, because they would be easy, too young yet to make demands—James Junior was five, Tommy three. The girls, he knew, would want to negotiate. Virginia was nearly thirteen, slender and pretty and good in school. He figured, rightly, that she would let her classes go for a while and agree to almost anything if he promised her a new pony. He leaned toward her to savor the kiss, as she threw her arms around his neck. He told her they would ride together across the plains, with the wind in their hair and herds of buffalo thundering in the distance.

He could not foresee what his younger daughter would want or say. She was a mystery to him, and thus his favorite, their first child together, his firstborn and named for his mother, Martha Jane, though everyone called her Patty. From infancy she'd had a bold look, as if wise beyond her years. "A sage," said Margaret's mother, when Patty was still in the crib. "This child's bound to be a sage, or a fortune-teller. Over in Virginia where we come from, I once saw a child had a look like this from an early age, and she had second sight."

Patty was eight and already seemed to be a very small adult. She had the thin, light bones of a bird, so light she appeared to defy gravity when she walked, as if floating, as if about to take flight. Her black eyes could look right through you. They looked through Jim, as he told her about the journey they would all soon undertake. She watched his face as if he were the one who needed to be taken aside and spoken to.

When he finished, she said, "Then, papa, I will want a very good pair of leather boots."

"And of course you shall have them, darlin'."

"I will need them to keep up with mama."

"Oh, you will all be riding in the wagon, you know. Just wait until you see what I have planned."

"I mean after that."

"After what?" said Jim, watching her brow furrow above the cryptic smile he never quite understood.

AS THE FALL of 1845 turned to winter, as pendulous skies lowered upon the valley of the Mississippi and the ground froze, the meadow-lands and villages along the Pacific coast grew sunnier and sunnier in the mind, and Jim carefully plotted the months ahead. He would bring cattle for milk and meat, and dogs for company, and keep a dozen oxen in reserve. There would be books for his children and medicine for Margaret and a bit of good brandy for himself. There would be two wagons to haul supplies and furniture, the flour and the lard, coffee and sugar and tools and cloth and spare parts and bullets, with hired hands to work the teams. A third wagon would be for the family, and he stayed close to his carpenters, making sure they got it right.

He was not going to be bound by what the average traveler expected a wagon to look like. He saw an opening you would enter from the side, through a swinging door, and step up into a sitting room with throw rugs, and with chests along the walls, and spring-cushion seats like a railroad car. There would be mirrors, and a woodstove with a chimney pipe rising through the roof, and drawers for books, and compartments for sewing gear. Built up on posts there would be a second level, with comforters and blankets and pillows. It would be a home away from home, a rolling parlor with sleeping loft attached. With a gang of restless children and an ailing wife who needed her daily rest, what better way to move across the plains and through the mountains? A man alone on horseback might make it in sixty days or so. A family, a household, could take four months, or five. What was the point of rumbling along like gypsies if you didn't need to?

Before they set out, the huge rig was much admired in the town. "My Lord, Jim Reed," said his neighbor's wife, "ain't nobody gonna hold a candle up to *you*!"

AFTER THE BUFFALO robes were returned, word quickly spread from wagon to wagon. The next morning, hearing that Lewis Keseberg pulled out before daylight, some said good riddance. Others were sorry to see him leave. They liked his wife, her ready smile, her raisin cookies. They hoped that in the long caravan of emigrants, some other party might find a way to take them in. Around the breakfast fires they wagged their heads, saying Reed did what had to be done. And yet some wondered about the way he did it.

"Like he's a colonel," said a farmer from Iowa, an Irishman named Patrick Breen, "and we are all his troops. But we are not an army regiment now, are we? We're just common folks trying to get from here to there, and you ought not to order a person out of the wagon party as if he has traded secrets to the enemy."

"Well," said his wife, sipping at her coffee, "what else do you expect from him who drives a wagon so big it takes a whole herd of cattle to pull it along? He thinks a lot of himself, this Mister James Reed. Who is he, anyhow?"

"He's bringing more animals than most anybody else, I know that much."

"Does it mean he has to have carpets inside and fancy chairs fixed up like a banquet hall?"

"I ain't worried about his wagon," said their nearly grown son, whose job it was to keep an eye on the family mules. "I'm still thinking about them Sioux. Ol' Keseberg leaving doesn't mean we get off scot-free."

Breen and his wife exchanged grave looks, their eyes asking, *Yes, what about them Sioux?*

All along the line, as fires were kicked out, and the teams hitched up for another dusty, plodding day, this was the first question in the air. Can Indians really tell one white from another? They might still come swooping down upon us for revenge. Double the guard, then. Stay close together. Keep the children inside, and keep the weapons loaded.

Such talk went on all day and into dinnertime. Late that night, Breen the Irishman sprang awake at a sound out of the darkness, certain his worst prairie dream was coming true at last, a merciless assault and massacre that would leave them all in pools of blood while the wagons burned. He listened for an hour. But the fearful noise, whatever it had been, was drawn back into the throat of the night, swallowed by silence, and the next morning the wagon train set out once again across the world of endless grasses, under a vast sky piled with clouds.

On a good day, over level ground, if they had no creeks to ford or rain to turn the trail to mud, they could make twenty miles. After a week of good days had passed, with the chief's scaffold far behind them, the fears of reprisal dwindled. They could think again of what lay ahead, what they would buy when they reached Fort Laramie, what equipment needed repair, which route they would follow once they moved past the fort and toward South Pass, where streams and rivers stopped running east across the continent and began to flow the other way.

Somewhere in Nevada

OCTOBER 1846

They had rolled out of Springfield with three families and nine wagons among them. Two months later they were forty wagons and twenty families plus the single men on horseback. There were companies ahead of them and others strung away behind them, strung for a hundred miles across the prairie, or so they'd heard. There'd never been anything like it. A thousand families for their thousand reasons had all decided to set out on the same trail in the same season, heading in the same direction. Before long the whole damn country will be on the move, they would say to one another during the nights of waiting for the next day's sun.

And yet the farther west they moved, the less they heard this kind of talk. As the weeks passed, patience wore thin. The hopes wore thin. The less they could agree among themselves on where they were going, or why, or which route to follow, or what they had in mind. They squabbled, and they subdivided. Wagon parties broke up and recombined. At the news that war had finally been declared with Mexico, rumors leaped from wagon to wagon, from fire to fire.

"I hear Mexicans are armed to the teeth," one fellow said, "and waiting for us at the border."

"Nonsense," said another. "There ain't no border."

"Well," said someone else, "if you was a Mexican in the middle of a war, would you just sit there and let a whole damn wagon train come rumbling into town?"

Some who'd been bound for California changed their minds, joined up with parties bound for Oregon, heading farther north until the smoke cleared. Some families who'd been waiting for any honorable excuse to give it up turned around and went back home. Others closed their ears to all such news but split off anyway, just for meanness, or for peace of mind, and traveled on their own a while. Some teamed up with total strangers, as Lewis Keseberg had done, falling back to linger on the trail until another band of travelers took him in.

Three weeks went by, and one evening there he was again, with his wife and children and wagons and all his animals, camped at the end of the Donner-Reed train as if he'd never left.

This time a council meeting was called. A vote was taken, and forgiveness carried the day. "I have paid for my crimes," said Keseberg in his own behalf, "whatever they were." His blue eyes looked penitent and sincere. "As for the Sioux, aren't they long forgotten now?"

"But why travel with us?" said Jim, who still mistrusted him.

"My wife has friends here. She misses her friends."

Jim saw more trouble coming. Afterward he regretted that he'd held his tongue that day. In hindsight, of course, it would be easy to see all the signs and portents. At the time, he let himself be persuaded by the eyes of Keseberg's pretty wife, shining with reunion, though she still wore a bonnet after sundown and wrapped her neck in scarves.

NOW THREE MORE months have passed. The lead parties in the long transcontinental parade have finally reached Oregon and the Willamette Valley or crossed the Sierra Nevada and arrived at Sutter's Fort and heard the news of the Bear Flag Revolt at Sonoma and the raising of the Stars and Stripes over the field of horned skulls and abandoned cattle bones that fill the plaza there. They have fanned out north and south into the Sacramento Valley or floated down the river toward the little town of Yerba Buena, where U.S. warships wait offshore, at the edge of San Francisco Bay.

Jim had hoped his wagons would be among the earliest. He once imagined appearing outside Sutter's Fort like Hannibal emerging from the Alps, with his herds and his handsome children and his wife dressed in the highest fashion of the day, and his letter of introduction from the governor of Illinois. But it hasn't turned out that way. He did not foresee that he would end up leading such a motley and cantankerous band, with their weapons and aggravations and rivalries. He did not imagine that he would ever fall this far behind and have to abandon wagons filled with mahogany furniture and the many dresses

Margaret might have worn. Supplies are running perilously low. Shrunken wheels are splitting in the heat. Many oxen have died or run away or been picked off by hungry Paiutes. The remaining animals are gaunt, worn down, and the emigrants are worn down too, following the Humboldt as it winds among old cinder cones.

Two days ago half the wagon party pushed ahead so that all the stock would not be competing for the same meager grazings. In this rear segment, twelve wagons have barely enough oxen to pull them through the ash-dry terrain. The nearest hills resemble slate. Along the riverbank, soil is so chalky almost nothing grows. The wheels and hooves send up plumes of dust that hang above the trail. It covers the beards and moustaches and hat brims and settles on the shoulders and upon the backs of animals. White dust clings to the eyebrows and the kerchiefs, making all their faces ghostly in the middle of the day.

There are no trees, nothing for the wind to rustle or rub against. Even the river is silent. Through this stripped country, the only thing moving, other than the wagons, is the narrow bend of water, and it is not at all like the canyon rivers they have followed, which spill and tumble. The water is very blue and very silent, and on this long afternoon members of the party are silent too, waiting for one of their wagons to make its slow way up a blistering, sandy slope.

By double-teaming, seven wagons have already made the climb. But one young driver has decided he doesn't need to borrow anyone else's team and yoke it with his. Perhaps he does not want to face the truth about how weak his animals have become. Perhaps the heat and short rations are working on him, as they work on all of them, and he has reached some kind of limit, so that no advice or good counsel can make a difference.

Four wagons wait in line behind him, while his wheels slide and sink. The emigrants watch him draw his whip and begin to curse, and they wait a while longer because they understand his fury. They are all at the edge of fury and outrage. Maybe they don't mind seeing some of it expressed by a fellow who has been well liked by all of them, sunbrowned and muscular enough to be a trapeze artist, and still handsome, even as his face contorts above the harnesses, the straining flanks.

This is John Snyder, a twenty-five-year-old teamster from Illinois.

He joined the party late in the crossing, a week after they left Fort Laramie, traveling with the family of Uncle Billy Graves, whose third wagon he is now trying to move. At the top of the slope Uncle Billy stands pulling on his beard and waiting. Beside him stands his daughter, Mary Graves, who loves John Snyder and plans to be his bride. They were sweethearts back home. She is the one who persuaded him to join her family for this expedition. She is the reason Snyder is here, and maybe he performs for her this afternoon. Maybe, for the hell of it, he has some point to make about his skills as a teamster.

But he isn't getting anywhere. His oxen are reluctant and irritable and tired, and the driver of the next wagon has run out of patience. This is Milt Elliott, who works for Jim Reed, a loyal driver and handyman. He has six oxen hitched to the Palace Car, and he has waited long enough. He is going to pass John Snyder and get over this hill so they can make a few more miles before sundown.

Milt snaps his reins and calls out to his animals. The lumbering double-decker begins to move, but very slowly, since it now carries everything the Reeds have left, an unwieldy warehouse, so filled to overflowing that the four Reed children must walk beside it. The wife who needs her daily rest, who still falls to her knees with blinding headaches, is walking the last three hundred miles to California.

"Be careful, Milt," she says. "Keep well away from John's team."

"Don't worry!" Milt shouts, loud enough for Snyder to hear. "Johnny might be climbing this here hill till midnight!"

Snyder turns sharply, and sees the crowd of oxen gaining on him. His scowl pleases Milt, who detests the other teamster for his good looks and his popularity. At the end of the long, difficult days, Snyder has been known to lift everyone's mood by dropping a wagon's tailgate and dancing jigs in the desert air. He is light on his feet and a charming singer. All the young women and some of the wives have crushes on John Snyder.

No one has a crush on Milt. He is tall and loose-limbed and homely. His jaw is crooked and his ears are large. He cannot sing or dance, nor has he been able to get a reaction from Mary Graves, whom he has coveted since the day she joined the party. But Milt is good at what he does. He can get a reaction from the cattle. With the reins he now urges them upward, while John Snyder, stuck in the sand, is standing at the wagon seat cursing his animals and cursing Milt, cursing the heat and the sky and the wagon that is gaining on him and the man who built the wagon. This is more than he can bear.

Snyder hates the Palace Car, the look of it, the size of it, the very idea of it. All he wants to do with his life is get to California and find some acreage with good water and a grove of trees and settle down with Mary Graves and work his ranch and raise a family and have a little extra time to sit on his front porch in the evening and contemplate his land. They could have been there weeks ago had they not joined up with this doomed wagon party led by a barn of a wagon that has held them back and slowed them down every foot of the way.

"Go easy down there, Johnny," Uncle Billy calls from the top of the hill.

John doesn't hear. He sees Milt's oxen next to him, and he remembers a covetous look he has seen when Milt's eyes have gazed too long at Mary. Jerking on the reins, he begins to flail his animals, causing his lead ox to flinch and stumble and veer, just as Milt's right front wheel hits a soft spot. The Palace Car tilts. The teams collide. Two wooden yokes somehow lock or overlap. Harness lines are tangled, and Snyder leaps in between the teams, beating oxen on the head with the butt end of his whip, first his own team, then Milt's team.

"You sonofabitch!" John shouts. "You sonofabitch! Damn you! Damn you! Damn you worthless sonofabitch!"

From behind the wagons a loud voice bellows, "Johnny! Johnny!"

It is Jim Reed, who rode off early with his rifle to hunt for food, and has returned in time to see the collision. Now he is out of his saddle and standing in the sand.

"Stop it, Johnny! We need these animals!"

For Snyder, the sight of Reed and his horse is another goad, the sight of a man who can roam around at will while the rest of the world has to drive teams and work the trail.

"What the hell do you know about animals?"

"I know we are dead without them! Now back away!"

"You and your goddam wagon!"

He still hammers on the heads and backs of the helpless oxen. Seams of blood begin to seep through their chalky, dusty hides.

"Milt!" Jim cries. "Unhitch the teams! Let's help John get his wagon up!"

Snyder shouts back, "I don't need nothin' from you or your teams!"

"Calm down, Johnny."

"You're the one got us into this mess!"

"You can't accuse me. I've been gone."

"I do accuse you!"

"I won't hear this!"

Snyder has climbed up onto the wagon tongue, brandishing his whip. Uncle Billy Graves is loping down the hill in long, sand-sliding hops, with Mary right behind him. Margaret Reed steps toward her husband, hearing in his voice a sound that frightens her. She moves toward the sound, as if her upheld hand might silence it.

"James, James," she says.

But Snyder and Reed both are deaf to the voices around them. Jim knows they have been saying this for weeks, laying at his feet all the blame for their delays. It eats at him. It's a sign of weakness, this blaming. When things go wrong, they dare not blame themselves. Late at night he has been thinking, Have I not done my best? God knows, I've given it my all at every turn. . . . Exhausted, yet he cannot sleep, worrying till dawn then arising to another day of sand and heat, as hour by hour his hold on the future turns literally to dust, crumbling around him, disappearing with the wind. Two wagons lost, eighteen cattle gone, his wife and children walking, all losing weight, their faces thinning in a way that can break a father's heart, yet still watching him with the child's faith that he will bring them through. And now to come back, after a morning's fruitless search for game, to find John Snyder beating on the head of one of his last oxen, as if he wants to beat the poor starving creature into the earth. Isn't this precisely what has brought them all to such a place? This senseless show?

Snyder stands above him on the wagon tongue as if to get a better angle on the heads and bodies of the animals.

"Maybe you're the one deserves a whipping, Mr. Reed!"

"Dammit, man, we'll settle this on top!"

"I think we ought to settle it right now!"

Jim is like another ox that has failed John Snyder. With the whip end for a club, he lands a slashing blow across the forehead, tearing loose a flap of skin.

Jim staggers back, dazed, gropes at the wound and feels blood oozing toward his eyes. When Snyder leaps to the ground, swinging wildly, Jim ducks, and this time the whipstock catches Margaret, who has rushed in to intervene. She is pitched into the sand.

He hears his wife cry out. He hears his daughters calling, "Mama!"

His right hand slides toward the Bowie knife he carries at his waist. Half blinded by the blood, he can't see much, but he knows another blow is coming. He draws his knife. Crouching, with the Bowie held wide, he lunges toward the sound, just as Snyder makes a move. The broad blade, strong enough and sharp enough to whittle oak into an axle tree, cuts in below the collarbone with such force that two ribs are severed and the lung is split.

Snyder's yell fills the little desert valley with his pain and his anger. When Jim pulls the knife free, Snyder keeps coming. Two more ferocious blows rip the scalp and drive Reed to his knees.

Milt Elliott and Uncle Billy are now close enough to get hands on Snyder, who will not be restrained. He pulls his powerful right arm free and raises it yet again, then lets it drop. As he turns to Uncle Billy his face goes blank. Beneath the dusty pallor, his ruddy skin turns whiter than white. He looks at Mary. His knees give way, and the old man catches him, eases him down into the sand. The shirtfront is red and wet.

"I am finished, Uncle Billy," he gasps. "I am done."

"No, sir," Uncle Billy says. "No, sir, that ain't true at all."

Jim pushes a sleeve against his brow, to slow the blood and clear his eyes, looking down in horror. "My God!" he cries. "My God, I didn't mean to do this!"

He hurls the culprit knife out into the blue curve of the river and drops to his knees. Margaret is behind him, her hair loose, streaked with blood and chalk, looking for some way to help, calling to Virginia and Patty to bring cloth, rags, anything. The daughters can't move. They have watched it all. They stand and watch their father kneel beside the dying teamster.

More emigrants come stumbling down the slope. They press in close, though no one is certain what to do. Snyder is wheezing. Jim tears open the shirt and with his kerchief tries to cover the hole and stanch the wound. Blood from his forehead drips into the blood trickling from one corner of Snyder's mouth. It is too much for Mary Graves.

"Murderer!" she screams. "Get away from him! Make him get away!"

He bends very close and says, "Forgive me, Johnny."

Snyder's lips part. He whispers, "I'm to blame," words heard only by Reed, who shakes his head and shakes his head as if pestered by a cloud of flies.

"No, no, no," he mutters. "No, no, no, no, no."

He watches the lips for whatever might come next, while others who have clambered down the hill push in behind a man who says, "What was that? Did Johnny speak?"

Again the lips move, but nothing more comes. The eyes spring wide, as if large with revelation, then squeeze shut against the tearing wound and stay shut as the last bloody breath bubbles out of him and the head lolls.

Above Jim the voice of Patrick Breen, the Irish farmer, is like a preacher's dire pulpit warning. "You've killed him."

"He struck me first."

"You ran him through," says Uncle Billy Graves. "I saw you do it, man."

With haggard eyes Graves looks around the circle and mimes the death blow. "That's what he did. Jim Reed pulled out his Bowie knife and ran Johnny through."

Jim brushes back the blood and tears and sweat from around his brows and eyelids. Through a blinking blur he sees a dozen faces watching him, filled with fear, suspicion, hatred, ready to condemn. He starts to protest, to defend himself, but his throat is so thick he cannot speak.

Uncle Billy hunkers next to the young man who would have been his son-in-law and takes the shoulders. Another man takes the feet. Jim reaches for the midsection, but Patrick Breen edges him aside and joins the two men as they lift the remains of John Snyder and begin to climb. As others fall in behind, they form a slow procession up the sandy slope and over the hill, leaving Jim and his family alone by the silent river.

Wounds

After the teams are untangled, Milt Elliott pulls the Palace Car around and parks it. He raises their small camping tent, and Margaret collapses there, stretched out under canvas, unable to speak. Snyder's whip handle caught her on the shoulder but didn't break the skin. The blood in her hair is Jim's. The girls sit with her, while he falls to the sand and leans back, propped against a wagon wheel.

Woozy, near nausea, he places his hands upon his thighs to steady them. He shuts his eyes, hoping to God this will be the last death. They come in threes, it is said, and this is the third. How can one company have such a string of hard luck? You lay your plans, you try to guard against every hazard you have heard about, then you stand there and watch the fates have their way with you. How could he have stabbed a man like Snyder, a man he has relied on all these weeks when others began to lose their will? Could he have backed away from the whipstock? No, Reed thinks. No, I had no choice. He gave me no choice. I wish to God he had . . .

He sees again his harnessed oxen squirming to evade a manic beating. He hears Patty's voice say, "Papa."

He opens his eyes and she is standing next to him, offering the canteen. He takes it and drinks. He would like to drink it all.

"How's your mother?"

"She fell asleep."

Next to Patty, Virginia waits and now moves in for a closer look. "These wounds need dressing."

Jim says, "Can you do it?"

"If you'll tell us how."

The girls are brave. They follow his instructions and bring a basin full of water, a sponge, a pair of scissors, some clean cloth. He bows his head. It is an act of surrender, and he has no trouble bowing before his daughters. He knows the gashes are deep. He needs someone to care for him, and they are eager, holding back their fears.

Around the bloody edges Virginia snips his thick, dark hair as close to the scalp as she can cut it, while Patty holds another pan to catch the clippings. As Virginia dabs lightly with the wet sponge, to clear away crusted shards of dust and clot, Patty holds the pan of water close, watching it turn pink. When Virginia drips iodine along the seams and swellings and closes the forehead flap torn loose, Patty rubs her father's neck with tiny hands. When it comes time to lay the gauze, she presses aside all the loose hairs around his wounds.

Finally Virginia wraps a clean kerchief over his head, knotting it behind. He raises his eyes to look at his daughters, and only then do Virginia's tears burst forth. In her stricken face, no longer girlish, womanly now, and far too soon, too soon—never had he expected this—he sees his wife. Jim takes her in his arms and says, "I should not have asked so much of you," and then sees Patty, standing back, not weeping, though plainly yearning that she too might be swept into her father's large embrace.

"Patty, hon. Sweet Patty. Here."

He flags one hand, and she steps toward him, a running step, her body stiff against him, and he is thinking of the last time he held them both at once.

He is thinking of their grandmother, Margaret's mother, who was too old to undertake such a journey, seventy and ailing, and yet she refused to stay behind and so set out, as if she were still a pioneer. She lasted until the end of May, expiring near the Big Blue River, where they buried her by an ever-flowing spring. Then he remembers the second death, the sickly fellow from Missouri who joined them late, too late, after they'd left Fort Laramie and all the bickering began. He had lost the power of his legs, and one wondered how he'd come so far, and why, since he could no longer ride or walk, had neither friend nor family, and should have stayed put at one of the forts. But he too refused to be left behind and begged for passage. He spent the last days of his tubercular life gasping and spitting inside George Donner's wagon, giving up the ghost just as they reached the white desert south of Great Salt Lake, where he was buried in pure salt. They dug a pit until the moisture came seeping from below. Again Jim sees his face, in the moment before they nailed shut the coffin lid and lowered him and began to cover him with shovelfuls of salt. His name was Luke. He was a Mason, they discovered, carrying in his trunk Masonic emblems—a white apron, a medallion—a gaunt and bearded man, twenty-five and looking fifty, his face a shaggy specter in that blinding sea of white.

Poor Luke, yes, he was ready to let life go. But Snyder? No. He was fit, supple, full of vinegar, reminding Jim a bit of himself in his younger days. And what about today? Will he have to watch Johnny's handsome face disappear? Under scoops of volcanic sand? Who has the makings of a coffin now, out here where nothing grows?

Uncle Billy and his son come sliding down the hill again with another yoke of oxen in tow, to pull their wagon free. Without a word they work the lines, move the animals into place.

Jim calls out, "I'll see you soon with some boards!"

Graves turns but still doesn't speak.

"I'll take them off my wagon!" Jim calls. "Johnny will need a casket and a proper burial. Me and Milt will bring it up."

Graves is dusted with chalk, from hat brim to boots. His voice is chalky too, dry and choked and distant.

"We don't need no part of your wagon, Reed. You can keep your boards."

He watches their team haul the wagon up and over the brow of the sandy slope, then shuts his eyes against the light, against the throb within.

Patty says, "Does your head feel better, papa?"

"Sit with me, girls," he says. "Don't nobody talk right now. Just sit here with me till my strength comes back."

Law and Order

When george and Jacob Donner and two other families pushed ahead, that left Jim in charge of the rear contingent. And who now will take his place? Something has to be decided. Everyone feels the need for a meeting, though no one announces it. They unhitch their animals. They slake their thirst. They tell their children to sit still and keep out of the way. One by one they move out from the wagons.

It is still early afternoon. The sun is bright. The scorched terrain looks as if at any moment it could burst into flame. But the air is not so hot now as it was a few days back. They stand in the sun and look at one another, derailed by this turn of events, twenty people who have come so far together stand in the midst of a treeless desert, strangers again, more estranged than before they met, estranged and abandoned. The Donners are out of sight somewhere ahead of them, and behind them there is no one left on the long trail, no one between here and Fort Bridger, three hundred and fifty miles east. Each family wishes they had never seen the other, yet by this isolation and by this killing they are bound. They have all been wounded today, a little community of the wounded, who need some kind of atonement.

The silence is broken by a heaving sob from Mary Graves. She stands behind her father, her pretty face bent with anguish.

He says, "John Snyder was a mighty good man."

Grunts and nods encourage him to continue. His voice breaks, in part from grief, in part from fear of speaking. In Illinois Graves was an able farmer, the father of ten, good with his hands and a good provider, never one to speak out like this, but with the Donners gone, he is the elder here. He is nearly sixty, and since all his children travel with him, as well as the husbands of two older daughters, he presides over the largest clan.

"I have lost a driver," he says at last. "And a good friend. Mary here . . . she has lost . . . She is hardly twenty, and now she has lost more. . . ."

"It's a crime against nature," says his wife, Elizabeth, who stands close to the sobbing daughter.

A burly fellow named William Eddy speaks up. "Did you see it happen?"

"I see the life gone out of John's body," the mother says. "I see Jim Reed with blood running down his hand."

William Eddy asks again, "But did you see it happen?"

"I saw it all," says Uncle Billy, indignant, coming to his wife's defense. "I was watching from the hill. I saw Jim pull out his Bowie knife and shove it in Johnny's chest like he'd just been waiting for the chance to run him through."

Patrick Breen the Irishman speaks up, an ardent Catholic and another family man, with seven children in his party. "We can't have a killing," he says. "We can't let one man kill another."

This starts heads nodding again.

"A man who has killed another has to pay," says Breen.

"That's right," says Graves. "If you ask me, Jim Reed has it coming to him."

"He's a willful and overbearing man," says Elizabeth Graves. "If it wasn't for him, we wouldn't be stuck out here."

A dozen voices swell in loud agreement, the loudest among them that of Lewis Keseberg who stands with his hands on his hips and his hat shoved back. His blond hair is matted across his brow.

"In Independence," he says, "I saw a man kill another man in a bar with a knife. And the very next day they hung him."

Patrick Breen says, "I heard about that fight."

Uncle Billy likes this idea. "An eye for an eye," he says.

Keseberg smiles with the confidence of a scholar. "An eye for an eye, a tooth for a tooth. It is the code of Hammurabi, and it must be our code as well."

"You ask me," says Uncle Billy, "Jim Reed deserves a hanging."

William Eddy takes his hat off and slams it against his leg. He was a carriage maker back in Illinois. He has a thick, square body and a face that looks hewn from oak. Disgusted, he challenges the circle with his eyes. "If George Donner was here, you people wouldn't have the guts to talk about a hanging."

"Well, George ain't here," says Uncle Billy, "and something's got to be done."

"The main thing that has got to be done," says Eddy, "is getting through the mountains. We'll need every hand we have. Let's wait till we make it to Sutter's, and we can settle it there."

"It ain't enough," says Uncle Billy.

"Why don't each one of us write down what we saw today," says Eddy, "and as soon as we get to Sutter's, we'll bring it before the magistrate."

"It's the wagon party's business," says Patrick Breen, glancing at his wife. "We're like a fort, or a town, or any other collection of humankind."

Breen has an apostolic face. His thick hair is wild and unruly beneath the dusty hat brim. He is a fiddler, and his eyes beside the bow have often flashed with merriment. But that look has not been seen in weeks. His eyes are hard, as if he has been recently betrayed. His wife's are the same, and he expects her now to agree with him.

"It needs settling," says Peggy Breen. "It needs settling today. But we don't want another killin'."

Breen looks at his wife with suspicion, ready to be betrayed again. Then he sees what she is getting at.

"Yes," he says, "I'm not at all sure we want Jim Reed's blood upon our hands."

"We'll take a vote," says Graves.

"On what?" says Eddy.

"On hanging the man who killed Johnny."

Eddy tips his head back and laughs a long, mocking laugh. "Where you gonna hang him? There ain't nothing out here higher than a coyote. Anybody thought about that?"

"Yes," says a voice from beyond the circle, "I have thought about that."

In front of his wagon, Keseberg has hastily cleared a space and moved his lines around and now lifts the long wooden tongue so that it makes a post twelve feet high. In this world of cinder cones and starving river grass, it is the straightest thing in sight. He hauls out some baggage and a wooden crate to prop up the tongue and hold it steady. As hanging becomes possible, a hush falls over the crowd. They regard him with horrified wonder, and Keseberg swells.

"This will suit him fine," he says.

Graves is pleased. He surveys the gathering. One third of these people are relatives. His clan alone could decide the outcome.

"We will mark on pieces of paper," he says. "Everyone eighteen and over has a vote."

William Eddy shouts, "Listen to me! You can't hang a man for defending himself!"

"He ran Johnny through!" cries Elizabeth Graves.

"You weren't there," says Eddy. "How could you see what happened?"

"We saw enough!" says Uncle Billy.

"Those were my animals Johnny was beating on," Eddy says. "Milt and me had hitched 'em together so he could pull the hill. Johnny was beating on 'em so bad Jim tried to put a stop to it. That's when Johnny turned on him and knocked Margaret down, and Jim had to pull his knife to hold him off . . ."

"Ain't the way I saw it!" Uncle Billy shouts.

"Well, hell, you were clear up on top!" says Eddy. "All Jim was aiming to do was hold him off. But Johnny, he was like a mad dog, and Jim never stabbed him . . ."

"Ain't the way I saw it, neither," says Elizabeth Graves.

"Johnny ran right up against the blade," Eddy says.

Now a rise of many voices fills the air.

Eddy shouts, "I was right behind 'em in the next wagon!" But he is drowned out as all the grievances against Jim Reed come pouring forth, some real, some imagined, some public, some private—from the men who have argued with him about which route to take and from others who have resented his excesses, his money, his clothing, and his hired help; from the women who wish their men had long ago turned around and gone back home and from the younger women now deprived of the graceful young teamster they could secretly adore.

God's Doing

From where he sits between his daughters, Jim can hear the tumult, can't make out many words, but he gets the drift. He stands up and tells the girls to go stay close to their mother. He tells Milt to get the weapons out of the wagon. Between them they have two rifles, a shotgun, three six-shooters, and four double-barreled pistols. Once everything is loaded, each man shoves two pistols behind his belt. They place the backup pistols within easy reach and prop the rifles where they can be seen, then they lean against the siding and wait.

After a while he says, "It was a terrible, terrible thing. But I didn't mean to kill him."

"No, sir."

"You know that, don't you, Milt?"

"Yes, sir."

"And we don't mean to kill anybody else today."

"No, we don't," says Milt. "I ain't never killed a person in my life, or even shot one, or wanted to."

"We just intend to let them know certain preparations have been made."

"Yes, sir."

At last the heads and hats appear above the sandy slope, the beards and the shoulders and the sweat-stained shirts, a row of men Jim knows too well, after days and nights together for all these weeks and months. Uncle Billy and his oldest son, a son-in-law who never speaks, whose opaque eyes seem bleached out by the constant sun. And Patrick Breen. And Lewis Keseberg. And William Eddy. They all come armed, and Jim has to wonder what Eddy is doing in such a bunch. Surely he's not one of them, packing his rifle and walking next to Keseberg as if they are trail-mates now. This isn't right. Ever since Salt Lake, the Reeds and Eddys have been traveling together, sharing animals and wagons. But as for Keseberg—ah, the German—Jim is not at all surprised to see him in the lead, with a coil of rope around his shoulder and a triumphant little smirk across his face. This is the day Keseberg has been waiting for, storing up resentment and biding his time.

They move down the slope, with some of the drivers behind them, and the women, and the older children. So many children, Jim thinks, as he watches them descend. He hasn't thought of it before. And until this moment he has not felt so distant from the others. They are a band of nomads who have come upon him in the desert, half of them wild children, ragged and dusty and thin.

They slide and lunge and kick up plumes, and he finds himself remembering the evening he passed by Keseberg's wagon just as a cooking pot fell into the fire with a clanging hiss. He saw the German's three-year-old cringe and draw back at the noise, and saw Keseberg strike his wife across the face, a powerful, open-handed blow that sent her staggering.

This was after Keseberg had rejoined the caravan. Jim was near his wagon by design, not by accident. At Margaret's urging he had become a spy. Other women were reporting sounds that woke them in the night, muffled cries. Now he saw Phillipine cowering, and next to her the wary youngster.

He called out, "Leave her be!"

Keseberg's eyes were very round, as he turned, surprised to be observed. Did he imagine that four walls screened off their kitchen from the world?

"It's no concern of yours," he said.

"It is now."

"You don't know this woman as I know her."

Phillipine was frantically waving one hand, as if to say, *Don't bother, don't bother, he doesn't mean it.*

"I know a brutal beating when I see one," Reed said.

"Are you calling me a brute?"

"I'm telling you this has to stop."

"Are you calling me a brute?"

At the nearest wagons, others turned from their cooking fires. Jim raised his voice, making it an address for all to hear, and as he spoke, he watched the redness rise to Keseberg's ears. "Is a woman no different from a mule? Do you beat her whenever she displeases you?"

Keseberg shouted, "This is no one's business but my own!"

"Every woman in this party is upset!"

"Then let them come and speak to me, not you."

"This will stop tonight," Jim said. "That is an order. Or you will answer to me personally. Do you understand?"

"I am not beholden to you," said Keseberg, "or to anyone else in this wagon train."

He took a menacing step toward Jim and tried to stare him down, but they both knew it was over, for the time being. The German backed off, as if he'd been waiting for someone to rein him in. There were fourteen years between them, and Jim felt then like a father disciplining a wayward son.

Now he watches Keseberg swaggering toward him like the son who finally has his father where he wants him. Jim almost smiles. He has expected this. He sees Keseberg as a dangerous child, who must be treated like a child. But why do these others allow him to take the lead? Who has listened to him? And why? It makes no sense. There is a kind of madness about it, thickening like a vapor in the desert air.

The men stop at the bottom of the slope, all but William Eddy, who keeps walking, with his rifle held across his belly like a soldier on patrol. He is the best shot in the company. Jim has seen him bring down deer and antelope. He has seen him pick off a moving jackrabbit at fifty yards. It occurs to him that Eddy has been appointed to be his executioner. For a moment his dread runs so cold he cannot draw a pistol to defend himself. In the next moment there is no need to, for Eddy walks right up to him and turns and aims his rifle in the other direction, toward the accusers, who do not seem to react. Jim understands it now. Something in them wants a show, some reckless desperation on the other side of weariness and thirst.

Uncle Billy says, "Step away from the wagon, Reed."

"We like it in the shade."

Keseberg has cocked his hip like an athlete. He says, "A vote was taken."

"You can't take a vote," Jim says, "without all council members present."

"Well," says Uncle Billy, "this ain't something we ever had to vote about before."

"What kind of vote, then?"

After a silence Patrick Breen says, "You've cast a shadow over the wagon party, Reed."

"You don't think there's a shadow over my heart, too? I had no desire to kill Johnny."

"But you did!" Uncle Billy's voice is shrill. "By God, you killed him in cold blood, and we aim to hang you for it!"

"He struck me first. You know that. Patrick, you saw what happened!"

As if spying a sudden movement on the nearest ridge, Breen's narrow eyes waver, glance away, then move back to meet Jim's. "Indeed I did."

"And your Bowie knife did the killing," says Uncle Billy.

"A death for a death," says Keseberg. "That was the vote."

In the German's eyes Jim sees a glitter of high anticipation. He looks at the son of Graves, and at the son-in-law who nods each time the old man speaks, and Graves himself, and Patrick Breen. Once workaday farmers, they are now unraveling, as their bodies shrink and their minds run wild, men with large families that must be fed, who put kin first, as any man would, hoard their provisions and hide their water, looking right through you most of the time, their jaws tight, their eyes screened over, drawn inward above the jaws, and so deranged that they call him a murderer. How dare they accuse him? Are they that far gone? Or is he himself so far gone he can't see what he has done? We will soon know who is deluded here.

He pulls his shirt open at the collar, ripping loose a button, exposing his neck and his white chest.

"Come on ahead, then, Mr. Keseberg. Place your noose around my throat. You and you alone."

With a glance at his colleagues, Keseberg lets the coil of rope slide down his arm until he holds it in one hand. Jim draws a pistol from behind his belt and pulls the hammer back. In the silence by the river, the click is like a lightning crack. Jim too is known to be a marksman, famous for his performance among the buffalo herds, firing from horseback like a legendary frontiersman.

Now Milt Elliott mimics his employer, draws a double-barreled pistol. Another click. Another crack. All the weapons rise an inch or two, not yet aimed for firing, but brandished. There is a readiness to fire. They are all like John Snyder as he started up the slope, and there is no thought for what the aftermath might be if one or two more should die and others fall wounded. The haggard face of Uncle Billy looks to be beyond despair, as if pulling a trigger would be some kind of blessing.

William Eddy breaks the spell, Eddy the survivor. "Damn you all!" he says. "Put down these weapons and listen to me. If we start shooting here, ain't nobody gonna make it across."

"Go damn yourself, Bill Eddy," says Graves. "Jim Reed has to pay."

"Then let him ride off alone," says Eddy.

"He has to hang," says Keseberg.

From the dusty crowd behind the leaders, voices rise in echo.

"Reed has to pay—"

"He ought to hang—"

Eddy cries, "He ain't gonna hang, and you know that! But what if he could ride ahead and just be . . ."

Jim looks at him. "What are you saying?"

Patrick Breen says, "You mean banished from the party?"

"I didn't say 'banished,' " Eddy says.

Jim shouts, "What is this, Bill?"

"I mean, separate yourself," says Eddy.

Breen is eager to pursue this. "Banishment now! That too might be a fitting price to pay."

"Damn it," says Eddy. "Banishment is not what I mean at all! I'm talking about a few days . . ."

Graves and Keseberg look at each other, they look at Eddy's rifle and Jim's six-shooter.

"How many days are we talking about?" says Graves.

"You'd better hang me, gentlemen, because I'm not going anywhere."

Breen says to the others, "I've told you before, I don't want his blood on my hands."

"Ay," says Breen's wife, "we've seen enough blood for one day."

Jim feels a touch upon his elbow and almost pulls the trigger in alarm. It is Margaret, suddenly next to him, gazing hard into his eyes. She reaches up to tuck an edge of the blood-wet kerchief wrapped around his head. When did she awaken? How much has she heard? And what is he seeing in her face? Anguish and fatigue and stern resolve. Her dark eyes looked bruised. Perhaps she did not sleep at all. Perhaps she has not slept in weeks.

She wears the hat she has worn every day, a straw bonnet tied below her chin with ribbons. Underneath its brim her forehead gathers against some chronic pain. With prim hat and bunched brow has she come to judge this mad display? When she turns toward the accusers, her gaze cuts through the rank of weapons, tells them all to hold their fire and hold their tongues.

William Eddy says, "If you can see your way clear, we could watch over Margaret and the young ones, me and Milt could."

He is baffled now, cannot comprehend this. Has he traveled so far, simply to ride off and leave them in an empty and unforgiving place?

With pressure on his elbow Margaret guides him, while they walk together across the sand, beyond the wagon, until they're out of earshot, entering a little pocket that swallows voices, a patch of desert that is the quicksand of all sound.

Her voice is soft. "Billy Eddy is right."

He looks at her, unable to speak. Is she as deranged as the rest of them?

"You have to ride ahead," she says.

"I will not!"

"It's our best chance."

"Leave you here?"

"They're crazy, James."

"We'll hold them off until this settles, then—"

"Then what?"

"We'll push on."

"The whole party?"

"Come morning they'll see the sense of it."

"Any one of them could kill you, James. Is that what you want? Keseberg would do it with his hands, you know he would."

"He wouldn't live to brag about it."

"Look at him. Look at Graves. They resent us. There's murder in their eyes. They would love to do you harm, and now they have their reason."

"We'll push on alone."

"How can we?"

"We'll just hitch up."

"We lack the animals to go it alone. The first hill, we'd be stuck again."

"Dammit, Margaret. This is my wagon party. I have to see it through!"

"Ride ahead, then."

"That leaves you at their mercy. It's unthinkable."

"They won't harm us, once you're gone. I'm sure of that."

"It's me, then. It's me alone they despise."

She looks away.

"It's the trail, James. The trail has addled every one of us. Bill Eddy sees it. Please listen. Go. As quickly as you can."

"That's running."

"Not if it's the wisest way. You think I want you proud and bull-headed and lying in the sand like Johnny? You think the children want to remember you like that?"

"I've never run."

"Milt is here. Bill and Eleanor Eddy are like family now. If you ride ahead, one man alone can make it through to the other side and find some help and send back more food, and horses. It could end up a blessing for us all. It has to be, James. You know I'm right. We want you alive."

He studies her face, her mouth, around her eyes the lines of wear. What has he done to this woman? The months of endless travel have added years of age. And how can he leave her here, and leave the children? They call her frail, but she is not, nor is she deluded like the others. Her eyes are clear. She is his anchor and his rock. His heart fills. His throat fills.

She waits, giving him time.

"I never wanted this for you," he says. "I never imagined it."

"No one could have imagined it." Her eyes brim. "Just tell them, James. Tell them that you're riding ahead. Please. For my sake. Tell them now."

For a long minute he stares out across the sand, where heat currents wave and distort the view. In the far distance a low ridge of hazy violet quivers as if about to detach from Earth and take flight. He shakes his head and looks again, and still it quivers. He walks back toward the men who would expel him, his judges and his jury.

"If I do this," he calls out, "I will take a horse and a rifle and a supply of ammunition."

They too have been talking among themselves. Now they look at one another. They look at their wives, whose lips are pursed, the faces closed.

"No weapons," says Keseberg, with his scornful smile. "We need every weapon for the trail."

Margaret exclaims, "My Lord!"

"And he can carry no food," says Graves. The white-bearded elder's face is burdened with the weight of such decisions. "There's none to spare."

"With our children going hungry," says Elizabeth Graves, "we can't give food to murderers."

"No one can survive out here alone without a gun," says Margaret, who finds herself a party to this monstrous proposal. "That's certain death."

"It will be God's doing, then," says Patrick Breen piously, "not ours."

from *The Trail Notes of Patty Reed*

Santa Cruz, California

October 1920

It rained all night the day I left.
The weather it was dry.
The sun so hot I froze to death.
Suzannah, don't you cry.

—*Stephen Foster*

Fʀᴏᴍ *our front stairs it is only five minutes to the beach. This morning I went walking early. I walked along the hard-packed sand under a high fog, the kind that stills the wind. The sea was glossy, smooth as silk. Waves were rising up so smooth and sharp, they looked like silver cutouts. Offshore all along here there are beds of kelp, where whole forests of slick leaves and bulbs and limbs sway just below the surface. As a wave lifts, the kelp appears like the broad shadow of some great bird flying through the fog. But you look up and there is no bird anywhere. There is just the shadow, the ghostly shape that seems to slide across the water as the wave moves on toward shore and rises and curls over and breaks and disappears.*

That's what held me this morning, the way they disappear.

I couldn't tell you how long I stood there, watching the waves, each one its own thing and finely edged, moving through the silky water, shining, leaping into a noisy burst of spray, then all of a sudden, it was over. It was just . . . gone.

You have to wonder at this, at the way it disappears. After so much buildup and clatter, it comes down to a slick of foam oozing toward your feet. And then not even that.

What I mean is, you get to my age you have to ponder such things. When you're younger, of course, looking at the Pacific Ocean, chances are you just dive in. You get past eighty you can stand on the beach till noon if you take a mind, or you can sit here on the porch and watch the water all day long.

It has sent me back again to the time of the crossing and the day our world would change forever. I can see now that a big wave had been rolling and rising and gathering force. After papa killed John Snyder it all came clattering down around us, and something disappeared. I could not have said quite what. But before you knew what happened, something you imagined would always be there was simply gone, sucked right on down into the desert sand.

I had never seen papa hurt the way Snyder hurt him. When we dressed his wounds he was close to weeping, but trying not to let us know. His head was bowed. I had to turn away from the gashes in his scalp. When I touched his neck I felt his whole body tremble. My sister finally broke down, crying for all three of us, since papa would not let us see him cry, and me, I couldn't. I felt like running. I could see us running along the trail ahead of the wagon party and making our escape before whatever was coming next. I did not know what that would be, but I already felt it rolling toward us.

That night after the opposing sides had backed off a ways, after we had fixed dinner and cleaned up the camp and made ready for bed, I saw papa walk out alone toward the riverbank. I was filled with the greatest fear I'd known up to that time. Grandma used to sing a song, a mournful ballad about a fellow who jumped into a river and drowned. I thought that's what he was going to do. I didn't know the Humboldt right along there was only two feet deep. I slid out of my bedroll and followed him down to the bank. At that hour, with everything as quiet as it only gets in the desert, you could hear the water slithering along like a snake on its belly, that slow, quiet hissing.

When he saw me next to him, he reached out his arm and drew me close, and I asked him if he was going to go away.

"I don't know, Patty."

"I saw what happened, papa. Johnny started it."

His voice cracked when he said, "That he did, darlin', that he did."

"If you go away, I'm going with you."

"Mama's going to need you more than ever, darlin'."

"Milt and Virginia and James Junior can take care of mama all right. But who will take care of you?"

"I'll do just fine."

"Please take me with you, papa."

"I didn't say for sure I was going anywhere, did I?"

"But if you do."

He picked me up and held me and pointed toward the east where the sky was glowing as if a forest had caught fire somewhere beyond the nearest mountain. Then the first glint of moon showed at a ridgetop, and we watched it swell up, round and yellow and nearly full, and spread its silver light across the long, long desert.

He and mama stayed up talking half the night, whispering under the camp tent. The next morning John Snyder was buried in the sand in a shroud, with one board below his body and one above, to discourage the coyotes. After the burial, papa climbed onto his mare and said good-bye.

I have already compared that river to a snake, and it was not by chance. Every river I have ever seen goes curving and looping from where it starts to wherever it ends up. The Snake River, which I have not seen, is one example. The Humboldt is another. For a while it was called the Mary's. But that is one they could just as well have called the Snake, in my opinion, instead of naming it for a fellow who never even saw Nevada. It makes an evil mark through a devilish place, and I am glad I have not had to go anywhere near it since the time we made the crossing. We had to stand by that river and watch papa ride out on a starving horse with his head wrapped in a bloody kerchief and his hat split to fit around the bandage. He was wearing buckskins then, like some of the other men, trousers and fringed tunic, so elegant when we left Fort Laramie all smeared and dark now with firesmoke and sweat, and nothing in front of him but sand and chalk and bare mountains. I can tell you it was the hardest day of my life up to that time, and the hardest day for mama too, though we would all have worse days before that trip was done.

She had put one husband in the grave. Now she had followed her second husband to the very end of the world and was surely imagining that she could be widowed again, at thirty-two. She looked as if it had been her who took the knife blow to the chest, not Snyder, as if it was her life that flowed into the sand beside the river. I know now that she wanted to fall down and quit right there, but she braced herself against the wagon, so she would not seem to falter. She had decided to be strong for the rest of us, and I have to say that from that day forward she was strong in ways none of us had seen before. As I have said, the stabbing of John Snyder changed all our lives.

That evening she made up a packet of jerked beef and biscuits. Where it came from, I still don't know. She wrapped up some powder and percussion caps too, in defiance of the terms of banishment, and passed them to Milt Elliott, along with papa's rifle. Under cover of darkness he and Virginia followed the river trail on horseback. They rode all night, caught up with papa, and got back to the wagons before dawn. I know she hoped papa would take her with him, to be his horse-girl companion, as she'd been all the way across the plains. I had wanted him all to myself. So did she. But he knew better than anyone else what lay in store for him.

After he sent Virginia back with Milt, she cried without letup. She cried until our wagons came upon the place where they had found him camping. There were the markings of the fire he had built, and scattered around it were the loose feathers of a bird he must have shot the next morning—which was his way of telling us he'd already made good use of the rifle and found himself something to eat. Mama said we would build our family fire on the same spot, as if the place held some of his spirit, or perhaps by making a fire there we would send our blessing forward to travel with him. Or perhaps it was just a family's way to keep the flame of hope burning from one day to the next, touching papa's campfire spots and, when we could, gathering one feather of a bird that had helped keep him alive.

A few days later, when we caught up with the advance party, we learned that he spent a night with the Donners before moving on. So we knew he made it at least that far along the Humboldt. They gave him another packet of food to carry and a partner to travel with, a young teamster who no longer had a team to drive with all the animals and wagons we had lost. Crossing the desert was too risky for one man alone. The Donners couldn't spare a horse, but they could spare a teamster. So papa and his new partner had one horse between them. They made a lonesome sight, I heard George Donner say, heading out at dawn, one mounted, one on foot. Getting through to the Truckee

River would be the test, he said. "Then there's water again . . . and after that . . . the Sierra Nevada."

George Donner had white hair and a deep, captivating voice, like a preacher's or like an actor playing King Lear in a huge empty theater. The way he said "Sierra Nevada" made it loom in my mind. Before long I would learn that it means "Snowy Mountains." But I didn't know any Spanish yet, so I didn't see snow. What I imagined was a soaring palisade of stone and timber that could only be crossed with the blessings of God and many angels. That night I prayed for all the angels in heaven to watch over papa, wherever he was on the long trail to California.

NUMEROUS PEOPLE have observed that our journey that year was a fateful journey. In hindsight anyone can see signs along the route and find a dozen or a hundred times when things could have gone some other way. Of course, they did not go some other way. Things never do. Things always go the way they're going to go. And I still have to wonder how much of it was fate and how much of it was papa's nature.

Every party on the trail had a hard time somehow or another. Everybody ran low on water and threw out furniture and shot oxen for meat and had arguments that would set one clan against the next. Our party, of course, had a special talent for arguing and disagreement. I can see that now. Surely there has never been a more mismatched bunch having to spend half a year trying to get from one place to the next. I suppose you can call that a kind of fate. It wasn't anything papa had planned ahead of time, though he was at the center of it all.

You take that day by the Humboldt. I still wonder if he really had to ride off like that. Maybe he already believed he had some punishment coming, even before he pulled his knife and started waving it like a man who is drunk outside a bar. Maybe he was yearning to be put through some kind of test even worse than the hell he'd already seen—to prove something to the rest of them, or take some scar upon himself for what he'd done, or failed to do.

Our stop at Fort Laramie was another time when things could have gone another way. And this was many weeks before the trouble started, while the animals were still healthy and the wagons were still loaded with provisions and the women still had time to think about what they'd fix for the Fourth of July, still holding on to the places they'd left behind, and in that way trying to make Fort Laramie an outpost of civilization, which it was not, though on the day we rolled in, there were more people congregated than you would have found anywhere else in the entire West. We saw buffalo hunters and shaggy, wild-eyed trappers with mules and squaws and furs to trade. Thousands of Sioux were camped outside the fort, along with half the wagons on the trail. Papa called out to men he hadn't seen since Independence. He saw a pair of mules he was sure he recognized, ones he'd sold just before we crossed the Missouri.

I remember a green meadow above the broad, sandy river we'd been following for weeks. Where Laramie Creek spills into the Platte, it looked like a park. I wanted us to stop, but we splashed on through the creek and climbed past the meadow until we came upon the fort, the long clay walls, the wooden gate, the blockhouse over the gate where riflemen could stand. Before dinner papa walked over there to look up the man in charge. He came walking back with a fellow he hadn't seen in fourteen years, since they had fought together in the Blackhawk War. Papa invited him to sit down for a cup of coffee, which was gratefully accepted. The man had not sniffed a cup of coffee in about six months, or so he said.

He was not with any of the westering parties. He was bound in the opposite direction. He had been a trapper and some kind of guide, and now he was on his way east from what the Mexicans used to call Alta California, said he was headed home to Illinois before these new crowds spoiled all the unspoiled places he had come to love.

Mama invited him to stay for dinner, but she didn't like him much. She had known him in Illinois, knew something about him from those days, though I think mainly it was the terrible smell that followed him like a shadow. All of those mountain men who wore the same clothes for weeks and months on end, you have no idea what a foul-smelling bunch they were. He wore moccasins and buckskin trousers and a buckskin shirt with fringes dangling from the sleeves, and his shirt was shiny smooth. Parts of it were nearly black with grease and smoke and weather. He carried a powder horn slung from his shoulder and a Bowie knife at his waist. He had so much hair you could hardly see his face, just his blue eyes peering out like he was inside a thicket.

I asked him if it was hard to breathe with all that hair around his mouth.

When the Mountain Man laughed, bad teeth showed through his beard, and gaps where other teeth had fallen out. The missing teeth gave him a bent mouth and a bent smile. "Sometimes it's hard to breathe," he said "but it catches all the bugs and skeeters 'fore they fly down my throat, so I don't mind."

After dinner papa opened one of his quarts of ten-year-old brandy, and they started talking. Around that fire they talked for hours. Papa had news about towns this fellow would be going back to, the prices, the state of the Union east of the Mississippi. The Mountain Man had news from all the places papa was so eager to see. He was the first person we met who'd actually been where we were headed. He'd just come over-land from Sutter's Fort, where things, he said, were "heating up." Papa wanted to know what he meant by that.

"Coming to a head," he said.

He was a storyteller. Before he began a story he would take a long pull from the brandy bottle. I can't remember all the stories he told that night, but I remember how his Adam's apple seemed to roll beneath the hair along his throat. And I remember the brightness of papa's eyes in the firelight when he first mentioned the name of Lansford Hastings.

"You're talking about the fellow who wrote the book," papa said.

"The very one."

"I wonder if you've read it."

"Don't need to read no guidebook, Jim. I've been to just about every place a person can get to."

"But you know something about Mr. Hastings."

"Know about him! Hell, I rode with him! We rode a thousand miles together, from this side of Sutter's, clear around Salt Lake, on up to Bridger's."

I could see the color rise into papa's face, which meant he was either angry or threatened or excited or drunk or all four.

"And what do you make of him?"

"He knows how to cover country, he surely does. He's been back and forth through there, I don't know how many times. But he is a talker, too. He will talk California till your ears fall off. You travel around for a while like I have, you find some people are content just to get where they're going. Ol' Hastings, he wants to be the prophet who will lead us all out of our misery. We were somewhere past Truckee River, bound for Salt Lake, and I looked at him, thinking, Hey, Moses, you are heading the wrong way if it's the Promised Land you're looking for, this feels like the road to Egypt. About the time we hit the Humboldt Sink I quit listening. Getting through that kind of country takes all my concentration."

Papa had walked over to his saddlebags and come back with a scuffed-up copy of <u>The Emigrants' Guide</u>, which he'd been looking at once or twice a day. As he sat down again he was flipping through the pages.

"When you came by Salt Lake, which way did you travel? To the north, or to the south?"

"Ol' Hastings, now, he wanted to try the way Captain Fremont took last spring. I went along with it because I hadn't seen that stretch since I'd rowed across Salt Lake in a bull boat. This might of been twenty years ago, and then some . . ."

He reached for a pull on the brandy bottle. Papa could see another story coming, so he broke in, reading from the book, real slow, like every sentence had to be savored.

By recent explorations a very good and much more direct wagon way has been found, about one hundred miles southward from the great southern pass. . . . The most direct route, for the California emigrants, would be to leave the Oregon route about two hundred miles east from Fort Hall; thence bearing west southwest to the Salt Lake; and thence continuing down to the Bay of San Francisco . . .

As he listened, the Mountain Man nodded. "Yessir, that's more or less it, and it ain't no route for wagons, Jim, if that's the way you're thinking. We crossed it last month. But we were half a dozen mounted men. With a string a wagons like this, cattle and all . . . I tell ya, it is some of the meanest land I have seen."

"According to Mr. Hastings, it's the nearer way."

"It's nearer, and that's a fact, if you don't mind a land God has turned His back on. After that you still have a lot more desert, and then you start the climb for Truckee Pass . . ."

"But why take a roundabout way when you can save three hundred miles or more?"

"I'll tell you why. You go north by Fort Hall you will get there. I guarantee it. That is the main idea, wouldn't you say? To get there?"

"We're already so far behind," papa said, "three hundred miles is something to think about."

"If it was me, I'd take the Fort Hall route and never leave it."

"But saving two weeks . . . we'd surely make those last mountains before a snowfall. Isn't that true?"

Papa made this a challenge, holding him with his eyes. He still had the <u>Guide</u> open in front of him. The Mountain Man looked at it like papa had a live lizard by the tail.

In the years since then, people have faulted papa for having more faith in what was printed on a page than in the man right beside him. What a lot of them don't know is that he had made promises to mama. He had made promises to all of us, and promises to himself. His own craving for the land where all the promises would come true ran so deep he dared not doubt the man who'd spelled it all out for him, page by page. It was a whole lot easier to doubt the foul-smelling survivor of a dozen expeditions through the country we were about to cross. That night at Fort Laramie there was a reverence in papa's voice, as if he were reading Scripture. After he let the covers fall closed, he held the little volume close to his belly, the way preachers sometimes hold copies of the New Testament.

The Mountain Man must have noted this. He'd known papa for quite some time, must have known how single-minded he could be, how important it was for him to end up on the right side of a discussion, and end up in California ahead of other wagon parties too timid to try a new and shorter route. The Mountain Man wasn't one to argue. He was at heart a lonesome fellow who cherished his solitude and carried with him all he owned. He savored human company when it came his way, but he didn't seek it out. Live and let live was his philosophy. He would tell you what he thought. If it didn't appeal to you, he would go his way, as he was about to do again.

"We still have some days to travel," papa said, "before we need to choose one way or the other."

"That you do. You'll have upwards of two weeks, from here to South Pass, then past there to Little Sandy Creek."

Having spoken his mind, he now sat looking at the fire. Papa passed him the brandy bottle, but this time the Mountain Man declined.

IT MUST HAVE *been two or three weeks later, I guess we were half-way through the Rockies, climbing the long grade to South Pass, when a rider came galloping out of the west. He had a message to read aloud, like a proclamation in the town square, though there was no town and no square, just a crowd of weary travelers starting to wonder why they had ever taken the first step on such a journey.*

He was riding from company to company with an open letter to all the emigrants on the trail. It said Lansford Hastings was assembling a new wagon train that he would personally guide along his new and faster route. Right now he was waiting at Fort Bridger.

Since then I've talked with some who saw that letter, written with flourishes in Hastings's own hand. They say it was somewhere between a travel brochure and a battle cry. Wagons ought to be bunching up in larger groups, it said, now that the U.S. had gone to war. No telling where we'd run into the Mexicans or how many there'd be. But if we all stuck together and followed his lead we would not only finish our trip in record time, we would join the ranks of a new society on the far Pacific shore. And somehow, while all this happened, Hastings himself would be at the forefront.

Well, you have never seen the kind of buzzing and scurrying around stirred up by this letter. It started an argument that went on for days, just adding to the squabble and disagreement boiling up ever since we'd left Fort Laramie. People argued till we reached the banks of Little Sandy Creek, where each family had to decide which way to go—north by Fort Hall, which is what most folks had done all summer long and continued to do for years to come, or south by Fort Bridger, clear on down in the bottom corner of what is now the state of Wyoming. There were long meetings, and papa was a fervent speaker. It was like an election, where politicians try to convince you who to vote for.

"I'm heading north," one fellow said, "and staying north till I git to Oregon, and California can be damned!"

"I'm sticking with Jim Reed," said someone else.

"Jim Reed can be damned, too," the first fellow said. "You can all be damned! I might just turn around and go back home!"

"It's too late to turn around," said someone else.

Papa's voice had the passion that could sway such fellows. He stood on a log and read from Hastings's book, while fire came into his eyes. He slammed the book shut and cried, "You think I would do this heedlessly? Risk the lives of my very own loved ones? By the southern route we can save two weeks of traveling time. And we NEED those weeks, people! So do our animals. Believe me! They'll be that much tougher for the final days of climbing!"

His voice was strong, and many listened and finally set out with papa and the Donners as one long line of wagons started south. And yet there remains the riddle I ponder to this very day. For all his desire to save time and make a speedy crossing, why had papa built that family wagon so big and cumbersome it slowed down everyone who traveled with us? The fact is, nothing like that wagon had ever been seen before. In its day it was the largest thing anyone had tried to move across North America. When I was eight I took it for granted that this was the way you traveled. Looking back, I can see how preposterous it was to imagine something that size could have a chance of rolling clear from Illinois to Sutter's Fort. Just getting as far as it did must have set some kind of record.

A few days after papa was banished, we were fifty or sixty miles farther along the Humboldt when that wagon came to its final halt and resting place. The poor creatures pulling us along just stopped in their tracks from exhaustion, and it was decided that we would have to abandon the wagon papa had designed. We would unload what we could and leave it by the side of a river that got smaller day by day, as we drew closer to what the Mountain Man called the Humboldt Sink, where the river finally plays itself out and trickles away into the sand.

It was another blow for mama. But she knew they were right. We spent the rest of that day moving what provisions we had left into one of the three Graves family wagons, along with a few odds and ends of clothing and ammunition and whatnot, and our little dog, Cash, who was the last of the pack of dogs we'd started out with, so skinny now he had to be carried half the time, but none of us could bear to lose him.

You might think it strange that we would be moving belongings into a wagon owned by one who so recently wanted to hang my father. It seems strange to me even now, and yet this is no stranger than anything else about those long-ago days. Uncle Billy could not simply leave us standing in the desert. He was already feeling bad for what he'd done and wishing papa were still among us, if only to lend his back and two strong arms to the daily struggle. William Eddy would tell mama what he heard others saying, how they would argue over who had been at fault, and how some who had not spoken out were coming around to papa's side. Already it was becoming clear, the folly of this vengeance. People who had been so eager to condemn, they would all do things as bad as papa had done, or worse, in the weeks and months ahead, and I would witness them, deeds that can still cause my gorge to rise. With their eyes they were already begging for forgiveness, begging ME, at my young age. Their eyes would say, You have no idea what grief and desperation can drive a person to!

I do not judge them. It is not my place to judge. Only to remember. But still, I have to ask, looking back, where was that spirit of forgiveness on the day they were ready to hang him for killing a man he never meant to kill? Maybe we saw a glint of it, like the first glint of the late moon, when we moved the shreds of our belongings into one of the wagons of Uncle Billy Graves, and his old worn-out eyes followed me around like I was the last one on earth who could save his soul.

When we rolled away from there the next morning, mama could not bear to look at all she was leaving. Papa had built the Palace Car, but she had supervised the packing of the wagons. She had shepherded all her prized possessions from our yard in Springfield, down to St. Louis, and across the Mississippi River, and then rode with them while our oxen plodded clear across the Great Plains and through the Rockies, up and down every gully and ravine in the Wasatch Range, across eighty miles of Salt Desert, and now there was nothing left of all that caravanning but a hulk out by itself among the cinder cones and dry ridges. There was still not a tree in sight, just our wagon, sitting back from the riverbank, a solitary testament to something. To what? My father's pride? The largeness of his vision? His fall?

While mama could not look, I could not take my eyes off the Palace Car. I sat in back, watching it get smaller and smaller, until a mountain spur blocked it from sight. I have imagined it standing like that for days and nights in the sand and in the wind, with the door flapping like the door of an empty saloon. The seats inside where no one will ever sit again are layered with sand and grit. Mama's mirror gazes out upon the tan and purple slopes of ash and spill, sending those colors back until the Indians finally come upon this unexplainable structure. Cautiously they approach it, wondering what kind of creatures are these whiteskins who make a thing so large, only to carry it out to such a place, an empty place where no one lives, and set it in the sand.

"Perhaps a Great One has passed away," says the scout who spotted it.

"No," says another, "they are crazy. The things they do. All crazy. Walking all day with the sun so high."

"Perhaps it is a trick," says another.

"Yes. We should burn it before they return."

They argue about what to do, and whether there is power in this huge tent, and can they be in danger if they touch it. And should they first take the parts and pieces that they like, or should they burn it all? And what if they do not burn it? Only a fool would leave it here and take nothing.

They circle and debate until the door is blown back by a sudden wind, and they see the mirror on the inside wall, the looking glass given to mama as a farewell gift. In the glass the Indians see their own faces. One by one they look, back away, look again, and tilt their heads, leaning toward it, peering. To have so many faces there inside the tent, this is indeed a kind of power. They look inside the door and see a clutter of bags and boxes the whiteskins left behind. They tear them open and find shoes and dresses and hairbrushes and shaving cream and medicine and books filled with pages of little black marks and coils of rope and empty drawers and a chamber pot and a pair of new suspenders and bedsheets and a flatiron and a brand-new stove.

At last the oldest warrior in the band takes the mirror from the wall with a whoop of conquest. Others scoop up bags and armloads of whatever can be carried, all whooping as the wagon is set afire. Once the flames begin to rise and lick, it goes fast, the wood is so dry. The heat is fierce and they back off, then leave it to ride away across the sand. And in this vision I am with them, on my own galloping pony. I am a desert Indian looking back over my shoulder at the flaming hulk that grows smaller as we ride.

Floating Pictures

Wᴴᴇᴇʟ ᴛʀᴀᴄᴋꜱ ꜰᴏʟʟᴏw the Humboldt south and west. The water here is bitter to the taste, harder to drink as the channel narrows. Far ahead he can see a faint edge of the long ditch it makes, like a pencil mark through the flatness.

The steady sun and the mare's plodding gait encourage him to doze. But he won't. He can't. His wounds still sting, sometimes throb. His eyes burn from the scanning and the lack of sleep. He looks back at the young teamster behind him, punching boots into the crusty sand like a man cast up on an endless beach. Jim is glad they aren't talking much. He doesn't want to talk. He doesn't want to think. He wants to cover ground now, get where they're going, and no telling how long it will take them, with one man mounted and one on foot, stopping five times a day to change places. But George Donner was right. A man alone is a sitting duck. Last week Bill Eddy was shot at, off hunting by himself, though he bragged that he was never in much trouble. For proof he brought an arrow back, rough-cut and primitive, not like the trim shafts they'd seen in the quivers of the Sioux. The bows of these desert tribes are small and weak and inflict damage only at close range. The great danger is at night when they come after animals—to injure, not to kill—hoping you'll leave the wounded behind. Right now they can't be far away, perched somewhere and watching, as they have watched all along the route.

His eyes roam. A layer of dry grass covers the basin, autumn dry, almost white. Clumps of sage show here and there. To the west, low ridges make a jagged line, and beyond them another line, another world of ridges below the arching sky, and now between the ridges and the river he sees something else. Bluish white. Is it moving? Is it water? Nothing that size is marked on any map.

He sees a shimmering lagoon, blue and seductive under midday sun. It looks to be bordered with beaches, and a darker border of what could be trees. He can't tell. Perhaps a row of enormous stones. If it's water the scene is blurred by undulating glare. A few weeks back he would have galloped toward this miracle, as he did more than once in the Salt Desert when water appeared on the hottest, driest days in the history of human life. He knows this lake is an illusion. Yet he studies it as he rides, as if still half persuaded it might be real.

He remembers the white flats and the rider who appeared to him when he thought he was entirely alone. It was another day like this. He'd left his family, to ride ahead in search of water. He remembers hooves crunching through crusted salt, like walking on icy snow, the salt thick and grainy, stretched out flat as a table, and the fierce light burning his eyes, when he saw another rider on another horse maybe fifty yards off, heading in the same direction. When Jim called out, the man didn't answer. Then a second rider was moving along at a similar gait, just beyond the first. When Jim raised his arm, both riders raised their arms. When Jim removed his hat, to wave it, both riders raised their hats and waved. More waving riders appeared, a whole platoon, wearing identical hats and beards. He saw then that they were all pictures of himself, reproduced by some bizarre alchemy of heat and light.

In his moment of amazement he turned to see how far he'd come from the family wagon, where Margaret and the children waited under canvas, in the heat. He turned to see his wagon shimmer and quiver and pull apart in the middle like a stretching gob of white taffy and divide itself into twin wagons, which lifted, floating, to divide again and again, until he saw a distant row of wagons like islands above the sea of salt.

That was while they were following the cutoff that should have saved them fourteen days but cost them thirty, and five wagons, and many cattle, and one human life. Though Lansford Hastings had promised to lead them across, he was already gone when they reached Fort Bridger. Sixty wagons answered his call and away he went, and the Reeds and Donners were on their own, pushing through the uncharted Wasatch Range, out into the blinding desert east of Great Salt Lake.

As Jim watched his family and his wagon subdivide into a dozen wagon-shaped balloons, the terror of that blighted place had gripped him fully. It was not the terror that comes upon you when water is gone and you feel your final body fluids drying up. Nor was it the terror when sight is burned away by days of glare and the searing whiteness turns black. This was a knowledge that the place could not be trusted. Deceit was embedded in the place itself and fed there and billowed around you like an invisible gas.

As he rides south and farther west beside the Humboldt, an inland sea calls out to him, the oasis of his wildest dreams. And the same fear wells up. What kind of land would trick you and deceive you day after day after day? And what kind of man is Hastings, who would fill such a land with promises as elusive as these floating pictures? His wagons are out ahead of Jim now, a few days farther along this trail. Jim is gaining on him. He can tell by the campsites and the trampled riverbanks. When Jim catches up with him, there are many questions he would like to ask this prophet and self-appointed leader of the multitudes.

He lets his eyelids fall. For quite some time he rides like a man asleep, lulled by bridle clink. When he opens his eyes the ridgeline has turned indigo. The lagoon is gone. In the far distance he sees that the long ditch the river makes is also gone, and this is not a trick of desert light. The sun is low. The glare is off the sand. In the nearby channel there's still a smear of water, but it doesn't seem to move.

The next morning they reach a sump of still and shallow pools slimed over with a yellowish residue. The air smells like some foul mix of sulfur and tar and fresh cow dung. Beyond these pools, parched terrain goes on for miles across the region the Mountain Man talked about, the legendary "Sink."

Jim surveys the miles ahead. It is unnatural for a river to disappear like this. Back where he comes from, a river always flows into a larger river, the way the Ohio meets the Mississippi, to merge with waters flowing down into the Gulf, where they spill out to join the waters that gird the Earth.

When water flows in and nothing flows out, it is like a room with all the doors and windows shut. Breath itself cannot escape. Arriving at the very end of water overwhelms him, makes this desert loneliness lonelier than any he has known. The gift of water slithers away into the sand, while all around them he sees nothing but crooked backbones of dry ridges, and the broad plain patched with white, quilted with the skeletons of long-dead grasses.

He says to Walter, "Where does it go?"

"Where does what go, Mr. Reed?"

"The water."

Walter studies the rim of mountains. " 'Bout like a horse pissin' in a dry field, I guess."

"What do you mean?"

"Horse can piss all day. The field just soaks it up."

They cross the sink and toward evening see a puff of smoke rising from an empty slope and figure it must mean Indians. Yet there is no fire, nor any sign of camp. They ride toward the smoke, watching it rise, white and filmy, tall as a tree. Jim sees it is not smoke. It's a tower of steam, a geyser spurting from the dryness.

They come upon a cluster of pools bubbling, spilling fluid across the sand. He thinks, This must be where the river comes back. The water travels all these miles and passes through some furnace down below. And is it yet another trick? Steal away your water, then give it back in pools and chasms of percolating steam that will probably burn your whiskers off?

Wispy plumes are wavering from holes in the earth, a hundred or more, bowls and fissures, some as small as a wash pan, some as wide as a barn door, rimed with yellow, or with white, crusts and coronas of mineral deposit. There are seeping pyramids of scarlet and purple, with steam curling as if from the barrel of a purple cannon aimed at the sky.

They roam around and find a pool that isn't boiling. It's warm, but calm, and potable. They drink until every cell is saturated, and let the mare drink, and then make camp. Walter lashes her to a clump of dry but deeply rooted sage, so she won't wander into a rocky pool and break a leg.

The air cools quickly once the sun drops out of sight. At four thousand feet, as darkness falls, the air is cold, but the steam is warm, and the ground so warm they don't need a fire. The heated earth is soothing. It's unnerving, too. This warmth coming toward them from who knows what source, it's uncanny. What kind of fire can send up steam and send these geysers twice as high as a man's head and make these freakish cones and spires?

As night spreads across the desert, the plumes make a hundred gauzy flags. Walter sees something out beyond the plumes. He has traveled with the party all the way from Springfield, single, restless, a steady fellow most of the time, but uneasy here. Seeing things. One dark, frosty night not long ago, when the Paiute wounded five of Donner's oxen, Walter was on guard duty. Now he sees those same marauders creeping through the steam. He isn't sure how many. Five? Six? A dozen?

Both men leap from their bedrolls, peering into the empty night. Jim sees nothing but vapor. Walter sees figures dancing in the steam, hears their groaning, night-piercing song. He shouts back, with threats and curses. When he lunges for the rifle, Jim grabs him and shakes him hard until the shouting subsides.

Afterward Jim has to calm himself. In the silence he thinks that no Indian would hazard such a place at night. He listens. There is nothing to hear. No wind. No voice. From time to time a whisper of releasing steam, which somehow makes the silence more complete. He would like to sleep. He needs the sleep. But his eyes won't close. The silence keeps him awake. He concentrates on it, as a way to ward off fear. No creatures here. No creature noise. No insect hum. No wind. The silent sand. The sprawl of stars in a silent sky, while vapor ascends and vanishes.

How has he ended up in such an empty and forsaken place, after all these weeks and months in the crowd of travelers, the loading of wagons, the cutting of trail, the settling of arguments, the abundance of mealtime, even as the food ran low, his daughters always there, his sons, his wife. His wife. His wife. He sees her standing by the wagon when he mounted, preparing to depart. Gazing at the sprawl of stars he hears her voice again.

It has to be, James. You know I'm right. We want you alive . . .

He hears the laughter of his children, long-ago and distant laughter from the yard in Springfield. He begins to hear the voices of his pals back home on the starry nights when they would step out onto a porch with their cigars and regard the Milky Way that spans the heavens like a million-pointed bridge and take comfort in its vaulting arch, sure evidence of the Guiding Hand that holds this universe in place.

Jim in exile, without the comfort of their full bellies and their many cigar ends in the balmy summer night and the scent of brandy on the air—Jim begins to wonder if there *is* a Guiding Hand. Could he be gazing at a million singular points of light, each one a ball of fire, as he has heard it said, our sun being one of them? And we revolve around the sun. Could this mean that other planets turn and float somewhere beyond what a human eye can see? And if that's so, how many? Might there be, somewhere, another like our own? A duplicate, perhaps? Another world with other empty places like this land of silent sand and rock and flags of undulating steam? Imagine yourself across the void, marooned upon the lonesome face of a far-off planet, a hundred million miles out into space, looking back upon this rolling speck, as small as the smallest pinpoint in the vault of stars . . .

It is a fearful thought. He lets it fade, glad for Walter slumbering nearby. At night a man needs company in such a place. "Walter," he says, and hears a wheeze, and waits, and hears another.

"Walter. You awake?"

ONE MORE DRY day and they reach the cooling channel of the Truckee River. Along its banks they see many footprints, some fresh, but they see no Indians. Maybe the Indians are going to stay out of sight and let them pass, these two bedraggled whites who have nothing but their blankets and one horse not worth taking.

Alders and cottonwoods tremble in the breeze above the water. Russet leaves and golden leaves make torches, a corridor of flame, which Jim and Walter follow until the river's winding canyon opens into a broad bowl bounded by dry and treeless slopes. A line of willows continues on through marshy meadowlands to mark the river's path across the bowl, the meadow spreading on the farther side, where the river leaves the Sierra Nevada Range.

These famous mountains are rising to the west, rising and rising, a light blue and hazy bulk against the sky, the higher peaks already capped with snow. Hastings described them. So did Fremont. But reading has not prepared him, nor has the look of the Wasatch Range prepared him. From the high plain his party followed out of Fort Bridger, the Wasatch made a subtler rise. These peaks, seen from the east, have a massive and eternal thickness that stirs the blood and makes the arm hairs prickle.

When the sun drops behind the farthest rippled ridge, a lemony glow sifts upward to fill the sky. The lemon slowly turns to tangerine. The snowy caps seem lit by fire. Now the crevices and creases are lost in shade. The canyon of the Truckee appears to be a low spot, a dip underneath the canopy of smoldering orange. The burnished sky softens, and the mountain contour almost looks benign, as if a way through this final barrier has been preordained, and all one has to do is follow it.

The next morning they set out from Truckee Meadows, passing through groves of tule higher than their hats. The river flows east, out into the desert, while they move west along its rocky channel, below thickening stands of yellow pine and fir. The second day in, they reach a lake with the same name as the river, named for the Paiute chief who guided an early wagon party along this route. It is a sparkling jewel of an alpine lake, profoundly blue, cobalt blue, between evergreen slopes of pine and fir and cedar.

Game is ever scarcer the higher they have climbed. Now they're out of food. For two days they've had nothing but berries and a few wild onions. Walter wants to stop and set up camp and hunt a while, but Jim won't do it. Beyond the lake a knobby barricade of stone swells for what looks to be a thousand feet or more. He knows they have to scale it. From here there is no other way. Meanwhile, the wind is colder. Clouds are gathering higher up. They're not prepared for heavy weather. He wants to make the summit before they lose their strength.

The looping switchback trail is broken by spills of scree and slick, treacherous granite chunks. Laboring upward, he imagines what it will be like bringing wagons over such a pass, with a track so narrow, toward the top, that a horse can barely pick its way. What do you do with a team of oxen? You lead them up one at a time, so he's heard, and reyoke them at the top, and down below you unload each wagon and carry your belongings on your back, however many trips it takes. As for the wagons, you take them apart. Axles, wheels, and wagon beds are fastened to ropes and chains. By block and tackle or by brute power of the teams, you haul them up the final yards of precipice.

From the top, looking back and down toward the blue oval of the lake, he imagines hauling up his double-decker Palace Car, the number of teams this will take, the number of hands, and wonders if the oxen have enough muscle left. Maybe he will be able to ride back this far with provisions and tell them to leave all the wagons down below and come ahead with whatever they can carry. Or maybe not. He'll see what lies ahead.

They are almost at the tree line here. Humps and parapets of granite soar above the trees. Wind like ice water spills toward them across the gray-white rock. They camp in a valley beyond the summit, spotted with patches of recent snow. The stream is low, waiting for another full winter to fill the many channels that flow both ways out of the high country. Up here all game has vanished. It is another night without dinner. Walter wants to shoot the horse.

"She's a lot worse off than we are, Mr. Reed. You'd be doing her a favor. Her and us too."

"We're not that far gone, not yet."

"Ain't doing us a lick a good."

"It can't be that long till we get where we're going."

Walter leaps to his feet and calls out toward the treetops. "Goddam it! We ain't gettin' nowhere if we don't find something to eat!"

"You think I don't know that?"

"Then gimme that rifle."

"We're not shooting the horse!"

Walter looks at the rifle, propped against a tree trunk. Before Reed can stop him he has grabbed it.

"Don't do this, Walter!"

"Cut 'er up. Jerk the meat."

Reed's hand is on his Bowie knife. "Drop the rifle."

Walter's eyes are large. He swings the barrel from the horse to Jim to the horse, and Jim is moving toward him.

"Right now!" he says.

He sees John Snyder's whip handle cutting through the chalk-dusty hides of the oxen, and that same anger rises. Why must animals be punished for our thoughtless misdeeds? Jim sees his racing mare, fallen over in the Salt Desert, dehydrated, too weak to lift her head. He had to shoot her there. It still haunts and burdens him. He would sooner take Walter's life. . . .

"We could keep going for days," Walter says.

"You shoot that horse, you better shoot me too."

In Walter's hand the barrel is a crazy compass needle looking for direction, pointing everywhere, finally swinging straight up beside his head. With a cry of anguish he fires into the overhanging branches. The blast startles them both, reverberating through the summit valley like thunder.

He looks at Jim and throws the rifle down and squats by the fire and spits onto a glowing ember and spits again and listens to it sizzle.

TWO DAYS LATER they are both delirious, wandering off the meager trail, finding it again, and losing it. They lead the horse, too thin and weary to bear a rider. Descending now, they come upon a wagon left to rot after a wheel tore loose. Where it veered into a trailside gully, it hangs at a tilt, like a schooner tacking in a gale.

They ransack the wreckage for any scraps or leavings, ripping boards loose, digging in the dirt. On hands and knees Jim the scavenger finds a tar bucket beneath the broken axle. He scrapes through black skin to uncover a layer of rancid fat, from the days when it had served as a tallow bucket.

He digs out a gob and sniffs it and draws back. But Walter does not hesitate. With greedy eyes and a triumphant shout he scoops it off the paddle and pops it into his mouth.

Hunkered next to the wagon, Jim watches to see what effect this will have. He digs out another gob and sniffs and again can't bear the smell, despite his gnawing hunger. Walter snatches it from the paddle, gives it half a chew and swallows it, and this too he manages to keep down.

They are both studying the bottom of the bucket. Jim digs out one more mouthful. If he doesn't swallow it, Walter will. He looks at Walter, who is watching the gob like a mountain lion ready to pounce. Jim takes it into his mouth, feels the tallow slide along his throat and instantly regrets the move. His shrunken stomach begins to convulse. It is like poison. It weakens his knees, makes him blind. His head is ready to explode. The world spins around him, and he falls to his knees, doubled with cramps. Cold sweat coats his body. His face goes white.

Walter is frantic, standing over him. "Don't die now, Mr. Reed! Please! Please! You can't die now!"

After ten minutes of agony he vomits out a vile and stringy yellow soup that looks like melting wax. Gradually the convulsive waves

let go. He can see again. Half an hour later he can stand weakly, leaning on the horse. Quelling his nausea, he moves one foot, the other,
staggers, finally walks. Before long they have reached another precipice, looking down into another valley where wagons are scattered
about. But these are not abandoned wagons. They see animals grazing, horses, mules, a few cattle standing in a well-watered pasture,
with a stream nearby, a long green meadow bordered with rising
stands of pine and fir.

Jim cries out "Hallelujah!" his voice cracked and feeble but full
of joy, as they lunge down the incline, the starving horse too weak
to ride, the beleaguered pilgrims tumbling and falling toward the
wagons.

His Dream

Oɴᴄᴇ ᴀɢᴀɪɴ ʜᴇ is at the summit looking down a rocky wall that drops and drops. Below, beyond, he sees the lake, from here a blue medallion in a bowl made of steeply sloping timber, but not a pleasing blue, not the blue you yearn to plunge into and swim away your cares. It is a heartless blue, the dark pit his wagon will fall into if the chains don't hold.

He hears the oxen grunt, straining at their yokes. How many, he cannot tell. Four. Eight. Twelve. More? Every animal they have. He hears the lash snap in mountain air so still and crisp each flicking whiplash seems to shatter it. He turns to see whose whip can crack open the air itself and knows before he turns that it is John Snyder standing on a rock above the heaving animals, lashing and snapping and cursing. It is Johnny in his trail hat, with his sleeves rolled back.

Jim calls, "Back off now! Let them be!"

But the teamster doesn't hear. Jim sees that chain links are spreading open. The load is too heavy. What's inside the wagon? Who's inside? Did Margaret unload all the children? Right beside his boot he can see the link stretch across a stony ledge, as the metal spreads and separates.

"Back off, Johnny! She's gonna tear loose!"

Again the whip falls on the backs of bleeding oxen. A link snaps. A chain breaks, then another, flying out above the void while the wagon is released to tumble down the cliff face. He watches it bounce from crag to crag, as boards fly loose and wheels spin away like pinwheels at a festival, and flour spills over the side. The wagon turns and tumbles, but it does not hit the blue-medallion lake, which grows smaller as the wagon plunges. A waterfall of flour spills from splitting sacks to coat the rocks with white dust.

A voice calls, "Mr. Reed."

Again he turns, expecting to see Johnny. But the teamster is gone. The oxen are gone. The wagon is gone. There is no lake below. He stands alone at the summit while the voice calls from farther away. It is not Snyder's voice.

"Mr. Reed!"

Nor is it Walter's.

"Mr. Reed! Wake up!"

His tongue is thick and dry as sand. His stomach is queasy. He holds still, waiting until the voice comes again, closer this time, very close. Is it right above him?

"Wake up. It's Charlie."

Behind his closed eyes Jim lets the summit dissolve. His head aches, feels larger, as if expanding, as if pushing outward from within. He feels his bones against the earth, his bedroll. On the whole long trail behind him and ahead of him, there is only one Charlie he can think of, pint-size Charlie Stanton. Jim remembers watching him ride away, so silly-looking perched atop his mule, so out of place, like a banker who'd been lifted off the streets of Chicago and carried a thousand miles west and dropped down in the middle of the desert. He remembers wondering if he would ever see this fellow again.

Jim opens his eyes to make sure it's him, then sits up with a hand outstretched. "You are a mighty welcome sight."

Charlie grabs his hand in both of his, seeming on the verge of tears. "Fella told me someone had come through on foot. I wondered if it could be from our party. But I swear, Mr. Reed, I saw you laying here and I hardly recognized you at all."

Charlie can't conceal his alarm. In the other man's face Jim sees how he must look to others now. He touches a hand to his gaunt and thinning features, his matted beard. The hair his daughters cut away has grown a bit but not enough to cover the unhealed welts, raw and crimson. Charlie is gazing at the welts.

"We had a few hard days," Jim says, nodding toward a nearby heap of blankets and oilskins. "Walter and me, we came ahead."

Charlie's eyes are full of questions he doesn't ask.

". . . to get more help," Jim says.

"How long since you've eaten?"

"We ate last night. Some folks here cooked up some meat. We're all right now. I think I'm all right. Walter might still be sick. He ate till he threw up . . ."

The words come slow. His throat feels closed and ragged. Charlie hunkers next to him, opens a shoulder pack, and pulls out what was going to be his lunch, a couple of biscuits, a strip of jerky. "Here," he says with a grin. " 'Bout time for breakfast."

"Walter," Jim calls, "you ready for breakfast?"

The heap turns, emits a miserable groan, falls silent.

"You're a good fellow," Jim says as he breaks off a piece of biscuit and begins to chew, slowly and deliberately. "One of the best."

He has never tasted such a delicious biscuit. With each bite his spirits rise. He looks at Charlie in amazement, amazed to see him here, a familiar face. If Charlie had been with them on the Humboldt, if the company by that time had not broken up into so many pieces, things would surely have gone another way. By some miracle Charlie had made no enemies. No one bore him a grudge. He always did more than his share, more than anyone expected, since he was not a family man. He is a bachelor, a loner, traveling without a wagon, who has had some wins and some losses in life, and the losses show around his eyes, a melancholy cheerfulness. For a number of years he was a merchant in Chicago, but fell on hard times and decided to head west hoping for a change of luck. He still dresses like a merchant, in his broadcloth coat, spectacles, bowler hat. He still has about him an oddly prosperous and well-fed look, even here in this wilderness valley, ruddy cheeks, a bit of belly pushing at his buttons.

When Charlie and Bill McCutcheon left the company a month ago, some predicted he was gone for good. McCutcheon will be back, they said, because his wife and child are with us. But why in the world would Stanton come back into this unforgiving land? "Would you?" Elizabeth Graves once asked, with an accusing eye. "If you was a single fella and no ties to anyone, nor any family calling?"

But here he is, a hundred miles north and east of the fort, with seven mules loaded and two more men, thanks to Captain Sutter, two Indians hunkered in the sun, watching and waiting. McCutcheon came down with a fever, Charlie tells him, and had to stay behind. It's malaria, Charlie thinks.

"You'll see him when you get there. Hard to believe a man that big and strong could get so weak he can hardly walk."

From Charlie he learns that the battle for California has already been waged and won. In the five months since they crossed the Missouri, the towns and bays and presidios all along the coast have been taken without firing a shot. It has been declared a U.S. Territory, with a military governor in charge. Sutter's Fort has been turned into an army garrison during what they call "the period of transition." Not all the Mexicans are happy about the new arrangement, Charlie says. Just last week he heard about some kind of rebellion in Los Angeles. Captain Fremont and his troops have already started down to take care of it. Fact is, everywhere you go you hear stories about our women getting captured and violated, and children getting kidnapped. The Mexicans are beasts, they say, torture their enemies and rape without mercy. That's why you see these wagons here in Bear Valley.

"They came over with the Hastings bunch. Some were here when I came through two weeks ago. Some are still here. People are sick, of course, or worn down from the crossing, or waiting for fresh animals to be brought up. But you'll meet some who are just plain scared. Hastings pumped 'em full of stories about how we got to band together and subdue the Mexicans and make room for a new place in the world. Then they got this far, and word comes trickling up the mountain about what the Mexicans are doing to our people. I heard one story about a fella from Virginia, got captured and forced to crawl around on his hands and knees till this vaquero rope-tied him like a calf and castrated him in front of his wife and children and then branded him with a red-hot iron. Ya see, some of these folks are afraid to move. It's too late to turn back, and there's no will to go forward. They're sort of paralyzed, waiting for somebody to tell 'em what to do. They curse Lansford Hastings for bringing them all this way and then riding off into the sunset. He doesn't have any wagons of his own, nor any family. He's just like me. He can come and go as he pleases."

"And what about the Mexicans? Is it true what people say?"

"Hard to tell," Charlie says. "I myself have yet to run into one."

"All the way from here to Sutter's Fort and back?"

"At the fort I saw two fellas looked like they could've been. But maybe they were Indians."

"What does Sutter say?"

"Well, now, Captain Sutter, he's a special case, since he will tell you he is part Mexican himself."

"I thought he was Swedish."

"Fact is, he's a Swiss."

"I believe Hastings described him as Swedish."

"That is just one more thing Mr. Hastings got wrong. Sutter comes from Switzerland. But he also happens to be a citizen of Mexico. That's how he got hold of so much land."

"I'll be damned," says Jim. "Whose side is he on then? Ours, or theirs?"

"I heard it depends on which way the wind blows."

These two could talk for hours, trading news, and they would, if this were after sundown instead of after sunup. Charlie feels the burden of his mission, pushing east now at a steady pace. Last night he camped lower down the valley. He wants to make the Yuba River today, and Jim is tempted to join him, tempted to turn around right now. Charlie and his two Indians, along with these fresh animals—it might just be enough to bring the party through.

He is tempted until he takes a close look at how much Charlie is packing, the many sacks of flour and beans and jerked beef.

Together they calculate the days it will take his mule train to reach the party, and where the wagons are likely to be found—somewhere along the Truckee?—and how many days from there to bring them past the summit. They figure how much game can be counted on, and how many mouths must be fed for that many days, and they realize, as they talk it through, that Charlie's provisions will not get eighty people all the way across. With no large setbacks, they might make it to the top of this valley. They might. Or they might not. But if food and fresh animals were waiting somewhere between here and the summit, well, that could make the difference.

As he studies Charlie's load, Jim's future takes its first clear shape. It is like a military campaign. In his mind the days line up. He will meet them right up there, above Bear Valley, and his accusers can be damned. His accusers! He will show them that it takes more than squabbling and blaming to bring a wagon party through. He sees his own mule train with another load like Charlie's, piled with fresh provisions. Already he sees the lead wagon coming toward him, as it clears a distant rise. He feels the thrill of that first sighting. By God, he will show them. . . .

Charlie beckons to the Indians, who wait near their horses. He calls them Salvador and Luis. They speak Spanish, but no English. They are not like the starvlings Jim saw in the desert. They too look well fed, full in the face, with clear eyes that do not connive or plead. They wear ranching clothes and are solidly built, muscular, alert. From the way they move the animals around, Jim sees that they're capable horsemen who could be good allies on the long trail back. They could turn on Charlie, of course, as soon as these wagons are out of sight and earshot, and steal the laden mules. But he seems to trust them, and they have some fear of Sutter, he says, who has threatened to execute them if any mules are lost.

Jim looks at Charlie, marveling again at the loyalty of this man who could have remained in the settlements, who has no earthly reason to take these hazards upon himself—none but his own sense of honor. How rare it is these days, Jim thinks, to find a man of honor. The thought grips him, and the idea that these seven mule loads are headed toward the dusty band still plodding along somewhere between the Humboldt and the Truckee. He feels tears welling.

"You're a prince, Charlie. Once we have all made it through, we'll have a banquet. We'll have the biggest damn banquet you or I have ever seen, and you will be the honored guest. I swear to you, this shall not be forgotten!"

Embarrassed by his outburst, Stanton has to turn away.

"How do you say 'thank you' in Spanish, Charlie?"

"They say 'grassias.' "

Jim knows he should be wary around any kind of Indian and never let his guard down. But the moment gets the best of him. He reaches for a hand, hoping to convey the depth of his gratitude for what they're all about to do. He wants to trust them. He has to. The lives of his wife and children now depend upon these men.

"Grassias," he says.

"They put 'moochas' in front of that," Charlie says. "Say 'moochas grassias, Salvador.' "

Jim squeezes the hand. "Moochas grassias, Salvador."

"De nada," says the Indian.

"Moochas grassias, Luis."

The men smile courteously, uncertain how to handle this. "De nada," they mutter. "De nada."

"And Charlie, please tell Margaret you saw me. Tell her I'm doing fine. No need to mention how I look, you hear? You tell her I'm doing fine, and we'll meet up again in no time."

"I surely will tell her that, Mr. Reed."

Charlie gives him one of Sutter's horses and a packet of jerked beef and flour. Then they move out in single file, Charlie and the Indians riding, the mules behind. Jim walks with them to the edge of the trees. He watches them cross the valley and begin the slow, torturous ascent up the wall he and Walter tumbled down yesterday. It looks to be six or seven hundred feet of loose rock where few trees have ever found a hold.

From the grove he looks across the wide meadow that runs the length of Bear Valley. For the first time in days his heart lifts. The sun is bright and warming him, making green things greener, the wild peas and mallow and the broad-leaved mule ear along the marshy banks of the stream. What a fine place this will be to bring his family for their first taste of California, an early moment of reward, where we can rest the animals before the final trek out to the settlements. Charlie has heard that last year the summit was passable until December, and that's still six weeks away. This morning not a cloud is to be seen from here to the farthest granite dome.

His Heart's Desire

WALTER IS TOO sick to move. The tallow has caught up with him. Everything has caught up with him. An Illinois family takes him in, people who traveled with Jim's party for a while along the Platte, lingering here a few more days to fatten up their stock. Jim is not much better off than Walter. He too should linger a while and fatten up, but won't let himself. After one day's rest he says good-bye to Walter and the mare and joins two horsemen from Tennessee heading for sea level.

The trail out of Bear Valley is the steepest yet, another drop where animals slide, where wagons will have to be lowered with chains and oxen led down one by one. His head pounds with each plunging lurch. Twice he nearly tumbles from the saddle. Staying close to the river, they pass Mule Springs and Steep Hollow Crossing. As they swing away from the river's narrow channel, to climb again, he falls behind the others, nearly blind with headache. Then they are clambering in and out of canyons. In Jim's wobbly condition the long westward unfoldment of the Sierras seems a maze of ridges and gullies without pattern, without end.

One day about noon, when a voice calls from high above, he does not understand the words. He doesn't react, keeps plodding up the raggedy slope toward a voice not aimed at him. From the top of a long rise he finally sees what the others see. After all these months the dreamed-of destination is laid before them, the valley of the Sacramento, still miles away but vivid in transparent light. Through the center a line of heavy growth marks the north-south course of its largest river, with tributary streams and creeks marked by lesser lines that fan and wiggle outward like the branches of a great tree spread across the flatness.

"Thar she blows!" shouts one of the men.

"Ain't she a beauty!" cries the other.

"Be goddamned if we ain't made it across!"

Jim nods his throbbing head and smiles and lets them do the shouting. His jaw and temples feel swollen. His belly hurts. He doesn't trust this view. He has been deceived before. He wants to get down closer to it, look for the trail that will take them into the lower foothills and the place Stanton told him about, the first outpost, William Johnson's ranch.

Two more hours bring them to a building, low and squat, sitting on cleared dirt with no road leading toward it or away from it. There appears to be a stretched cowhide for a door. In the ten weeks since Jim left Fort Bridger, it's the first sign of any settlement at all, a two-room shack, half adobe, half timber, set back from the Bear River, with pens beyond, a rickety corral. No fences. No barns. He sees a few more wagons scattered among the nearest trees, and unyoked cattle grazing.

Though there is no gate, Johnson is a kind of gatekeeper at this end of the emigrant trail. They find him behind the shack, where two naked Indian men are layering adobe bricks. Their bodies are dark and muscular. Their hands and feet are covered with gloves and stockings of chalky brown mud. Johnson's trousers are muddy to the knees. He wears an ancient felt hat but no shirt. He too is brown, barrel-chested. He is cursing the mud and the sun and welcomes the chance to leave this task and see to his visitors. He has a rough, wind-worn face, a reddish beard streaked with gray, the rolling walk of a man who has spent some time at sea.

Johnson seems accustomed to strangers, used to their hungers and their dazed wonder at having survived this far. He acts as if he has been expecting Jim and the Tennessee men, says he doesn't have much to offer, but there might be some cheese and milk and bread.

"I ain't been here hardly a year," he says.

As Jim dismounts, his knees give way and he drops to the ground. In the midday heat it feels like high summer. His cheeks and brows glisten. They drag him into the shade and prop him against the timbers. Johnson calls out in a language Reed doesn't understand.

He lets his eyelids close, waiting for the wooziness to pass. When he opens them an Indian woman is hunkering at his side. She studies the welts festering on his scalp. She doesn't speak. Her face is young and pleasant. Her eyes are oval. Her black hair, held by a tightly rolled bandanna, falls past her shoulders in two thick strands. When she stands and leans over him for a closer look, he sees that she is wearing a short skirt of furred skin, perhaps deer, with bits of shell around the waist, and a necklace made of shell bits, but nothing else. Her flesh is very smooth. Her breasts are large and pendulous, much larger than Margaret's. He wants to look at her, but again his eyelids close. He falls into a long, dreamy sleep, a half-wakeful sleeping dream, during which the woman twice appears. When he wakes he is alone inside the dark cabin, and he thinks she may have been a phantom, but soon she is next to him again. Her hands are gentle as she applies to his scalp a sticky poultice that smells like pine.

This time he sleeps for sixteen hours and wakes to find his companions gone. He tries to rise, as if to follow and catch up with them, but he doesn't have the strength. And so he lingers another day at Johnson's Ranch, and then another, while she applies the sticky poultice, and a pulp of heated roots, and feeds him bowls of a bitter, medicinal brew, and murmurs words strange to his ears. He tries to learn her name, but she won't tell him. He offers her money, but she won't take it. Johnson tells him, with a satisfied grin, that she doesn't know what money is. "And the less she knows, the better, wouldn't you say so, Mr. Reed?"

One night he feels well enough to sit up late. He and Johnson eat large chunks of recently slaughtered beef that have been skewered on pointed sticks and roasted over the open fire. They eat without plates and throw the bones and rims of fat into the flames, where they blacken. Their hands and faces gleam with the grease. From a jug they sip aguardiente brought up from Sonoma by way of Sutter's. Jim can't remember how long it has been since he's had a drink. A month? His last bottle of brandy is packed away somewhere in the Palace Car, in safekeeping for a moment such as this, to celebrate his arrival in the promised land.

The liquor goes straight to his head. He will have to pace himself. This is a night for swapping the stories of their lives. Where do you come from? Where have you been? What curious twists and turns have brought each of us to this particular place at this odd time? Yet there are certain things he shouldn't talk about tonight. His fight, for one. On this side of the mountain, why spread the news around? Until the rest of them make it through, who's to agree or disagree?

On the other hand, why can't he revise the story here and there? With the aguardiente warming his insides, Jim is tempted to make the knifing of the teamster a tale of high danger and desert bravery. But no. No. Better not to risk raising doubts in any mind, when you're going to need all the help you can get.

Already he is looking for allies. Already he knows Johnson's will be the leaping-off place. When you've come from overland, this is your first stop. Heading out the other way, as Jim knows he soon must do, it is your last stop. So he deletes the murder scene, as he relives all the rest, the thirsty days, the mountain nights, the plight of families left behind.

Johnson listens and scratches his chest. He scratches his thick, grease-polished beard and wags his head in near disbelief, as if Jim is claiming to have landed from the moon.

"I'd go back in there with ya," he says, "but I wouldn't be much good, since I never been up as far as you fellas been. Farthest I've traveled is one day's ride out the Bear River canyon. That's my limit. I'm no mountaineer and got no cause to be, though I don't mind the view. It's pleasant having mountains to look at from time to time. You want to know the truth, I have had my fill of snow. That's why I shipped out when I did. I'd had my fill, and when I heard about the South Seas, that sounded like the place for me. But what with one thing and another . . ."

He'd been a ship's mate and had sailed around Cape Horn, touching all the famous ports, Santiago, Acapulco, San Pedro, Honolulu, Sitka. Six years ago he stepped ashore at Yerba Buena and left the sea behind to become a riverman working cargo on the Sacramento.

Then this land came up for auction, he says. "Me and a partner located a hundred and fifty dollars and made our bid, and lo and behold, I got me a rancho now and a herd of cattle and two young squaws to keep me company at night."

His laugh spills upward with the fiery sparks, a loud and raucous laugh full of mischief and wonder. Johnson is still astounded at the way his life has turned out.

"You mind if I ask how much land you got for a hundred and fifty dollars?"

Johnson scratches his neck, as if he minds a little. He finds something there, a tick or a chigger, squeezes and tosses it aside, flinging his arm wide in helpless surrender to his windfall. "Haven't had time to find out where all of it exactly is. Somewhere in the neighborhood of twenty thousand acres . . ."

"You say twenty *thousand*?"

"Or twenty-two. Maybe it's twenty-two. And I paid a whole lot more than the last fella paid. You know what the word 'grant' means? It means free for the asking. That's the way the greasers do it. They just pass out ranchos to each other like pieces of birthday cake. First one to have this spread got it straight from the gobernador."

"And where is he now?"

"The gobernador?"

"The one who had the ranch."

"They hung him."

"Who hung him?"

"You have to understand there are two kinds of greasers. Them from Mexico. And them from California. And they hardly ever get along."

Johnson drinks from the brandy jug and passes it to Jim, who drinks and settles back to listen to the story of Johnson's Ranch. Soon he will be hearing such stories wherever he goes. The struggle with Mexico has been brewing for years. In the province known as Alta California no one has ever been in charge for very long. The land is vast and empty. The laws are feeble. The men in power appear and disappear like coyotes.

Until last year, Johnson tells him, the gobernador was a politician sent up from Mexico City. The local rancheros never liked him much, and they were getting ready to run him out. When Captain Sutter got wind of their plan, he tried to send a warning down to Monterey, since he was then on the side of the gobernador, angling for more land grants of his own. Sutter's messenger, a fellow called Pablo, was the one who used to own this ranch. He and Sutter had been together for years, ever since they'd worked the Santa Fe Trail together back in the 1830s. Before Pablo left the fort, they fitted him out with a special boot that had some kind of false sole where the secret message was concealed. Alas, it didn't stay concealed for long. Some Californios captured him on the road to Monterey. They searched him up and down. They tore his saddlebags apart, and his saddle. Then they tore his boots apart and found the message written by Captain Sutter to the hated gobernador who had been appointed by indifferent officials three thousand miles away. They hung poor Pablo right there by the side of the road, just south of San Jose, hung him without mercy, says Johnson, "the way them greasers do."

"Next thing I hear, there is going to be a land auction down at Sutter's Fort. When you been out here a while you learn to strike while the iron is hot. Captain Sutter, you see, he'd had a hand in this deal from the start. In these parts he is the judge and the jury and the land agent and the bank and the chief of police and just about anything else you can think of. Him and the gobernador were thick as thieves—that is, before the gobernador got run out. When Pablo petitioned for all this land, Sutter spoke up for him, and that was good enough for the gobernador, who signed the grant. Now the gobernador is long gone, back to Mexico City with his tail between his legs. And Pablo is dead, God rest his soul. And I got the land. And Captain Sutter, far as I know, he kept the hundred and fifty dollars, though that is none of my business, as long as each man gets what's coming to him."

STARTING SOUTH the next morning, Jim still hears this story as he rides, wondering how much of it is true. He has never heard of one man possessing so much land. And for so little! A hundred and fifty dollars for twenty-two thousand acres? Why, that's less than a penny an acre. It is hard to believe. Yet he wants to believe it. He wants to believe that in this new country all things are possible. As he follows the Bear River he doesn't think about the muddy-footed bricklayers or the woman who ministered to him, whose people have lived here for so many thousands of years. Nor does he think about the governor from Mexico who has never been near the huge tract he signed over to a fellow from Santa Fe. Jim is thinking about the extraordinary timing and Johnson's luck. The earth here is rich. Already many bushels of wheat have been gathered. They make their own bread. Their own cheese. And water flows all year long, flowing down from the Sierras.

Beyond the river, rolling foothills gradually level out, across miles of pastureland and open country. How much of it belongs to Johnson? There's no way to tell. He has so much land his cattle run loose, without fences, like buffalo.

Jim follows the Bear to its junction with the Feather and from there heads farther south through marshy bottomland even richer than the pastures higher up. Today his eyes seem sharper, his head clearer. He looks at this place with clearer eyes, yet what he sees is like a dream. Between the long mountain ranges east and west, it is a vast park, perfectly flat. He figures crossing it would take a day of steady riding. The channel of the Feather is lined with oak and sycamore. Wild grapevines wind through the undergrowth along its banks. He sees unfamiliar creatures here, cranes and pelicans. Around him groves of oak trees decorate the broad and level plain, their canopies like sculpture. He sees elk and blacktail deer. Under gnarled, spreading limbs he sees a herd of pronghorn antelope, two hundred animals at least, who take no notice of his passing. He sees ponds where wild ducks feed, and more ponds, a chain of mirrors under a sky without clouds, until a cloud of ducks obscures the sun, flapping and veering, a thousand ducks, or five thousand, he cannot tell.

Silently he mouths "Hallelujah!" The virginal abundance is like an alcoholic fume. Wonder fills his heart, and stronger than the wonder is a welling desire that intoxicates him. He is here at last. Yes! He has made it, though not in the way he once imagined he would make it, never dreaming he would arrive alone, with so many miles and days between him and his family. Perhaps it is a blessing to have arrived at all, and he gives thanks that he may have arrived in time to possess some part of this unspoiled place, to inhabit it, make his mark upon it and make it his own. Make it *their* own.

This time he speaks the word aloud. "HALLELUJAH!," an outburst to ward off an unexpected pang of doubt. Somewhere inside this wondrous spectacle he feels a menace. What it is or where it is, he cannot say. His eyes are following a shadow thrown across the valley by the thick cloud of ducks, so many they eclipse the sun. It occurs to him that it might be too soon to bring a family into such a wild place. Are the Mexicans as dangerous as they are made out to be? Should he have waited another year to try this journey?

By early afternoon he has crossed the American River, so low at the ford this time of year the water is no higher than his horse's knees. The trail here is heavily used, passing through more level country, spotted with oaks. He sees a village, a cluster of domes covered with dirt and built close to the ground. He sees the smoke of cooking fires. He passes a field where cowboys are cutting longhorn cattle out of a herd. They are local Indians, he later learns, working for Sutter. One fellow does something Jim hasn't seen before. He rides with a coil of rope in one hand, throws it toward a moving bull, and the loop falls deftly around the horns. Jim watches another fellow do this, and another, then they lead the reluctant creatures toward the fort, now a mile or so ahead, on a swell of land well back from the river.

There are deep ditches here, four or five feet wide, to separate the unfenced rangelands from broad stubbled fields where grain has been harvested. Closer to the fort he sees a few emigrant wagons with the clutter of their rustic campsites under oaks. He sees corrals and storage sheds, then the whitewashed walls are rising ahead of him—after all these hundreds of empty miles, an adobe bulwark three times higher than a man is tall, with corner blockhouses notched for artillery.

Compared to Fort Bridger, with its log-cabin trading post and picket-fence stockade, this is a fortress. This is a castle. A white building shows above the walls, and on a pole rising from the peak of its sloping roof an American flag now flies.

A broad dirt track leads up to the gate. In front of it, two Indian soldiers in military jackets and buckskin trousers pace slowly back and forth, underneath a wizened face that grins down at all who pass. Above the gate, a human head has been impaled upon a spike so that it too, like the flag, can be widely seen. The eyes are long gone, pecked out by birds. The skin is dark, sunburnt and shriveled, drawn back from yellowing teeth. Strands of black hair dangle past the neck.

Another Man with a Secret

At a second-story window John Augustus Sutter looks out across his compound toward the south gate where yet another emigrant stands seeking entrance. Who is it, he wonders, and what will he want? A bed? A fresh horse? A sack of flour? A job? How many has he seen this year? How many more will be coming, the longed-for multitude that now fills his days with apprehension?

Sutter wears an unbuttoned military jacket so that a pot belly is revealed, pushing against his shirt. A moustache curves above his upper lip. Beneath his mouth there's a small triangular goatee, a bushy medallion on his chin. The hair across his scalp is almost gone, or perhaps has been relocated to the long, full sideburns that drop past his ears. Alone at the window, he stands erect, with his shoulders shoved back, as if inspecting a squad of recruits, wishing he were a captain again, instead of second in command at his own fort.

He is thinking of the courier who rode in this afternoon from Monterey, who ran sweating across the plaza in search of Fremont's anointed lieutenant. Can things get any worse? That message should have come straight to *him*! Until this summer, all couriers from Monterey came looking for John Sutter. Now, in his own house, he is the last to learn what is going on. Two hours later the news came trickling across the compound, mouth by mouth, and who knows how much truth remains in the story he has heard, of American forces at Los Angeles Pueblo being beaten back, driven to their ship. A hundred marines had sailed down from the Bay of San Francisco to quell the insurrection, and now we're told they have been defeated, with six dead—or sixteen? or sixty?—and the southern pueblo once again under Mexican control.

Did he, Sutter, make another mistake by letting the Americans take charge here and fly their flag above his fort? Is it possible that the

Mexicans might somehow win this struggle after all? Surely they can't last much longer. They have no ammunition, no defense against ships of war. Their troops are untrained, their artillery useless. This remote, badly managed province was abandoned years ago.

But suppose that policy has somehow been reversed? What if reinforcements have finally found their way north? You hear rumors about shiploads of Mexican troops landing in the dark of night. Has it all been too easy—each port and pueblo taken like a man caught half asleep? Were they simply buying time?

No. No, he thinks. It's out of the question. That kind of foresight would be out of character.

From the decanter on his desk he pours half a cup of brandy and sniffs and swirls it and sniffs again and gazes into it before he sips. His third this afternoon. He doesn't like to drink alone. Companionship adds savor. This fellow at the gate, should he be invited in? Or could there be another family waiting somewhere out of view, the wife, the ragged children? Never has he seen so many wives, so many children as have passed his way this year. For months they have been coming, and still they come, and why does the sight of it fill him with misgivings? Hasn't he dreamed of the numbers that would one day gather here and provide the strength to wrest this land from the Mexicans, who have never had a clear idea of what to do with it?

These Americans, they think like he thinks. They see the same opportunities. There is a recognition, a sizing up of one another that is familiar. He likes that. And yet he does not like it. There are so many now. So suddenly. While their warships fill the bays, the horses and wagons roll over the Sierras, or down from Oregon, family by family, and before you know it, the men turn into soldiers. They call themselves soldiers, though many are not. Vagabonds and bullies—that is what they become. Captain Fremont, who now calls himself a colonel, would like the world to believe he commands a military company. But under whose authority, Sutter has to wonder. They have no uniforms. They roam up and down the province, stealing what they need. They come here where Fremont knows he has always been welcome, and they steal this fort away, put another man in charge, an infant who has never marched in battle, who marched across the continent in Fremont's shadow, a twenty-three-year-old lieutenant replacing *him*, John Sutter, and removing his very name from the map of the region he himself transformed. They call it Fort Sacramento now. What a humiliation! What a joke! Despising Mexicans, they give the fort a Mexican name.

From his window he can see corrals and fallow fields and garden plots and sheds. Were it not for him, there would be no cultivation here, no sheep or cattle, no blacksmith shops to make new shoes for Fremont's horses, no barracks for his so-called troops. There would be no grapes, no melons, no tomatoes, no brandy. There would be no fort. There would only be the meager huts of the tribes who awaited Sutter when he sailed up the river and chose this spot and set up his cannon and fired off a few rounds, sending unknown forms of thunder up and down the valley to let them understand who had come to stay.

Does Colonel Fremont appreciate this, he asks himself? Not for a moment. He thinks we have too many friends among the Mexicans. Because the flag of Mexico has flown here, he thinks I can't be trusted. He forgets that you do not survive in such a place without allies and alliances. He forgets that when I built this fort the Americans north of San Francisco Bay could be gathered into a single room. He forgets how many I have befriended, offering refuge in a hostile land. He forgets that I formed the first militia here, to subdue the tribes, and now they work for me! They work for me by the hundreds. And I feed them well. And many come to me in friendship . . .

Across the compound he sees the new emigrant looking up at the face of a man who used to be such a friend, the shrunken head of the Mokelumne Miwok chief. Once a respected ally, he had been persuaded by the commandant from Monterey to turn against this fort. Sutter had to hunt him down and execute him, and mount his head above the gate as an example to all the others. I try to be generous and just, he tells himself. I am not at heart a brutal man. But some of them will never comprehend justice. They only comprehend fear. At the edge of this wilderness, fear is a necessary tool.

Now a messenger is crossing the compound. Sutter waits for the knock below. He sips his brandy. He listens. He waits for Manuiki, who will bring this message to him. Her bare feet make no noise upon the stair, but he knows she is ascending. She appears at his door.

"A visitor," she says.

She stands regarding him with her large black eyes. The luminous glow is gone, like a fireplace of coals banked for the night. Her face is a mask, as it has been for two days. Too bad, he thinks. Too bad I have to put up with this. Too bad she has to be so nosy about my habits.

"Who is it?"

"Mister Reed."

Sutter nods.

Reed.

Where has he heard this name? Was it from the fellow who led the mule train out of here last week? Yes. The small fellow. Stanton told them all the story of that unlucky company, the last bunch on the trail. And Reed, yes. Isn't he one of the leaders? Maybe they have finally made it through.

"James Reed?"

"I think so."

"Is he alone?"

She shrugs. "Who knows?"

"I'll meet him at the gate, then."

She turns to leave.

"Manuiki."

At the door she waits but doesn't turn. She wears a plain cotton dress that covers her arms and legs. Her black hair is gathered on top of her head. Her neck is the color of chocolate, darker than the Indians. He has always liked her neck. He has had silver earrings delivered just so he could see them hanging there. Too bad she now behaves so much like a wife and cannot be the tender, pliant thing she used to be when they sailed out of Honolulu and he brought her here to be his Manuiki, his little bird. She is putting on weight. Her hips are spreading. Is she pregnant again? That could be it, though he prays it is not. There have been enough children.

He says, "Why are you unhappy?"

She doesn't move or speak.

He lifts his brandy cup. "Come. Have a drink with me."

The stairs squeak, but her feet make no sound as she descends. He sips. Down below he hears her voice speaking to the messenger. She must know I brought in the new Indian girl again, he thinks. But is that any business of hers? I am still in command here, no matter what Colonel Fremont and his lackeys may believe.

·　　　·　　　·

BEYOND THE GATE Reed stands waiting. Sutter observes his filthy buckskins, his battered hat, his unruly beard, the lean, fierce look of prolonged hunger. What a test it is, he thinks, getting through this country. What it takes out of a man.

Sutter is known for his hospitality and courtesy. It pains him to tell Reed that he cannot be invited inside these walls, nor can he be offered a place to sleep, without the approval of Fremont's lieutenant.

"You are already known to us," says Sutter, with a charming and self-deprecating smile. "If it were up to me, you would enter now and receive a royal welcome."

Where he sleeps tonight, says Reed, doesn't matter. As soon as possible he's heading back along the trail, a hundred miles or so, maybe more, and he needs provisions, horses.

"You have already been generous. We'll be very grateful for what-ever else you can provide. I have a wife and four young children still out there, with the company . . ."

Reed's voice breaks. He averts his eyes in a way that touches Sutter, who can see that Reed has some cultivation, rough-hewn, but a cut above so many who appear at this gate and never leave. He hears grief and passion in this voice. Against his will, Sutter is reminded that he too has a family waiting somewhere else. He prefers not to think about this, but the urgency of the father standing here takes him by surprise. The thought of his wife makes Sutter long for a drink. He does not miss much about Europe, but he misses the quality of the liquor. His taste buds are stirred, as if the aroma of schnapps has traveled eight thousand miles in an instant. He can smell it. Saliva gathers around his tongue. It makes him thirsty, it makes him sentimental. His eyes are wet. He misses his son, his firstborn, who would be twenty or more. He must send for them all. Yes. Too much time has passed since he left Burgdorf, though who knows where they could live, now that his fort has been stolen out from under him, and what could he offer them here? It is too late in the year, of course, to ask them to make such a journey, with the winter approaching. But in the spring he could send for them. Most definitely. Yes. In the spring. In the spring . . .

"Do you have sons?" he says to Reed.

"Two sons, yes, and two daughters."

"And a wife, you say?"

"Yes."

"And you left them all in the mountains?"

"We had not reached the mountains yet. We fell behind. The herds we started with were half gone. Supplies were running low."

It is very odd, thinks Sutter, that he would be the man to come ahead, a man who appears to be a few years older than himself, a man of some position in the company. A younger man would have been much better suited for that ordeal. Watching him talk, Sutter knows there is more to it. Reed is concealing something. But then he thinks, Who isn't? We all have things to hide. And he is drawn to Reed, as another man with a secret.

"Somehow these adobe walls are no longer mine," he says, "thanks to Colonel Fremont. But the herds, the corrals, the sheds, these things I still control. You tell me what you need. I may find one or two vaqueros to help you with the animals."

"We are indebted, sir. We want you to know that George Donner, who was elected captain of our party, will stand behind all our obligations."

From inside his shirt Reed pulls a folded scrap of heavy paper with a letter of guarantee, signed in Donner's hand. Sutter glances at it.

"When the time comes we can settle these details. I know of George Donner. We get wind of travelers long before they arrive. Much of the country you have passed through is known to me. Though I have not seen the Wasatch Range or the Salt Desert, I have already heard of your struggles there, thanks to your friend who recites William Shakespeare with such enthusiasm."

"You mean Bill McCutcheon."

"I have read some of Shakespeare's work, of course, but long ago, and in translation . . ."

"Is he still laid up?"

"I believe he is walking again. I saw him at noon."

"So he's here at the fort."

"At this moment he is probably in a meeting to which I have not been invited, though I am sure you will be welcome. Everyone there is an American, or so I have been told."

Sutter's voice is rising. His eyes are red-rimmed with sudden anger.

"How can I reach him?" Reed says.

"They are drinking my brandy, you can be sure of that. But they no longer care for my opinions. No one trusts me, you see! General Castro thinks I am aligned with the Americans! Colonel Fremont thinks I am aligned with the Mexicans! While he gallops up and down the province with his battalion of vagabonds, I am not to be trusted with the command of my own domain. Now men who have been in this region but a few days or weeks gather in a room in this fort I have built, and there they make plans that I am not privy to!"

From the look on Reed's face he can tell he has said too much, or spoken too loudly. He softens his voice, saying he will send a messenger to Fremont's lieutenant on Reed's behalf and request an entrance to the fort. Sometime soon, Sutter adds, he will look forward to inviting Reed to dine with him.

NOW HE STANDS in the dining room, pouring himself another cup of brandy while he waits for Manuiki, who will soon come in to set the table. This Reed, he thinks, seems like a decent fellow, a man he's glad to help. Providing these travelers with what they need, of course, is a form of insurance. When the party finally makes it past the mountains, Sutter will get his mules and his Indians back. He will also get paid for the flour.

Doing business has been the good part about emigrant traffic. And there will be more of it. More business. And more traffic. As the Reeds of the world keep coming and keep crowding him.

That's how it feels. The future is crowding him. Sutter's hope is that the Mexicans cannot hold out. If they give up the fight, Fremont will lose interest. He and his followers will move on to the next adventure, and Sutter will have his fort back. Yes. But then what? What next? There was a time when he thought he knew. These days who can know anything, with the world transforming itself at such a pace. He grows weary of these unforeseeable changes. He grows weary of his fort, the burden of his fort. Days like this he would like to be rid of it. If the Americans are so taken with its virtues, perhaps he should let them have it. Perhaps he should simply sell them this accursed fort, pay off all his creditors, and be a free man at last! He has heard that the naval commander from the Bay of San Francisco might soon pay him a visit, to inspect the site, perhaps to pay for the shipment of flour recently purchased for his fleet, perhaps to make an offer on the fort itself. Would he sell it? Should he? Well, of course. He would sell it in a minute, if the price were right . . .

When Manuiki steps into the room, he is gazing out the window thinking how much he would ask, somewhere between thirty-five and forty thousand dollars, depending on the amount of land to be sold with it, and whether or not he includes the cost of the flour. He doesn't hear her feet upon the boards. He doesn't move until one dish clinks against another. Startled, he turns and sees her watching him with cautious eyes. Sutter seldom appears in the dining room until his food is on the table.

He says, "I have something for you."

She looks away and waits.

He holds out a small carved box. "Something from Monterey."

This is not what she expected. Her face perks up.

"What you like," he says.

"Let me see."

"First, have a drink with me."

"I don't want a drink."

"Of course you do."

"They make dinner now."

"Dinner can wait."

He opens the box and shows her the earrings of hammered silver, shaped like fish. In the muted light of late afternoon they seem to glow.

"Oooooh," she says. "So pretty."

He has already set a cup on the table. He pours it half full and hands it to her.

"We will drink to your beauty."

She laughs a small laugh, half pleasure, half disgust.

"You make fun of me."

"I don't make fun. Here. Drink a toast. Then we will try them on."

They raise their cups. Manuiki sips and squinches her face. With glittering eyes he watches her. After she sips again, he lifts one earring and attaches it and stands back for a better look. She runs into the next room, where a small mirror hangs near the door, tilts her head, swings sideways.

"My special kind," she says.

"You see? I don't forget. We will drink again, then try the other one." He has followed her, with the bottle and the cups.

"I have work," she says.

"We all have work. Life is work. You must sometimes give yourself a little vacation from your work. Here."

This time she doesn't grimace. Her eyes, too, have taken on a glitter. When he fastens the second earring, she lolls her head and lets his fingers graze her neck.

He says, "Let me see you from the front."

She turns and lifts her black eyebrows as if awaiting the answer to a question. When he reaches to take her by the waist, she steps away.

She says, "You like the Indian girl too much."

"She is nothing."

"You like too many Indian girls."

"I only like you."

"Then why keep her?"

"Why do you flirt with the miller?"

"I do not flirt."

"Why do you flirt with the blacksmith?"

"We only talk."

"I saw you making eyes again."

"You say I cannot talk?"

"If you spend all your time making eyes at the blacksmith, what am I to do?"

"Keep the Indian girl."

He glares like a stern pastor. "Did he give you a present?"

"No."

"If he did, I will have him flogged."

Her eyes expand with fear, and it arouses him. Why are Hawaiian eyes so maddeningly expressive? His mouth curves in a thin smile. "I am a very jealous man. If this continues, I will have both of them punished, the blacksmith and the miller too! I will have them flogged and thrown into prison. I will have the blacksmith hanged! I can do it, you know!"

He says this with an exaggerated fury, swelling out his chest like a rooster. He starts prancing back and forth across the room in a way that makes her giggle.

"I have executed many men. I will execute this blacksmith without mercy if I see him so much as glance at you one more time. He will hang by his neck, and his feet will kick like the feet of a baby in a crib, and then all the world will know that Manuiki is my little bird and mine alone!"

Now she is laughing. He hands her the brandy cup. Again they drink together. Above the rims of the cups their eyes meet. This time when he reaches for her waist she does not step away. His hand slides toward her buttocks, a heavy, calloused hand grasping at the skirt, bunching it so the cloth slowly rises to reveal her thick calf, her thigh, her solid haunch. She wears nothing underneath. As his hand moves across the bare dark skin, she makes a face of mock disappointment, gathering her brows.

"Augie," she says. "No need to sneak."

She unties the sash, lifts the dress over her head and lets it fall.

Patriotism

Cloud cover has rolled in from the north, bringing an early dusk. In the still air, voices carry. From many yards away, Jim can hear their exclamations. He opens the door, and the voices subside as the heads turn, as if by sudden command. The room is lit by one kerosene lamp. Half a dozen men gang around a low table where cups and a jug have been set out. With pen in hand one fellow hunches over a sheaf of paper. Jim knows these men, or knew them once, knew them in what now seems another life—all fellow travelers on the trail west, though at first their names don't come to him.

His hesitation is matched by theirs, the eyes remembering yet unsure. He has changed so much, thinner now, older and shaggier.

McCutcheon is the first to move. He hulks near the door, as if prepared to make a quick exit, so tall and broad he alone fills half the tiny room. Lunging toward Jim with an outstretched hand, he barks his head on the ceiling but doesn't seem to notice.

"Goddam, Jim! When'd you get here?"

"I just rode in."

"God*dam*!" says McCutcheon, furiously pumping his hand. "Good to see you, Jim, I swear it is!" The broad face opens in a silly grin. "And you do come most carefully upon your hour!"

These last words are from a play, Jim knows, though he couldn't say which one. When Mac is excited he will quote from the Bard, or spout something that sounds like a quotation. Jim never knows how to react to this. Mac himself seems surprised by these words and the pleasure he finds in speaking them. He has a big voice, a boyish face that quickly fills with color.

"I ran into Charlie on the trail," Jim says, watching the grin grow wider.

"Then the company made it through," Mac says. "They're all here!"

In his eyes there is an unnatural luster, whether from drink or a lingering malaria or the spark of hope, Jim can't tell.

He shakes his head. "I've come alone."

The wide grin fades. "What about Amanda?"

"Holding up just fine, her and the baby both."

Mac's feverish eyes absorb this news, Mac the huge young father from Missouri who hasn't seen his family for six weeks at least. Jim wants to tell him more, tell him why, but he can't. Not now. Other men push forward to grab his hand with cries of astonishment and welcome, men who only recently made the crossing. They swell anew with the kinship of survival.

The fellow at the table has shoved his chair back and reaches to shake his hand, and here is a face Jim remembers well, lean and handsome, though darker now. Weeks of sun and short rations have given him an Indian look. Jim is glad to be meeting him again, a reporter, a scribbler, a note-taker, a man always looking for his notebook. He gave up a good newspaper job in Louisville to join the great migration and claimed he was going to write a book about it. Jim hopes he'll write about one memorable day when they drank together on the banks of the Platte.

It was the Fourth of July. The whole wagon train took out some time to celebrate Independence Day. There was a parade, back there in the middle of nowhere. Exuberant weapons were fired into the air. Jim opened another bottle of his ten-year-old brandy, and they toasted the seventieth birthday of the Republic, toasted the Founding Fathers, who had the nerve and the will and the vision to claim this land for their own and all future generations.

Was that only last July? It seems a century ago, and Jim has not seen the Scribbler since. He was in a party of single men who left early and rode ahead on horseback. Lord, how Jim would like to sit down and hear this man's story, his opinion of the Hastings Cutoff, maybe find out where the prophet has gone. But there's no time for catching up, not with today's news hanging in the air. The war they thought had been won is in danger of being lost, unless every able-bodied man comes to the aid of Colonel Fremont, now preparing to march on the Mexican rebels and take care of them once and for all.

The Scribbler refills the cups on the table. In Jim's honor he toasts again the Declaration of Independence, and toasts the men who have gathered in this room.

"To the new Founding Fathers, who have come this far west to complete the job they started back in 1776!"

"Hurrah!"

"To the Founding Fathers!"

"Hurrah! Hurrah!"

"And we cannot fail," cries Bill McCutcheon, with flushed face and burning eye, "if we screw our courage to the sticking point!"

The Scribbler lifts a cup. "Very good! To the sticking point!"

He is the one who called this meeting, in a rush of national pride. Now he is writing again, hunched over the sheaf of paper as he drafts a pledge that all men present will begin immediately to recruit volunteers to ride in the California Battalion. In the companies they assemble they will serve as officers, and at the earliest moment they will join Colonel Fremont.

As the sentences flow from his pen, the others watch his moving hand. It's a heady proposal. John Fremont is a legend, a Marco Polo, a Napoleon of the West. No one in this room has met him. Only the Scribbler has seen him, and then from a distance. But all have heard the stories and read his book, or had parts of it read to them. In their bones they know why he is called the Pathfinder. He blazed the trails they all have followed. If Fremont wants to lead a charge down to Los Angeles, what American man who loves his country would not be proud to follow? Last summer, wasn't he behind that show over in Sonoma, the Bear Flag business? Didn't he run the Stars and Stripes right up to the top of that goddam Mexican flagpole?

The Scribbler was in Yerba Buena on the day Fremont sailed for Santa Barbara with a hundred and fifty men. They were going to retake that town, commandeer some horses, and ride on south. But now comes this courier to announce that they didn't make it. The battalion had to turn around when a northbound ship told them not a horse remained in Santa Barbara. All the ranchos down that way had been raided and stripped. So Fremont sailed back to Monterey, where he is forming up to take his battalion overland. He needs all the horses and all the men he can find.

"What in hell has got into them greasers anyhow?"

"Damned if I know."

"We been too easy on 'em, that's all. It's time to rise up."

"How many did they have down there?"

"Four or five hundred, is what I heard."

"What about us? How many'd we have?"

"Three hundred or thereabouts."

"Well, damn their eyes!"

"I'm ready to pick off a few."

"I have shot some buffalo on the way across. I'd sooner shoot me a greaser."

"I guess you'd have to chase him a whole lot farther."

"Haw haw haw."

"You'll get your chance, boys," the Scribbler says. "Quicker we head down there, quicker they'll know who's running the show."

Jim empties his glass and fills it again and raises it high but he holds his tongue. He has been in this territory less than a week. He has yet to see a Mexican. What he knows of California is the eighty miles between here and Bear Valley, where there are four ranches held by Americans and Germans, and forty clusters of earth-covered domes, and this fort watched over by the shrunken face of a beheaded Indian, and inside the fort a room filled with men whose eyes remind him of the day he stood by his wagon facing those who wanted to string him up or die trying, that reckless readiness to shoot or lynch or ride head-long into the night. He knows the mood. He feels it rising in himself.

He looks around. They are mostly single men, without families to consider. Perhaps it's just as well that Margaret and the children are somewhere else. It occurs to him that if the wagons did not make it through the mountains, if somehow they found a sheltered spot where they might last out the winter, it might be a gift in disguise. For them. For him. It is turmoil here, with armies clashing, the towns under siege. He could join up with these men and ride south and start to make this runaway region a safer place.

He isn't sure. He cannot speak. In his silence the others see strength. It tells them something. They remember how he used to prance at the head of the wagon party on his racing mare. He has the air of a leader, a willingness to take command. At forty-six, Jim is the elder in this room. He has a seniority they respect. It seems foreordained that he

walked in when he did. They want him to take charge of their uni-
formed company. Again they raise their glasses.

"To Captain Jim Reed!" they cry.

"Hurrah! Hurrah!"

"By God!" says the Scribbler. "I would ride anywhere on earth
with this fellow! I swear it!"

And oh, how this appeals to Jim. To lead again. To be a captain. To
surrender to the fervor and the ferment. What a tonic, after where he's
been and what he's left behind, the long, silent, dusty days and the
tedious passage of collapsing wagons. Here at the fort, large matters
are at stake. His nation's honor is at stake. He has seen the waterways
and the bottomland and the boundless herds of game, seen enough to
know that he must sooner or later join the fight to secure it all for the
nation it rightfully belongs to. And here—tonight!—he can become
the officer in charge of a company that will march with the California
Battalion. There is glory in that sound, and he is tempted.

He says, "How far from here to Monterey?"

"Four or five days on horseback."

"I'd say six," says the Scribbler.

Jim says, "How about Los Angeles?"

"No telling. Could take a month. Depending on weather."

A month to Los Angeles? A month to get back? He is tempted.
Tempted. But he can't say yes. It's too soon to be a captain. Too soon
to fight. The wagon party is not going to stop. They have no idea what
awaits them here.

Jim wags his head, to clear away the brandy fumes, and tells them
what is in his heart, tells them he has to ride north again, not south.

"I cannot speak for Mac," he says, "though I suspect he will be riding that way too. Of course, we'll look for recruits as we go. If we can
sign them up, why we sure will."

The Scribbler isn't satisfied. "A lieutenant, then," he cries. "I will
put you down for a lieutenancy. And whenever you join up with us,
Jim, there'll be a place! What do you say?"

"Ay," says Jim. "That'll do just fine."

There is another round of drinks, a round of toasts to the offices
they have created for themselves.

"To the lieutenant!"

"Hurrah!"

"And congratulations!"

"We salute you, sir!"

"Salutes to all!"

"Bravo! Bravo!"

Now Jim is shouting with them, toasting, drinking deeply. The brandy makes his eyes wet with patriotism and comradeship. They begin to brag and boast, drinking to deeds past and yet to come. Their shouts and noisy promises drown out the patter of rain that starts to fall upon the fort, a light rain at first, soaked up by wood and thirsty soil.

Gradually the sound becomes a clatter, as the puddles form and rain spills off the roof to splash down into the puddles. Soon water falling on the roof is like a drum, and the outside splatter is so loud they stop to listen.

"What's that?" says Jim.

"Sounds like Indians," one fellow says, "doing a harvest dance up there on the roof."

They all laugh.

"Could be Mexicans," the Scribbler says. "Maybe they have us surrounded. A hundred Mexicans pissing on the wall."

"Rage and blow," McCutcheon says, "you tornadoes and you cataracks. Spout till you have drenched our steeples and drowned our cocks."

"The steeples, yes," says the Scribbler. "Drench the steeples! But Lord, don't drown our cocks!"

Another round of laughter. And another raucous round of drinks, then some quiet sipping as they listen a while to the first rain any of them has heard since crossing the Sierra, sobered by the new force of this downpour, wondering how long it will last and thinking of the roads they'll have to travel tomorrow.

ALL NIGHT IT rains and into early morning. Jim rises with a dull ache behind his eyes, steps out of the bunkhouse and feels a colder edge on the air. He steps past the outbuildings toward a clearing that opens to the east. The clouds have rolled on. Rain has cleansed the atmosphere. He can see for a hundred miles or more, and now he knows where the cold breeze comes from, sweeping across the valley. In the Sierras he sees snow where there had been no snow. Overnight the nearer and farther peaks have been blanketed with white.

A voice behind him says, "Strange weather."

It is Sutter, in a thick walking coat and knitted hat, looking like a Swiss burgher on his morning constitutional in the shadow of the Alps.

"I have never seen it so low on the slope so early in the season."

"What does it mean?" asks Jim.

"Who knows? Every year is different from the last. You learn to be careful about predictions."

"Will there be snow across the entire range?"

"I think so. If the storm comes from the north, as this one did. It takes us by surprise."

While the recruiters fan out south and west, Jim and Mac spend a day rounding up their gear, loading the animals with jerked beef and beans and flour—enough, they hope, to bring eighty people through one last week in the high country. While they work, they watch the snow line. Jim tells himself that even with this bad turn in the weather, time should still be on their side. Nearly a month has passed since he said good-bye. On his mind's trail map he has followed their progress day by day. He calculates that they should have just about cleared the summit. At that altitude Margaret and the children would have had a hard night, a miserable night. But the worst part should be behind them now. He prays that this is so.

On the second morning after the rain Jim and Mac start north with thirty horses, one mule, and two of Sutter's Indians. At dawn their caravan fords the American River, heading back toward Johnson's Ranch.

from **The Trail Notes of Patty Reed**

Santa Cruz, California

November 1920

Our journey had advanced;
Our feet were almost come
To that odd fork in Being's road,
Eternity by term.

—*Emily Dickinson*

Ducks *swoop in across the lake and settle, as they have done for who knows how many thousands of years. Wild ducks and geese mix with the gulls that float above the beach on shoreline breezes. The lake is inland from the beach, bordered with tules. They call it a brackish lagoon, half runoff from the wintertime rivulets and rained-on slopes, half salt water seeping under the sand. We have a boat moored down below the house, a little dinghy tied to our spindly pier. It will get you across the lake and back, and I have been out there a time or two, but I'm too old for boating. Sitting still seems to suit me fine. Late afternoons I watch the wind move across the water, and the odd effect it has.*

You expect water by the ocean to be flowing toward the larger body. But here it seems to be the opposite. Sea wind keeps the surface moving inland, back the way it has come, and the movement gives the afternoon sheen a rippled look. The lake seems to jump with light, like a million tiny minnows out there leaping for joy, and the glare so bright you can hardly see beyond it.

The brightness burns my eyes. But I don't mind. If I gaze right into it I can almost see papa moving across the lake, looking the way he used to look. After all these years I still expect to see him coming back, just as I expected him all the time we waited. Waiting for papa. Waiting for anyone.

If I gaze long enough I am eight years old again instead of eighty, and it is the day we finally reached the Truckee River, after two days of the emptiest country you have ever imagined. Things out there were so flat you could see the river coming for miles away. The line of trees was like a lifeline stretched across the sand. It was the first sign of hope we'd had in days, though some people wouldn't believe it. We were all so maddened with thirst, this could have been another mirage. The animals told us otherwise. They smelled the water hours before we got there. Oxen that looked to be breathing their final breath were suddenly straining at the yoke. A horse bolted, the one carrying mama and my brother Tommy. She couldn't hold it back, and they went galloping away ahead of us.

Virginia and I were walking. Just about everyone was walking, to lighten the wagonloads. I wonder how many of us could have lasted another day out there. But now we had those trees to guide us in, and what a welcome sight they were! When we finally reached the riverbank, people fell into the water with their boots and shirts and dresses on, like a whole crowd of children splashing and ducking in the sweetest water we had ever felt or tasted.

How sweet it was to drink our fill and then lie back on wet green grass and look up into the leaves. By that time it was the middle of October. Trees along the Truckee, alder and aspen and cottonwood, looked like they had caught fire, the colors were so bright and crisp. That afternoon Virginia and I began to gather autumn leaves, just like we would have done back home. There was every different kind of yellow, pale yellow, chalky yellow, lemon yellow, lime-tinted greenish yellow. Some leaves had a persimmon tinge, and some were red as blood. Sunlight coming through these leaves made an actual glow above the river, and the light dancing on the water was like the light out here dancing across the lake today. It was strange and wondrous water, moving in the wrong direction.

For three weeks our guide had been the Humboldt, winding through the desert from east to west. Now here was the Truckee flowing the other way. To my young eyes the river was flowing backward, and this added to the magic of that afternoon. Somehow it pushed the light right at you. I remember how the yellowy persimmon light reflected up onto the faces, so that everyone looked younger and fresher, their faces shining like saints, as if we had finally arrived at the golden place of all our dreams.

We saw tracks of hare and fox and deer along the river. Pretty soon Bill Eddy came back with nine geese to pluck and cook. We rested there a whole day, and drank and drank, and didn't want to leave. But we had to. Time was running out. So on we went, along the eastward-running river. I guess it was a day later we met some men on horseback riding toward us. We had just come around a bend. It was afternoon again. We were heading toward the sun, with light filtered through a blaze of autumn leaves. All the air around the river seemed to shine, and right in the middle of that light we saw a figure in the lead. The glare was so bright you couldn't see who it was, but I knew who it was, and I started running along the bank.

Every day I'd expected to see papa come riding into view. I didn't know how far it was to Sutter's Fort, a day, or a month, or a year. But he had already gone off twice—once while we were crossing the Wasatch, and once while we were crossing the Salt Desert. Both times I'd watched and waited, and both times he'd come back.

Virginia had spotted him too. We were both running along the riverbank calling out, "Papa! Papa!"

Even after we got close enough to see that it wasn't him, I wouldn't believe it. The man on the horse looked shorter than papa, and thicker, and wore glasses, and a silly-looking derby hat. But I kept trying to make him look different than he looked. I waited until I could see his face, and I tried to make it into papa's face, find a way to see papa's eyes and mouth and beard, and only gave up when I heard the folks who'd run along with us begin to call out, "Charlie! Charlie! By God, it's Charlie Stanton! He's come back! Thank the Lord! Look at them sacks, look at them mules! God bless you, Charlie Stanton!"

Men and women crowded in to grab his hand and throw their arms around him and kiss him and call his name, and mama was right among them, wanting to know if Charlie had seen papa anywhere along the way. Charlie looked at her and grinned and said, "Yes, ma'am. We had breakfast at Bear Valley."

"Where's that?" she said.

"Day or so past the summit."

"You mean he made it across?"

"Yes, ma'am."

"And he was all right?"

"Fit as a fiddle, Mrs. Reed. He looked just fine."

Her thin shoulders dropped, as if a load of wood she'd been carrying for miles had just dissolved. She sank onto the riverbank and sat with her face in her hands. She was wearing the hat she'd worn all the way across the plains, whenever the sun was out, a Shaker-style hat like so many of the women wore, made of leghorn straw and curved almost like a hood so it held in all her hair. The ribbons underneath her chin were trimmed with red roses. I don't know how it had lasted so long. The worn-out sweetness of that hat, the rose-tinted sweetness of the dangling ribbons, made me want to weep. Virginia went over and put her arms around mama. I did too, imagining she felt as brokenhearted as I did then, though I was wrong about that. Through her fingers the words came spilling. "Thank God." She said it over and over. "Thank God. Thank God."

Much later I would understand that her relief that day was mixed with something else. From the gentle way her shoulders shook, I could feel it, though I couldn't yet speak it. Much later I would learn that as often as she had prayed for papa, she had cursed him for bringing such a fate upon his family, cursed him because she was the one who had to talk him into leaving the wagon party, cursed him for the looks she had to take from those who now held her responsible for Johnny's stabbing, and cursed herself for ever marrying such a man. That day by the Truckee she trembled with gratitude and shame.

We all wept with her, but not for long. Mama soon stood up and wiped her eyes and said with a brave smile, "C'mon, let's see what those mules are packing."

Everyone else was drifting toward the mules, eager to unload the sacks. Charlie told George Donner what all they were carrying, and George took charge of passing out the provisions. We ate biscuits for the first time in many days, and boiled beans, and some pieces of a rabbit somebody shot. With all the water flowing by, Milt and mama made coffee again that night, to drink with dinner. Coffee still tasted bitter to me, but I already loved the smell. Somehow it stood for the comforts of regular life. To my eight-year-old nose, the smell of coffee underneath the trees along the riverbank meant things were almost ready to be normal again.

. . .

NOWADAYS IT'S HARD *to imagine how isolated we were out there. Charlie brought the first news we'd had from anywhere in many weeks. There weren't any roads, no mail or newspapers, or telegraph lines or telephone. This was even before the Pony Express. The whole government could have fallen and Washington, D.C., gone up in flames and we would never have heard a thing about it. Our one and only link with the rest of the world was Charlie Stanton, and he brought back a whole lot more than food. He brought back stories of the place we'd all been imagining. I would say he brought back our faith that such a place was actually somewhere up ahead and waiting for us. He restored our belief in something we had almost stopped believing in. He had been to California, and here he stood, human proof that a person could get there and live to tell the tale.*

He was a hero in every way but one. What in God's name—some people wanted to know—had possessed him to travel in the company of these two redskins? Even if they'd helped him get through the mountains, did we really want to let them join our party, after all the trouble we'd been having with the desert tribes?

Along the Humboldt we'd lost dozens of cattle, and it hurt us bad, slowed us down, doubled the work for the teams that had survived. In hindsight I suppose you could see the Paiutes had about as much right to our cattle as we did to the buffalo herds back there on the plains. Of course, you could not have told that to any of the families whose animals had been shot at. You would have died with those words in your mouth. If thousands of buffalo were running around loose, why it stood to reason they must belong to ANYBODY WITH A RIFLE. But these cattle here, well, they are different. They all belong to US.

Papa's shadow hung over the presence of Charlie's two Indian companions, the way it seemed to hang over everything that came along to divide up our company. I would not say papa was partial to Indians, but neither did he despise them on sight, the way some folks did. Just a couple of nights before the stabbing, he had let two Indians creep in close to our campfire, gaunt and underfed and making friendship signs.

Uncle Billy raised his voice in protest, as did several others, but papa wouldn't listen. He let them hunker next to our fire. Pretty soon they began to talk, as anyone would, on a cold night—sit by the crackling flames and talk. They might have done this before, with other wagon parties, since they knew a few words of English. With sign language they were trying to explain something about the trail farther on, when some sparks from the Graves's family fire suddenly leaped into the blanket of dry grass that spread out from where we'd camped. In no time a sheet of fire was flashing and licking all around. It was a frenzy there for the next few minutes. While some folks stamped their boots and some flailed bedclothes and some ran to the river with buckets, the two Paiutes sprang into the fire. They had skins wrapped around them. They rolled across the burning grass with a speed that could scarcely be believed. They jumped up flailing and seemed to be everywhere at once.

After the fire was out, their eyebrows and hair were singed, but their dark faces glowed with pleasure. There was no question that without their quickness and the risks they took, three more wagons would likely have been lost. Everyone agreed on that. So papa told them to eat with us, which they did, using their fingers and slurping food right off the plate. Yet they were so grateful and so happy you didn't mind the sound. The way they curled up next to the fire, I figured they had joined us and now we'd have some Indian guides to help us get across the desert.

The next morning I was as surprised as anyone else to wake up and find them gone. They took a yoke of oxen belonging to Uncle Billy, and one of his favorite shirts—losses he immediately blamed on papa for befriending these scoundrels, for being soft on Indians and forever doing things that added to the burdens of our journey.

On the day papa fought with John Snyder, Uncle Billy was smarting from those recent losses. And two weeks later it was still on his mind, as he cautioned Charlie Stanton that when it comes to Indians you can't ever afford to give an inch. If those first two had been chased after and scalped, he said, we might have saved ourselves a lot of grief. If it was up to him, he would scalp these two right here and now and hang them by their heels and let them be messengers to all the other cattle-rustling bandits that had been dogging us ever since we hit the Humboldt.

I have to hand it to Charlie. He stood firm. These men aren't Paiutes or Shoshone, he said, they are from the valley of the Sacramento, and they are Christians too. Captain John Sutter himself had vouched for their good character, and so would Charlie. What's more, Sutter had warned these fellows that if anything happened to so much as one of his mules, he would have Salvador and Luis hunted down and hung. They were on their best behavior, Charlie told us all, and they would be a great asset to the company.

The next morning mama led me toward the one named Salvador. He was going to hoist me up onto his horse. By that time I had seen a lot of Indians, but I'd never been this close to one. The night the Paiutes sat by our fire, I had kept well back, just watching and, I have to confess, mighty disappointed. We had all grown up on Indian stories. Those Paiutes, they didn't have tomahawks or headdresses. They were the skinniest two people I had ever seen.

Salvador was not skinny. He looked pretty well fed, compared to the rest of us. But he was another disappointment, at first, since he was dressed about like everybody else you saw those days—shirt and trousers made of homespun, heavy boots, a dirty hat.

I held back until his head tipped up and I saw his face. He had a look that quickly won me over. His eyes were so brown they were almost black. He wasn't smiling, yet he seemed about to break out in laughter, as he pointed to himself and said, "Salvador." He put the accent at the end. I thought he was speaking an Indian language.

"Sal-va-DOOR," I said.

"Si," he said, then pointed at me.

"Patty," I said.

"Pat-tee," he said.

"Si," I said.

He slapped his horse. "Caballo."

"Ca-ba-yo," I said, thinking this was the horse's name.

He held out his hands, and this stopped me. I looked at them as if they were detached from his body. I had never touched an Indian, or been touched by one. I looked at his hands, afraid to move. Finally mama said, "Get on, Patty. Hurry up now. Folks are waiting. We have to go."

Charlie had given her one of the mules to ride. Tommy was already perched up on its back. Thanks to Charlie, we would all be riding now. He could see how our family was down to nothing. But since he hadn't witnessed Johnny's stabbing, he didn't have to take sides on that, the way some still did, holding mama herself responsible.

James Junior was going to ride behind Luis. Virginia was going to ride behind Charlie. They were all mounted now, watching me.

I raised my arms, and Salvador grabbed and lifted. "Cuidado, señorita," he said, as he set me on Caballo's rump.

He swung up into the saddle, with a look back at me and said, "Bamanos."

"Ba-ma-nos," I said, though I did not yet know it meant "let's go."

Charlie and the Indians knew more about the route now than anyone else, so we were in the lead. As Caballo began to move, I placed my arms around Salvador's waist. He had worked cattle in the open country around the Mission of St. Joseph and also around Sutter's Fort, so he was a very fine horseman, good with all the animals. He was strong and firm. Underneath his coat his body was as hard as a tree. He didn't talk much at all, but little by little he taught me my first bits of Spanish. Buenos dias. Adios. Muchas gracias. Por favor. Me llama Patty Reed. Each time he lifted me onto his horse he would say, "Cuidado, señorita." Take care, little lady. And I finally learned to say, "Y usted también, señor."

It was our ritual, our trail game.

He wore a thick wool coat. Sometimes, holding on tight, I would press my face into his back and feel the rough wool against my cheek and smell the heavy smell of woodsmoke and horseflesh and sweat, with some dampness added to the smoky scent, first thing in the morning. To this day I can close my eyes, sitting here above the lake, and the smell of Salvador comes back to me.

THE RIVER FINALLY brought us to what was called Truckee Meadows, where the town of Reno stands today. A silence fell over the company when we saw the Sierras rising ahead of us, with fresh snow showing all across the peaks and looming cloud cover everywhere you looked. Soon after we'd set up camp near the river, it started to rain, a cold rain very close to snow, and that started people arguing about what to do now, whether to linger a few days here where grass was thick, so the animals could fatten some before we started into the mountains, or to push on before the weather turned. It was only the end of October, some said. By rights, they said, we ought to have another month at least.

"I've heard of parties crossing close to Christmas," one man said, without much conviction.

from The Trail Notes of Patty Reed

Such stories did not change the long line of snowy peaks to the west, nor did they change the desperation in the air.

This was where a young fellow named William Foster shot his own brother-in-law in the back for no reason anyone has ever been able to agree on. He had been with us all the way, part of the Murphy clan. His relatives tried to call it an accident, but I still have my doubts, considering some things Foster did later on. He had a mean streak in him. According to the story we've been told, his brother-in-law, William Pike, was cleaning a pepperbox pistol. The two of them were getting ready to set out for Sutter's, hoping to bring back more supplies. When his wife called for some firewood, Pike stood up to fetch it and he passed his pistol to Foster.

You don't see pepperbox pistols much anymore, except in museums and fancy gun collections. Even in those days you didn't see them much, because the six-shooter had already come along. But William Pike still carried an old pepperbox, which was an early form of six-shooter, with six small barrels in a ring, one for each bullet. It was an awful-looking contraption, and a mess to clean. But men love things like that. Foster had been itching to get his hands on this pistol. Moments after Pike handed it to him, the gun went off. Pike was shot in the back, and he died by the fire with his wife and children watching.

Did Foster have some family grudge against his brother-in-law and choose this moment to pull the trigger? Or did the gun go off by itself? Or did it somehow explode in his hands, as his relatives claimed?

It was just one more event to divide us, with the animals down to skin and bones, and the resentment and aggravations swelling day by day—this family unhappy about traveling with Indians, that family still arguing about who had started the knife fight and whose idea it was to take the Hastings Cutoff, the next family squabbling over whose fault it was so many cattle had been lost. Now they were all wondering how a man could get shot in the back for no reason, though this time you did not hear Lewis Keseberg demanding "an eye for an eye," since he had run a long thorn through his foot and it had swollen up so bad he couldn't walk. Nor did you hear Patrick Breen say, "A killing cannot go unpunished." His animals had made it across the desert in better shape than anyone else's. He was eager to get away from Truckee Meadows, figuring he could now make better time on his own. Council meetings were a thing of the past. It was each family for itself.

Then came the sight we all feared most. The day they buried William Pike, the cold rain turned white, and the skies hung over us like the heavy cloak of God. They had buried grandma by a bubbling spring. They had buried Luke Halloran in salt, and John Snyder in dry sand. Now they buried William Pike in the first snow.

By the time we started into the mountains we weren't a wagon company anymore. We were just a scattering of wagons and cattle and mules and horses and frantic people strewn for miles along the trail. When we came at last to Truckee Lake, the one they now call Donner, a foot of snow had fallen around the shore. The lake was gray as a rifle barrel, and all the trees above the lake were white. The Breens had pushed ahead and had already tried the summit trail and run into drifts too deep for their oxen. Five feet, they reported. Men were saying we'd have to leave the wagons where they stood, pack up whatever the animals could carry and press on before all traces of the trail were buried. It was our only hope to clear the summit.

After that it was bedlam by the lake, the panic in the air thicker than the falling snow, with some men still lashing at their fallen animals, and others berating frozen hands as they struggled to unyoke the teams, and wives screaming at their husbands about what to leave behind and what to carry, the food, the money, the blankets, the extra boots.

Salvador was in the lead again once we started climbing. Since he'd seen the trail and was the best rider, they had given him the strongest mule. I held on to his woolen coat, certain he could get us through. Indians were supposed to know everything about trails and forests and canyons and so forth. He'd already been over this pass. His mules had made the journey too. As long as I had hold of Salvador's coat, his mule would make it one more time.

Back behind us I could see wagons tilting where they'd lost the trail. I saw other mules and oxen up to their bellies. Some had already pitched into the snow. I saw mama and Tommy on another mule, and Luis right behind us, with my baby brother, and farther back Virginia riding with Charlie Stanton. With one arm I held on to Salvador, with the other I held on to little Cash, our dog. Back at the wagons he had barked until I scooped him up. Now he was curled inside my shawl. Somehow, I imagined, if we could all make it to the top, papa would be waiting there. I didn't know what the top looked like, or how far it was, or how papa would get himself there. But my mind was working to see a way through, and this was my vision. If I held tight enough, Salvador would lead us to the summit and get us past it to a sunny place where papa would be waiting.

I did not have any idea what the weather had in store, or what snow can do to you at that altitude, nor did I know that Salvador and Luis were valley people just like all the rest of us, flatlanders from the fertile valleys of California. We were farmers and blacksmiths and carriage makers and mule skinners from Illinois and Missouri. That is the heartbreaking part, as I look back, all of these flatlanders finding themselves at six thousand feet in the blinding snow and trying to climb to seven thousand feet.

Salvador was in the lead. But he didn't know much more about what to do in this kind of weather than anyone else pushing for the summit that day. His tribe had learned long ago to stay out of those mountains in the dark of the year, and you have to wonder what was going through his mind. You have to wonder if he wasn't asking himself, *How did I get up here breaking trail for these crazy whiteskins where only a fool would be?*

In the High Country

UNDER A CLEAR sky the great valley sprawls behind them now—four men and thirty animals strung along the rocky trail. Up ahead, snow-covered peaks and slopes loom closer, ever closer, glimpsed in and out of gathering clouds.

As they move through the foothills, above Bear River canyon, Jim observes the curving hunch of Mac's great shoulders, his slouch hat pitched forward, his long legs bent. He likes riding with this man, likes his spirit, a man who loves his family, who always goes the extra mile to do his share and more, and doesn't talk much unless he's stirred up or drinking. In his saddlebag Mac carries a trinket for little Harriet, his one-year-old, something he picked up at Sutter's, a miniature whistle on a rawhide thong. Jim has seen it, a short, polished tube of wood with a hole notched. It makes a trilling birdlike note.

Jim remembers when the McCutcheons joined the wagon company, outside Fort Laramie, young and eager, remembers seeing Mac's generous face and massive frame, thinking, We can use this kind of muscle. Mac and Amanda had to leave another company when he came down with fever, had to lay low for ten days and sweat it out. At the time Jim didn't think much about it, Mac seemed so strong and fit, as if the rest had done him good. But the fever has stayed with him, flared up again when he reached Sutter's, and Jim can still see it in his eyes. They are too bright. The color in his cheeks is unnatural. Today his voice has a raspy edge.

When the rain finally hits and revives his cough, Mac looks bewildered, as if he himself cannot believe a man of his size could be afflicted for so long. He does not complain. He will never complain. He will ride until he drops. But Jim doesn't want him to drop, or come close to dropping. Four men on such an expedition is already too few.

They climb through a cold and muddy downpour. It rains for

hours, steady, soaking everything. At Mule Springs they see the first scatterings of snow. A while later all the ground is white. The rain turns to sleet. On the long steep ascent into Bear Valley they plod through sleet, prod and pull the animals upward, and make camp in a night so wet they can't build a fire.

From here on, they tell themselves, the wagon party could turn up anywhere, anytime. This hope gets them through a damp, bone-chilling night, and through the next day, as they cross Bear Valley, now under two feet of snow, and climb the wall Jim and Walter slid down.

They climb its slippery zigzag trail, and Jim can tell the Indians don't like the work at all, up this high, driving thirty horses through thickening snow. For two days he has not heard either of them speak. What are they thinking? Do they really know what this trip is for? Do they care? Are they doing it for wages? Sutter uses threats to keep his men in line. But does Sutter's arm reach this far into the mountains?

Above Bear Valley the snow is waist-deep. The night is colder as they bed down, and utterly silent under the pines. A restless clatter from the horse herd rouses Jim and Mac. They call out to the Indians, who have camped apart, but get no answer. They hear hooves crunching through icy crust. They are up and running in the dark.

Jim stays with the herd while Mac resaddles, to give midnight chase down the long incline, plunging back the hard way they have come. But the Indians elude him, and once again he climbs the slope out of Bear Valley, returning before dawn to tell Jim their wranglers have disappeared, along with three horses.

When they have finished damning the runaways and damning Sutter and damning the snow and the cold and the endless night, after Mac has fallen exhausted into his bedroll, Jim lies in the darkness wondering how long Charlie's Indians stayed loyal to the cause. They seemed to be trustworthy fellows. But so did these two, as they left the fort, giving their Indian promise to bring all Sutter's horses back. So had the Paiutes Jim let hunker by his desert fire.

The next morning it begins to snow, a dry, windless, powdery fluff that gradually fills the trace of the trail. Jim rides in front of the pack train. Mac rides behind, as the snow deepens, hour by hour, soft and feathery, up to the bellies of the horses, up to their haunches. Under heavy loads of flour and beans the animals struggle. Some give out, stumble and fall, unable to rise. Their mouths and noses lift for air, as if coming up from underwater through foamy surf.

Jim has never been this high so late in the year. With the Indians gone and the horses floundering, it seems hopeless. Yet it is not hopeless. He won't let it be. He does not know this Sierra weather. But he remembers the terrain. Didn't he already cross it once? He thinks he knows where he is and where the summit is likely to be. He calls back that they will leave the herd and ride ahead on saddle mounts, just the two of them.

Mac shouts something in reply, but Jim doesn't hear it. He doesn't want to hear it. He is thinking that Margaret and Virginia and Patty and Tommy and James Junior are now caught in something similar, somewhere not very far from here. Perhaps they struggle toward him as he pushes toward them. Perhaps ten miles away. Maybe less. They could be an hour away. Or half an hour! At any turn in the trail, at any clearing he could have a glimpse of the first mule or campfire flame.

In his mind's eye he sees the whole route, the soothing trees along the Truckee, the wide bowl where the river spreads thick with tule, the eastern Sierra face. He sees the oval lake and the summit beyond the lake, the bleak grasslands higher up, the alpine valleys, then the crossing and recrossing of the Yuba, right on to this very spot where his horse heaves its chest against the mounds and heaps of white.

Nearly a month has passed since Jim and Charlie Stanton went their separate ways. By all calculations the party should have come this far by now. Where are they? Did Charlie make it through? Maybe his Indians did something worse than take off in the night with a few animals. Or maybe the snow stopped all of them somewhere before the summit. But no. That doesn't figure. Something else went wrong. Could other fights have broken out? Lord knows, they were on a hair trigger, the whole company, day and night. Maybe Keseberg thought he'd try to hang somebody else, and this time succeeded. Right now Jim would like to have that moment back, facing Keseberg with the weapons loaded. He should have shot him while he had the chance. Yes. If he had that moment back he would shoot Lewis Keseberg in the heart and gladly watch him die. This spurs him on—the thought that one day he will have another chance.

He urges his panicky horse to drive forward, drive against the chest-high drifts. Each slow, bucking plunge moves the wheezing animal one yard closer to collapse.

At last they can go no farther. Jim dismounts, sinking in up to his belt. He throws a pack and bedroll over his shoulder and hurls himself at the white field, as if a refusal to stop will cause the snow to melt away in front of him.

Mac shouts, "Jim!"

He doesn't turn.

"Jim, what the hell are you doing?"

"We have to keep going!"

"We can't get anywhere in this stuff!"

"C'mon! C'mon!"

Jim is certain now that the party is within shouting distance. They could be holed up just past this ridge. They have to be. It stands to reason. He calls out, "Hallo! Hallo!"

They don't have snowshoes. Neither of them thought of snowshoes. Where Jim comes from you don't need snowshoes, and they weren't mentioned in any of the guidebooks. They make another hundred yards, descending through powder up to their armpits. Downhill it is a slow floating fall through banks of cotton. They reach a ledge with a view along a white and empty slope toward the course of the Yuba. It has stopped snowing. Again Jim calls, "Hallo! Hallo!"

They listen.

They peer.

Not a sign. Not a sound. Not even an echo. The whole mountain range is empty. No one here but two snow-spattered men with heaving chests and steam puffing over the drifts, and silent flakes falling again, closing off the view ahead. All the streams are gone, buried. The Yuba's gone. Perhaps he hears it hissing down below. Perhaps not.

At last Mac gets his breath. "This has got to be it."

"This can't be it."

They look at each other, eyes red-rimmed under frosted brows. Mac stifles a wet, phlegmy cough, and Jim hates his cough, tells himself this is Mac's fever talking, another body giving out the way the horses gave out.

Mac says, "We have to go back."

"Goddam it, we can't go back!"

"Even if we got through, what good is it without the pack herd? Wherever they are, they need food, not two more bellies to fill."

Jim can't bear this thought. Neither can he bear to speak his own heart. He knows Mac is right. He, too, is ready to collapse. He could bury himself right here in the powder and sleep for a year. He waits and lets Mac speak the terrible truth, the voice low and hoarse, words breaking in the breezeless cold.

"We're stuck, Jim. They're stuck too."

"We'll get back down to Sutter's . . . get some more horses."

"Horses can't make it through this, don't ya see?"

"He'll stake us to whatever we need."

"Fifty more horses. A hundred and fifty. Don't make no difference. We're all stuck, us and them, and right now there ain't a goddam thing on earth you or me or anybody else can do about it."

His words join the flakes that drop between the thick coats and their stoic faces, spoken, then gone, swallowed into the huge, white, all-surrounding silence. The men don't move, as if still waiting for any distant flicker of a sign, a sound, perhaps a reaction from the place itself, some recognition that they have come this far to stand and listen. The indifferent snow falls lightly on their hats, their shoulder packs, their sleeves, the laden pines.

—PART TWO—

ORCHARDS

A Ray of Hope

THEY TURN BACK. But he hasn't given up. They dig out the packhorses and at Bear Valley stash sacks of flour and jerked beef high up in the pines, still hoping that by God's grace the company, or some part of it, might get this far. As they wind their way down toward the lowlands, he is already calculating what it will take to recross these mountains, spotting sites for backup camps.

They went about it all wrong, he sees that now. We'll need a base camp below the snow line. We'll need a forward camp higher up, and enough men to hold them while a lead team pushes for the summit. We'll need tents, heavier blankets, and mules as well as horses, and a dozen men next time, or more, if we can find them. That means packing twice as much food for the trip in, and enough stored along the trail to get everyone out.

In the valley again, on the level plain, they follow the Feather. By midmorning it warms up. They've had some sleep. As Jim feels his strength again he scolds himself for listening to Mac. Another mile or two might well have brought them face-to-face with the families at last. He wants to get back up there. He wants to push on through. And soon. Soon! SOON! The sooner the better. In his mind the plan of rescue comes to life, the route, the catalog of details large and small—gloves, saddles, beans, flour, coils of rope . . .

Mac's mind is filling too, though he has doubts. "I just don't know," he says repeatedly. "I just don't know."

"Don't know what?" says Jim.

"I'll give 'er anything I've got."

"I know you will."

"I sure don't see how we'd make it past where we were."

"We are going to!"

"Goddam it to hell, Jim . . ."

"That's all there is to it."

"I want to bring my family through same as you . . ."

"What are you saying, Mac?"

"When I think what it was like, with us not near the summit and . . ."

"And?"

"You have to wonder what it'll be like once a full winter sets in."

"So we leave them all in the mountains to freeze."

"Did I say that?"

"I don't know what you're saying."

"You think I'd say something like that? Hell, no. Any more than you would say something like that! But if a man can't get through, he can't get through. I just wish to hell I'd never left. I should've stayed with the company. I'd sooner be on that side now than this side, I can tell you that. But I ain't. And you ain't. And I sure can't see how to get there!"

Jim doesn't want this kind of talk. He wants to tame the snow, tame the high country, get back to Margaret and his children before the season's full force overwhelms them. He wonders now if the malaria could still be working on Mac, even though the high color has subsided and the coughing only comes in early-morning darkness, when the air turns damp.

As they ford the American River again and see the fort, Jim is counting on Sutter to reassure them. It all depends on Sutter. His settlement is close enough to the mountains and big enough to outfit the kind of rescue team they're going to need. As soon as the captain hears our story, Jim figures, he'll understand what has to be done.

And Jim is right. Sutter understands it all too well. When they appear before him, shabby and weathered and worn down, he is moved by the plight of the two gallant fathers, the two husbands.

This time he invites them to eat and drink. They sit on wooden benches, at a plank table made of pine. Overhead, in elegant incongruity, hangs a candelabra of hammered iron, with twelve unlit white candles. The table is furnished with kerosene lamps and a brandy jug, three sterling silver spoons to catch the light, and three china bowls steaming with potato soup that smells of garlic and pepper.

Outside the walls, Indian guards pace back and forth in blue jackets of heavy cotton, their ancient muskets pointed toward the sky. Inside, the compound seems oddly altered. When Jim and Mac stepped through the gate, a few Indians could be seen, a scattering of half-breed children, half a dozen troops. But the place has the look of a town emptied by news of rising floodwaters. In Sutter's rustic dining room a woodstove fire crackles, and he is eager for some company.

Jim is struck by how ordinary he looks for such a famous man. In the pages of the travel books he stands larger than life, a wilderness legend. Fremont is "the Pathfinder." Sutter is "the Empire Builder," self-appointed ambassador at the farthest edge of the civilized world. Upon close inspection, he is a short and balding fellow who has difficulty sitting still, as if pestered by a boil on his backside, or some affliction of his private parts. He wears his unbuttoned military jacket, blue with gold braid beginning to unravel. From a distance he still has a youthful look, his smile cordial, even jovial. From across the narrow table one sees the webbing around burdened eyes that seem to say he knows a truth too troubling to speak.

Sutter has been drinking for hours. His eyes are too steady now, his cheeks bright red, his voice animated yet maudlin. As he fills their cups a third time with his fort-made brandy, he apologizes for the runaway Indians.

"They would rather steal a horse, you know, than raise one from a colt and feed it and make it their own."

Jim and Mac give their full attention to the soup. Bathed in aromatic steam, their eyes grow large and fill with the water of gratitude.

"They take pleasure in the stealing," Sutter says.

Mac lifts his eyes but not his head. "I chased 'em halfway down the mountain, captain. They got clean away."

Jim says, "We meant to bring back every last one of those horses."

Sutter's smile is ironic. "When my own vaqueros are the thieves, I can hardly hold you gentlemen responsible. What saddens me is the loss. Each animal is so precious, now that Colonel Fremont has taken every horse we had for his so-called battalion. Do you have any idea how many animals it takes to work the fields and ranches here?"

Jim hears belligerence creeping into this question and thinks it's aimed at him. "We'll make it up to you, captain."

"Not long ago we had four hundred horses. Today we have your herd and a drawerful of receipts, the colonel's way of saying thank you. Knowing Fremont, I'll never see him again *or* my horses. I suppose I should be glad he made the gesture. It is the territorial policy now, to give receipts for whatever is commandeered. When they will be honored, or by whom, is anyone's guess. This war has stripped us, gentlemen. Not a hand left at the fort, or in the valley. Nor any horses. Indians steal them. Californians steal them. Americans steal them."

When Sutter pauses to sip, his anger has subsided. He is not one to spoil his own dinner party with grievances.

"What do you mean," Jim says, "not a hand left at the fort?"

"The recruiters did their work too well. You yourself were one of them."

"Yes, sir. At Johnson's we signed up half a dozen."

Again Sutter smiles the resigned and ironic smile of a man outdone by circumstances.

"Dozens more have been recruited. Emigrants. Hired hands. Drifters. Every able-bodied man up and down this valley has gone south to ride with Fremont."

Jim looks at Mac, who is watching him with fearful eyes that seem to say, Didn't I tell you we were stuck?

"You people may have to wait the winter out," says Sutter. "I don't see what else you can do until the worst of it is finished and the snow packs down."

"And when will that be?" Jim demands.

"February, I would say . . ."

"Good God!"

"At the earliest. Maybe longer."

"That's two months, captain!"

"The war is against us now. The weather, too."

Jim's stare is almost suspicious, as if Sutter and Mac are in collusion, both bent on raising obstacles. Why did you let so many go? he wants to ask, though Jim knows how close he came himself to joining the battalion.

Mac says, "We saw some weather, all right. Snow got so deep we flat couldn't move a hand or a foot."

Jim pounces on this. "I guess the captain's news suits you just fine!"

"Hell, no, it don't suit me, Jim!"

"How can you sit here like this when we were so damn close to making it across . . . ?"

"You're sitting here too!"

"You think I want to be sitting here? You think this is my idea?"

Mac winces, as if poked with a knife. Jim's face is flushed. His hands grip the table edge, ready to push back his chair and challenge his huge companion.

Sutter the peacemaker spreads wide his open hands. "Gentlemen. Gentlemen. Please help yourself."

An Indian fellow has appeared, to gather up the china bowls and replace them with a large tin platter of beef, half of it boiled, half fried, surrounded with fried and boiled onions.

Mac leans across the table with a wink. As if to make amends for their manners and any possible show of ingratitude, he says, "This castle has a pleasant seat, captain, a very pleasant seat."

Sutter returns the wink. "Now you test me, Mr. McCutcheon. That has a familiar ring."

"What I just said?"

"It's from a play, if I'm not mistaken."

"I believe it's from *Macbeth,* sir, and a fine play it is."

"Of course, of course. Years ago I saw it performed, by a traveling company passing through St. Louis."

With another wink Mac says, "May good digestion waste your appetite. And health on both."

"Indeed," says Sutter, delighted, as he lifts a ceremonious fork. "And health on both."

Jim has already surrendered to the meat. Now Mac forks two slabs from the platter and in the same move somehow slices and shoves a chunk into his mouth.

Sutter says, "I hope you'll forgive the primitive conditions."

Through working teeth Mac says, "We're mighty content, after nothing but dry jerky and half-cooked beans . . ." He winks. He chews.

"You have no idea how difficult it is to obtain the most rudimentary conveniences of modern life. A ship from Boston can take three months. An order sent to San Francisco tomorrow will be filled half a year from now, and then must come up the river from the bay, which takes another week or more, depending on the season and the tide. To have a watch repaired you might send it across to Honolulu, though you run the risk of never seeing it again."

Sutter likes to talk and hear himself talk. His guests only half listen.

While Mac assaults the beef, Jim is dabbling, distracted, gazing at his brandy cup, stunned by Sutter's news. Seeing this, the captain tries to ease the blow. He wants these men to know they're not alone, that others have been delayed by bad weather and made it through.

He empties his brandy cup and begins the story of a wagon party who crossed the Sierras two years back, led by a tough old Irishman named Murphy, the first party to bring wagons overland to California, though they decided to leave three at Truckee Lake rather than pull them over the summit. One fellow stayed to guard the belongings, built a cabin, and spent a winter there alone. Those who went ahead hit heavy snow right along the Yuba. They were driving cattle and didn't want to lose them, so some kept going and drove the cattle down into this valley ahead of the worst storms, while a couple of men stayed behind with a dozen women and children, who put up shelters and lasted through almost till spring.

"The men who went ahead," says Sutter, "they finally packed back up there and brought the others out. It wasn't an easy time. But no one died, Mr. Reed. No one died. In fact, they added to their numbers. A baby girl was born, right there by the river. They are quite a clan. Catholics, you know. Murphy Senior had nine children, and some of those had traveled with children of their own. They are spread from here to San Jose, with herds and ranches, and to hear them tell it, they all came through in fine fashion."

Jim listens hard, calculating as he listens. He and Mac made it to the Yuba and saw no sign. Had the families camped somewhere higher up? Or did they stop at Truckee Lake like the fellow who stayed to guard the Murphy wagons? What about Charlie Stanton? How many of his mules survived the crossing? And how long did those two Indians last? Jim is counting head of livestock now, counting out loud, remembering the size of the teams and herds on the day he last saw George Donner, on the banks of the Humboldt.

With a reassuring smile, Sutter nods. "If they have that many cattle, if they slaughter them in time and conserve the meat, they should have enough to last them, gentlemen. They should have enough."

Jim examines his plateful of beef and onions and begins to eat, sawing off large forkfuls. Sutter is eating. The three men chew with noisy vigor, their jaws pumping and flexing and crunching as they devour the meat, the onions, washing down each bite with water and with brandy. Jim's head hums with the elixir of food and drink. But still he can't relax.

Between mouthfuls he says, "Yes, sir, they might do fine. Then again, they might not. My boy Tommy is three years old. Mac's girl is only one. Young ones like that, all winter in the mountains . . . it's a big risk to take."

Jim chews a while and swallows.

"We're new in these parts, captain, don't know our way around yet. Seems like there has to be somebody somewhere can give us a hand. I have money. George Donner has money. We pay our way. I hear Californians are the best horsemen in the West. They can't all be thieves and kidnappers. I'd hire Californians if they could be found . . ."

Sutter sips, wags his head. "Some are quite honorable, Mr. Reed. Hearing your story they would weep from their hearts with compassion, as I myself could weep while we are sitting here. They would pour you a drink, man to man, as I pour you a drink . . ."

He refills the cups, raises his in a little toast, and they all sip. Sutter shrugs and laughs his melancholy laugh. "But your country is at war with these people. Your warships are anchored in the Bay of San Francisco. The skillful horsemen you have heard about, why should they ride up into the Sierras in the dead of winter to rescue a band of foreigners? What would be the point, in their eyes? There are already too many foreigners in California."

Above the smeared and greasy plate, Jim's face sags. He is getting drunk. They are catching up with Sutter, who now regrets his last remark and wants to lift the mood, be the bearer of better tidings. Like a prophet he lifts his arms above his head.

"But the warships! Aha! Now there is a ray of hope! There you will find more of your countrymen. Americans. And American resources. It is worth a try, yes it is. If I were you, Mr. Reed, I would call upon the military command in the Bay of San Francisco. A strong case can be made that they have a duty to look after emigrants in trouble. Isn't that so? I would go straight to the commander of the fleet!"

As if this settles something, Sutter slaps his hand upon the table, causing plates and cutlery to leap and clatter.

Jim looks at his ruddy face, his glittering eyes. "And who might that be?"

"Well now, it is Captain . . . I've been told his name is Captain . . . Captain something, yes. Though at the moment it escapes me. A new man has been put in charge of their Northern Command, and there is some confusion, since he may have less seniority than another captain on another ship whose name also escapes me. Commanders there have changed so often, no one can keep track of it from so far away. But no matter. Whichever man is now in charge, please bring greetings from Captain John Augustus Sutter, formerly of His Majesty's Swiss Guard. We have not met, of course. But he will know me. Please assure him that when he has the chance to visit us here he will be most welcome. I am eager to cooperate . . . most eager . . . ."

Again the Indian fellow appears to clear the plates. Not a scrap remains. Every morsel has been consumed, every speck of grease and gravy. This time Manuiki follows with the final course, a platter of fresh-baked breads, pale green slices of melon, a block of cheese. She sets it in the center of the table, with a slow glance at Sutter. He nods his approval and touches her arm.

"Gentlemen, meet my kanaka."

"My goodness," says Mac, leaning toward her for a better look.

"She's from the Sandwich Islands," Sutter says.

"I've heard of the Sandwich Islands," says Jim. "I've heard the whalers stop there."

"All the trade goes that way now. You fellows ought to visit those islands. The men are sturdy and good-humored. All the women are just like her." Sutter winks a lewd wink.

"Well, captain, I salute you," says Mac, his cup raised high. "The hostess of our tavern is a most sweet wench."

Groping at her waist, Sutter leans back with a proprietary and self-satisfied grin. She regards him with neutral eyes.

"Manuiki keeps the garden here. The vegetables we eat have come from her garden, though I of course taught her how to make the soup. Potatoes are not common fare among the kanakas in their native land."

"Mighty fine vegetables," says Jim, nodding toward her with a wrinkled, brandy grin. "What's that name again?"

"Manuiki," Sutter says. "It's kanaka. It means 'little bird.' "

"She know any English?"

Sutter turns to look up at her, his eyebrows raised, like a professor encouraging a prize student to speak.

Manuiki's sudden smile is radiant, seeming to fill the room with light. She gestures toward the melon. "Please. Eat," she says, then steps back, gliding through the doorway.

The visitors are transfixed. "I'll be damned," says Jim.

"First time I have seen a kanaka up close," says Mac.

With another wink Sutter says, "I highly recommend it."

There is one knife to slice the cheese. They break off dark chunks of bread, holding bread and cheese in one hand, melon in the other. Jim has not tasted anything this succulent and fresh in months. He thought the hearty soup and slabs of meat had quelled his hunger. The sight of Manuiki stirs all his appetites anew. He takes his time, sipping brandy, sucking in the melon's juice, regarding Sutter now with a kind of wonder. He regards the unlit chandelier, the table heaped with fruit and cheese. Another jug of brandy has appeared. Who is this balding and potbellied man in his officer's tunic in the midst of an untamed, trackless country? How did he find this distant valley? Jim feels a kinship with Sutter, who got here ahead of almost anyone and saw the possibilities and staked his claim. He is a charming man, and generous, and Jim would like to trust him. Perhaps he is vain and drinks too much and talks too much, but Jim wants to trust his advice. He has to. He can't think of a better plan, and he needs a plan.

He lets the melon juice spill over his lip and trickle through his beard, ready to hear the next story, the one Sutter most wants to tell, about his trip across the Oregon Trail to the Rocky Mountain fur rendezvous of 1838 and from there to points farther west—so far west he left this continent behind. It was winter when he reached the mouth of the Columbia, where they told him that with so much rain and snow, no one could make it south to California. From Fort Vancouver he caught a merchant ship bound for Honolulu. He remembers dolphins leaping along beside them in the crystal blue water, a sign of good luck, he says, a sign that he would soon have his wish and find another ship heading back the other way.

Jim listens, munching, sipping, trying to stay with him, as Sutter recounts his days among "the influential people of the islands," the consuls and traders, the plantation families, and the king himself. They all wrote glowing letters recommending Sutter to the officials here. Months went by. At last he found the ship that would take him east again. When he stepped ashore at Monterey, he brought such high reports of his character and reputation the gobernador had no choice but to grant him even more land than he petitioned for.

This is the part Jim wants to hear, about the land, how Sutter found it, and so much of it, countless thousands of acres. But the story has wandered into the night, with asides and anecdotes and laborious digressions. The brandy fumes have reached Jim's brain and plugged his ears. He listens but can scarcely hear. He glances at Mac, whose eyes are slits, whose long torso is bent, in shadow. Only his face and arm are seen, a cupped hand beneath the chin.

When Sutter pauses to drink, Mac's eyelids lift with great effort. "Good night," he mumbles.

"What's that?" says Sutter.

"Good night, sweet prince . . . and flocks of angels sing thee to thy sleep . . ."

The eyes have closed. In the half flight of flickering lamps, Mac's wide, bearded face looks like the disembodied carving of a head upon a pedestal.

Sutter's tale is all for Jim, who sits up straight blinking, blinking, straining to take it in. Words come toward him, in broken clumps.

"At Yerba Buena we hired a schooner . . ."

". . . two weeks on the Sacramento River . . ."

". . . a kingdom of savages, Mr. Reed . . ."

Jim's body has filled with sand. Though he hears the voice, the words mean nothing. His eyes droop. His lids have a will of their own. They slowly close. His shoulders slump, his body folding like a sack of grain.

Jim's chin falls against his chest.

Voices

MANUIKI IS WAITING in the bedroom. She hears him talk. She waits to hear the voices of the others, and to hear the wide door creaking open as they leave. There is only Sutter's voice, then his bootsteps heavy across the floorboards.

He falls against the bedroom door, lunges in, colliding with the bed, and she knows that once again his guests have been left dozing at the table. Still talking, he fumbles with his boots. He falls backward upon the mattress and lies there looking at the ceiling while he tells a story she has heard before but barely follows, too many words she does not know. Names she has no faces for. She listens to the sounds. She knows the word "commander" means a famous chief.

"When he buys my fort we can move away . . . just you and me . . . move to the farm, Manuiki . . . Ma . . . nu . . . i . . . ki."

He rolls against her. She smells the reek of liquor on his breath, feels his hands upon her body, pressing, sliding. She knows his hands will soon be still. His voice is thick and getting smaller, going away, a thin voice breaking into pieces. At last it stops. The searching hands settle, one upon her bosom, one upon her neck. His breath goes softly in and out, and it is quiet in the upstairs room, quiet in the house, quiet in the compound and around the fort and in the corrals outside the fort.

One sound rises in the valley night, a husky groaning call from the village out beyond the grain fields, a chanting call of many voices, mixed with shouts and wails from the dance house of the village. She did not understand the story of the man wheezing next to her, but she understands this, the distant voices rising late. They touch her. They are not the chants and songs from the islands of her youth. But they have the same feeling, from the same place in the heart and in the throat, as they celebrate the new points of grass brought forth by the first weeks of rain. All day, all night they dance and chant and sing to the rain and the earth and the grass, and their song draws other voices. In Manuiki's heart and in her throat she hears them. They gather in the air.

Her mother.

Her grandmother.

Her *tutu*.

Her *kupuna*.

She throws the cover back and steps to the window and opens it and listens to the voices from the dance house and other voices traveling across the water to speak to her in the long night. They call her back. She listens, and silent tears fall as she sees her mother on the day the chief told them Manuiki was to go with this man, John Sutter. Soon she found herself upon the water, bound for a place she had heard of in the voice of the chanter, bound for *kaleponi*, beyond the water, in the direction of the rising sun.

Sutter gave the chief a piece of paper, and the chief gave him ten kanaka, and they all came to the Bay of San Francisco, and up the wide river with nine white sailors, the kanakas rowing in the first boat and Captain Sutter in among them, pointing, talking. She thought he knew where they were going. Her mother told her white men must be wise because their boats are so large. In his own land, her mother said, this man must be a great chief.

On the river Manuiki saw that he did not know where he was going, and her fear was great. For days they saw no people, though white feathers hung from the trees. Clumps of feathers dangled from the branches, telling them the river people watched. One day the bank was filled with men painted black and red and yellow. She feared that she would die at the hands of the river people. But the captain went ashore and spoke and offered gifts. The kanakas lifted their oars again and rowed upstream, and at last the captain found a place to land. They made houses there from river grass, kanaka houses, island houses. The men found slender limbs to weave. Manuiki gathered grasses as soft as *pili* grass. In the heat they worked while welcome breezes came up the river with the salty smell of the bay and the sea.

The river people stood and watched the grass houses rise, until the captain fired his cannon. Then they cried out and ran away. . . .

A clatter breaks her reverie. She hears a door open. The two men stumble down the stairs. She sees them veer across the compound and find the barracks and stagger inside, scolding the doorway and the darkness. It is quiet again around the fort.

She knows that tomorrow these men will be gone. But where do they go? Where do they come from? So many men moving. How far do they ride? The tall one, she can tell, has a body made of iron. But he will not ride far. He has a sickness. So many men are sick. The older one has a good spirit, but there is too much hunger in his eyes. These white men, their eyes never rest. Their eyes burn.

She sees her father on the rocks, hurling his net to gather in the fish. Her father's eyes are liquid. Steady pools. She sees her mother.

She hears the tribal voices in the night, the groans and shouts and keening wails. The river is low. The salty, fishy smell of the sea drifts northward from the bay, and she knows how the island voices reach her. They come with the water. She knows now how the voices will return, and how she will follow them. One day. This river flows into the bay, and the bay opens into the sea, and the sea is a wide, wide road. . . .

Wild Horses

THE SHORTEST ROUTE is downriver. But Sutter's vessel left four days ago, his schooner loaded with wheat and emigrant families, wives and children bound for the coastal valleys. Nothing else sails for a week, they say. Perhaps two. Or three. Jim can't sit still that long. He is like Sutter trying to reach California from the Columbia River in midwinter. He has to keep moving, even if it means taking the long way round.

He'll ride on down past the maze of delta lands where the two great rivers converge and feed mountain runoff into the bay. It is large enough, they say, to be an inland sea, a two-day sail from one end to the other, a bay so wide and deep, he has heard, that whales cavort as if it is their private swimming hole. He'll skirt the lower edge, by way of San Jose Pueblo, then head north up the long peninsula to the port of Yerba Buena where the U.S. forces have their anchorage.

He leaves Mac hungover in the bunkhouse, Mac who wakes with a moan and swears before God and all the hosts of heaven that he will never taste another drop of liquor until the day he dies. He is going to join the Temperance Union and help other men to put away this vile habit.

"And I am your earthly witness," says Jim, whose tongue is thick and head seems filled with broken ice.

They're splitting up. Mac will ride across the valley, through the coastal mountains to Sonoma, where there's another U.S. garrison. Ranchers out that way might be willing to help, according to Sutter.

Mac looks gray, perhaps from drink. In the predawn chill Jim heard his cough, a deep, wet, wracking early-morning cough.

"Where'll we meet up?" Mac asks.

"Hard to say. Back here, most likely."

"You mean the fort?"

"Or could be Yerba Buena."

"I haven't been there."

"Nor have I," says Jim.

"Where in Yerba Buena?"

The way his head throbs, Jim can barely think. "You stay put in Sonoma. I'll send a letter when I can."

"A month from now."

"Good."

"That'd make it Christmas Day."

"Or thereabouts."

"Sooner, if you can."

"Yes, sooner," Jim says. "Sooner would be fine with me. But in the meantime you lay low right here a day or two. You hear me? You need the rest."

Jim should take his own advice. Slumped in the saddle, he sees nothing until the sun is halfway up the sky. He does not note the shriveled grin of the decapitated Miwok bearing witness from his perch above the gate, nor does he note the Nisenan sentries standing guard in threadbare jackets, shouldering their ancient muzzle-loaders. He sees nothing but the ten feet of trail in front of him, sometimes puddled, sometimes damply dry. The rains that began a month ago have continued off and on. So far, the flat earth has soaked up most of it.

As the sun climbs, as his head clears, he begins to notice the fecund land, the many oaks, the fields of wild oats, with stalks as high as his stirrups. He has been told to watch for grizzlies, but has seen none yet. He sees a herd of elk grazing like cattle, a thousand animals, perhaps two thousand, spread across the plain, elk as thick as the largest herd of buffalo they spied back in Nebraska. Some bulls have wing-shaped antlers scooping outward. Where water stands in marshy wetlands a multitude of geese come rising from beyond a tule forest. They lift and rise, white geese with black-tipped wings, their slender necks extended as if invisible leashes pull them toward the sky.

It is a paradise of creatures here, deer and elk and cranes and pigeons, jackrabbits, geese beyond the counting. With his eyes Jim sees it all. Yet he does not see. His mind roams other country, unable to take much pleasure in this great show.

As his head clears, the weight of their predicament comes bearing down upon him. Margaret and the children trapped. George and Tamsen too, and their five girls. Charlie Stanton. Milt Elliott. Bill and Eleanor Eddy and their two young ones. The whole company stuck somewhere and no way for him or anyone else to reach them. Not for weeks, John Sutter says. Nor can he find a horse to borrow, buy, or steal. No able-bodied men. And had he twenty men, or fifty, what difference would it make, when the snow gets deeper day by day?

He wants wings. He wants a catapult. He wants to vault across the snowy ridges. He can't sit still. Yet what can really come of this trip to Yerba Buena? How long will it take, in the middle of a war? And who, after all, is this nameless naval captain? A friend of Sutter's? No. A man Sutter has *heard about* and, in midnight drunkenness, salutes.

What a lame, half-baked, and slippery plan. Jim feels his control of things sliding away. He needs an outcome up ahead, a clear goal to set his sights upon. There's no future now, none he can see. He sees only his past mistakes. Old doubts push to the surface as he rides. Like bad dreams he hears again the voices of the women in the company, the voice of John Snyder, too, as he brandishes the butt end of his whip.

You're the one got us into this.

Maybe you're the one deserves a whipping . . .

An eye for an eye, and a tooth for a tooth.

It's your doing, Reed.

It's all your doing . . .

They fill the air around his head, voices louder than the honking from the cloud of geese. Margaret's voice is now among them.

They won't harm us, she says, standing next to him in the sand, with the armed accusers waiting, *once you're gone.*

Once you're gone . . .

Is it possible? Could they have all been right? Was he the culprit? Would he bring such a fate upon himself? Upon his family?

He can't listen to these voices. He did his best. What more can you ask of any man? Hasn't he always strived to do his best?

He hears Mac's cough, sees again the fever in the young man's face, and is relieved to be riding on another trail, away from Mac's heated eyes, as if he could ride away from fever itself. In this land where sickness is unknown—according to Lansford Hastings—it is everywhere. Fevers. Agues. Aches. Cramps. Boils. Rheumatism. Sudden blindness. Coughing in the night. Why did he ever open that book and listen to such concoctions? Back in Springfield the winter's fuel would now be stacked, the house snug against the weather. The laughter of running children would be his music.

Hearth music.

Holiday music.

THREE DAYS SOUTH of the fort, where the marshlands narrow and the river finally shows its shape, he swims his horse across the San Joaquin. On both sides tules are higher than his hat, a riverine world of tule stalks as thick as axe handles. He rides through them, bearing west across a plain rutted deep with trails cut by the abundant herds—more elk, more deer, more antelope. Vapor rises from the damp terrain, covering it with a skin of steam. In the distance he sees a pack of wild horses grazing, dream horses whose legs are lost in vapor.

When they notice his approach they bolt toward him from a quarter mile away. There could be two hundred in this herd, maybe more—inquisitive, apocalyptic horses galloping through steaming grass, until they're close enough to see it's just another human, atop another horse. They wheel, lunge back the way they've come, then abruptly stop, swarming, restless horseflesh. The sleek heads swing and snort and turn to graze again, snouts disappearing in the steam.

The land begins to undulate. The broad plain wrinkles westward, makes a rise. Grasses thin out, where the soil gets shallow. Off the trail and up a slope he sees a line of bones, longer than any skeleton he would recognize. He rides toward it, climbing, and finds a bleached pattern laid across the grass as if it fell from the sky. Too long to be a cow's remains. Or an elk's. The oblong shape, the skull, the ribs have the dimensions of a giant fish. Perhaps a whale. But how? There must still be a hundred miles between this spot and the ocean shore.

Jim looks back the way he has come. The mist has spread. Below him it's a lake of mist. He can imagine that the endless valley may once have been another kind of lake. If water somehow had risen to the level of this slope, some poor creature who had swum too far became marooned when the waters receded. The sight fills him with reverence and a rush of dread at the strangeness of this huge skeleton spread across otherwise empty terrain, as if waiting for the water to return.

He rides on, and the low-lying vapor follows him. It rises, gathering, a wet, enshrouding fog so dense he cannot see the trail. He lets the horse pick its way. When they finally climb through it, the fog breaks into shreds, revealing a corridor of green-skinned slopes.

After the Sierras, this crossing seems to him no more than a bulge of foothills. The trail climbs smoothly toward a notch, an easy pass between two steep slopes, emerald under gauzy cloud cover that obscures the topmost ridges. Too easy, it seems to Jim. Beyond this range, he has been told, the Californians have built their towns and laid out their largest ranchos. This narrow passage, it's one of the gateways to the Californian enclaves—in times like these, the kind of place you would expect troops to lurk.

He stops to listen, tries to peer into the cloud barrier, then heads toward it, and through it, as the trail descends to another valley. Isolated oaks emerge from dense mist, backlit silhouettes. Late sun pushes underneath the mist to make luminous curtains around the trees.

It is a well-watered valley where longhorn cattle roam at large, like Johnson's herds, without fences, but somehow more sinister. They seem to regard him with suspicion. Is this the untamed herd of a Californian's rancho? They seem wilder than the elk or antelope.

Another pass leads into another valley, which slopes toward yet another notch, another wooded ridge where riflemen might wait. But where are they? Why don't they show themselves? Do they watch from a distance, like the desert Indians watched? He feels exposed. Again he is a sitting duck, and what in hell is he really doing here? What is the point of this tedious excursion? He should have waited for the schooner. The trail is too long, too chancy, and it takes him in the wrong direction—west—when he should be heading east with food and horses. Each day has taken him farther from where he ought to be, farther south, now west again, and how many more days before this southern loop bends north at last?

Jim feels that he has lost his way. The land is lovely, bowls of pasture, stands of oak, the succulent country he has yearned to possess. But after all these months of dreaming, after all these years of knowing where he was headed next, and why, today he is like the great fish once marooned back there, in the wrong place at the wrong time, with fins and undulating rudder tail suddenly useless. In this alien place where the maps and guidebooks cannot be trusted, he is adrift, a householder with no house, a father with no children, a wagon master with no more wagons to lead.

ON THE AFTERNOON of his second day past the river he is climbing toward a ridge that seems burnished. From somewhere beyond it, an aura probes the sky. A final corridor opens out, and he sees another plain spread before him to the west, blazing silver. He dismounts and gulps from his canteen. The late sun appears to bounce off a sheet of water, light shimmering so brightly he has to squint to see through it, to make out the low range of indigo mountains bordering the farther side. This is like the beguiling mirages that followed him so many times across the Salt Desert, that delicious dazzle off the still water. He half expects it to lift or wobble, yet the water does not move. No pieces break and float away, nor do those distant mountains waver in the heat. They can't. There is no heat. It occurs to him that today is the last day of November. The air is crisp and clean. But cool.

A briny scent is rising. He remembers that he smelled it long before he passed through that corridor. Your eyes can fool you. But the smells are real, the smell of marshy wetlands where salt collects. Surely this is the southern arm of that large bay pictured on maps, named by the Spanish for Saint Francis. The water extends as far north as he can see, bordered by those low dark ridges. Yerba Buena must lie that way.

He studies the curving edge of water. Out in front of him, where the long bay ends, a basin continues farther south, wide and flat, and seemingly empty, but for its glinting rivulets and scattering of trees.

Jim gazes until his eyes burn. He dips his hat to shield his eyes against the blazing light. From somewhere behind him he hears a voice.

"Don't turn around."

As he reaches for the rifle in its scabbard by his saddle, he hears the click of a hammer cocked.

"Don't do that either."

Jim waits. How did someone get this close?

The voice says, "Where do you come from?"

"John Sutter's fort."

"You're American."

"That's right. I have a letter of safe passage."

"From Sutter?"

"From the lieutenant in charge of the garrison there."

He hears the man spit.

"An idiot."

"That may be so," Jim says, "but he commands the valley of the Sacramento now."

He hears a low, sardonic chuckle.

"I'm going to turn around. I mean no harm here."

"Hands away from the body, please."

The fellow sits on a fallen tree trunk as if posing for a portrait, one boot propped on a rock, a dark hat tipped to shade his eyes. His jacket has a vaguely military cut, though it isn't military, the collar high and circular, a tapered waist. A rifle in the crook of his arm points toward the ground.

"I'll look at that letter now."

He has a black tuft of chin beard and across his cheeks unshaven stubble. A thin mocking smile tells Jim he is being toyed with, in some little game this fellow seems to enjoy. He holds a hand out, palm up, not like a highwayman, but like a creditor collecting on a debt.

From the leather pouch slung inside his coat Jim withdraws a smudged and flimsy folded page. He has noticed movement beyond some trees. Now three more men ride toward them, leading half a dozen horses. They all carry rifles, wear wide-brimmed hats and heavy coats similar enough to seem like uniforms, though they are not. Dust and grime are embedded in these coats and in the bulging beards. They look as if they have been traveling on horseback for months, or years.

They watch but do not speak, as the one on foot returns Jim's letter. The hat brim has been pushed back, revealing fixed blue eyes, implacable eyes that hold him with a haughty gaze. Do they taunt him?

"Meet Mr. Reed. He'll ride with us a while."

Is this an order or an offer? The fellow mounts one of the horses and waits for Jim to mount. The riders bunch around him as they set out together on the downslope trail.

For a couple of miles they ride without speaking. Has Jim been captured or befriended? He can't quite tell. There is something menacing about the leader's face under the shadow of his tilted brim. In profile the tufted chin protrudes too far. Jim considers making a run for it, but knows he won't. Not yet, at any rate. Where would he run to? He studies the three in overcoats. He is sure he recognizes one of them, a tall and lanky fellow.

After a while Jim mentions Fort Laramie. The fellow nods. He was there in July. And yes, he thinks the name Reed might ring a bell. A younger man, riding next to him, nods and grunts. "Ain't you the ones fell so far behind?"

They all know something of the story, the last party on the trail in this year that a thousand wagons made the crossing. Scraps and bits of lore and gossip have traveled through the passes like burs and seed-pods in the furry coats of animals, to spread out into the valleys where the emigrants have gathered.

These men too are land-seeking settlers, now plunged into a struggle with the scoundrel Californians who cannot seem to get it through their heads that the newcomers are here to stay and not about to be pushed aside or trifled with.

The lanky fellow has a wife and three children parked down below. "Most everybody rode south with Colonel Fremont," he says, "but some of us had to stay behind to protect the families."

Two weeks ago he joined the volunteer militia out of San Jose. This patrol of four is about to give up the search for a band of troops rumored to be forming in these mountains. Stock has been stolen, so they've heard, though whether by Californians or by Indians, it's hard to say.

Jim looks at the string of unsaddled horses.

"So you found the animals but not the troops."

The man grins and looks away. "Let's say these critters been repossessed."

"They're wily, them greasers," the younger fellow says.

"Chickenshit's what they mostly are," says the third.

"They could be clear to Mexico City by now."

Jim hears these things from the men in overcoats, not from their jacketed leader, whose name is Valentine. He keeps a brooding silence on the trail. The way he rides reminds Jim of someone. Though aloof, he sits in the saddle like a performer who insists that you notice him.

Later on, the lanky fellow tells Jim he was among those who made it to Fort Bridger in time to join the party led by Lansford Hastings. "I guess we come through just ahead of your bunch," he says, with a grim, commiserating nod. "And I don't have to tell you it was a tough old road. We lost some wagons. Just barely made it, if you want to know the truth. Then come to find out this fancy new republic he claimed he would lead weren't nothing but hot air, since the United States Navy had got here first. But we did make it through, I'll give him that."

"And where is he now?" Jim asks.

"Long gone."

"Gone where?"

"On south with the rest of 'em. Some kind of officer, is what I heard. That Hastings, he don't miss a step. I'd wager he's halfway to Los Angeles."

Jim feels the stab of envy. It irks him that Hastings is there while he is not, riding with Fremont's battalion. It irks him more that the man has escaped interrogation. Jim has imagined him in some California town filling other heads with far-fetched promises. Jim has imagined finding him and throwing a rope around his neck and walking him up to that ridge above Bear Valley where they listened to the empty snow-fields, so that Hastings might contemplate the miseries he led them to.

Part of him would head south right now in pursuit of the battalion, while part of him listens to the fellow pilgrim who followed the prophet from Fort Bridger and made it all the way across with his family intact. Could it be that Jim has misjudged Hastings and his cut-off? He wonders, as they ride, and he resigns himself to waiting. The war can't last forever. In this uncertain land, in such uncertain times, he'll have to wait a while longer to learn who to hold accountable for the suffering and the setbacks on the journey he thought he'd planned so well.

Valentine

THE SUN IS about to touch the farther rim of mountains when another rider overtakes them. He comes up from behind at a gallop, wearing high boots and the tight-waisted jacket of a Californian, although he is not a Californian. His face is brown, his cheekbones high, an Indian face, and on his head a wide blue cap, flat-topped and circular with a short bill. Sitting tall and straight, he rides next to Valentine, says a few words in Spanish, then drops back.

They have crossed a table of land between the tawny foothills and the bay's dark curve, and now they come upon a low compound of tattered buildings. San Jose Pueblo still lies half a day's ride south, beyond the bay. This is the Mission of St. Joseph, or what remains of it. Valentine decides they'll spend the night here.

Along one side of the road, a lopsided row of adobe huts, half brick, half mud, are melting back into the soil from which they rose. They face a chapel, a long, squared-off barn of adobe brickwork, covered with flaking whitewash. The peaked roof is made of earth-red tiles, though many have slipped loose and lie broken. There is no bell tower, no steeple, no cross rising—only a door in the windowless facade, held loosely shut by a padlock on a rusty chain.

With a cryptic nod Valentine says, "There is the true enemy."

Jim looks at him. "The Church?"

"Neglect. Indifference."

Though the mission looks abandoned, in one of the shacks they find a woman who is willing to prepare some food, a very short woman, well under five feet, dark and round and hunched, with a braid of silver hair down her back. When Valentine speaks to her in Spanish about the food, her eyes grow bright. To the men he says, with a leer, "Her bed is too small for all of us together. But she will take us one at a time and guarantee our satisfaction."

The men chuckle. The woman and a granddaughter of ten or so scurry around a cooking fire. The floor is dirt, swept and hard-packed. There is one small window. On the low benchlike table they set out platters of tortillas, beans cooked with beef chunks, and chili colorado. The men eat with their fingers. They eat as if they haven't seen food in weeks, hot juice running across their hands, dripping onto the platters. They joke about the lack of forks and spoons.

"My daddy never even saw a fork till he was nine," the lanky fellow says, "then it was just for pitching little bitty bales of hay in this field that was owned by a midget."

It is near dusk when they lead their horses past the outbuildings that surround the chapel and through an unlocked gate in the low adobe wall. They pass long porticos outside the empty dormitories, collapsing sheds where thatched roofing has been torn by wind, and warehouses where olive oil and dried fruit and grains and wines were once stored. Staves lie scattered where the barrels fell apart among the shards of broken jugs. Rickety looms stand idle, gray with cobwebs and rotting yarn. Farther in, there is a courtyard covered with debris, twigs and limbs and birds' nests blown from trees, strewn around a gurgling fountain, and beyond that the long-neglected vineyards and olive groves and orchards.

At night the place is ghostly. The fountain splash is like a light burning, as if someone just stepped away and might return at any moment. Jim peers into the falling darkness.

As if to the others, yet somehow attuned to Jim's uneasiness, Valentine says, "We have been looking in the wrong place. There are no troops within miles of here. If we find them at all, it will be in the mountains to the west." With soft sarcasm, he adds, "Tonight our only company will be a few goats, and the old woman across the road, who waits patiently to see which of us will be first."

He offers a laugh. But his joke wears thin. The others ignore it.

Under the vast limbs of an elderly fig tree they lay out bedrolls and build a fire in a pit where other sojourners have built fires. A bottle of aguardiente appears. After it has passed around the circle a couple of times they begin to talk, all but Valentine, who now maintains a dramatic silence. Whenever the bottle is offered he passes it on, while he stares at the fire with chin in hand, as if rehearsing for the role of a character whose complex fate weighs heavily upon him.

The others pay little notice. They are curious about Jim. Why did he leave his party? Why is he bound for San Jose?

With every telling of his story the desert has grown wider, the mountains higher, the snow deeper, the need for animals and food more urgent. Hearing of his hopes to mount a rescue team, the listeners glance away with hooded, guilty looks. They sip again, poke sticks at the edges of the blaze, and confirm Jim's fears. We sure do feel for your kinfolk, they say, and it's a terrible thing to admit, but when the whole Bay of San Francisco is on alert, who has a spare moment to think about people stuck somewhere three hundred miles away?

One fellow tells a story that he too has told and retold, about a firefight two weeks ago, below San Jose, where five brave Americans were killed and six Walla Wallas riding with them and twice that many Californians.

"What right did they have to stand in the way of our boys moving horses from the Sacramento down to help out Colonel Fremont? They had us outnumbered three to one, but our boys hunkered down and made 'em wish they stayed home on that particular day. Served 'em right, I'd say. Our boys wasn't out to do battle, just driving this herd of horses from one place to the other."

"Trouble is," the lanky fellow says, "the greasers got no respect for human life."

"Nor the Stars and Stripes, neither," says the fellow next to him, who turns out to be his son. "Two times it was run up the pole there in San Jose. Two times in the dark of night they crept in and tore it down."

"Thieving cowards is what I call 'em."

"Treacherous," says the third, a stout barrel-maker from Indiana. "Lord, you have never seen such treachery!" And he recounts how all the towns had surrendered peaceably, even the new capital of Los Angeles. But the next thing you know, they turn right around and rise in insurrection. The word now is that Mexican regulars are sailing up the coast from Mazatlán or some such place, with artillery and fresh troops by the hundreds . . .

His tale is interrupted by the low, thick, insistent voice of Valentine. "Perhaps someone can tell me something."

He still gazes at the fire. They all look at him and wait.

"When these troops arrive, what do they think they are coming to defend?"

The lanky fellow starts to speak but holds his tongue, as Valentine's frowning face opens with a slow chuckle. It rises to a hollow laugh.

"Look around you. Look where we are camped. Look at these buildings. If you can call them buildings." He reaches out, as if to embrace the compound. "*This* is California, gentlemen! Do you think it is worth defending? This is what happens when Californians are in command!"

He steps toward the fire with his hands on his hips, a defiant stance, as if waiting for someone to challenge him. Something about the old mission kindles his anger. Rubbing his wrists as if they itch or burn, twisting them inside his cuffs, he begins to pace.

"A thousand Indians used to work these grounds. Did you know that? Carlos was among them . . ."

He flings a hand toward the guide, who sits slightly apart, puffing on a corncob pipe. Carlos has not been drinking. Beneath the unbuttoned jacket he wears no shirt. His brown chest is smooth, the muscles etched. Intense eyes give him a warrior look, yet his manner is anything but warlike, with the pipe smoke curling upward. He doesn't seem to know enough English to follow what's being said, nor does he seem to care.

"And where are they now?" says Valentine, with accusation in his voice. "What happened to that multitude? I'll tell you where they are. They ran away, as the family of Carlos ran away. They worked for the padres. They tilled the soil. They made the bricks. They pressed the grapes and ran the cattle. They worked for Spain. But Madrid was so far from Mexico, the Spaniards could not hold this land. The Church lost its power. The padres lost control of the Indians. And away they went. You can see what it has become! You can see how quickly it has been allowed to fall to pieces!"

His rising voice is hoarse and urgent. Lit from below, his tufted chin seems large. His cheeks make upward shadows. The skin below his eyes seems wet, as if watered by the passion of this speech.

Jim takes a long pull on the aguardiente and watches Valentine, reminded of the desert, when men deprived of food and water became delirious and woke up raving in the night, or at midday for no reason would grab you by the shirt. You forgave them, knowing how near you were yourself to such an outburst. But Valentine is not delirious. He looks well fed. He's a young man too, fit and trim. Jim glances at the others, who have listened without any show of wonder or alarm. Have they heard all this before?

Peering into the heavy branches overhead, Valentine says, "Do you know where you are, Mr. Reed?"

The question startles him. Where does it come from? Again, Valentine seems to enter his mind and know his doubts. Unaccountably he feels his arm hairs prickle.

"More or less," Jim says.

"You may know that these mountains behind us are named for the devil. The Spanish called this range Diablo. Who knows why? They say a band of Spanish soldiers were defeated not far from here by Indians whose leader was a medicine man of strong powers. The Spanish claimed they were devilish powers. Do you think such things are possible?"

"Out here everything seems possible."

Valentine regards him with an approving smirk. "Aha! A very good answer, Mr. Reed. The correct answer. But now tell me this! Why would someone establish a mission in such a place, named for the very father of our Savior, Jesus Christ, and built in a region that is named for the devil?"

Jim has no answer. He has never heard of such a thing. All this delights Valentine. His blue eyes gleam. He wraps his arms across his chest and rocks in the firelight.

"It is wicked to do this. They are a wicked people! All of them! Is it any wonder the Indians ran away? Any wonder that the mission is in ruins? The Spaniards thought the Indians were devils. The Indians thought the Spaniards were devils. We are certain that the Californians are devils. And the Californians? Who knows what they think? Perhaps these mountains are well named after all. Wouldn't you say so, Mr. Reed? Each man can find here the devil of his own making."

Valentine's long laugh echoes across the broken tiles of the empty courtyard and the crumbling adobe walls.

Out of the Wilderness

JIM'S SLEEP IS fitful. Twice the fountain wakes him, and he lies on his back, gazing into the swarm of branches while he retraces the route. Again and again he revisits each mile, from the curve of the Humboldt, across the sand, along the Truckee, into the Sierras, over the summit and through to Bear Valley, trying to imagine the safest spot, trying to place them there, bedded down, somehow protected . . .

The third time he wakes, a predawn breeze has stirred the leaves. Little clicks and the overhead chatter of twiglets rouse him, and he is up before the others, walking out among the rows of trees, where a few pears and apples can still be seen, brown or mottled yellow, clinging to the gnarly limbs. Valentine is right. They haven't been pruned in many years, nor has the soil been turned. His boots move through a dense mulch of fallen leaves, years of leaves decomposing, sending up a moldy hard-cider scent, half sweet, half vinegar, from the near-rot of windfall apples and bird-eaten pears composting with the leaves.

These hills are called Diablo, says Valentine. That doesn't trouble Jim. He won't let it trouble him. Hills are hills, and apples are apples, and a name is just a name. He breathes deeply, takes in the smell of trees and earth, all doing their work, a comforting and heady smell, floating on a subtle light. Though the orchard is in shadow and the sun still hidden, the air around him has come to life. He turns and sees that the bay and the slopes beyond the bay already catch the sun's first rays and send them back to tint the limbs and yellow globes.

He falls to his knees and digs his hands down through compost until he touches soil. Out of the leaves he lifts it toward his face, a dark and crumbling handful, holds it close and sniffs, then inhales deeply. It brings water to his eyes, the moist and loamy cider scent of orchard soil. How can Valentine call this place devilish? There is something sacred about an orchard in late autumn, approaching winter, the silence of the leaf-stripped trees, the patience of the trees, turning inward. Trees in summer are sacred too, in another way, their limbs weighted with the produce that the miracle of fertility sends forth—fertility plus cultivation. The long rows stretch out around him, acres and acres of apple trees, pear trees, plum, and quince. Could it be the reason he has come this way? To feel this soil, unlike any he has known, to see these trees sprung out of the wilderness in perfect rows?

Again he smells the soil and imagines the abundance. In his mind he sees the year turn, he sees the pruned limbs sprout new buds. He sees the pears and plums spring forth, burdening the limbs. He sees his children climbing among the branches, and scurrying between the rows to gather windfall fruit.

The Sight of His Flag

AFTER BREAKFAST, as they ride down the slope, Jim asks aloud, to anyone, "Who owns those orchards now?"

The other emigrants look to Valentine, whose answer is a muffled laugh.

They follow one of the many streams that flow toward the bay, bordered with sycamores and willow thickets and fields of high mustard. The plain is turning green with the shoots of new grasses. Ancient oaks are everywhere but set apart from one another, growing singly. Spaced among the trees, the longhorn cattle stand like distant statues.

"No one," says Valentine at last. "The finest land for miles around, and no one gives a damn. Would you like the mission orchards, Mr. Reed? They can be yours for the asking."

One arm stretches forth, as if he is this valley's first citizen, as if to say, "All of this I present to you!" Again he laughs at the exhilarating folly of such a place. These missions, he tells Jim, once had lands that went on forever. Now it's all in the hands of the ranching families. But alas, the ranchers don't like to work for long among the fruit trees. They prefer to speed up and down the valleys seeing to their cattle. To cultivate an orchard would mean getting off your horse. "A man on foot," he says, "is thought to be no man at all."

"If I were an orchard lover I would seize the chance and sit myself down upon that land with some loaded rifles and claim it by right of occupation. Of course, I am like all the rest of them now. I have been in California too long to accept any task that separates me from my beloved horse!"

With an exuberant cry he removes his hat, whacks the animal's rump, and gallops away. The trail bends around a grove of oaks, and

Valentine disappears, his hat held high, as if he leads a parade along a boulevard filled with admirers.

By the time they catch up to him they are near the pueblo, which can't be seen until they're almost upon it. The first buildings are low ranch houses set out by themselves, with plots of vegetables and corrals made of tilting limbs, chickens running loose and tethered goats, the yards littered with cattle bones and skulls.

Now Valentine and Jim ride ahead of the other four, and Valentine's manner has changed. They ride almost shoulder to shoulder, at a slow trot. He speaks softly, intimately, telling Jim he has a rancho of his own, beyond the town, with corrals and a flour mill. He knows exactly the man to talk with about those orchards, the vineyards, the other mission lands. It is not like the old days, he says, when you petitioned for a grant of such and such a size and then, in order to receive it, became a Catholic and a citizen and swore allegiance to Mexico. That time is gone. The rules are changing every day. Perhaps there are no rules.

A sly and covert glance from Valentine tells Jim this history lesson won't come free of charge. With an apologetic grin, he confesses that he recognized Jim's name on the letter of safe passage. Not long ago he met the men who signed the proclamation at Sutter's Fort, when Jim accepted a lieutenancy in their half-formed platoon. He wants Jim to ride with him. Valentine leads this local militia unit, and tomorrow they'll be riding out again, this time toward the western mountains, taking more men. He needs thirty to police the town and thirty to ride. He could use another lieutenant.

Is this a request? Is it an offer? Or an order? Jim can't quite tell. Yet from Valentine it is somehow a flattering proposal, as if he alone can fully appreciate Jim's qualities of judgment and patriotic zeal.

As for Yerba Buena, he adds seductively, there is no point in trying to get through. Not now. Half the American fleet is anchored there, it's true, but the port will soon be under siege, with these Californians in revolt and more troops on their way from Mexico. A man alone bound for Yerba Buena would risk his life, and all for what? No one at the port or in the town can think of anything but holding their position.

"Whether here or there, Mr. Reed, you would be conscripted. And we need you here. You ride well. You keep your own counsel. You do not drink too much, as these other buffoons are inclined to do. In the end, of course, the United States will prevail. There is no doubt. Then the men you hope to find will be more than ready to lend a hand. I guarantee it. I know this place. I know them all. The travelers. The families. The officers who now preside over Alta California with their fleet marines at the ready. I know the high-handed rancheros and the little *mamacita* who heated our tortillas last night. I know them, Reed. I know their hearts."

The town—El Pueblo de San José de Guadalupe—has no pattern, no grid of streets. The road from the north lies between two meandering waterways, rough-hewn irrigation ditches, and the houses are strewn here and there, some facing water, some facing the road, some thatched, some tiled, some with gardens, some with nothing in the yards but the heaped horns and ribs of cattle. The road widens into a dirt plaza, damp from recent rain, free of dust. The tallest building is another whitewashed adobe church. In the center of the plaza, the courthouse is a one-story adobe with a tiled roof, where an American flag flies from a high pole.

Beside the courthouse a U.S. Marine stands guard. Half a dozen more lounge with rifles and bayonets at the ready, beyond a deep moat that looks recently dug. The moat is five feet across and makes a square, and the dirt from the moat has been thrown against a breastwork of stakes not quite as high as the tallest marine. At first glance it is hard to know whether this little fortress has been created to protect the random scattering of cottages and sheds that surround it, or to protect the marines from the inhabitants of the town.

Jim is looking at the flag, the way its colors fold into one another, stripes of white and scarlet overlapping chunks of indigo. His throat thickens. He looks at these young men in their navy jackets. How have they come so far? By ship, no doubt, around the southern cape—in miles, ten times the distance he himself has traveled these past few months—to raise the Stars and Stripes at the farthest corner of the continent. In the muddy plaza of this foreign town, the cut of their uniforms stirs him profoundly. He is a lieutenant, after all. At Sutter's he signed the paper. He swore the oath. The very sight of the flag tells him he must travel with Valentine's militia. In his heart he has already joined them. Sutter was right. *Until this war is done, there are no men to call upon for aid.*

If there is a better way for him to go, he can't think of it. Not today, with the marines right here in front of him and his flag flying. His nation is at war with Mexico, and he knows more now about what that means, having seen so much country in these recent days, the long valley with its multitude of creatures, and the rippling coastal ranges, and the smaller valleys where longhorns graze, and the fertile plain around this pueblo, and the orchards too. The dawn-burnished apples are in his mind somewhere, not *on* his mind, yet gathered there along with all the rest that he has seen and somehow feels closer to, as if crossing it on horseback brings him that much closer to possessing it.

Yes, he is willing to join them, to ride on across the plaza, though he knows this man is too full of himself. Outside the moat, Valentine speaks to the marines as if he commands their unit, too. One acknowledges him with a finger to the hat. He rides on, like a general reviewing troops. Even his horse seems to strut.

Of all the northern towns, he says to Jim, importantly, *we are the largest. We are also the most vulnerable, with so many men gone south to join the colonel. The port of Yerba Buena has its warships. Here in San Jose we have no ships, and no presidio. These marines came down from the fleet to help us hold the town. Thanks to them, my Volunteers are free to roam the outskirts.*

They pass an alleyway where a dozen men circle two battered bantam roosters. One bird is tearing out the eye of the other, stabbing at the dark socket with a bloody beak. The men shout wildly, among them two marines, their faces flushed, their jackets loose, suspenders showing. "Pronto!" they cry. "Vamoose! Vamoose!"

Valentine leads him toward a low-slung adobe already filled with voices in the early afternoon. Inside, the light is dim, the tables full. At the first table they stop, and a cry goes up, a call for drinks. These are militiamen, playing cards. Jim is introduced as a new Volunteer, just down from Sutter's. Another fellow seems to recognize the name. Hands reach out. Chairs shove back to make room at the table. The bartender, a swarthy Californian with a large, engaging smile, brings a new bottle and some glasses. He calls Valentine "mi capitano." To Jim, with elaborate courtesy, he says, "Buenas tardes, señor. Bienvenidos a San José."

Jim finds himself in a swirl of toasts and noisy drunken greetings. As the welcoming subsides, as the game resumes, as his eyes adjust to the murky light, he notices three vaqueros heading for the door, like insulted citizens walking out of a public meeting. Their spurs clink with disapproval. Are they scowling at him? At Valentine? At other tables, in among off-duty marines, other moustachioed vaqueros seem aware of nothing but their cards. From a corner Jim can't see he hears a sound he hasn't heard in weeks, or months, the alto peal of female laughter. He glimpses a white blouse, a bare shoulder and another blouse. They are playing cards with two marines. He shifts his weight for a better look, but two large men block his view, pulling chairs in close to Valentine.

Around the cards the men are swapping opinions about a report that came in today by courier from Monterey, where militant rancheros are said to be gathering in the hills. It follows hard upon yesterday's report, dispatched by launch from Yerba Buena—advance parties of the Mexican fleet have been sighted as far north as Santa Barbara, sailing up from Mazatlán with orders to capture and execute all foreigners. Here at the pueblo, two mothers camping with their children—women who narrowly survived the crossing of the continent and now await the return of husbands traveling with Fremont—these mothers say that dark-complected men on horseback surrounded them one night, brandishing swords and swinging lariats, and then laughed hysterically as they rode off into the darkness.

With each story the voices grow louder. The eyes grow wide with drink and indignation. One by one the card-playing vaqueros leave the cantina. Then the women leave. And the bartender too. Valentine, rising to his feet, vows that this time his men will not return empty-handed.

He Doesn't Want to Think

THEY SET OUT early, thirty mounted men and a caballada of fifty horses, heading westward toward dark green ridges, the last low range before the land ends and the sea begins. Above the mountains some distant probing light off the endless water lends its silver to the morning sky.

From timbered slopes the rivulets and creeks come spilling down to stripe the valley. Carlos rides far ahead, toward a winding canyon they will follow into the foothills, and Jim is moving ever farther from where he wishes he could be. He is pulled two ways. Yesterday he was glad to be with Valentine. Today he is cursing the war and the weather and the mushy trail and the Indian guide who chose it and the manzanita bushes grabbing at his stirrups, and cursing Valentine, who rides with shoulders thrown back like a general at the head of a regiment.

Jim knows now who this man reminds him of. Why hadn't he seen it sooner? The smugness. The theatrical horsemanship. Is he not, in certain ways, like Lewis Keseberg? About the same age. Similar build. A friendlier Keseberg with a caustic humor and a satanic laugh.

The possibility alarms him. Yet he is drawn to it, drawn to Valentine, whose contempt for the adversary somehow suits Jim's mood, his rising self-disgust. As they ride, Valentine mutters to himself and to anyone who's listening. They pause in a clearing, to consider the route, and Jim lets himself be prodded by the words.

"These people don't deserve California, Mr. Reed. They don't know what they want. They are their own worst enemies. You saw them playing cards with Americans. They are glad to see us in the town. Yet they have brothers and sisters who despise all foreigners and all Mexicans too. No two of them can agree on anything. Families fight with families. How else do you think sixty marines who are usually drunk can hold a town of eight hundred souls?"

As they climb, scouting parties head out to explore the higher ridges. Jim volunteers to lead half a dozen men through a shaded, nameless gully and upward to the topmost pinnacle. Valentine calls after them, bellowing instructions. As his voice rings through stands of pine and redwood, these searches take on a hectic frenzy, a headlong lunging here and there. The horses sweat and fight the muck and rear back wild-eyed on the steep ascents. It's exactly what Jim wants. He doesn't want to think, he wants to ride until he drops and fall into a sleep of bottomless fatigue and wake to ride again.

THEY ARE TWO days making the summit, two days making the descent. A westward-flowing creek takes them down through dense timber to the narrow valley of the San Lorenzo River, lined with more redwood groves and cottonwoods and sycamores and willow. They cross and recross the river, searching for any sign of an enemy encampment, until it passes at last between two promontories set a mile back from the sea.

Here two villages face each other across a marshy delta. On a bluff above the river, dissolving remnants of an adobe compound cluster around old Mission Santa Cruz, named for the Holy Cross. Its bell tower still lies toppled in a heap where it fell during an earthquake. To the east and up a gentler rise, they see the low tiled roofs of Branciforte, colonized by convicted criminals sent up from Mexico, says Valentine with his mocking smile, and named for a Spanish viceroy now long gone.

Adobes are scattered along a mile of dusty boulevard. The caravan parades its length, the throng of horses, the thirty armed riders with bridles clinking. Men stand by their porches waiting to learn who this motley band may be, what they'll ask for, relieved to learn that all they'll want today is information and something to drink and a couple of steers to barbecue. In the cantina an American rancher tells Valentine they've seen no ships or heard of any passing in the night, though marauding bands were sighted down the coast, or so they've heard. Whether these were rebellious Californians, or Mexicans on the march, or reckless Indians posturing in western garb, it's hard to know.

They move on, heading south around the bay's curve, across table-lands and down through dunes tufted with seagrass, onto a sandy beach where white surf spills over blue-green water. It's Jim's first look at the Pacific, such a spectacle that he is almost glad again for a moment, glad to have come this far. The tide is low. On packed sand the horses kick up flecks of foam and bits of kelp. If only his children could be riding with him on such a day to witness the swarm of seabirds rising off the beach ahead, sandpipers, pelicans, gray-white gulls, squawking and flapping in exuberant protest.

Another river delta turns the caballada inland, searching for the ford. Now Jim sees his family as if they have suddenly joined him here. He sees them as they looked in Illinois, but standing under pine boughs, Margaret, Virginia, Patty, James Junior, baby Tom. Around them a grove of pines makes a kind of barricade. Beyond the pines a bulge of granite, the mountain swelling up from Truckee Lake. Yes. That has to be the place he has looked for, as he has traveled and retraveled the long route in his mind, searching for a spot that can hold and protect them through the wintry weeks ahead. He needs to know that such a spot exists. Finally, like a vision, it has come to him.

He sees the grove, the pale circles of the stumps rimmed with saw-dust where trees were felled to make logs to build the cabins. Again he counts the cattle and the horses. Wagon by wagon, family by family they walk through his mind. One by one he counts them. The animals are alive. Then they have been slaughtered, cut up in a timely fashion, and jerked, and the meat will keep, thanks to the cold. And the cold can be fought off with fire. Limbs have been cut and stacked for kindling. Yes. This winter will be hard, but they won't freeze or starve before the snows recede enough for him to make it through. All the things he would have done have now been done by someone. Milt. Bill Eddy. Charlie Stanton . . .

The picture is so vivid, Jim himself could be standing in snow beside a cabin. He sees this scene, and holds to it like a drowning man who will grasp at anything that floats, as the Volunteers ford one river, then ford a wider river and swing back toward the curving shore, where a fishhook point makes a sheltered cove for the presidio and custom house at Monterey.

from *The Trail Notes of Patty Reed*

Santa Cruz, California

December 1920

The wilderness has a mysterious tongue
Which teaches awful doubt . . .

—Percy Shelley, "Mont Blanc"

PEOPLE *tend to think all the beaches on the Pacific Coast face west. Ours happens to face due south across the bay. This time of year the tide runs out so far, sometimes you can imagine you could walk on sand for twenty miles, clear across to the old presidio where Spanish cannons used to guard the Point of Pines. Young men go clamming on days like this. They gather up big, thick pismos by the gunnysack and don't even need a fork. The wet sand is flat and glistening, and the white shells stick out, sometimes clusters of shells. It's called a minus tide. The fuller the moon, the farther out the water goes. Sometimes the rising moon is huge in the east, just as the sun sets in the west, lighting the sky on fire, and the fire is reflected in the smooth mirror of a thousand acres of wet sand.*

It is glorious then to walk down toward the water's faraway, receding edge and think that where your head and shoulders are, fish were swimming not long ago, and sea otters and glossy seals out diving for their dinners. Where the water has been six feet deep and soon will be that deep again, you can walk along through air still somehow owned by the sea.

At one end of our beach, cliffs jut out. When so much water draws away from their rocky sides, a wonderland is revealed to you, whole colonies of long black mussels, tiny limpets and barnacles by the thou-

sands, and anemones that will suck the end of your baby finger, and here and there an abalone too. I have seen them a foot wide, curving, crusty saucers clinging to the rocks. These are the shells some people gather up for ashtrays and fireplace decorations and borders for their lawns. Here in the house there is a piece of abalone shell I have kept now for over seventy years, though when I first saw it I didn't know it was abalone. I did not yet know that word—which is an old Indian word the Spaniards first heard right around here somewhere, along the shores of this bay—nor had I ever seen anything that gleamed in its particular way, as if light from underneath or inside were shining through.

Home from the beach today I opened up my keepsake box and poked through the ancient souvenirs, my grandmother's pincushion, and a lock of her hair I kept after she was buried on the trail, and a miniature doll I'd carried with me all the way across, and this curved bit of abalone shell I hold here in my lap, about the size of an eyeglass, silver-pink. High in the Sierra Nevada Range, when I was eight, it held me mesmerized. It still does, and sends me back. It sends me thinking back. I move it this way and that, and the light moves around its pearly sur-face. Sometimes I see a river there. Sometimes I see a swarm of silver clouds . . .

AS MANY HAVE observed in the decades since that winter long ago, our party reached the summit trail twenty-four hours too late. Who can say which of our delays was the culprit? Who can say which of our numerous setbacks stole away the one last day that might have made the difference? Who could have known that the snow would come so much earlier than anyone expected?

On Captain Sutter's mule, Salvador and I had climbed halfway to the summit. When the mule gave out we tried to push ahead on foot. I tried to step where he stepped, but my legs were too short, so he lifted me up in his arms. I was carrying Cash, and Salvador was carrying both of us. His arms were strong, and he held me tight and close, but his chest was heaving. The climb right along there was so steep he couldn't make it and carry me and Cash too. All signs of the trail were gone. The summit was lost in gloomy overhang. Charlie Stanton still thought we could get across. He and Luis had been right behind us on the other mules. He told mama to stay put with us kids while he pushed on with the Indians.

After a while he came tumbling back down the slope yelling for everyone to get on their feet. If we kept climbing, he yelled, we could still make it before dark. A crowd of us had fallen down in the snow in a sprawl of bodies and bundles and baskets, exhausted from the altitude and the cold and what seemed like the longest day of the whole endless journey. Charlie ran around tugging and pulling at people, but no one had the will to move on.

Someone had set a pine tree on fire. A raggedy circle took shape around its crackling flame. Under another tree mama spread a blanket. The four of us children fell onto the blanket. She laid one on top of us and sat there hunched over, brushing back the flakes. She said, "Hush," and I dozed off.

It seemed like only a moment later something woke me, though several hours must have passed because the sky was light. From up the mountain I heard a distant howling that I thought at first was a wolf. I listened. It wasn't a wolf. It was too forlorn and human. Later on I would find out it was Salvador. His howling, groaning call became a chant, an incantation, the same lonesome words called out over and over again.

Mama's eyes were open too, and we looked at each other, listening to this long lament for what the night had given us. She had stayed awake brushing the flakes away, but she hadn't been able to hold back the snow. Her shoulders were white. All the blankets under all the trees were white. There was nothing to do but to retrace our steps back down to the shore of Truckee Lake, where we made camp as best we could.

In the years since then I have often thought about Charlie and Salvador and Luis standing at the summit on that stormy afternoon. They knew it was only twenty miles more to reach Bear Valley. If they'd kept going, the three of them could probably have made it through. They were all strong enough then. They knew the route. I still have to wonder what called them back to our bedraggled crowd of wanderers scattered across that slope like old limbs fallen from the juniper and sugar pine.

That lake—the one they renamed Donner—is about three miles long, set in a valley among the higher peaks. Toward the eastern end, in the trees, it was nice and level. The snow was sparse enough, men could get right to work putting up cabins. Charlie and the Indians and Milt Elliott worked on ours, felled the trees, fit the logs, laid limbs across the top and covered those with the hides of cattle people had already started to slaughter for meat. We had one half of a double cabin, with a wall between us and the other side, which was occupied by the Graves clan. It was a test, I have to say, being thrown in so close with people who'd been resenting us for so long. Mary Graves still mourned the loss of her beloved. Elizabeth, Uncle Billy's wife, behaved as if mama herself was the one who sent the snow that blocked our path to the summit.

The fastest way to get shelter up, of course, was to make one wall serve two cabins. You had to share it with somebody or another, though in all other ways people seemed reluctant to share much else. When I think back, if we'd wanted to make the best of a bad situation, we could have tried to make a kind of village there in the mountains, a little community. But at the time nobody wanted it that way—as if the various families were so fed up with one another and the fix we were in, they'd rather live in solitude, like hermits.

At the lake camp there were three cabins, set so far apart whole days could go by when you didn't see anyone but whoever lived right next to you. From our place to where the Breens and Kesebergs camped it was almost half a mile through the trees. It was another two hundred yards past the Breens' place to where the Eddys were and the widow Murphy and her clan.

If mama had had her secret wish we would have shared a cabin with one of the Donner families. But they had fallen so far behind, their camp was five miles back. The front axle had broken on George Donner's family wagon, which some folks saw as just one more sign of the curse that had fallen on our party. He and Jacob had to make a new one on the spot. They got out their tools and cut fresh timber and were shaping it to size, when George drove a chisel into his hand, tearing back a chunk of flesh. It shows you what a hurry they must have been in. Papa always said George was one of the handiest carpenters he'd ever known. It cost them another day, and there were no days to spare. When the next snow started, they set up some tents and lean-tos. And that was where they stayed, with their teamsters and some of the other single men, clear through to the end—a day's hike farther back, on the banks of another creek that fed into the Truckee River. They were mama's closest allies, the ones she and papa planned the trip with from the start, and we didn't see any of the Donners for another month at least.

The first concern, for all of us, was food. By that time our family was worse off than just about anyone else. Back in April we'd been the most prosperous-looking family on the western trail. Now we were down to nothing. The Graveses, right next door, they still had a wagon and a dozen cattle or more, raggedy and bewildered, but still a supply of food that could get them quite a ways. By November every one of our cattle had wandered out into the Salt Desert or been picked off by Paiutes or starved to death somewhere. We had our clothes and some bedding and the final hoarded scraps of the provisions mama and papa had hoped would last six months and had just about lasted seven.

On the morning after we moved into the cabin, mama and I were walking back from the creek when she ran into Elizabeth Graves, who had just come around from behind their ramshackle wagon with her one-year-old daughter on her hip. They hadn't said a word to each other in at least two weeks. Mama steeled herself and spoke first.

"Good day, Elizabeth."

She just nodded.

"Looks like we'll be neighbors for a while," mama said.

"Looks like it."

"We finally got ourselves moved in."

She nodded again and turned away.

Mama stepped around so she could see her face. "I'd be grateful if you would talk to me, Elizabeth."

Mrs. Graves looked right at her with that blaming look. I could tell it took all mama's will not to walk away.

"We don't have much left," mama said.

"Nobody does."

"I'd like to buy some beef."

"Not from us. There's none to sell."

"Our supplies are just about used up."

"Whose fault is that?" asked Mrs. Graves.

"Whose fault?"

"Some of us have took care of what we brought and some of us have not."

"My God, Elizabeth! I have four children here, four hungry children . . ."

"Mine are hungry too. And I've got twice as many mouths to feed. I got this baby here, helpless in the world without me to feed her . . ."

"What are we to do, then, if we run out?"

"Should have thought about that a whole lot sooner."

Mrs. Graves was a big woman, bigger than mama, and a good deal older, by fifteen or twenty years, almost old enough to be her mother. Her tight face had that kind of look, a mother scolding a daughter. Mama wasn't used to being talked at like that. Usually she was the one did the scolding. It took her by surprise. A frightened, girlish look crossed her face, and Mrs. Graves went after her.

"You should have thought about that when you were building a wagon so big it wore out all your oxen hauling it through the mountains! You could use them oxen right about now, couldn't you? If it wasn't for you people slowing down the whole party, by this time we'd all be in California! Johnny would still be alive, too! Now we're just plain stuck! Lord knows how long till we get outta here, and we can't be feeding anybody but our own!"

The skin around her eyes had turned pink. Her mouth was twitching. I knew mama wanted to shout back at her, but she held her tongue and took a deep breath.

"I'm sorry for what your family has been through, I truly am. Someday I hope we can make it up to you . . ."

"Can you bring a dead man back to life?"

This time mama couldn't hold it back. Her eyes started flashing. "You think James _meant_ to kill Johnny?"

The mouth of Mrs. Graves twitched into a crooked smile. "Didn't he pull a knife? It was him pulled the knife . . ."

"He loved John Snyder!" mama cried.

Her smile got bigger, a crazy and triumphant smile. "Why'd he stab him, then? If he loved Johnny so much, how could he stab him in the heart in cold blood and stand there and watch him die?"

"Don't you think he took his punishment for that? Don't you think we all have—with him gone off now . . . who knows where? You have any idea what that is like?"

Mama's voice broke. Mrs. Graves looked away, blinking, maybe blinking back tears of her own, though I couldn't quite tell, nor could I *tell if these blinks were for John Snyder or for her daughter Mary Ann or for herself and for mama and all the other wives and mothers marooned up there.*

When she spoke again her voice sounded different, gentler. "We ought not to be parting with any beef."

Mama closed her eyes and gathered herself together. "I'm not asking for your best animals. Whatever you can spare. One or two. Just to get us through."

Mrs. Graves looked out among the pines where the cattle stood, mournful and shivering, as if they had lost their way, with no idea where to turn or which way to move. Getting across the desert and up into these mountains had been harder on them than it had been on the human travelers. The pathetic creatures that had survived were all that stood between us and starvation. Mrs. Graves pointed toward the two worst-looking of the lot.

"We might could get along without them two."

Mama looked at the cattle.

"Back in Independence," said Mrs. Graves, "they'd draw twenty dollars each."

"My Lord, Elizabeth, they can hardly stand up."

"Beggars can't be choosers."

Mama pointed toward another clump of trees. "I'll tell you what. Give me those two over there, and when we get to California I'll pay you back with two fat healthy cattle, the best ones we can find."

Mrs. Graves stood with her hands on her hips. Whatever softness she might have been feeling had hardened again.

"Up here," she said, "the price is double."

"Double what?"

"Seeing as how we have to wait a while to get paid back, it'll be two cattle for each one of these."

Mama felt betrayed. I wanted to kill Mrs. Graves just then. I think mama did too and might have tried it if she'd had a club or an axe close at hand. But she stood her ground, knowing there'd have to be something to eat if we were going to get through the next few days and weeks. She held back her tears and kept her shoulders straight.

"Thank you, Elizabeth. We do appreciate your generosity."

Her voice was full of sarcasm and contempt, but Mrs. Graves didn't seem to hear it. She had that crazy grin again, lopsided and victorious, as if she believed she had not only avenged John Snyder's death but somehow righted all the wrongs of history. Then she went and got a little scrap of paper and called Mary and told her to write out a bill with a promise to pay back the Graves family four cattle for two.

At the time this seemed to be one more way to humiliate mama, as if her word wasn't good enough and only a signed receipt would do. And maybe that's what Mrs. Graves had in mind. But as I look back now, my heart fills, thinking how that little piece of paper was also an odd and twisted form of hope. All that winter, even through the darkest times, as those who had more kept trading and selling things to those who had less, they would write out receipts and IOUs, as if there were no doubt at all that on some future day beyond the snow, beyond the mountains, all such obligations would be settled and all accounts put right.

AROUND THIS SAME time William Eddy borrowed a rifle and started hunting. If there was anything out there, he would find it. He hated to come home with nothing. One day he brought back a coyote, another day an owl. Then we got word he had taken a grizzly bear. He had shot it twice and clubbed it to death. The men who went and helped him haul it out of the woods said it weighed eight hundred pounds or more. Eddy was a hero, and our hopes soared. A kill like this from time to time would solve half our problems! Part of the meat came to our family, thanks to him, and we lived off it for many days.

That's how it was for the first month at the lake camp. We were wilderness gypsies, making our way from week to week.

Charlie Stanton and the Indians stayed in our cabin then. Mama didn't have to feed them—they foraged on their own—but at night they were inside, along with Milt and our whole family, in a room no bigger than our woodshed back home. I'd never been that close to snoring men, nor had I known nights as dark as some of our nights there at the lake. We had no windows, just one low door, and a chimney to let the smoke out. At that altitude the stars are so bright and numerous they can make a silver blanket across the sky, but in our cabin you could never glimpse the stars. No moonlight leaked in. Sometimes the wind would come up strong and whistle through the cracks and chinks and blow out the coals, and then it was as dark as the whale's insides must have been for Jonah.

The days were somewhat nicer, at least in the early weeks, when most of the early snow had melted off the valley floor. The lake hadn't frozen over yet. When the sun came out, the sharp blue sky made the evergreens greener, and the blue lake bluer. Sometimes I would take Tommy on a long walk to the lake and make up stories about all the things we'd do when we got to California. I would describe the armies coming across the mountains to rescue us. When we got to the shoreline I would point to the pass and tell him that's where they would come from, hundreds of men with horses and bugles and wagons full of biscuits and buttermilk and johnnycake and cornmeal mush and fried bacon and apple pie. I would tell him we would see papa first. He would ride through the pass waving his hat, and his horse would rear back and kick its hooves high in the air.

By the time I finished such a story I would be hearing papa's voice. The first time I heard it, I thought he was already at the top of the summit, calling down to us. Later on I knew his voice was inside my head, and he was talking right to me from wherever he might be, and I would answer. I'd tell Tommy to wait by a big log. I'd walk down to the water's edge, and we'd have conversations.

"I didn't forget you, darlin'," he would say.

"I know it, papa. We didn't forget you, either."

"How do those boots feel now?" he would ask.

"Some folks have worn out their boots. But these are still snug."

"Well, you know I try to take care of my little girl."

"We miss you, papa. Will you get here pretty soon?"

"You just sit tight, darlin'. It won't be long."

"Don't give up, papa," I would say. "Don't you ever give up."

Sometimes I'd go walking by myself, just to talk to him. Late one afternoon I was standing like that when I heard rocks click behind me. I thought it was Tommy, or Virginia coming to call me back to the cabin. But it was Salvador, heading for the water with his fishing gig.

He looked down at me with an odd smile on his brown face, as if whatever I was doing he approved of—talking to the water, talking to the mountains, talking to papa. Maybe in his mind it was all the same thing.

He hunkered next to me and looked out across the lake, the way I was looking. It was getting cold, but I didn't care. I liked having Salvador next to me like that, with our frosty breath and the water lapping right in front of you.

After a while he said softly, "Pat-ti. Tu padre 'sta bien."

I was pretty sure this meant papa was all right, though the words themselves could have meant just about anything. The very sound of his voice was like a wave of comfort through the air. My chest was thick with gratitude. I threw my arms around his neck and nearly knocked him off balance.

With wide eyes he said, "Cuidado, señorita."

"Si, señor," said I, holding tight.

His free arm squeezed me, then he stood up and walked on along the lakeshore toward an outcropping of rocks where he could stand.

Salvador had tied some points of bone to the end of a pole. Late in the day, when the glare was off the water, he would try to spear some trout, though he never had much luck, since they seldom came in close enough. Some days he'd get one or two, which was more than the other men would get, who fished with hooks but had not fished for trout before. In the three weeks between when we got there and the lake froze, they never did seem to figure out the bait.

TWICE MORE THAT *first month Salvador and Luis and Charlie Stanton had started for the pass, leading small parties who hoped to get through and bring back some help. Both times the snowdrifts higher up had stopped them. They had hardly returned from the second attempt and begun to thaw out, when Bill Eddy called at each cabin, saying they had to give it one more try.*

"We can't wait around for somebody else to come and find us," I heard him say. "We'll just flat starve to death."

About the time a third bunch was ready to try the pass, a storm hit us, a big one. There was nothing much to do but burrow in and wait. For eight days it snowed without a break. Nobody at the lake camp, except for Uncle Billy Graves, had ever seen such snow or heard of it or imagined that something from the sky could simply bury you like that. Years later I would look through the guidebooks everyone had read before we started out. Not one of them says anything useful about snow of any kind, apart from advising you to leave Missouri soon enough not to get caught in it.

Our cabin was buried to the roofline. Milt Elliott had to climb out through the chimney to dig away snow so we could use the door. Elsewhere, the people with animals still alive had lost them all. They wandered off and fell over frozen and got covered where no one would find them for months. It was disastrous. With that kind of snow there'd be no more game. Bill Eddy had probably shot the last grizzly roaming around loose that winter. Rations had to be cut, and it started another round of blaming.

You can imagine the accusations, as families blamed one another, blaming whoever had been fool enough to let their cattle wander, blaming the storm, blaming Lansford Hastings again for leading us there, and some of them still blaming papa, though they also hoped some miracle would bring him and Bill McCutcheon through the snow with a rescue party. They couldn't make up their minds about papa. One day he was "the Villain." The next day he was "the Deliverer." I heard Bill Eddy say the Jim Reed he used to know would be doing all he could, but if it was <u>this</u> hard for a person to get out, wouldn't it be just as hard coming in from the other side?

For Eddy it was all the more reason to try the mountain one more time. Families had to cut through their differences, he said, and pool whatever supplies they had and plan one more expedition.

Some agreed. Some did not. Some were already too discouraged, running out of food, running out of energy, running out of will. Some just wouldn't budge. There was no leader anymore, no one in charge. George Donner was five miles back, at Alder Creek, and no one else had been elected captain. Patrick Breen had slaughtered most of his cattle early on and had enough frozen beef stored away, he figured his wife and seven kids would be better off sitting still. As for Lewis Keseberg, he couldn't travel more than twenty yards. The thorn in his foot had got so bad he seldom left his cabin. Maybe he was like Patrick, and figured he didn't need to—not yet. For all his failings, Lewis was well organized, a good planner, a good packer. He knew how to store things and maintain his equipment. Back in the desert, when everyone else was running low, he still had provisions stocked, flour and sugar and coffee and so forth. Some had made it clear to the lake camp. He and Patrick both figured they could last awhile, so they were going to stay put. But the Eddys, they were like us, living one meal at a time. In Bill's view the only chance to save his family was to make it across while he still had some muscle for the trip. I'll say this much for him: he was never one to give up without going to the limit.

And I'll say this for Uncle Billy Graves: he finally remembered something that would give these hikers a lot better chance. Using rawhide thongs and strips of hickory that came out of the oxbows, he had fashioned some snowshoes. Why he hadn't thought of it sooner is still a mystery to me. Maybe the big snow took him back to his early years, before he'd settled in Illinois, when he spent a few winters in Vermont.

There must have been sixty of us in those cabins near the lake. Fourteen decided to go, including Uncle Billy and his older son and his daughter Mary Ann, and Bill Eddy, and William Foster, and Charlie Stanton and the two Indians, who were leading again since those three had already traveled the whole route. I remember that Charlie's derby was gone. His beard had grown down to conceal his throat. He had scarves wrapped around his head and a floppy cap he'd made out of a scrap of tenting.

The day they left, the skies were clear, one of those dazzling times when you want to believe the world is a kind place after all. Nowadays you will see postcards of Donner Lake featuring just such a scene, with a caption across the bottom saying, "Sierra Winter Idyll." I know people who collect such cards. I can't look at them for long. They remind me of the day the Snowshoe Party said good-bye.

You don't set forth into that kind of country in December unless you have more to lose by staying than by going. We all knew they were risking their lives. At the same time, fourteen people leaving meant fourteen fewer mouths to feed. It's humbling to think back on how little food they took for the journey, one strip of jerky per person per day, each strip about twelve inches long. They had a six days' supply. That's how long Charlie imagined it would take to make Bear Valley.

To lighten the loads, they were taking only one rifle, and I remember that William Foster carried it. It seemed wrong that he would be the one, considering he had shot his brother-in-law in the back with that pepperbox pistol. But I guess it was his rifle. After that shooting, Foster's eyes always had a startled look that repelled me and intrigued me too. I never saw him blink. As his cheeks sunk in, from the short rations, his eyes seemed to grow. I would never go near him, but I remember watching him strap on the rifle, fascinated by his wide, staring eyes.

Foster was leaving a young wife behind and a four-year-old son. Uncle Billy, he was leaving six children behind. I remember him trying to say good-bye to his wife, how hard it was to speak. He was in his late fifties then. He looked twenty years older. The long privation had caught up with him. He was the oldest person at the lake camp, a kind of elder who might have taken charge, but he was not a man to take charge. This too showed in his haunted face. His eyes seemed to say that if he himself had been capable of more, things might have gone another way.

Maybe it was this very look that caused Mrs. Graves to turn and cry out and run back through the trees with arms flapping out from underneath her shawl. The night before, I'd heard them arguing, on the other side of the wall between our cabins, arguing about who was to leave and who was to stay. What was she supposed to do, she yelled, with her husband gone away, and taking her older son, and taking Mary Ann too, the only daughter she could count on?

I heard Uncle Billy's mournful voice. "It has got to be."

"We come all this way! We ought to all go together or stay put together!"

"Charlie says it'd be too hard on the young'uns. They're too frail now."

"Charlie? Charlie? What does Charlie know?"

"He's been up there."

"He don't have no young'uns!"

"Just hush up now."

"You can't run off and not come back! Jim Reed did that! You can't do that!"

"I said hush up. If I do wrong, God will punish me, not you."

"I ain't gonna hush up!"

"It has got to be . . ."

"WHAT HAS GOT TO BE?"

Years later I would understand what she went through that winter, what all the women went through, Mrs. Graves, and mama, and Peggy Breen and Keseberg's young wife, and Bill Eddy's wife. I had to grow up and get married and have a family of my own before I could begin to know the terror and the turmoil they had to live with and somehow hold inside, so they could just get one foot in front of the other, get from hour to hour and not be broken by the utter hopelessness that seemed to fill the valley, as their children shrank before their eyes, with snow covering the cabins now, and the cabins themselves nothing but half-trimmed logs thrown up so fast they hardly fit together.

Until that day I had seen Mrs. Graves as a witch sent to persecute mama. That morning I saw her as a wild snowbird flapping her wings, desperate to fly off through the trees.

As Uncle Billy watched her go, his face did not change. He watched her, then he took mama's hand in both of his and gazed at her. His voice was raspy and faraway.

"Good-bye, Margaret," he said at last. "May God forgive us all."

"God has," mama said. "And we will meet again in California."

His eyes held hers, as if drinking in something he saw there that he would see only once. For me, at age eight, it was too painful to watch. It filled me with fear.

I had to turn away—and there was Salvador with his snowshoes strapped on. He had shuffled over next to me. He squatted down, so skinny he did not look like the same man who'd come riding along the Truckee River in October. Yet his eyes glowed in the same way when he spoke our little ritual exchange.

With a thin, sad smile he said, "Cuidado, señorita."

"Si, señor," I said. "Y tu también."

He reached inside his coat and his shirt and pulled out a pendant that hung around his neck. He took off his hat, lifting the pendant over his long black hair, and handed it to me, a piece of shell on a fiber cord. I had seen seashells once or twice but never anything that could shimmer with its own inner light, pearly white and silver, with soft, rosy streaks that moved when the shell moved. Later on I would learn how people from his region had traded for centuries with the coastal tribes, skins and nuts for shells and salt. On that day I knew nothing about trading routes. I knew nothing about Indians. I knew nothing about the ocean or its creatures or where something this unique and beautiful might come from. I stared at the shell, then I turned to Salvador. He was look-ing at me the same way Uncle Billy had looked at mama.

"Vaya con Dios, señorita."

"Gracias, Salvador. Muchas gracias. Y vaya con Dios."

The others had shouldered their packs and bundles. He joined Luis and Charlie at the head of the line, and they started out, plodding through the pines. Those snowshoes were clumsy, homemade hoops, but they worked. Like the crisp blue sky overhead, it seemed to be a good omen, something we could hang new hopes on. This time the hikers would stay on top of the snow instead of sinking into drifts. I had no clear idea what awaited them up there. I imagined impossible peaks, and great mounds of snow, then somehow, beyond the pass, somewhere beyond all that, a wide sunny field spreading on forever.

We followed them as far as the iced-over lake, where we stood watching as they moved away along the shoreline, shuffling and plodding toward the white wall some of them had already climbed three times and would now have to climb again.

Somewhere in California

DECEMBER 1846

THE CABALLADA RODE on toward Monterey where U.S. Marines were bivouacked in the long adobe barracks called El Cuartel, restless young men from Salem and Providence and Allentown, eager for news. They welcomed the Volunteers. That night in the cantinas they all sang patriotic songs and lonesome marching songs—"Yankee Doodle," "The Girl I Left Behind Me"—and swapped stories, rumors, gossip, lore: The Mexican ships are close to Santa Barbara. . . . Eight or ten, they say, each with a hundred fighting men aboard. . . . They're going to land just south of here . . . or maybe north of here, at Santa Cruz, and march overland to Yerba Buena. . . . Who knows, they might sail clear into San Francisco Bay. . . . And the thieving Californians, they are forming up close by, you can count on it, to come at us from the flank . . . unless we stop them first . . . and by God, THEY WILL BE STOPPED!

> O, father and I went down to camp
> Along with Captain Good'n,
> And there we saw the men and boys
> As thick as hasty pudd'n.

> Yankee Doodle, keep it up,
> Yankee Doodle Dandy.
> Yankee Doodle, keep it up,
> And let the boys be handeeeeeeee!

It was a night of drink and wild vows and toasts to each of the twenty-eight states, while weapons were fired into the fog that had descended upon the cannons and the cypress trees and the white-washed customhouse. The Volunteers fell asleep and woke in foggy dampness.

Now they ride groaning out of town, hunched over their pommels, to loop inland again, heading north. Bloodshot eyes scan the hills, the arroyos, the borders of the road, for a sign or signal that hostile troops have passed this way.

Though Valentine did no drinking, he is in a darker mood than any of his men. Having come so far and seen nothing, he is despondent. He needs something to show for these long days of riding. In a foul humor, he spews out orders the men only half respond to, since it's clear to all but Valentine, and perhaps to him, that there is no campaign to wage in this unthreatening terrain. Though they wouldn't mind a skirmish, no one believes an enemy lurks anywhere within striking distance. Something has changed. They all feel it, though none will voice it.

They let him shout his vain commands, as if these tirades will call forth the enemy he needs. And finally it seems to work. The next morning, an hour before noon, a patrol comes loping back from a wooded notch between two folds of the Coastal Range. They escort three mounted Californians and a small herd of horses.

Valentine regards the three with disdain. They wear high-crown hats and leather chaps. They are not soldiers. They are vaqueros, a rancher and two sons of perhaps twelve and fifteen years, hoping they would go unnoticed in a grove back there until the Volunteers had passed.

In Spanish Valentine demands to know why the father carries a pistol.

The man shrugs. With a careful smile and a glance at the crowd surrounding him, he says these are dangerous times.

Does he know it is against the law for all but United States forces to carry firearms?

Yes, he says, surrendering the pistol, he knows that.

Valentine the interrogator wants to know what he is doing with so many horses?

Moving them to higher ground, the father says, in case of flooding along the river.

Nonsense. You are taking them to the soldiers.

There are no soldiers.

What do you mean?

They have gone.

You are lying.

They have fled to the south.

Some have fled. Some are coming back. This we know.

The father shakes his head.

You lie! cries Valentine. Tell us where you take these horses, or you will all be killed. We will hang you from that oak!

Hang us, then, the father says, sitting taller in his saddle. We were moving them to higher ground. There are no soldiers now. We have been abandoned. They are cowards. They have fled to the south, the officers, all of them. They will not be coming back.

This man too is despondent. He speaks with a cynicism that Valentine recognizes and begrudgingly trusts. On this expedition there will be no glory. Once again he will have to settle for plunder. He looks over the herd, all sleek and healthy, in better shape than the animals his men ride now. He orders the Californians to dismount.

Desperation shows in the dark eyes of the father. We need our horses, he says. Without them how can we work the ranch?

We too need them, Valentine says, for protecting the pueblo.

He cocks his rifle. Other Volunteers follow suit, pushing in closer to the three surrounded men. It is three against thirty.

Jim speaks up, Jim the lieutenant. "Should we give them a receipt?"

Valentine jerks toward him as if a weapon has been fired.

"A receipt for what?"

"So he knows he gets his horses back when it's over."

"I'll decide that!"

"Otherwise, how does anybody know where they went?"

Valentine's eyes burn with anger and alarm. "Whose side are you on, Mr. Reed?"

Jim eyes burn too. "You know whose side I'm on!"

"You soft on greasers?"

"We just can't be stealing horses!"

"You feeling sorry for these boys?"

"Goddam it, Valentine! Don't you shout at me!"

"This is wartime! You forget about that?"

"Even Fremont gives receipts. He gave a bunch to Captain Sutter . . ."

Valentine's laugh is forced and empty, ringing across the glade.

"Sutter says anytime you conscript animals . . ."

"Captain Sutter is also under house arrest, Mr. Reed! So what difference does it make?"

With an accusing eye he watches Jim, who stares back in consternation, but says nothing more. As if the skirmish they've all been hoping for has at last been waged and won, Valentine calls to the others, "Round 'em up!"

Fifteen horses are added to the caballada, leaving the Californians without a weapon or a lariat or a saddle or an animal to strap a saddle to. Valentine knows this is an insult perhaps worse than hanging.

The father's lean, weathered face strains against his anger. Do you expect us to walk? he says. Our corrals are half a day from here.

Don't complain, says Valentine with a satisfied grin, or we will also ask for your boots and your sombreros.

The father and his sons stand in the grass, furious, humiliated. The sight titillates several Volunteers, who take sweet and secret pleasure in having someone at their mercy. As the caballada moves north again, the yearning to pillage sends five men riding off to visit a nearby rancho. Sometime later they return with cocky grins and six more horses. They brag of this adventure and laugh at the helplessness of a Californio woman and gray-bearded grandfather who tried to block their entrance to the house and barns, where bridles and saddles had been hidden away, and inside some saddlebags a pair of handsome pistols.

Jim listens to their tale of conquest, still thinking about Valentine's outburst. He has not let the matter go. What right has Valentine to challenge his loyalty? Or was that a challenge at all? Maybe it was another scene, performed at Jim's expense. He grows weary of the posturing. He grows weary of this vain man who lets bullying run unchecked and always seems to be onstage, prancing along now like a military hero homeward bound.

Jim is remembering Lewis Keseberg's saddle style, prancing and disdainful, on that evening so long ago when they met beside the Platte. He was right to part ways with Keseberg in the middle of Nebraska, and he should never have let him rejoin the party. Think how differently things might have gone. Maybe the time has come to put some space between himself and Valentine. How has he ended up in this cavalcade of strangers, in hot pursuit of an enemy none of them has seen? He should be riding out of here. He should leave today. Yes, he should. But then what? Where else is there to ride to? Where else to go if Yerba Buena itself may soon be under siege? Jim has seen what lies this side of the Sierras—Johnson's Ranch, Sutter's Fort, abandoned missions, adobe villages, endless miles of open land, all of it wet, with winter coming on, and getting wetter, a pueblo, a presidio with cannon barrels rusted shut . . .

Valentine interrupts his silent debate.

"I know you'd rather be somewhere else, Mr. Reed. But don't give up on me just yet."

It is the mellow voice of the intimate companion, the confidant who seems once again to be reading his mind. Valentine rides next to him. Their knees almost touch. He inclines his head, speaking so softly Jim can barely hear the words.

"You are right, of course. About the receipts. In this interim time of martial law, it is the policy of the Northern Department. But it only applies to Americans and other foreigners whose possessions must be put to military use, wouldn't you say? Among these Californians, a receipt for livestock would be meaningless, since none of them can read. They don't deserve receipts. Their ignorance is appalling. Matched only by the vastness of their lands. They have no clear knowledge of what they own, or where it may begin or end. I imagine that fellow back there has more horses than he can count. And most are running loose. These ranches, you know, they have no boundaries. In the great valley to the east, there are horses beyond number, horses that belong to no one. They run wild by the thousands. Plucking one of these horses is like plucking a blade of grass from the floor of the valley. You and I should not be disagreeing about such trivial details."

A slanting hat brim covers his brow. The eyelids droop with conspiracy and comradeship. Jim knows he is right about the wild horses. For the rest of it, he tells himself he's too new in this country. In such times it's better to be safe than sorry, and so he rides a while longer with Valentine, who led him to the orchards and now leads him back toward San Jose de Guadalupe.

By late afternoon they are heading for the courthouse moat. The

Volunteers are boisterous with shouts and rearing horses. Townspeople appear cautiously, one by one, to see the source of such commotion. Women leave their cooking fires. Men step out of the cantinas. A priest stands in the door of the church, and children gaze at the ragtag band of mounted men led by Valentine, with Carlos at his side in flat-top bill cap and leather jacket, while behind them and around them men wear greatcoats, carry powder horns and Bowie knives, their trousers made of buckskin or homespun or military wool, some with hats, some long-haired and hatless, wearing rolled bandannas, Apache-style. As if they might be in the mood to attack this island stronghold, the dusty, bearded riders and their frothing herd make a full turn around the courthouse and its bemused guard of curious marines.

Ahead of them, on the far side of the plaza, a gang of young men on horseback seem to take no interest in this display. Their eyes follow one of their own number, who comes galloping out of an alleyway at full speed, as if in a race, though he is alone. He swings his body down until his hand nearly touches the earth. A live rooster has been buried to its neck in the spongy dirt. Without slowing, he grabs the rooster's head. As the body pops free, the liberated wings flap frantically. The lad's excited yank has nearly torn the head loose, but tendons still connect it. He swings the bird like a lariat, as he hurtles toward the Volunteers.

Shouting "Bienvenidos, mi capitano!" he snaps his wrist, so that the body flies free over ducking heads. A few coats and shirts are spattered red before the bloody carcass meets the upthrust hand of Carlos, who rises in his saddle to make an astonishing midair catch.

The young rider has crossed the plaza, picking up speed as he sprints along the King's Highway. His laughing allies scatter, disappearing among the sheds and heaps of cattle bones. With a battle cry, Carlos whirls in galloping pursuit, hunched over the mane, until he is close enough to hurl the rooster. It strikes the young vaquero squarely between the shoulders, a perfect shot that propels him toward the edge of town. The Volunteers are cheering, all but Valentine, who brushes at his hat and spotted waistcoat.

"Sonofabitch will pay for that," he mutters. "They will all pay dearly."

In a corner of the plaza the rooster flops and squirms, then lies still.

Townspeople drift away, and the scouting party drifts toward the cantina. Having seen nothing, they nonetheless have much to report, already telling one another stories that will swell into the saga of their fruitless expedition.

"Ol' Valentine, he cracks the whip. He worked us day and night. But by God we stayed the course . . ."

"Never seen fog so thick as what rolled in at Monterey. Might as well had your head inside a gunnysack. For all we know, them Mexican ships snuck right by us in the night . . ."

"I know they're out there. We flushed up a gang of greasers runnin' horses for the army. You think they wasn't scared? I had me a bead on one of 'em. If he'd a moved a muscle . . . *ka-pow!*"

A Call to Arms

LATE DECEMBER NOW in Santa Clara Valley, getting close to Christmas, when dark falls early and the evening air is cold, drawing forth a steamy ground fog from flat pasturelands where the longhorns have grazed all autumn. Low ranges east and west are black lines against a blue-black sky, while to the north a faint light, the memory of afterglow, still hangs above the vast waters of the bay.

Smooth, unruffled water stretches past the long peninsula, where deer will gather at the shoreline to lick at patches of salty residue. The water stretches north to Yerba Buena, where the U.S. fleet waits just inside the channel John Fremont named "the Golden Gate," and stretches farther north, past seal pods fishing for dinner off Alcatraz and Angel Island, to the village of Sonoma, beyond the water's northern edge, where thirty men overran the garrison last June, raised the image of a grizzly bear above the plaza and launched the season of turmoil that now is nearly done.

In Sonoma Bill McCutcheon, still sweating in the night, waits for some word, any word, having found two men who might—just might, if the price is right—ride with them back into the mountains to help bring out their wives and children . . . Mac at one end of the bay, Jim at the other, and they'll both have to wait a while longer, since the returning Volunteers have been greeted with a fresh report, delivered today by yet another launch sailing up the river that winds inland from the bay.

While the Volunteers were on patrol, hostile forces captured six sailors from the U.S.S. *Portsmouth* and the acting mayor of Yerba Buena, a ship's officer named Bartlett, only recently appointed to the post. Though they were armed, and though they may have been scouting out some territory as they went, they weren't looking for trouble. They'd set forth in search of beef cattle to feed the town and feed the personnel aboard the ships—only to be surrounded, deprived of their weapons, and abducted. A marauding band has twice been sighted in the coastal hills, a hundred riders at the least, some say two hundred, maybe more, traveling with these hostages in tow.

Tonight, at the end of a wagon road lined with oak, a meeting has been called in the home of the Alcalde, the first official of the pueblo. He comes from Massachusetts, has the beefy looks of an English country squire but the outfit of a California ranchero. He wears snug buckskin leggings with stitched edges, split almost to the knee so the white underleggings show. His ruffled shirt is so white it almost shines. Jim has not seen a shirt this white in months, the cloth pulled smooth across an ample belly, underneath a jacket a size too small, a jacket made of maroon velvet, with twin rows of silver buttons down the front and buttons along each tight-fitting sleeve.

His wife is also here, a California woman, gracious, cultivated, younger than the Alcalde. She speaks no English, or perhaps chooses not to. Though she stands apart, she presides over the arrivings, the removing of heavy coats and weathered hats. Her erect and elegant posture says, "This is my home and you are welcome."

On her adobe walls, framed mirrors catch the light. There is an oak sideboard, highly polished, a mantelpiece above the fire, with bric-a-brac and silver candelabra, and several chairs, some with upholstered seats, some with seats of woven straw.

Jim savors what he sees. He covets it, the first true home he's set foot in since leaving Illinois. The woman's touch awakens old domestic hungers. He cannot keep his eyes off the Alcalde's wife, who wears a low-cut red dress, her broad shoulders covered with a shawl, her skin deliciously smooth and white. Dark silky hair hangs in a thick braid.

She says, "Bienvenidos, Señor Reed."

"Tengo mucho gusto, señora," says Jim, trying out a phrase he has heard some others use. I'm pleased to meet you.

"Nuestra casa es su casa."

Her smile is polite, yet expansive, showing healthy white teeth. He gropes for more words, hoping to keep it alive, the most generous smile he's ever seen. Alas, it comes and goes too quickly. She steps away to welcome someone else, then she's gone, as if called to an emergency in some other part of the house, and the Alcalde is refilling Jim's glass, his florid brow creased and burdened.

The Alcalde is hospitable yet agitated tonight, pouring wine and liquors from his various decanters into goblets of cut glass for Jim and Valentine and three other Volunteers, for the red-bearded captain who commands the marine detachment, and for the young naval officer in charge of the launch. Like a host at a banquet, he has moved from guest to guest, pouring, nodding, sharing each man's version of concern or alarm or outrage.

He says, "Heady times, Mr. Reed."

"Indeed."

"The pueblo is grateful for your help."

"I believe in people sticking together," Jim says, with a self-deprecating nod.

The Alcalde likes this. "I wish more of our compatriots felt that way."

"Taking care of any town can keep you busy."

"Do you mind if I ask where you're staying?"

"A bunch of us bunk next to Valentine's mill."

"You're welcome here, you know. It's not lavish, but it might beat that shed."

"Why, thank you, sir."

"I'm sure you know we've heard about your people stranded in the mountains. We're very sorry, too."

"That's much appreciated."

"A terrible thing."

"Others have made it through a winter there. Our people will make it."

"Even so, our prayers are with you."

The Alcalde is a softhearted man. This story, what he's heard, as it has trickled toward him from Johnson's and from Sutter's Fort, has softened his heart a bit more. He wants Jim to know there will be a place for the Reeds in Santa Clara Valley.

"I may take you up on that," Jim says. "I like it here. I like the look of things."

"I hope you mean that." The Alcalde's eyes glisten with pride and fellowship. "I hope you'll bring your family and settle down among us. You have already performed a service above and beyond the call of duty. This will not be forgotten."

"It's been mostly sitting in the saddle, sir, riding along from one day to the next."

"We're grateful to have a man of your substance in our midst. So many loose ones around now, you know. Here today, gone tomorrow."

The Alcalde reminds him of George Donner, a fatherly man who will keep certain confidences. Jim is moved to talk with him in a way he cannot talk with Valentine, who is like a boy, like a wayward and impetuous son.

The fleshy face is open, congenial now. Jim wants to tell him what he saw in the orchards of the Mission of St. Joseph, when leaves and limbs sent back suffused light off the waters of the bay. In memory these acres glow, the rows of limbs, where new shoots wait under crusty bark, where layers of damp mulch carpet the earth.

"We slept there. And very early I awoke and walked out among the trees. I imagined that once my family was safely across I would bring them there to camp beneath the boughs while the crop is being harvested. Someone should gather all that fruit, you know, perhaps to dry, perhaps to ship . . ."

The Alcalde is blinking. If he were a younger man, he says with misty eyes, he would join such a venture. This is the kind of spirit the community needs and the valley needs.

"And yet I've heard that no one owns the orchard now," Jim says. "Has it truly been abandoned?"

The Alcalde shrugs. "Some say it still belongs to the Church. Some say to Mexico. Some say to the brother of the gobernador, who may have bought the land a year or so ago."

"From whom?"

"Why, from the gobernador, of course—though both of them have now fled for Mexico City, or so I've heard. How strong is your interest, Mr. Reed?"

"Very strong."

"Some say the pueblo will soon have jurisdiction over all such lands. I suspect a petition addressed to the Alcalde would get some serious consideration."

He winks, touches Jim's arm. "We'll talk again, just the two of us, when we have more time. Right now . . ." He nods toward the men who fill his parlor.

The Alcalde moves toward his fireplace, clinking an upraised glass. In candlelight his head of abundant white hair has a glow. His voice is large and captivating, a politician's voice.

"Gentlemen. Gentlemen. Once again, welcome. As you all know, the good captain has called us together tonight. Though we meet in secret, there is no secret about why we are here."

He looks down at the commander of the marine detachment, who leans from his chair and scans the room with unblinking eyes. The Captain has been drinking since midafternoon. His eyes are as red as his beard. His thinning hair looks wet. The aguardiente gives his voice a ragged and persuasive edge. Everyone knows the story he's about to tell, but something ceremonial is required here, and the red-bearded captain has a ceremonial style.

As he describes again how seven men set out in search of food to feed their comrades, an indignant murmur crosses the room. His cheeks turn a deeper red, new moisture rises to his ruby eyes. Three months ago in Los Angeles, he says, a rebellious spirit broke the truce, and now it has reached the northern towns—seven of our finest men held captive, taken unawares, without warning, in an unprovoked attack.

"Murderous bastards," someone mutters.

"They'll regret this day."

"We heard they was comin'," says a Volunteer, "everywhere we went we heard it. They must've landed farther north and come up from the beach."

"We don't know for sure yet who we're dealing with," the Captain says, "or how many there may be. But this is not just another phantom report. These riders have been sighted. They are roaming the peninsula between the pueblo and the port, and the time has come to take action before more damage is done!"

He stands up, his voice raw, compelling. We were sent here, he says, to defend the town. But we can't do it alone. This will take all the troops in San Jose and Yerba Buena together, regulars and volunteers. Tomorrow a courier will ride to the port, instructing those units to head south at top speed. The San Jose units will move north, leaving the enemy nowhere to turn. Long before they reach this pueblo they will be forced out into the open.

He frames a bracket with his hands, reminding them that the peninsula is bounded on one side by San Francisco Bay, on the other by cliffs and narrow beaches facing the Pacific.

"We will flush them out, you see! Like a fox on the run!"

He turns to Valentine. "Can we count on your militia?"

The Captain's fervor has lifted Valentine from his seat. "By God, you can, sir! Isn't this the day we've waited for?"

Another murmur, a swell of agreement, from all but the Alcalde, who seems to tolerate Valentine the way you tolerate an unruly relative. He has listened with a mounting agitation, as if he did not expect this scenario. He lifts his thick and meaty hands, his face more burdened now, his wiry brows bent.

"We are given to understand, Captain, that the men who did the kidnapping were not soldiers or Mexican regulars. They were ranchers from up that way."

"It happened on a ranch, that's true. As to who all were involved . . ."

"If they have taken hostages, my guess is they want something. They want to negotiate."

Valentine interrupts. "It's too late to bargain!"

The Alcalde ignores him. "Before we rush into battle, the prudent move would be to make contact with their leaders, find out what they want. I'd do that first."

The Captain's face is fixed in a drinker's smile of elaborate courtesy. "Perhaps you can tell us, sir, what it is they want."

Unsure of his ground, the Alcalde hesitates, intimidated by the ruddy marine. "Ranchers around here . . . have all lost stock. Fremont's men took everything that walked. I myself gave up dozens of horses, though not as many as some."

"There were orders for that," says Valentine with loud impatience, "directly from the Northern Department."

"Who had orders to strip the ranches?"

Valentine sighs, as if they've already gone through this too many times. "There was authorization from the Commandant himself."

"Yes," the Alcalde says. "And that gentleman has now sailed away. Am I correct?"

"Many have sailed for the fighting farther south."

The Alcalde's voice is trembling with anger, his frail composure broken. "How long must we endure this? These officers arrive, drop anchor and sign edicts that shape our fate, then sail again before the costs are known! Families come to me, law-abiding families who have been treated like animals!"

"Some will whimper," Valentine says, "but troops need horses."

The Alcalde glares at him, shakes his head. "With all due respect for the good captain, the threat of Mexican regulars landing this far north is just another fantasy. You navy men don't know our region. You don't know these people. Nor do you speak the language they speak . . ."

The Captain has unrolled a long page of heavy paper and rattles it dramatically.

"According to our intelligence the enemy was two days ago assembled in force at Point San Pedro, a dozen miles below the entrance to the bay. I repeat *in force*, sir! Does that sound like disgruntled ranchers? We may well be facing a full-scale invasion!"

The Alcalde looks trapped. His eyes search the room. The Captain seizes his advantage.

"They've taken the mayor of Yerba Buena. Who do you think will be next? Every official in this region is now at risk."

The older man's uncertain silence seems to be a form of surrender.

Valentine chimes in, grinning with confidence. "We'll set out in the morning." He stands beside the Captain as if together they have hatched this campaign. "A scouting party will ride ahead, a dozen men, to find out where they are, which way they move. Then we mobilize. We strike. We bring them to their knees!"

A Volunteer speaks up, an Indiana man who recently settled in the pueblo. "Some of us got families and need a day or two to take care of things. We been riding for more'n a week. Some are about give out, you want to know the truth, and might not ride at all if we got to start again first thing . . ."

Valentine looks offended. "You think the greasers are going to rest up? We don't have time to wait, wouldn't you agree, Captain?"

"Not when American lives are in grave jeopardy."

Alarmed, overwhelmed, the Alcalde says, "Hold on! Hold on! You cannot simply sally forth and leave this pueblo undefended. That is your solemn duty, Valentine. Why else were you appointed to the post? For weeks on end we do not see you . . ."

"I defer to the Captain, sir, a man of wide experience in the art of war. Oftentimes the best defense is to go on the offensive. We can sit here and wait to be attacked, or we can move with speed and gain the upper hand."

"We have an agreement," the Alcalde urges them, "to treat all citizens with respect."

Valentine has been flexing his fingers as if preparing for a fistfight. Compulsively he grabs one wrist, pressing, massaging. "Respect, you say! Perhaps you can teach that lesson to the California horse gangs who strip their own ranchos when it suits them. What difference does it make who gets there first?"

Again the Alcalde tries to speak, one arm raised, like a preacher in a pulpit with a warning for his congregation. But Valentine has ignited the room. Now all talk at once, on their feet, pouring their own drinks, animated, planning and protesting, agreeing and lecturing one another. Glasses are raised again, and Jim's is among them, his voice as loud as anyone's, though he has his doubts. For all the stories he has heard, for all his riding up and down the trails of Alta California, he has yet to see with his own eyes one Mexican ship or the uniform of any nation but the United States.

He watches the Captain tilt his head and empty a tumbler of brandy in a single gulp. He watches Valentine do the same, a man who claims never to drink but is much taken with the Captain and his naval tunic, as if they are veterans posing side by side. Jim knows he is the veteran of something. He has heard that Valentine once was kidnapped by a band of Californians and so foully treated he bears a grudge against them all, soldiers, ranchers, elders, priests. Who knows? Perhaps he feels some special bond with the seven captives.

Jim watches the Alcalde, wondering if he could be right. He's a wiser man than Valentine. Jim wants him to be right, now that he has offered the mission orchards, or seemed to, almost as an enticement. Jim wants the smoke to clear so he can sit down with this fellow. And maybe that's what the Alcalde was driving at—help us get this smoke cleared, wherever it comes from, then we'll talk. Jim isn't sure. The Alcalde is another man pulled two ways, like Captain Sutter, out here long enough to be divided within himself, half American, half Californian. He can see it in the Alcalde's eyes. In times like these, with our boys taken hostage and a pueblo threatened, you cannot be of two minds. With a war on, you have to be of one mind, like the Captain, a fellow who sailed around Cape Horn with the Pacific Fleet and up the long coast of South America and on past the ports of Acapulco, San Diego, Santa Barbara, Monterey. He told Jim he was sent here with fifty men to defend the town and not to stray beyond its edges. After a month of waiting he is sick of rutted alleyways and windowless adobe cubicles and interminable nights in the dim cantina playing cards with women who can't pronounce his name. He is fed up with his superiors in Yerba Buena who will not make decisions. "A maddening situation there," he said to Jim. "Two men of equal rank cannot agree on who's in charge, so one contradicts the orders of the other, and here we sit." The Captain is itching for something to happen. He doesn't much care what it is. That's about how Jim feels too, impatient, unable to sit still now, though his eyes burn with fatigue.

As he thinks of setting out again tomorrow, his shoulders feel weighted with sandbags. Yet moving seems better than not moving. A foe of any kind is better than the void of not knowing where to turn. He can't turn back, that much he knows. He can't stay put. And peace, he tells himself, peace must be restored at any cost. If families are going to settle here and thrive, isn't peace the first step?

Strangers

LATE INTO THE night they talk and scheme. The next morning Jim wakes to the ranch bell. The Alcalde is up ahead of him, riding out to check his herds and confer with his foreman. Indian servants lay out a hearty breakfast, coffee, tortillas, eggs with chorizo sausage, the finest breakfast he's had in a month. He could get used to this ranchero's way of life. He feels born again, his head abuzz, as he steps into the crisp morning air.

He is halfway to the barn when he comes upon the Alcalde's wife. She stands between the barn and a smaller shed, with a rebozo pulled tight, covering her head against the chill. In the yard she looks smaller, more vulnerable. She is listening to a vaquero whose face, at first, is turned away. Jim's sudden appearance catches her off guard. She offers a careful smile.

"Señor Reed, buenos dias."

"Buenos dias, señora."

She glances at the vaquero, then at Jim. With a hand held outward she says, "Mi primo," and adds haltingly, "my cuz-zin."

He turns, a lean man wearing leather trousers and a close-fitting jacket of dark suede. Jim has seen him before. But where?

On the plaza?

In the cantina?

With the bartender there?

No.

No, this is the fellow they stopped south of the pueblo, the fellow with the two sons and the fifteen horses.

As they regard each other, the man's black eyes go wide with recognition. His swarthy features do not move, but the eyes look Jim up and down. His back seems to stiffen. Finally he forces a thin smile, a curt nod.

"Buenos dias, señor."

"Buenos dias," says Jim.

To the Alcalde's wife he says, "My apologies. I didn't mean to interrupt. Again I am most grateful for the hospitality here. I have slept well and eaten well. Moochas grassias. Moochas grassias," nodding as he moves toward the barn to saddle up.

When he leaves the ranch, heading for the plaza, they are still talking. Cousins, Jim thinks. Did Valentine know this when he commandeered the horses? Perhaps such things cannot be avoided. He has heard that sooner or later they are all cousins, these Californians. It is strange to observe the two of them. It makes him feel strange. For just a moment Jim feels foreign, a man who has peeked into the window of a stranger's house and seen something he did not expect to see.

Consuela

In the morning chill she stands alone, thinking she will go to the church and light a candle and pray. Yes, in spite of his warning she will go to the plaza and enter the church and light a candle. But what will she pray for?

First, for guidance. She will ask the Virgin to guide her through the confusion of these times.

Then she will pray for Antonio, the son of her mother's closest sister. He is like a brother. They grew up together. He is the brother she never had. She watches him ride off across open pasture, heading north. She knows where he is going, and she knows he is filled with bitterness, the kind of bitterness that can only bring harm. She knows he cannot forgive the Americans. She will pray that he can somehow look into his own heart and find patience before he gets himself killed.

He cannot win. These insurgents with their hostages, they do not have a chance. The Americans will not be stopped. In the harbor at Monterey she has seen their ships of war. Until today she believed there was no reason to try and stop them. She has believed that in the hands of the United States, California would be a better place than it has been in the hands of Mexico. Her husband has told her of his homeland and still promises to take her there one day. He has told her of the many houses made of wood. Every town has a school, he says, and a mill, and many kinds of shops. She has been to Mexico City, where her great-uncle Rosario lives. She has seen how they look down upon those from Alta California. Even the nuns in the convent school took pity on her for having to return to such a far-off and barbaric place. The Mexicans have never cared for us, her father used to say, so we must care for ourselves. They do not know this land as we know it, he would say, How can they know our hearts? Her father thought California should be a separate country. Antonio still thinks so.

She remembers the day her husband appeared in the plaza. It seemed incredible to her that this handsome foreigner should be suddenly in their midst, as if he had dropped from the sky. So many years ago now. The first American she had seen. He rode a fine palomino, and his hair was still blond. Everyone talked about him. He spoke Spanish, and he went to Mass. Women schemed to meet him. Today Americans occupy half the houses in the pueblo, while more come every week. They park their wagons under the trees, or her husband invites them to spend the night.

Her husband likes this fellow Reed. Antonio does not. Before he rode away, Antonio told her Reed and Valentine led the band that stole his horses. They had a disagreement he could not understand. But in his view they are the same. Consuela isn't sure. Reed has a feverish and driven look, but he is not a vicious man. He speaks with courtesy. Her husband tells her he has a wife and four children. Antonio tells her not to be fooled. The Americans arriving now, he says, are not like the Alcalde. They are worse than the Mexicans, he says, and Valentine is the worst of all, a thief with no mercy.

It is the third time Antonio's ranch has been raided by foreign soldiers, or by men who claim to be soldiers. They say they need horses for the war and cattle for their food. But where does the war come from, Antonio says. The Americans bring the war. Then they use it as an excuse to take whatever they want. All the ranches are suffering, he says. Ships have come to Monterey to trade for hides, and men have missed the shipment for lack of horses and saddles to round up their stock. One by one they join the forces gathering south of Yerba Buena. Who knows where their desperation will lead them or where they will strike first? If San Jose is attacked, says Antonio—and this is what he came to tell her—she will not be harmed, nor will the Alcalde be harmed, as long as they both stay close to the rancho and do not venture toward the plaza where the marines are stationed.

You are the one who will be in danger, she told him, not I. You cannot win against the Americans. Do you have ships? Do you have cannon?

Try to understand me, Antonio said. We cannot let these foreigners simply walk across our borders and treat us like slaves in our own land. Isn't our honor worth more than certain victory?

She can still see him, far across the field, the cousin who could be her brother, who loves this land as she has loved it. And if you die, Consuela thinks, what then is all your honor worth?

After he disappears among the distant oaks, she is gazing at the land itself, broad pasturage where her father once presided, until he passed this piece of his holdings on to her and to her husband. Consuela was born one mile from where she stands. The long valley of Santa Clara, with its rim of mountains east and west, is the world of her childhood, the world of her marriage and her married years. She shivers with cold and with a rush of sentiment for the spectacle before her. This hard, crisp chill is the bite of winter coming on, the Christmas bite, she calls it, as familiar as the hills of summer when dried grasses give the rising contours a tawny lion's skin.

By late December the hills are green, the mornings blue, and the town prepares for a pageant at the church. Yet now Antonio comes to warn her to avoid the plaza where American marines have built a fortress around the *juzgado*, the old adobe courthouse. Why are they here? And who could have imagined the plaza could become such a dangerous place? Her husband says they came to protect the pueblo. Yet they only bring more danger. In her heart she knew this from the day they arrived, though she has tried not to know it. Today, with Antonio's warning, she feels it all around her, like a dark mist rising from the valley grass.

A Common Enemy

THREE DAYS PASS, three days of rain, windless days with water
spilling down upon them. The Volunteers can't remember when it
began. This is the eternal rain, with no beginning, no end. For the
scouting party the trails are troughs of goopy muck. Riders follow the
margins of the trails where hooves churn up the grass. Water leaks
inside their slickers and into their saddlebags.

Enemy troops are out here too, somewhere, hunkered down perhaps, or on the move, using weather as a screen. The scouts bring back
reports of a large campsite among redwoods in the mountains to the
west. Fire pits were seen, cattle bones charred and scattered. In this
rain it's hard to say how recently men camped there, or how many. But
there is evidence enough for Valentine and for the Captain, who sends
half his men to plod along behind the mounted Volunteers, two dozen
drenched marines in mud-thick boots.

On the fourth day a new report tells them what they do not want
to hear. The unseen foe has looped behind them, passing in the night,
or under cover of wooded groves that stripe the foothills. It is New
Year's Eve, but celebrations will have to wait. They swing around
and head back the other way, joined by forty men who have marched
down from Yerba Buena, a few more marines, another militia, and
men from the port who thought they could not take off for three
months to travel with Fremont but who can't stand idly by when
attackers might soon be right outside the gate. They bring a small
ship's cannon, an eight-pounder on a two-wheel carriage, pulled by a
yoke of glum and dripping oxen.

The next afternoon, under sheets of drizzle, the whole party—
numbering a hundred, plus their mules and horse herds—veers westward to avoid a broad mudflat where the cannon would sink to its
hubs. Sighting a benchland above the plain, they clamber toward it. As

darkness falls they reach two shepherds' huts, which offer a rickety and worthless gathering point.

It is the first of January. The night comes quick and early, with no sunset, just a dimming of light under murky clouds. As Jim Reed turns in, he prays for this wet campaign to lead him somewhere, anywhere, and soon. The troops from Yerba Buena saw nothing on their journey southward, which must mean the entire enemy force is maneuvering for an assault on San Jose. They can't be far from us, he thinks. Tomorrow they will show themselves. They have to. As he falls into a troubled sleep, he feels tomorrow heading toward him like the herd of wild horses in the San Joaquin. He turns and squirms and calls out in the darkness and dreams a now familiar dream . . .

He sees a cobalt sky, a world of blue both pure and perilous. Granite peaks loom large against the blue. He hears the wheezing grunts as teams of oxen strain to haul canvas-covered wagons up a final cliff. He hears the whip and sees the teamster with his sleeves rolled back, his trail hat tilted, slashing away at their bony ribs and haunches. But wait. This man is not a teamster. He has the golden beard and moustache of Lewis Keseberg, that arrogant smirk. With every slash the thick-butt whip draws blood.

Jim hears himself cry, "Back off, Lewis! Back off now!"

Keseberg doesn't turn. He doesn't hear. The arm lifts. Under his lash the dry flesh quivers. Again Jim sees chain links strain against the edge of broken rock, while oxen heave to pull the wagon clear. He sees the iron linkage spread across the stone and break. His family wagon plunges. Silently it plunges toward the distant oval of the lake. Whiteness gushes from the split sacks inside the wagon. This time it is not flour spilling forth. It's something colder, as cold as the white salt that covered the nighttime desert. Yes, this white stuff is cold salt that somehow spills from the family wagon to cover Jim . . . so cold and white he springs awake, his eyes wide.

He sits up and finds his bedroll covered. Is it frost? He touches it. Snow has fallen and covered the encampment. And snow could fall again, it's that cold. Too cold to sleep.

With scavenged kindling someone stacked inside a shed, he builds a fire and sits beside it. There is half a moon. Under its feeble light he sees that the plain below is also snowy, as well as the mountains to the east, across the bay. It strains belief. Another dream. Just now, what was he dreaming? He can't remember. He remembers the early snow-fall seen from Sutter's Fort, while looking eastward toward the farther peaks, ominous and unwelcome. How long ago was that? And has the same snow followed him to the Bay of San Francisco, to remind him again of the families still waiting? If it pains his hands to gather kindling here and strike a flintstone, what must the cold be like for them, after all these weeks? And when he wants to be there, why is he perched here, waiting for the day to melt this crust of white?

What an odd sight, this milky stillness under the humpbacked moon. What an odd prologue to the day he feels approaching, and to this year that comes so suddenly upon them all.

Is it 1847 now?

He tries the number on his tongue. How curious it feels. What an unlikely ring. Where has the time gone? How can a century be so far advanced, already near its halfway point? Where has his life gone? It occurs to him that sometime in the past few weeks a birthday came and went. Somewhere on the trail to Bear Valley, or while trekking back from Bear Valley, he turned forty-seven. My God! He too is near the half-century mark, while these men sprawled around him, in their damp bedrolls and in their tents, they are in their thirties. Some are in their twenties, young enough to be sons of his, men half his age, who can drink twice as much, and spoiling for a fight. At their age Jim, too, was spoiling for a fight, enlisting in the Indian wars and chasing bands of renegade Sauk and Fox up the Rock River Valley clear into the Wisconsin wilderness. How long ago it seems. Another time. Another world. And he was another man. Back then. A single man. With just himself to care for. He had thought that was warrioring enough for one man's life. Nowadays the trail gets longer, the saddles get harder, the foe more and more elusive. He wonders how much longer he can keep this up.

The mountains to the east are moon-white down to the shores of the bay. What are they called? The Diablo Range? Maybe there's some truth to that name after all. Some say the devil's realm is fire. Some say ice. Under the winter moon the slopes and peaks are carved of ice. On such a night this entire land seems devilish. Maybe Valentine is right. Maybe it needs some kind of purging. And maybe, yes, maybe he wouldn't mind another skirmish, one more go-round. A man needs some satisfaction. Sometimes any enemy will do. If he can't catch up with Hastings, if he can't get his hands on those cowardly accusers who sent him into exile, he may as well take whatever foe comes toward him, and when the fighting's done, when the way is cleared, who then will listen to those small voices from the past . . .

The night's deep silence is broken by the crunch of boots. He turns and sees a figure with a hat pulled tight and a long leather traveling coat around his shoulders. He waits. It's Valentine.

"I saw your fire."

"The snow woke me."

"As it woke me too."

"Then warm yourself."

Valentine hunkers next to him, breathes puffs of steam, gazing into the flames.

After a while he says, "Do you believe in omens, Reed?"

Jim looks at him, expecting the sardonic leer, but sees something else, something unprotected.

"I think we all do, though many claim they don't."

"This district is famous for its mild winters, you know. Snow is seldom seen. You think it's a sign? Coming on a night like this? A day like this?"

"Depends on the kind of day you think it is."

Valentine's voice is almost a whisper. "The day we meet the dreaded foe. You've heard the news."

"Maybe I haven't."

"During the night, another report came in. They're not far from us, not far at all, sighted at a rancho this side of San Jose. No soldiers seen. But many horses, and rancheros bearing arms. Day by day their numbers grow, according to the scouts . . ."

"You say no soldiers?"

"None reported. But what difference does it make? They have the hostages. They're farther south than anyone expected them to roam. How they got past us, I still don't know. But they won't get much farther. We'll cut them off before they reach the pueblo. I can taste it now, can't you?"

"Something's in the air."

"They can't be far, and it won't last long, once we flush them out. I know these people. You may have heard that I once rode with the Californians."

"I have heard that, yes."

"What have you heard?"

"Sooner or later, fellows talk about everything."

"Let me tell you something, Reed."

Again Jim waits. This is not an order. It is an offer. Or a plea. With a stick, Valentine stirs the fire, and new flames leap up.

"We once had a gobernador from Mexico. A prissy and bureaucratic man, liked by no one. A war was fought to send him back and you could side with him or you could side with those who wanted to be rid of him. But you really had no choice. The Californians made me a captain. We were comrades in arms, you see. When the fellow and his lackeys finally fled we drank many toasts to his departure. The new gobernador—a man from California, not from Mexico—gave me a bit of land, as they will do, to show appreciation. But the times changed. Times always change. My comrades had a new adversary and again they summoned me to join their cause, this time to take up arms against men like you, Mr. Reed, against Los Americanos."

Jim wants to be wary of this tale, but something needful and naked in the voice compels him to listen. It has the sound of a confession, or of a last letter home on the eve of battle.

"I had a close friend, an officer at Monterey. When I refused this offer, he was insulted. You are a citizen here, he told me. You accepted land. I told him the Americans would not be stopped. I could see the future coming. I spoke friend to friend. Make peace while you can, I said, spare the blood of your soldiers. As you might expect, he hated me for saying this. We are traveling south in search of reinforcements, he said, and you are coming with us. He could not forgive me for refusing to serve in their army, and so they took me prisoner. We ran short of horses, and they made me walk. I had to walk along behind a horse at the end of a rope like a goat led to the marketplace. The rope was new and lashed around my wrists and made wounds kept open by the blazing sun. Would you like to see them? Here. Even now they throb."

Valentine pulls off one leather glove and shoves back a jacket sleeve to expose the welts, red and shiny as if still bleeding. Jim stares at the wounded skin. Under his hat brim his own welts seem to throb, though they have nearly healed over now, itching from time to time as hair grows back around the tender edges. His fingers push in under the brim to touch the welts and the new hair. He lifts his eyes from the wrist and sees that Valentine has turned away, as if scanning distant terrain. It could be an actor's theatrical show of grief, but Jim wants to believe this story now. The wounds persuade him. The voice grows softer, somehow lighter, with a blaming in it that Jim knows well.

"We passed Los Angeles, then moved out across the desert, bearing east almost to the Colorado, where they set me loose. They were running low on food, you see, and weary of feeding me. I was worth nothing to them, even as a hostage. They cut my ropes and left me while they rode on, claiming they would return with cannons and a thousand men. Then I saw the true nature of their character. A man I had once called comrade left me alone in the midday sun with no horses, no weapon. I had to make my way on foot, back across the southern desert. It took many days to reach a town. I can't recall how many. You can imagine what this journey was like. It stole away my strength. My body shrank. I fell into a fever and passed an entire month half blind. To this day I have spells of fever and my mind begins to reel . . ."

He turns and looks hard at Jim. "But today my mind is clear."

Valentine rises from his crouch and opens his hands toward the faint rim of light along the snowy ridge tops across the bay.

"Believe me, Reed. Beware of the Californians. They are not like us."

Around them the mud-stained camp has begun to move, as men wake to pee and splash water on stubbled faces, boil their coffee, munch biscuits and molding jerky strips, and marvel at the snow. One man moves with more deliberation, picking his way among the soggy bedrolls and sagging tents. When Valentine stands up, he quickens his pace and calls, "Señor." It is Carlos, back from a predawn reconnoiter. Beside the fire he speaks quietly, in rapid Spanish.

Valentine nods. "Ah, good. This is good indeed."

Very early, he explains to Jim, an armed patrol left from the rancho, but not toward San Jose as had been feared. They were soon followed by a larger group evidently bound for an open plain some five miles from here. "They're gathering up," says Valentine with zeal. "They're going to show themselves at last."

Carlos also likes this news. His eyes are very keen for so early in the day. Jim sees that he too is spoiling for a fight. "He does not like the greasers," Valentine once told him, "any more than we do. He'd rather ride with us, and that blue bill cap he wears at such a jaunty angle is his badge of honor." Carlos won it fair and square, Valentine has said, arm-wrestling a young marine from Baltimore, a fellow half again his size.

As they stand by the fire, reaching toward the flames for one last bit of warmth, Jim sees that the scout's hands are large and thick, look to be made of leather. Beneath the serape his shoulders are wide. His hawk eyes seem to miss nothing. As Carlos walks away, it occurs to Jim that in stance, in stride, he is much more alive than the sentries who plod back and forth in front of John Sutter's double gates. Jim doesn't envy the young marine who lost his cap to Carlos. He would not want to tangle with him one on one. He is glad they're on the same side today, yes, glad they've found a common enemy, he and Carlos and Valentine and all the others assembled here to right old wrongs, to fight their many fights.

As they saddle their horses and mount up and begin their descent out of the foothills, Valentine's story still moves through his mind. Jim has known that kind of treachery, expelled into the desert without a weapon, forced to make a lonely crossing, suffer wounds that would not heal. His scalp welts throb again, and he is ready for whatever comes.

At sea level the snow has melted. A crust of frozen mud beneath the snow has melted too, adding new moisture to the slush. They push southward, and reports come one upon the next. More troops were sighted here! An armed party was sighted there!

"How many?" asks Valentine.

"Hard to tell," says one excited scout, "the way they snaked along."

"What do you mean, 'snaked'?"

"Like they was skulking in and out of the trees."

Shouting commands, Valentine rushes off to see for himself and soon comes galloping toward them from a grove of stately oaks.

"We've spied the entire force!" he cries. "A mile from here! Form up! Form up!"

Somewhere beyond that grove the enemy waits, as if finally prepared to step out into the open and take a stand.

"But why?" one man wants to know. "Why here?"

"Why now?" asks another. "Why have they waited so long and led us in such a circle?"

Valentine seems delighted by these questions, delighted by flurry and chaotic swirl. "It is in their nature, man! Expect no rhyme or reason!"

The Mustard Thicket

UNDER COVER OF the spreading oaks the pueblo Volunteers fan
out along a wide left flank. The Yerba Buena units hold the right,
while four dozen musket-bearing marines take the center. They see
nothing until they leave the grove and step out into a broad and
muddy plain, half covered with stands of water. Three creeks wander
through it. From a quarter mile away a swarm of mounted men are
watching, as if positioned there for days, for weeks, expecting the
Americans to track them down. Ponds of water shine like mirrors in
the midday sun. Patches of snow still show on the nearest hills, while
off to the south a bell tower can be seen, an incongruous relic, rising
from what remains of another Spanish mission.

A few riders prance out away from the waiting throng and begin to
turn, to wheel, in a circus show of horsemanship that causes the
advancing troops to slow their pace. Uncertainly they gaze, amazed at
the skill, the lifted hooves and whirling lariats, wondering if this is the
prologue to a charge.

They see horsemen standing in their stirrups as they ride, or leaning low as if plucking objects from the ground. Some brandish what
appear to be long lances. They wear serapes of many hues, high-
crowned hats, the split leggings of the vaquero. Their horses lift and
rear and turn, race back and forth as if in competition. But are they
going to charge?

"They are cowards!" cries Valentine. "They are staying out of rifle
range! Advance! Advance!"

The Volunteers move ahead, and Jim is as eager as Valentine, until
he's stopped by swampy weeds. His horse sinks to its knees. Nearby
marines are also trying to advance, but the first ranks flounder in mud
and pools of glistening overflow, and now the eight-pounder has
rolled to a halt, bogged down crossing one of the creeks. Ten men are

dispatched to wrestle the cannon and its yoke of oxen onto firmer ground.

Seeing this, a few dozen prancing horsemen are emboldened to make a scattered charge, splashing through the puddles and bogs with shouts of "Viva California!" Some hold swords or lances. A few fire pistols wildly as they ride, a damp and motley regiment, still two hundred yards away, firing into the air or straight ahead—*pop, pop, pop*—while Americans hunker down to return the fire.

At last the cannoneers get off a round of grapeshot, then another, which sinks the carriage wheels deeper into the creekbank, but these rounds take the charging horsemen by surprise. With shouts and threatening blades held high, they wheel and splash back the way they've come.

Their numbers are much smaller than reported. A hundred men at most. Where are the others? Where are the hostages? Where are the Mexican regulars ferried up from Mazatlán? Could a reserve force be gathering somewhere else? What about the banks of these overgrown streams? Snipers could be lurking there, or an entire company ready to ambush.

Before the horsemen charge again, two squads of Volunteers spread wide to search the perimeter, one led by Valentine, with Carlos riding point, one led by Jim, who sends his men into the willow groves and stands of mustard along the banks of a shadowy creek.

Soon he finds himself alone, groping through a thicket where the green stalks are ten and twelve feet tall, so dense and leafy they block his view of anything ahead. They muffle the sounds from the nearby plain. The shouts and intermittent pops seem to recede, while the sounds close by seem larger, louder, the slow ripple of moving water, the suck of lifting hooves. On a mushy embankment, with a wall of stalks behind him, he stops to listen.

Stillness.

A little globe of stillness, where overhead leaves filter the light.

Then stalks are rustling somewhere back in the thicket on the farther bank. Another horse is struggling toward him. It could be someone from his own patrol. But maybe not. He reaches for his pistol. He would love to have a clear shot.

A horse pushes into the tiny clearing, and Jim sees the startled eyes of a rider who has lost his way. He carries an ancient sword. He wears a ranchero's jacket, heavy leather chaps. Under the sombrero his face is lean and swarthy, the cheeks shaded by days of dark stubble. Jim knows this face. It is the cousin of the Alcalde's wife, haggard in the way Jim is haggard, from days of riding long hours in the wet and the cold. He has been using his sword like a machete, to cut a path through the mustard stalks. Seeing Jim, he lifts it overhead. With a cry he urges his horse across the stream. Jim hears a voice that echoes in his own heart, a cry of grief and pride and furious defiance.

He shouts, "Hold it! Hold it!"

The ranchero seems to recognize him now, but not with any pleasure, spewing oaths as his horse splashes into the creek. The man and his sword are almost upon him. If Jim doesn't fire, his head will be chopped off. But he cannot shoot the rancher. He has to shoot the horse. A bullet to the tawny chest, then a second, spraying blood, and the animal lurches, stumbles, drops to its knees.

The ranchero is thrown sideways into the mud, where he sprawls, spitting words Jim can't understand. He scrambles to his feet and stands backed against the stalks. The horse is dead. His sword is at the ready. Jim could shoot it from his hand. He could wound the ranchero and have a hostage to take back for trading. But the thought repels him. It has all come clear. The Alcalde was right. His adversary is a man of his own age, with a proud eye and two young sons wondering when he will return, and a wife somewhere, perhaps a woman like the Alcalde's wife. Jim remembers how the sons stood that day, erect and unflinching, next to the father.

From somewhere back in the thicket he hears other horses, American voices. To the ranchero he says, "Get out of here. Get away."

The man stares at him, at the pistol.

Jim flings his free hand outward. "Go! Go! Vamoose!"

The ranchero doesn't hesitate. He turns and is gone. Jim plunges back into the mustard grove, calling to his men, cursing his luck, filled with shame for he knows not what.

THE TWO PATROLS emerge from the thicket. Valentine and Carlos heard muffled voices and sounds of movement, saw no one. Another futile outing. They all yearn to rejoin the fray, but there is nothing to rejoin. Out on the swampy plain the taunting horsemen have twice more charged, each time riding nearly into range, turning back, repulsed by muskets and by grapeshot from the mired cannon. Now, after a final charge, serapes and sombreros are once again retreating. As horses disappear among the oaks, heading toward the foothills, the Volunteers watch their common enemy dissolve.

The encounter lasts two hours, with one mule lost and one American injured, burned across the face and chest when the cannon back-fired. On the wide field of battle no bodies can be seen, no sign of any casualties from the other side. Valentine would ride after them, while they're on the run. So would the men who marched down from Yerba Buena. But the senior officer here, the red-bearded captain of marines, observes the darkening sky. With more snow likely, it's too late in the day to give chase. They can't get far.

"We'll wait," the Captain says. "We'll ride to that mission, to dry ourselves off and quench our many thirsts."

Spoils of War

Next morning, in the early sunlight, a patch of white appears across the field. It could be a patch of snow, caught among oak limbs, except that it moves a bit. Now the upright lance is seen. The white flag flutters from its tip. A bundled rider carries the lance, and his horse seems to walk on water, as a far-off delegation skirts the edge of a glistening pond. Eventually they stop under the limbs of a massive, ancient oak that occupies its own island among the ponds and puddles.

From the mission yard another white flag moves out to meet them, carried by the captain of marines. Riding with him are Valentine, the militia leader, and Jim Reed, his lieutenant, and the Alcalde, who will repeat in Spanish the Captain's words and repeat in English the words of the delegation's leader, a grizzled man of sixty or so, known to the Alcalde, the patriarch of a ranching clan. The leader's eyes are darkly circled. All night he has been debating with his comrades about their next move. Behind him three young Californians sit straight in their saddles, pistol butts showing at their belts. Among them sits the ranking hostage, the mayor of Yerba Buena, in poncho and naval cap, age twenty-six and looking ten years older, the line of his muttonchops almost obscured by two weeks' growth of dense black beard.

The Captain says, Are you prepared to surrender?

The leader says, We have come to talk.

There will be no talking until this man and the others are returned to us.

We will return our hostages when someone returns our horses.

You seem to have your horses under you.

I refer to our stock. How do we live without the horses and saddles and all the rest your soldiers have taken from us?

You have provoked an attack on the territorial government of the United States.

On the contrary, Captain. I believe you have provoked us.

It is not your place to accuse me, sir!

You tell us horses are needed for the war and cattle to feed your soldiers. Yet in those mountains to the east I have seen some of my own horses under guard and grazing . . .

"Captain," Valentine mutters at his ear, "I have never heard such insolence."

"At ease," says the Captain. And then to the leader, This is a serious charge, an outrageous charge.

You brought this war into our land . . .

"These men should be whipped," says Valentine, "and dragged through the plaza!" He touches his pistol, as if to draw.

Jim grabs his arm. "Let's hear them out."

On both sides, men raise their voices, place hands on their weapons. The Alcalde removes his hat.

"Señores! Señores! Por favor . . ."

As the voices subside, the leader continues.

We have no desire to do battle with your troops, or to demean your flag. We do not speak for Mexico. We speak only for ourselves, as ranchers, as common men.

To the weary, waiting hostage the Captain says, "Lieutenant Bartlett, your command of Spanish is fairly good, as I recall."

"I get by."

"What are these men up to, then? Is this a trick? Are there reserve troops in hiding?"

"Not at all."

"Are we vulnerable to new attack?"

"I'm afraid he speaks the truth."

"So you are being released today. Is that what's going on?"

"Not yet. They want you to see that I am well."

"And are you? Have you been tortured? Are they forcing you to speak?"

"I've been treated rather cordially, sir, all things considered."

Valentine leans forward. "Sir, they have filled his head with nonsense."

"You hold your tongue, Mr. Valentine. I'll do the talking here."

The Captain looks long at the leader and the men behind him. He looks at Bartlett.

"What then do you recommend?"

"Return as many horses and saddles as you can, with a guarantee of public safety."

"And for that they will return the hostages?"

"I'm sure of it."

"We have orders to wipe them out, you know. The Commandant wants a clear and certain victory."

"It would be our loss, Captain."

"I don't follow you."

"We could kill them all, I suppose, or put them in irons, and turn our own troops into cowboys. But what would be the point? We have relied on these men for beef to feed us and to feed the people of the port."

"So we send them all back home?"

"I would recommend it."

"They will not turn on us?"

"It isn't likely, given what they have to fight with—half a keg of powder left, and that is damp and useless . . ."

"Their weapons . . ."

". . . for the most part have already been confiscated."

"By us."

"Indeed."

"I see."

The Captain's cheeks fill with a color to match his beard. His jaws flex and pump. To the Alcalde he says, "Ask him why in God's name they forced us to the field of battle!"

Our only desire, the leader replies, was to be heard.

Why didn't you take your grievances to Yerba Buena?

We did so, Captain, several times.

In person?

Yes.

And in writing?

Yes.

And what was the response?

There has been no response.

Nothing at all?

We understand that two senior officers there cannot agree on who is in command. Perhaps this explains why certain decisions have been delayed.

UNDER THE LIMBS of the great oak tree a truce is declared. They agree to meet again, and the Californians retire to their foothill encampment. The Americans retire to the mission compound. Three times they meet in the open field, while couriers gallop back and forth the fifty miles to Yerba Buena with terms and counter-terms. On the eighth day after the skirmish, two facing columns form outside the crumbling walls of the mission called Santa Clara. While a horse-drawn carriage passes between them, the rancheros, one by one, drop their remaining weapons in the wagon—forty-three rifles, nine pistols, ten swords, nineteen lances made of poles with hunting knives attached.

A herd of horses is driven up from San Jose to the mission corral. The Californians walk among them, speaking to animals they recognize, touching their favorites, a reunion of loved ones, as they sort out the horses they will ride, the ones they will lead away. Once the men are content with the return of animals most longed for, the hostages are ushered down out of the foothills, Bartlett and six unshaven young sailors damp and shivering in the clothes they've worn since their capture, but none wounded or mistreated. They've been fed well enough. Their eyes are bright with liberation.

By early afternoon the insurgents have started home to their ranches. Some Volunteers head home to their families. Others join the marines riding into San Jose, where a keg of brandy has appeared. In the cantina they toast the release of their countrymen. There are toasts to the Union, to the flag, to President Polk, as all begin to brag, embellishing their exploits, the captives and the warriors, laying groundwork for the legend of this episode, the dogged pursuit of a determined foe, the daylong battle, the harrowing firefights, the armistice.

While Jim's voice is loud among them, his glass held high for every toast, he makes no mention of the sword-wielding ranchero. He takes no pride in the shooting of another man's horse. In this dubious victory he can't find much at all to celebrate. Yet in the end it gives him what he needs. Jim has new allies now, and the path ahead seems clear at last. They were riding in to the pueblo when this Bartlett fellow told him that he too has heard of the plight of the wagon company now talked about in every California town. Once he's back at his magistrate's desk in Yerba Buena, Bartlett said, he might be able to stir up some support for a rescue.

"When things are settled here in San Jose," he said, "you call on me. We'll do everything we can."

In the crowded cantina, where revelers spread out toward the plaza in spite of the cold, the Alcalde takes him aside. His cheeks are rosy, his eyes merry with drink and relief now that his pueblo is safe again. He wears his Spanish hat. A black cloak lined with crimson hangs nearly to the floor.

"We should have listened to you," Jim says.

"Yes, the navy might have saved itself a good bit of trouble. But things are taken care of now. And we're grateful here."

"So am I. Glad it's finally over."

Dropping his voice, the Alcalde says, "I want to add that our family thanks you."

"I beg your pardon?"

"We know you spared our cousin's life."

Jim looks away. "No need to spread that news around."

"Oh, we don't gossip out of turn. Our cousin has no desire that the facts be known. Suffice to say, we're thankful for your services in these days of crisis and uncertainty."

With a raise of his glass the Alcalde tells him it might not be a bad time to stop by the ranch house and draw up that petition for the orchard lands. Now that the United States has a firm hold, petitions have been coming to him thick and fast for parcels of every size and shape.

"Fact is, Reed, another fellow has his eye on the acreage there. But I would much prefer the title go to you." With a fatherly wink he adds, "Wouldn't hurt to move the date back, you know, to give you the earlier claim. I'm sure the good Captain at the garrison will endorse it for us, on behalf of the command."

As their glasses touch, Jim says, "I'll do that, sir, I'll do that the very first thing."

The marines and the Volunteers are joined by gaunt emigrants whose wagons have been parked near the pueblo and by citizens who rode out to watch the armistice. All are relieved that hostilities have ended with no men lost and daily life can now resume. One fellow brings along a fiddle. Another has a banjo. Men with stiff hands tune up, breathe on their fingers, and begin to play. In some forgotten seam of his saddlebags a man finds a harmonica. Soon a clumsy square dance has flared around the room, lit by candles and dusky kerosene lamps.

Standing at the bar Jim feels a hand upon his arm, and here is Valentine with his sly, conspiratorial smile.

"Well, Reed, life is full of its surprises, wouldn't you say? We knew the Californians had no stomach for the contest. Who would have thought our own marines would back down too? But in the end, it's all the same."

His jacket is loose. His hat hangs down upon his shoulders. His black hair is combed straight back. His face looks gleeful, as if some secret dream has unexpectedly come true.

"They were right about the horses, of course. On a ranch not far from here I have quite a number well secluded. Why don't you come in with me? These are superior animals, well bred and broken. We can drive them inland and name our price. With your share you can mount the rescue team you're going to need. I guarantee it. Then, when you've brought your family through, we'll go into partnership. Out here it's hard to find a steady man who knows what he wants."

"What sort of partnership?"

"Why, buying, selling, trading. I know you've done some of that. It's wide open now. There will be no more resistance in the north. Nothing stands in our way."

Valentine once again seems to know his mind. Here's what Jim is searching for, the money to hire men, to buy supplies for a month or more. But does he dare rely on such a fellow? There is something perverse about Valentine. He should be in disgrace today. Yet he seems to revel in all this. He has no shame. Wasn't the militia formed to solve the very problems he and others like him had created? Jim remembers their first meeting, when Valentine told him no man alone could get through to Yerba Buena. Surely he knew that wasn't true. Surely he knew what the Alcalde already knew. If Jim hadn't listened to him, he might long ago have traveled north and reached the port. And yet . . .

and yet had he done so, the battle would not have ended any sooner, nor would he have seen the orchards or this long, fecund valley. Or met the good Alcalde. Or met Bartlett.

Who can say, in hindsight, which route is the nearer or the better one? The route itself would seem to have a will, and each of us is bound to it.

With his cocky smile Valentine says, "Believe me, Reed, no one is watching now. California is like a bank with the front door open and the safe unlocked and the banker gone away on a year's vacation."

"I'm not sure I like the sound of that."

"Of course you do."

"I like to know there's a banker somewhere sitting at his desk. I want a county clerk who keeps the deeds and documents in order."

Valentine throws his head back in a laugh of disbelief. "And yet with a single nod from the snowy head of our dear Alcalde, you'd gladly snatch up the mission's keys and all the orchard lands . . ."

"Such fine trees deserve some care. Those lands belong to no one now."

"And how did you come to know *that?*"

"Well . . . as a matter of fact, from you."

"That's right! You learned it from me! I have gone out of my way to befriend you, Reed. And yet you would turn your back on me. An abandoned orchard is one thing, you say, but a surplus of horses is something else."

"Everyone knows where those horses came from."

"I suppose you disapprove."

"By God, I do!"

"You draw a fine line. Too fine a line for me."

"Don't sneer."

"You should have been a lawyer."

"I'm in no mood tonight for mockery."

"You have a very legal mind."

"I have a family. Can you imagine what that means? I want some safety for them here. I don't want a lawless land. I've had enough of that."

"You are too cautious, Reed, far too cautious. The time is ripe. Ride with us and you'll have all the money you need to bring your family out."

His blue eyes glitter with amused and erotic intensity, as if he's just told a bawdy tale among cigar-smoking cronies.

"Think it over, Reed. You and me and Carlos, we'd be quite a team."

"Why Carlos?"

"Where we're going he knows all the tribal leaders," says Valentine with a rascal wink, as he moves out among the gangly dancers. "We'll want to keep the tribes in line."

In some nameless jig/fandango he begins to leap and strut, while the banjo strums and the fiddle whines and the harmonica hums and warbles. Valentine's partner is one of the local women, bare-shouldered and vivacious. Her skirt flares wide. He does not so much dance with her as dance around her, grinning and prancing in the dusky light from candles and from the little tongues of flame inside the lamps.

from *The Trail Notes of Patty Reed*

Santa Cruz, January 1921

"Over the mountains
Of the Moon,
Down the Valley of the Shadow,
Ride, boldly ride,"
The Shade replied,—
"If you seek for Eldorado."

—Edgar Allan Poe

SOMETIMES *in the very winter of the year we will have a run of warm days here, five or six in a row, when it seems like spring has come along three months too early. The fruit trees in our yard will start to show their tiny blossoms, pink and white, and someone who has not lived here long, someone who recently arrived from Ohio or Alabama will shake his head and say it's an enigma and perhaps a crime that nature would deceive these poor trees, get their hopes up and call forth these innocent shoots so soon, only to have the frosty nights come back and nip them in the bud.*

What such a person has not yet discovered is that the trees know more than we know about how they are to get along in such a place. Somehow they do just fine. They take advantage of the warm days, and get through the frosty days, and in due time the fruit comes, the pears and the apples and the plums and tangerines.

If we get a warm day in January, we have to learn from the fruit tree to let some little bud of expectation peep forth. It's not a trick of nature. It's a gift. I'm past eighty, but I'm not too old to get outside on such a day, sit on the porch and let the light call things into the open. A warm day like this makes it easier to think back on the cold weeks of 1847 when our cabins were sometimes under ten feet of snow. Even though I was there, it's hard to believe we had to cut ramps and ice steps to climb out of the cabins and get back up to the light. We were like Eskimos, I guess, but with our igloos down there below the surface. One day we'd have falling snow. The next day a roaring wind would come and a blizzard that penned us in for a week or more. When it was over we might have five new feet of snow to dig through. Then the sun would be so bright and the sky so blue you couldn't look at it. You'd have to shut your eyes and let the tears run down your face and give thanks. It amazes me now, in spite of all we'd lost, how often we'd find something to be thankful for.

After a week went by and the Snowshoe Party did not return, as the earlier exploring parties had, we gave thanks that they'd made it across. At least that's all you heard anyone say about it. No one would mention out loud that they might have got lost in one of those storms that kept us underground. It was too awful to think about. So mama and Milt calculated how much time it would take them to get back with a rescue team. Everyone had some kind of vision of their route, since Charlie Stanton had many times described his travels to Sutter's Fort. He had figured six days to get from Truckee Lake to Bear Valley and three more to make Johnson's. The next question was, How long would it take them to return? The first trip had taken him a month. He'd had mules to ride, of course, but then he'd also had twice as far to go. "If he's lucky," I heard Milt say, "he might cut that time in half."

"Depending on the weather," mama said.

"Depending on a lot of things," said Milt, his crooked jaw working back and forth.

Everyone was counting on Charlie and Bill Eddy and the Indians. Some folks had given up on papa. If he was coming back, they would say with a scowl, he'd have been here by now. In my own heart I had not given up on papa. I still expected to see him any day, pushing through the trees. Meanwhile, I had another hero standing in reserve. His name was Salvador. I had his abalone amulet around my neck. Whenever the sun was out I'd keep an eye on the pass above the lake. I did not know if they would come together, or one at a time, but I knew they'd come.

In the first part of January, something happened to mama. She didn't think she could wait for papa any longer, or for the Snowshoe Party, or for any other kind of party that might be coming toward us from the west. She was going to hike across the mountains herself, she said, and bring back help.

It was a crazy idea. We all begged her not to go, but she was frantic. We were nearly out of food. She couldn't see how any of us could make it through a winter on the pitiful scraps remaining. Before the snow fell so thick and fast, we would sometimes capture the tiny field mice that crept into camp, and roast them, and make a soup. For a while mama had doled out strips of beef the size of your forefinger, each little strip a meal. About the time that was running out, she told us she had trapped a rabbit. It was already skinned, she said. That night each of us kids got a paw, and it was good, I have to confess. It was skinny but succulent. We sucked every last speck of meat off the little bones. We sucked the bones and held them in our mouths for a long time. The next afternoon I noticed that our dog, Cash, had been gone all day. I asked Virginia if she had seen him. I asked Tommy. We all asked mama if she had seen Cash. She couldn't answer. She turned away as if she'd heard a noise somewhere. So we knew what she'd done, and I scolded her. I said I'd rather die than eat off the rest of Cash's body. Virginia joined in. She was crying. "He came all the way across the plains with the family," she said. "It's like killing one of us!"

For all our tears and our remorse and guilt, once we smelled the next pieces cooking over mama's fire—the skimpy legs, the ribs—we ate up every last morsel. There wasn't much left of him, either. It still amazes me how Cash survived that long with nothing to nibble on but bits of bone and bark and who knows what else. But mama made that dog last a week. And I learned then that hunger has no boundaries. For me, at age eight, this was no different from what others would be doing in the days ahead. Cash had become a member of the family and we stood in line, James Junior and Tommy and Virginia and me, while mama served up his ears, his neck, his tongue, his very eyes.

After that we started eating hides, which boiled down to a gummy gelatin that was the worst-tasting mess I have ever tried to swallow. First you'd have to cut a hide into squares about a foot across and burn off the hair and scrape it down with a knife, then boil the pieces for hours and hours. Some people couldn't eat it, no matter how hungry they were. It would make them gag and retch. What was worse, for us, the only hides we had were ones we'd used to cover the cabin. Not only were we reduced to eating this undigestible glue, we would soon be eating the very roof from over our heads. That's when mama decided to try and hike out. If she took Virginia and Milt, she said, they could go for help, and it would also mean three less mouths to feed.

She had no idea what it would take to cross those mountains in January. All the food she had to carry was a few last strips of jerky she had stored away. James Junior and Tommy and me, we pleaded with her to take us too. We ganged around her, wailing and pulling on her skirts. She said we were too young to do the climbing. She said she was doing this for us.

"I'm going to bring you all back some bread," she said. "Wouldn't you like some warm bread to eat?"

I had forgotten what bread tasted like. All I wanted was to go wherever mama was going. How could she take Virginia along and not take me too? I hated Virginia.

"You have to be strong," mama said to me, "to take care of Tommy and James until I get back. You're the big sister now."

"If I'm strong," I said, "why can't I go with you?"

"We won't be gone long, Patty. We won't be gone any time at all."

The way she said this, my hatred for Virginia turned to terror. Mama was past arguing or thinking clear. Her eyes were wild. While we three young ones stood and watched, she and Virginia and Milt moved out through the trees the way we had watched papa move out across the flatness of the hot, blank desert. I don't have to tell you what it felt like to be that age and have both your mother and your father disappear into country that seemed to have no beginning and no end. Her crazy look was the same look I'd seen on the face of Elizabeth Graves the day Uncle Billy left with the Snowshoe Party. I realize now I knew something about Elizabeth Graves I had not known before. I knew where her screams had come from, though I myself could not yet scream.

Mama had parceled us out among the other families—James Junior to the Graveses, Tommy to the Breens, and me to the Keseberg cabin. We had never been split up like this, with the whole family broken into pieces. Mama had told me to look out for my baby brothers, but they, too, soon disappeared, carried away to the other cabins, and I was alone, shivering in the snow, too scared to descend into Keseberg's cave. No one had seen him for weeks. Maybe he was dead. I imagined his corpse lying down there in the darkness, and I could not move. Finally his wife Phillipine came up the snow stairs and said something in German and beckoned with her hands. Her eyes were full of grief, but she had a sweet and motherly smile, so I climbed down the steps behind her.

In the dim light I could see him lying under a pile of filthy blankets. His face was to the fire and his eyes were open, but he did not speak. I slunk down next to the wall, as far from him as I could get, which wasn't more than a few feet, since their cabin was smaller than ours, just a lean-to built against one side of Breen's cabin. I watched him a while, thinking maybe he had died with his eyes open. Then I saw his beard move. His blond beard had grown down to cover his throat. He was wheezing like an old dog underneath the porch. Later on, when he got up from his bed to relieve himself, he groaned and whimpered. The thorn he had stepped on, way back by the Humboldt, had festered until his foot was too big to fit inside his boot. It was dark and swollen and wrapped in rags. He could barely hobble across the room, let alone get up and down the stairs. I heard him pee against the wall. He staggered back to the bed and fell into his heap of blankets.

The foot couldn't bear any weight at all. So Phillipine was doing everything. She brought in the wood and split the kindling. She brought in snow to melt for water. I helped her as much as I could. Their young child, Lewis Junior, was pale as chalk. He wasn't quite a year old. Their daughter, Ada, age three, was sickly too and whimpering like her daddy. Poor Phillipine was at her wits' end. I can still see her trapped inside that lean-to with Keseberg, who had often beaten her while we were on the trail, as everyone knew. She was only twenty-three, a small woman, and still pretty in spite of all she had endured. Every one of us had traveled a good way to reach this stark rendezvous at Truckee Lake, but no one in the party had traveled farther than Phillipine. She had left a prosperous town somewhere in Germany to follow her husband across the Atlantic Ocean and clear across North America, hoping to make some kind of new start in life, only to end up in this smoky igloo with one child dying and another sick, and a gloomy tyrant filling up the room.

If he had any feeling for her, it didn't show while I was in their care. His own pain seemed to occupy his full attention. He was too frail to hurt her much, but she still bore her fear of him and served him as if to ward off beatings later on, if he got his strength back.

Once in a while he would speak to her in German, in a gruff, demanding voice. He never spoke to me. Not one word, the whole time I was with them. I thought it had something to do with papa. I knew the two of them had argued. On the day they tried to hang papa, Keseberg had carried the rope. I remembered that rope. I remembered his hungry grin. I thought he hated me for being papa's daughter. Much later I would understand that he would have treated anyone the way he treated me. He didn't want any stranger in his lean-to seeing him so helpless, nor did he like a stranger anywhere close to his stash of meal and jerked beef. All we had to eat, my brothers and I, were pieces of hide, which I boiled every day over Keseberg's fire. Tommy would come from Breen's cabin next door and join me to choke down some of the sticky gelatin, and then I would take a gob over to the Graveses' cabin for James Junior. A couple of times, while the Kesebergs were eating, Phillipine passed me little bits of meat, and he looked at her as if she had just stolen all his money.

I WAS ONLY with them four days, though it seemed like four months. One afternoon we heard a voice calling, "Help us! Help us!" a thin, cracking voice that would break your heart no matter who was doing the calling.

Phillipine and I scrambled up the ice steps and out into the snow, and there was mama stumbling through the trees, with Milt behind her carrying Virginia. I ran out and threw my arms around mama's waist. She fell against me, just collapsed, and we both tumbled into the snow. I lay there waiting for her to move, but she didn't. I wriggled out from under and said, "C'mon, mama, get up, get up. You made it back. You'll be all right now, mama. C'mon, get up."

She didn't answer. I tried to lift her, but I had no strength. Thank goodness Phillipine was there. Between us we half raised her. By that time Milt had put Virginia down. He came and lent a hand, and we dragged mama to the cabin.

All three of them were near dead from exposure and exhaustion, too cold to talk, too cold to cry. Later on we would learn how they made it to the summit and a little way past, then lost the trail and wandered off *for two days through drifts and crags. They had run out of food and slept three nights in the snow, tormented by the howls of timber wolves. One morning they woke up at the bottom of a bowl of snow. The fire they'd built had melted through the crust and made a hollow, and during the night they'd all slid to the bottom of the bowl. By sheer will they scratched and scrambled their way to the top. Virginia's feet were frostbitten. She couldn't walk. They saw then how impossible it was and so turned back. Providence had a hand in this, I know. If they had stayed one more night up there, or if they'd made it to Truckee Lake just one hour later, all three of them would have died in the worst week of blizzard we'd seen so far.*

AFTER THAT MAMA *was different. After she thawed out, the craziness left her. I never saw that look in her eyes again. She knew there was no way for any of us to leave that place, and there was nothing else to do but wait. It was a kind of waiting that was different from giving up, and in my mind this is a very big difference. When a person gives up, the spirit goes out of the body, a last gleam goes out of the eyes. By this time we had all seen someone die that way, not only from lack of food, but from hopelessness. They say this is what happened to George Donner's older brother, Jacob, in the camp at Alder Creek. He just stopped eating, sat for days with his head in his hands, and finally gave up the ghost.*

Given what faced us after she came back, I don't know where mama found her reserves of hope. With half the hides gone from the roof, our cabin leaked so bad it was useless. We had to move in with somebody else. In that little snowbound world we were suddenly destitute, begging for shelter where there wasn't near enough to go around. Keseberg had nothing but a lean-to. The widow Murphy still had eleven in her cabin, plus Bill Eddy's wife and their two children. The cabin next to ours was filled up with fourteen members of the Graves clan, and Elizabeth was delirious half the time, calling out for her husband and accusing people of all manner of deception and treachery. Every day or so she would accost mama and demand payment for those two scrawny cattle she had sold us. Her eyes had sunk back into her skull. "You owe me!" she would cry. Mama would walk away from her, and Elizabeth would shout mournful predictions into the wind. "Am I supposed to wait until my children waste away? You owe me, Margaret Reed! And God will punish you for all your sinful deeds!"

Mama knew she would not last five minutes in the same cabin with Elizabeth. So it was Patrick Breen who took us in, Patrick who had not wanted to see papa hang but had allowed him to be banished into the wastelands of Nevada. He said he'd let us in on two conditions. First, he did not have room to take Milt Elliott, who would have to fend for himself. Second, the Reed children should never have to see what the Breens had to eat. Patrick was a prudent man, who had seen right away what the future held in store. He had slaughtered all his cattle early, and jerked the beef, and started in eating the hides before his stock of beef was gone. As the third month of our isolation began he still had some beef and a bit of flour and some tea. "It's our family's food," he told mama. "It's God's will that a man feed his own family first. But I would spare your young'uns the pain of watching others eat."

Their cabin was sturdier than the others, built back in 1844 by another bunch who got stranded at that same spot. It was bigger than the others too, though not by much. Sixteen feet wide and twenty long, with a fireplace and chimney at one end. The Breens and their seven children were already packed in there like cordwood, and along came the five of us, filing through his doorway with our bedding and our patchwork bundles. A sheet was hung midway between the walls. On nights when we dined on snow water and the foul-tasting glue of boiled hides, we could not see their meat, but we could smell it, and we could hear their jaws working, as they muttered among themselves.

Some have written of Patrick Breen's penurious ways and called him selfish and heartless for hoarding food while all about him people were slowly starving to death. Others have praised his generous spirit during those dark weeks, as a man who did as much as he could do with what he had. "Be thankful for this shelter," mama would tell us. "Without it we would all be frozen stiff." Still, you have to wonder what it does to a man, watching another's children shrink while his own have food— especially in such close quarters. By that time we were so skinny there was no flesh on our lips. We could see the line of one another's teeth behind the skin. I remember once I counted Tommy's teeth while his mouth was closed.

.   .   .

IN THE BREENS' *cabin there would be two or three days at a time when you couldn't get outside. We'd just sit tight, mama and the four of us kids, Patrick and Peg and their seven. As long as the fire was going, we could stay warm. The piling snow was a good insulator. It held in other things besides the heat, of course. Lice liked the warmth as much as we did. We all had lice in our hair and in our clothes. And the smells—I don't want to linger on how things smelled inside that cabin with fourteen of us in a space the size of a chicken house, and Peggy's youngest only one year old. It is just awful to think about now, with no way for anyone to bathe and sometimes no way to get outdoors to do your business.*

We did a lot of sitting and scratching and waiting. Mama would read to us when she could, though her headaches had come back and might keep her laid up for half a day. Somewhere along the way Patrick started reciting a Thirty Days Prayer. He would recite it both morning and night. The Breens were the only Catholic family in the party. Something about the dim light and Patrick's voice made his cabin feel like a church, a little chapel in the wilderness. His readings had an eerie power that worked on me, and I know they worked on my sister, Virginia.

All we had for light were short pieces of kindling that we kept burning on the hearth like little candles. She would sit next to him while he read and hold up one of the pieces of kindling so he could see the pages. He had a high, reedy voice with an Irish lilt to it. After all these years I can still hear Patrick reading:

Ever glorious and blessed Mary, Queen of Virgins, Mother of Mercy, hope and comfort of dejected and desolate souls, through that sword of sorrow which pierced thy heart whilst thine only Son, Jesus, our Lord, suffered death and ignominy on the cross; through that filial tenderness and pure love He had for thee, grieving in thy grief, whilst from His Cross He recommended thee to the care and protection of His beloved disciple, St. John, take pity, I beseech thee, on my poverty and necessities . . .

Between prayers Patrick would read passages from the Bible. Sometimes he would read the same verse over and over and over again, as if trying to commit it to memory. One day he was reading from the story of John the Baptist.

"*Prepare ye the way of the Lord, and make his paths straight*."

He raised his head from the page, and it seemed to me then he looked like John the Baptist, with his craggy face and scraggly beard and his hair pushed out and firelight glinting in his gaunt and red-rimmed eyes. He read the verse again.

"*Prepare ye the way of the Lord, and make his paths straight*."

He read it again.

And then again.

He must have read it ten times, until his wife ran out of patience and called at him to move on to the next verse.

By that time Patrick may have been a little demented, talking to himself as much as to God. He had a bad case of kidney stones. Sometimes he would curl into a ball and lie there in silent agony until the pain passed. Eventually he would sit up and smile like a fool and talk about the sunshine, even though a bitter wind might be howling overhead. Looking back, I can see that we were all a bit demented from the hardship and the lack of food, seeing things and hearing things. I don't think this takes away from the regularity of his devotions or from what Virginia heard, the passion in his voice that spoke to her own deep need.

With her feet frostbitten she had to crawl around the cabin. She was so weak she believed she was going to die at any moment. Each day when she woke up she did not know whether to give thanks that she was still alive or ask to be taken soon and get it over with. Two or three times, when Patrick was out of the cabin, Peggy Breen took pity on Virginia and slipped her bits of meat. Those precious morsels surely saved her life. Saved her body, that is. Something else saved her spirit.

Our family would all sleep huddled and mashed up together, holding close to mama and to one another. One of those nights is still vivid in my memory, when I heard a voice right next to me. I thought it was a dream voice. I opened my eyes in the blackness and lay still and listened, and I knew then it was Virginia, close by, kneeling on the blankets and speaking quietly.

"Please, God," she was saying. "Please send us a rescue. Please, God, send somebody to help us escape from here. Please send us a rescue. Please, God, let me see papa again, and I will be a Catholic. I promise. I will always go to Mass, and I will live a good life. Only, please send somebody to help us escape from here. Please, God. Please, God. Please."

I wondered if mama was awake to hear this too. Our family was Presbyterian, and you weren't supposed to give any kind of credit at all to the Catholics. If papa had been there to hear such statements he would have put a stop to it right then, even though part of her prayer was to see him safe and sound again. Papa's mother, who had come from Scotland and grew up in Ireland, had taught him never to trust a Catholic. Their persecution, she used to say, was what drove her to leave for America. Maybe this had something to do with why papa and Patrick never did like each other much. They were both born in Ireland, where the Protestants and the Catholics hardly ever get along. Being my father's daughter, I have to confess that I too had my suspicions, at age eight. To this day I have never set foot inside a Catholic church. But in my mind, looking back on what I heard that night in Virginia's pleading voice, it was not the Catholic part that got to her. It was the yearning toward something larger than yourself that you can put your faith in. That is the thing. Your faith needs a place to put itself. I remember envying Virginia the radiance that soon came into her eyes. Whatever she had heard in Patrick's voice gave her something to hold on to. It persuaded her that someone was out there with us, listening. After that she prayed with him every day, saying Catholic words out loud in that deep forest of pine and snow-laden Douglas fir where such words had never before been heard.

I envied Virginia then. I envy her even now, as I think back. She was fourteen and had found God and trusted Him to get her through. I was still too young to believe in something as large and vast and invisible as God. I could only believe in mama and papa and Salvador, and when mama left a second time, as she soon would do, they'd all be gone.

—PART THREE—

ANGELS

Yerba Buena

A CIVILIAN ONCE again, Jim rides alone between timbered foothills and the glassy bay. He has thrown away the buckskins he wore last summer and through the fall while they crossed from Laramie to Sutter's Fort. He wears Mexican boots, homespun trousers, a government-issue jersey shirt. His rifle hangs in its scabbard by his leg. His Spanish hat has a round, stiff brim. His dark beard and moustache are recently trimmed. A jacket is strapped behind his saddle. In the middle of the day it's too warm for a jacket. A very unwintry winter sun—a molten gold piece in the southern sky—warms his shirt, moistens his chin, makes his beard itch. He reaches up to scratch it, thinking, Strange weather.

In such uncanny warmth the place itself seems coated with a foreign light, though it should be familiar to him now. This is country the Volunteers crossed in driving rain—broad and open, with grand oaks standing singly and clumped in groves as far ahead as he can see. Their zigzag branches angle out over rolling lawns of new grass. The oldest trunks are checkered gray, with bark broken into rows and tiny blocks, like sleeves that have been shattered yet hold tightly to the trees. In front of him two elegant blacktail deer leap from an unseen gully and spring across the trail. Hawks float above the trees. Jim would like to linger here, lie back in the new grass and watch the hawks, let the sun bathe his face and neck, and ponder the mystery of flight, the mysteries of climate and unaccountable change. He cannot linger. Time is running out. Time presses down upon him and pushes from behind him like a posse on the trail of a fugitive.

Did he stay too long in San Jose? No. No, he had to stay. In the northern towns the trouble was over, yet no one knew what had happened farther south, whether Fremont's battalion had retaken Los Angeles, or had arrived at all. What if they'd stalled again for lack of horses? They had four hundred miles overland to cover. What if they'd been cut down by hordes of Mexican regulars who had landed at Santa Barbara or somewhere farther down? And if they'd lost the south, what then?

For two weeks Jim waited. By boat he sent a letter up the bay to Bill McCutcheon, hoping it would find him in Sonoma or Napa, to tell him everything depended on the outcome of the southern campaign, but if all went well they could meet again within the month.

One afternoon a courier came clopping up the Monterey road and into the plaza, an exhausted fellow who'd been riding day and night. At the courthouse moat he slid from his horse. The marines revived him with whiskey while a crowd gathered to hear his parched and jubilant voice announce that Colonel Fremont had accepted a final surrender from the rebel Californians. Los Angeles had been reoccupied. American warships controlled the harbors.

Men fired their pistols at the sky, shouting, "Hallelujah!" and "Glory be to God!" as they headed for the cantina to toast the conquest, to brag, to dream of statehood. Both north and south the insurrections had been put down. Once again the United States had full control of the ports and towns, and this time they would not let it slip away. At the long, murky bar men outdid one another drinking to a nation that soon would spread from coast to coast.

The next day Jim took his discharge from the Volunteers. He has it in writing, tucked away among the papers in his flat leather pouch. A set of keys is in there too, the elderly keys to the gate at St. Joseph's mission, presented to him by the Alcalde, who quickly granted his request to lease and work those fields.

Riding north, he nears the end of the long peninsula and stops for water at another mission, the one called Dolores, named for a stream winding toward it from the west. A salty edge is on the air. The stream winds past a cemetery and broken-down corrals, and flows on through wetlands and tules toward the Bay of San Francisco, two miles off. Jim dips his cup into the stream and drinks. He dips his canteen in and lets it fill and looks at the chapel, whitewashed adobe with a tiled roof. Round white columns frame its entry and support a fragile balustrade. Around it, sheds have fallen in. Where workers lived, the low walls are eaten away by rain and fog. The columns have a Roman look, reminding him of courthouses back in Illinois, though there is something lonesome about four Roman pillars out here in such a windswept place, something odd. To the west, beyond the chapel, two matching conical peaks stand against the sky.

A few emigrant wagons are parked near the mission. Here and there tents are pitched. Jim chats long enough to find out where they're from, what news they bring. Several are Mormons who arrived last year by ship from New York, hoping to found a new community in the far Far West. One cantankerous fellow says that with the last gobernador they had a clearcut understanding that the whole of Alta California could be theirs. He is blaming the United States for starting a war and spoiling their negotiations with Mexico.

These Mormons, Jim thinks, they are always blaming the United States, always eyeing enormous parcels of uncharted land they can lay claim to. He has heard their men take several wives at once, though why anyone would choose to do that is beyond him. They set themselves apart, call themselves "Saints." Yet this man's face doesn't shine with a purer light. His tent is just as porous as the next fellow's, his cooking pots blackened with the same soot. Jim is glad he reached Santa Clara Valley ahead of the Mormons, glad to hear this fellow say California may already be too far gone, already tainted and no longer worth his precious time.

He rides on, thinking of the Mormons, thinking of "his" valley, and of Valentine too, of the money he might have made selling horses. It would have been easy money, the first of many lucrative schemes, according to Valentine, on the night the pueblo celebrated the final conquest, when they drank together one last time. Yes, it would have been easy to scheme and laugh with him and ride out on one more escapade. Drinking with Valentine was like being single again. He drew you in, made you a comrade, made you remember an old recklessness still yearning to be let loose. But Jim looked into Valentine's blue and glittering boyish eyes and knew he had traveled far enough with a fellow who so delighted in plunder and seemed entirely untroubled by the enemies he made.

Why should Jim share the many enemies Valentine gathered in that last campaign? It is too great a risk. Someday he will return to the valley of Santa Clara and to the Mission of St. Joseph. He can't say when. But someday. The sooner, the better. He carries a piece of paper signed with the Alcalde's flourish. He carries the heavy iron keys.

Pressing his hand upon the pouch, he feels the keys outlined against his ribs.

He follows a well-worn wagon track that cuts through scattered scrub oak, tangled thickets of wild currant, gooseberry, rambling rose. He sees cattle grazing, a far-off adobe ranch house. Three miles beyond Mission Dolores he tops a hillock. Ahead of him the cove called Yerba Buena is a little crescent scooped from the inside edge of the peninsula. Thirty or forty buildings hug the crescent, upslope from a narrow beach. The slope rises toward a bare dome that protects the cove from hovering fog. There are no piers, no fortifications. From all Jim has heard, from all the talk of "imminent danger" and a head-quarters for "the Northern Department," somehow he expected more. Compared to this shoreside village, San Jose is a metropolis. A bay so broad and long, he thinks, deserves a bigger town.

Out beyond the cove, the navy ships and merchant ships and schooners rest at anchor on placid waters. From this vantage point they could be toy boats floating in a tub. Between the cove and the ridges of the farther shore, out beyond the ships, there is a rocky island capped with what looks at first like new-fallen snow. Centuries of seabirds have left their droppings, countless wild geese and pelicans and cormorants and gulls. They swarm around the island, lifting off in great flocks, landing together on white escarpments, to flap and squawk and scan for prey, and soar away again.

THE MAYOR'S OFFICE is a two-room adobe that joins one of the hotels, a block uphill from the beach. When Jim walks in, Bartlett pushes his chair back and reaches a hand across the polished desk. A wide grin lifts all the planes and angles of his carefully barbered muttonchops and handlebar moustache.

"Welcome, Mr. Reed. I've been hoping we'd meet again."

"It's good to be here at last."

"Can you beat this weather? I've never known a day in February to be so warm."

"I'm starting to think a fellow needs two sets of clothing with him, year in and year out."

"The hotel bartender says tomorrow or the next day there could be hail."

"Well, it's good to see you indoors for a change, with a bit more than an oak tree over your head."

Bartlett laughs a hearty laugh. "We did get wet, now, didn't we, Mr. Reed?"

"Not as wet as the Californians."

They both laugh. Bartlett offers Jim a chair.

"They're not as frightful as some would make them out to be, you know. During my captivity one fellow taught me to twirl a lariat."

"So you're a vaquero, too."

Bartlett's eyes glint with youthful well-being, perhaps with mischief. Above his head he turns an invisible rope. "I believe I could be, with a little practice."

He is a small man, stoutly built, with the posture of a good cadet, though he wears no navy braid or brass. He was appointed to the post last summer, when the Americans first claimed the bay. Once ashore he stored his lieutenant's uniforms and adopted the look of a prosperous banker. A tailored coat hangs over the back of his chair. He wears a ruffled shirt, a vest of maroon satin, with sleeve garters to match. He enjoys these clothes. It is like a costume. He enjoys the job. The town is small, a village, and his duties are light now that the insurrection has been put down. In the next room there are more chairs and another polished desk, where he hears cases and settles complaints from local citizens.

"You know why I'm here," Jim says.

"Indeed I do."

"The men in San Jose have forwarded a petition on my behalf."

"So I've heard. The Commandant received it yesterday."

"And he's the one I need to meet."

"I've already told him I expected to be seeing you."

"For that I am most grateful, lieutenant." Jim lifts the flaps of his leather pouch. "I have other documents, you know, that might support my plea . . ."

Bartlett waves his hands as if the room is filled with smoke. "My goodness, Reed. No more documents. I have paper enough to last me several years. Everyone knows your name by now and why you're here. Everyone knows you were with us on the plain at Santa Clara. It's just a matter of finding the best way to go about this."

"The best way?"

"We'll start with the Commandant, of course. This time of day he should be at the customhouse."

Bartlett drops his voice, glances through the door, as if an eavesdropper might be lurking. "He has a good heart, Reed. But be forewarned. He is not known for his boldness of approach. This job of mine is heaven, compared to being on board certain ships under the command of certain officers who shall remain nameless. Later on we'll retire to the hotel saloon, just you and I. We have some catching up to do."

As they step out onto the porch of the mayor's adobe, Bartlett spots the Commandant heading toward them from the beach. He has just come ashore. Jim watches him with high anticipation. For two months he's been trying to reach this man, and here he comes, plodding up the hill as if called to an appointment made long ago.

He looks to be about Jim's age, give or take a year, a lean man, tall and very thin, his neck a wrinkled tube. His cheeks are high and hollowed out. His naval jacket hangs loosely from narrow shoulders. He walks as if his shoes pinch, planting each foot, lifting it before it bends.

When he reaches them at last, Bartlett makes the introductions. The Commandant shakes Jim's hand but will not look at him for long. The weary eyes graze Jim's face and swing toward the water. He seems glad to have a reason to stand still.

"Yes. Yes," says the Commandant. "Good job, Reed. You've found us. Excellent. Excellent. As you can see, we're settling in. Bartlett here, he'll bring you up to date. He's a busy fellow. But then we're all busy, aren't we, Bartlett? Busy as beavers. At this very moment I'm on my way to the customhouse. A bit of business there. Come along, Reed. Perhaps we can find a place to sit and talk things over, though the accommodations leave a great deal to be desired. It's rustic. Exceedingly rustic. Before we dropped anchor here I had no idea what we'd be in for. The skies are lovely, as I'm sure you have observed. Those hills we see across the bay are called the *contra costa*, 'the other shore.' Last evening as the sun set, the color there was quite astonishing. Still, one sometimes feels we have arrived at the very ends of the Earth. Will you be long in Yerba Buena?"

"No longer, sir, than I have to be."

Again the Commandant glances at him. Jim sees his eyes are filled with fear, though fear of what is hard to say. It's also in his voice, a deep and practiced voice, round and resonant, yet lacking in conviction. If he speaks deeply enough—this voice seems to say—he will believe what he is saying. As the Commandant steps out across the plaza he pats his hands up and down his jacket front and upon the seat of his trousers.

"I have your petition, Reed, sent up by courier. It's in my pocket here. Or perhaps it's lying on my desk. I must say they make a case on your behalf, they surely do, some of my own officers among them, along with leading citizens of the pueblo. You evidently made a fine impression. Nonetheless, I feel compelled to say that I remain troubled by the outcome there, deeply troubled that the Mexicans got off so easily. We needed something more, as I believe my orders repeatedly conveyed. We needed a resounding victory!"

Jim would like to say, "Why weren't you there?" but holds his tongue, trying to like this man on whom his future may depend.

"Well, sir," Jim says, "they did surrender. And they did lay down their arms."

"And now they run around loose again. I see them in the streets and on the roads. Is that a victory? We need to let them know who rules the West! We should have pursued them when we had the chance. When they retreated from the field of battle, when we had them on the run, we should have seized the advantage and trimmed them down to size!"

"With all due respect, sir," says Jim, whose respect is slipping fast, "they still held seven hostages whose lives could have been at risk, Mr. Bartlett here among them."

"And they were, of course, civilians, sir," says Bartlett, "not soldiers, not regulars as we once suspected."

"I know that, Bartlett. Or so I've heard it said more than once in recent days—though all of our informants told us otherwise. We had every reason to believe that a sizable force was on its way. Nonetheless, what you say may in the end be true . . ."

The Commandant walks at a forward tilt, with hands clasped behind his waist. As he carries on some inner debate, his jaws are squeezing like a chipmunk's.

"All right, then," he says. "Let's say it's true, for the sake of argument. Let's say you have a point there. In the end perhaps it has worked out for the best. We're not butchers, after all. We are men of goodwill. There seems to be a calm across the water. Only time will tell, of course. But there it is. There it is. And we are appreciative, Mr. Reed. We are indeed, all of us, most appreciative."

They have reached the long customhouse. The Commandant stands outside a door as if he has decided to cut short this interview and must now move on to more pressing matters. With a cordial farewell smile, he extends his hand.

"Very good to have you here. With Lieutenant Bartlett, you're in excellent hands."

Jim is stunned. Is this man as foolish as he seems? He looks at Bartlett, who has placed a hand upon the door, as if to push it open, but in fact bars the way.

"About Reed's petition, sir . . ."

"Certainly. Certainly. I was getting to that." Again he pats his jacket and his hips. "I have it here about me. Or perhaps not. At any rate, I have weighed it in my mind. These things are terrible to contemplate. We have all read the story in the *California Star* . . . travelers struggling through a mountain winter, women among them, babes in arms. I sincerely wish there were something we might do on your behalf. As Commandant of the Northern Department I have certain resources at my disposal, but who is to say how long this peace will last. Are there any guarantees that these hot-blooded and inscrutable people might not rise again and wreak havoc in the towns . . ."

"I beg your pardon, sir!" says Jim, louder than he meant to speak. "You're not saying you cannot help us mount an expedition!"

The Commandant's eyes dart anxiously up and down the porch. "A month's supplies for a team of men, plus wages, and the animals required—I simply cannot authorize such a thing without the approval of the Commodore himself, as Governor General of Alta California. And he remains in San Pedro, as far as we have heard, a week's sail to the south, and even he might wonder if the Department of the Navy in Washington would honor such expenditures when our mission here is to hold the harbors in this period of adjustment and supervise the governance of the towns . . ."

To Jim's ears the sonorous and endless flow of words is like the snowfall that blocked his way back in November. He leans toward the Commandant.

"My God, man! Have you ever seen that country?"

The Commandant steps back, as if to avoid a blow.

"Eighty people are trapped up there!" Jim shouts. "My wife. My own children. They'll have beef for another month at most. At *most*, sir! And poor beef at that. We have to bring them out. I was told that the military here could lend a hand . . ."

"By whom? Who told you that?"

"Why, John Sutter himself, who has helped us in every way he could."

The Commandant relaxes. A smile plays across his thin lips, a cautious and condescending smile. "I don't believe this Sutter fellow can speak for the United States Navy."

"He knows the land. He calculates that February is the earliest time anyone could try another crossing . . ."

"As I recall, he once fought for Mexico, and may still be a citizen of Mexico. Certainly he is not an American. I am afraid, Mr. Reed, that his proposal, whatever it may have been, cannot be taken seriously."

Jim lifts the flap on his leather pouch and draws forth a sheaf of letters. In a hand quivering with anger the heavy pages rustle and scrape.

"Sir," Jim says, "I beg of you . . ."

The Commandant takes the pages and gravely leafs through a letter of discharge after honorable service with the San Jose volunteer militia, a letter of safe passage south signed by the U.S. Army officer commanding at Sutter's Fort, now renamed Fort Sacramento, a letter of guarantee signed by George Donner, leader of the wagon party, a letter of recommendation to all concerned, signed by the Governor of Illinois . . .

These documents seem to affect him in ways that spoken words do not. Into his eyes they bring a deeper fear, perhaps the fear of other letters that might find their way to Washington if the wrong decision is made today.

He glances toward the water, as if expecting some signal to appear on the mast of his ship. He seems to scan the offshore islands where seabirds swarm.

"I'm going to give this a great deal of thought. I'm going to consult with my counterpart, who commands the *Savannah*. I'll bring this to his attention at the earliest moment. He knows these waters almost as well as I. Between us I have no doubt that we can work something out.

Bear with us, Reed. I understand your concern. I admire your spirit. Believe me, I do. I most certainly do. If you'll bear with us here just a short while longer."

Jim can scarcely speak. "How much longer?"

"As I've already pointed out, these decisions are not mine alone to make. Whatever can be done *will* be done, and at the earliest moment, I assure . . ."

Jim turns to Bartlett, who does not look alarmed. He almost seems amused by these procrastinations.

"Sir," says Bartlett.

"I don't like to be interrupted!"

"My apologies, sir."

"What is it, then?"

"Another possibility has occurred to me."

"Don't just stand there. Don't keep it to yourself."

"As mayor I have the authority to call a public meeting. While the options are being considered, there might be another way, in the interim, to raise some funds."

For the first time the Commandant smiles broadly, revealing long and separated teeth. His narrow shoulders straighten.

"A public meeting?"

"We'll pass a box around."

"Splendid, Bartlett. Very good indeed."

"I believe we'll find considerable support."

"Excellent. This has my full endorsement, my full and unqualified endorsement."

He blinks as if afflicted by a speck of sand. Suddenly his eyes are moist, whether from compassion, or relief, or gratitude, it's hard to tell. "Democracy at work! And isn't that why we've come so far, by God? To bring the democratic way!"

Yet again he pats his seat, his pockets. "I'll tell you what. You put me down as the first to make a contribution. This is personal, you understand. As commandant, alas, my hands are tied. But I do wish to be kept informed. I am your ally in this enterprise. Do you follow me, gentlemen? Yes. Put me down for fifty dollars."

He opens the door—"I'll leave it to you, then"—and steps into the customhouse.

After a moment Bartlett says quietly, "Forgive me for intervening. I simply felt that time is of the essence."

"I'm glad you did. I was about to take him by the throat. But now he's given us fifty dollars. Fifty dollars!"

"And there's more to come," says Bartlett, with a grin that spreads the whiskers in his dark moustache.

Kinship

His call spreads quickly through the inns and sheds along the beach and over the dunes to the compound at Mission Dolores, and out across the water to the anchored ships. That night in the hotel saloon all the tables are crowded. Men stand shoulder to shoulder along the bar and around the shadowed edges of the room. No one remembers a gathering this size in the town of Yerba Buena, two hundred men at least, and more pushing in from outside. The chatter is high. They are drinking fast and talking fast, talking about victories and the price of land and the fate of this unfortunate wagon party lost somewhere in the Sierras, which calls forth tales of their own brushes with disease and injury and death as they made their various ways across the continent or across the Pacific or around Cape Horn.

Now Bartlett is banging on the bar with an empty bottle. He bangs until the chatter settles. He wears his tailored coat, his maroon vest. Like a bantam rooster he stands with feet planted and swelling chest.

"Gentlemen, gentlemen!" he proclaims. "It is my duty and honor to call this meeting to order."

"Good luck, your majesty," calls someone from the bar.

Bartlett lets the laughter ripple and subside.

"As I'm sure you're all aware, this is a historic occasion. The citizens of our town have never before been called upon to contribute from their own pockets to a common cause. But never before have the families of our countrymen found themselves in such dire straits. I have spoken with the Commandant, who assures me that he will do all in his power to support our efforts here tonight. And with his permission"—nodding to a nearby table—"I will read to you a most timely petition sent up by courier from the Pueblo of San Jose."

With a town crier's flourish he unfolds the document and begins to read, his voice formal, striving for dignity:

"We, the undersigned, citizens and residents of the Territory of California, beg leave respectfully to present to your Excellency the following memorial, viz: That, whereas the last detachment of emigrants have been unable to reach the frontier settlements . . ."

Everyone has heard the story. But they are willing to hear it again, eager to hear it, a tale that gains power each time it is retold. Bartlett speaks so convincingly, with such a rising fervor, the crowd gives him a round of applause. Men pound the tables and stamp their feet. Before this thunder has entirely died down, he calls upon Jim Reed to describe for them what the rescue effort will require.

Jim has been sitting at a table with the Commandant and a few others. As he stands and turns to face the room, a voice from the back calls out, "Hey, boys, I want to tell ya. Ol' Jim, now, he was with us there at Santa Clara. We rode together, Jim and me! We cut them greasers into a thousand pieces! I swear we did!"

From another table an arm swings up to clap Jim on the shoulder. "God bless you, brother. I heard about that show."

From the bar comes a shrill voice. "I was with 'em too!"

"And so were we!" cries a big marine from a table of marines who are standing with glasses raised. They call for a toast to the Battle on the Plain of Santa Clara.

"Hurrah!"

Then a toast to the fleet.

"Hurrah! Hurrah!"

And a toast to the defeat of Mexico.

"Hurrah! Hurrah! Hurrah!"

Again, Bartlett bangs the room to order. They all wait for Jim to speak.

"Thank you for this opportunity," he says at last, with a nod to Bartlett. "My thanks to all of you for coming here tonight. It touches me deeply to know that so many can find it in their hearts . . ."

He has to stop. His chest feels wrapped around with heavy rope. He stands gazing at a spot high up the farther wall, above the heads of his listeners. He waits a while, amazed by the swelling in his throat.

He tries again.

"Last fall Bill McCutcheon and myself we took a party in from this side, hoping to get across with some relief. But our horses soon were stuck in drifts above their shoulders, and I saw then what it would take to get back in there and bring the others out. As some of you may know, my own children are among them and my wife, Margaret, who . . ."

This time his throat closes. He can't go on. It is the sound of her name. He has not spoken it aloud or heard it said since day he rode away from the wagons.

Margaret.

Mar-ga-ret.

The room blurs. The syllables stick where he swallows. He sees her face. His shoulders begin to shake. His hands cover his eyes as he drops into his chair and the tears spill down.

A man sitting next to Jim leaps to his feet. He wears the black coat and round white collar of a cleric. He has the blazing eyes of an evangelist.

"Men of Yerba Buena, listen to me now! These are not the tears of a weak man who has given up in the face of difficulty. No, not that at all. Quite the contrary. Our good brother here, James Frazier Reed, has reason to weep. These are the tears of a strong and courageous American who now throws himself upon your mercy and the great generosity of your spirits so that he himself can rise up again, like Lazarus wrapped in his winding sheet, and continue the quest that brought him here tonight!"

His voice rings out. His face glows with inspiration. Some here already know him. Some do not. On the emigrant trail he was known as the Reverend, a man who moved from wagon party to wagon party, to pray at burials, bless the births, preach the Gospel. Some say he rode away as soon as he had emptied the collection plate into his own saddlebags. Others saw him as a phantom minister who appeared when needed and was gone again before the sun rose. Tonight he embellishes the story that Bartlett began to tell, the saga of the long trek west, the dreams and hazards all have shared. He speaks for Jim, as if sent from on high, though Jim does not hear these words.

He sits lost inside his embarrassment and grief, weeping for Margaret, suddenly gripped by the fear that he might never see her again in this life, weeping for his young ones too, and for all the waiting of these past few weeks, the time lost waiting, waiting, waiting. He weeps with shame for shooting Antonio's horse out from under him, and for the loss of John Snyder, poor Johnny long buried in sand by the slithering Humboldt, and for the many brave oxen who shriveled up in the sand and died of thirst. After three mugs of ale and three brandies he weeps maudlin tears of humility for this crowd of new comrades gathered around. Losses, terrors, gratitudes all fountain up and spill out to move the other men, who recognize this grief.

The Reverend's pulpit voice makes them a congregation of believers. While some wipe back tears of their own, others feel the long-lost call of home, the call of family and women left somewhere back in the States, who but for the grace of God could be out there now among the snowbound sufferers. And wrapped around the call of home is the recent news of conquests, a newfound pride in territory won. Compassion for Jim's plight swells up, along with their common sense of history in the making. For this night at least they share an urgent kinship. This land is their land. The people in the mountains are their people. While passion rises in the Reverend's voice, a hat begins to circulate. Money leaps out of pockets and into the moving hat, wrinkled bills and gold pieces clinking and glinting in the smoky saloon.

"They are all fine people," the Reverend shouts. "They are just like you and me!"

"Yes! Yes!" a man exclaims.

"God bless you, Reverend!"

"We're with you, Jim!"

"They've got some bad trouble, that's all! Now they need our help. They need volunteers to go back up there with Jim to bring 'em out. If you can't volunteer, then dig deep, brothers. Dig into your pockets. These are American families who started west to take their rightful place out here at the far side of this great continent, and by God they deserve every chance!"

"All I got is one dollar left! But here it is!"

"Here's one for Jim, and one more for a drink!"

The owner of a shipping company calls out that he will offer a launch.

The bartender calls out that the next round is on the house.

A great cry fills the saloon. The Reverend lifts Jim up and grabs him in a bear hug. Others crowd in close to shake his hand, as more upturned hats move around the room.

One by one, men come forward, half a dozen men, red-faced and teary-eyed, a deckhand, a mule skinner, a man who can pilot the launch.

"I'm with ya, Jim," another deckhand says. "Wouldn't want no young'un of mine stuck for long in a place like that."

When the coins and bills are dumped out upon a table, they make a heap that looks to be at least a thousand dollars. A committee is appointed to count it and to go around tomorrow to collect some more from anyone who might have missed this chance to invest in the future and in the common good.

In the North Wind

OVERNIGHT A PLAN takes shape. From Yerba Buena to Truckee Lake, it's about two hundred miles. With a launch donated, they can travel more than halfway by water. They will bear north and east across the bay toward the delta, then follow the Sacramento River to the mouth of the Feather, heading overland from there to Johnson's Ranch, gathering more men and horses as they go. No one has ever attempted this—traveling in wintertime from San Francisco Bay back into the Sierra Nevada Range. The clothing they can find is for sailors or for ranchers. They'll have to improvise. Another committee is formed to find and pack the goods, the mittens and long underwear and oilcloth, the tents and ropes and kerosene and flour and beans and salt pork and tobacco.

Two days later they are ready to set sail. The supplies have all been ferried out and loaded. Jim and a warehouseman are standing on the porch of a storage shed, waiting on the tide and watching the water. The day is cold. An icy wind blows out of the north, chopping up the surface of the bay.

The workman says, "Look there."

"What is it?"

"That launch beating ahead of the wind."

Jim has seen it but not seen it, just a pair of white sails half a mile out. "They're making pretty good time."

"It's curious, though."

"Why so?"

"That's Cap'n Sutter's vessel, the one goes back and forth between here and his fort. Seems like they was just here. They're not due back for another two, three weeks."

"You think there's trouble at the fort?"

"No telling. It's gonna worry some folks, if they got goods to send that aren't packed up and ready."

They watch it veer toward the cove and come to rest. The sails go slack. A boat is lowered and two men are rowing toward the beach as if pursued by killer sharks. Something in the heaving of their powerful backs gives Jim a pang of apprehension. They are not here with cargo. They bring some news he does not want to hear. With the warehouse-man he joins half a dozen others who have spied the launch and gather on the beach wrapped in heavy coats and scarves and hats and knitted caps. As the keel scrapes sand, a rower leaps out, splashing.

"Any of you the Commandant?" he shouts. "I got a letter for the Commandant."

They crowd in close.

"What's up?"

"What's the news?"

He tries to break past them, but they bar his way.

"Captain Sutter needs men," he says, with great importance. "Them folks stuck back in the mountains all this time, some of 'em have made it through."

Jim's heart begins to pound. "What's this? What's this you say?"

"Captain Sutter wants to bring out the others."

"Who made it through?"

"Ain't my place to tell it," the fellow says.

"My God, man!" Jim shouts. "How many?"

"This letter's for the Commandant!"

He shoulders past them, heading up the slope with men beside him and behind him, yammering, tossing questions back and forth among themselves, while others step out of shops and inns and boarding-houses to tag along, breathing steam and slapping arms against their sides as they climb.

Hearing this clamor rise toward him, the Commandant has stepped out onto his porch. The sailor with the message doffs his cap and passes across to him a packet, which the Commandant receives and steps back inside and shuts the door.

The sailor is surrounded by men with urgent questions, Jim fore-most among them. "Who made it through?" he demands. "Where are they now?"

The sailor doesn't know where to begin. Something happened at

Johnson's Ranch. A rescue party is forming up. Most of all he'd like a drink. Doesn't anybody have a drink?

Someone produces a small flask. As the sailor tips it for a swallow, the Commandant's door swings open. An orderly rushes out, pushing past the crowd. They watch him sprint across the plaza to the mayor's adobe. A moment later Bartlett appears, pulling on his coat against the February wind. As he passes the waiting men he says, "G'morning, gents."

Jim calls, "What the hell is going on?"

"We'll soon find out."

Now they murmur among themselves, stamp their feet and speculate, but Jim can't bear the waiting. "Goddam!" he says. "I'm going in there!"

He mounts the steps, has his hand upon the door, when it opens once again and there stands Bartlett. His young eyes are wide and fixed, as if he has just witnessed an execution. In his hand he holds a sheaf of paper. To Jim and to the suddenly quiet crowd he says, "All of you should hear this."

They follow Bartlett through the wind and into the hotel saloon, where they spread out among the tables. He stands by the bar, gazing at the first page, as if to be sure he has the gist of it. His eyes move, but nothing else, neither face nor hands. He stands so still he seems to be holding his breath.

Slowly he begins to read aloud the story of a small party that set out two months ago and more. Fifteen had started for the pass, ten men, five women. Jim listens to the names, listens for Margaret's name, for Patty's, Virginia's. He doesn't hear them and wishes Bartlett would go through the list again. Then he's glad he didn't hear the names. Only seven of the fifteen have survived, among them Mac's wife, Amanda, and William Eddy, who made it down to Johnson's, where he dictated this account of their grueling ordeal.

It was a trip, the letter says, "impelled by the scarcity of provisions at the cabins." They had hoped the crossing would take a week. It took a month. During most of that time they were hopelessly lost, penned in by blizzards, with no shelter, and almost no food. The first to go was Charlie Stanton, left behind to die alone. Before long half a dozen others died, Uncle Billy Graves, the Indians Salvador and Luis. At last the survivors resorted to the unthinkable . . .

Bartlett's voice dwindles, then stops, as if the handwriting here might be hard to decipher. When he reads again he's nearly whispering.

In the afternoon of this day they succeeded in getting a fire into a dry pine tree. Having been four entire days without food, and since the month of October on short allowance, there was now but two alternatives left them—either to die, or to preserve life by eating the bodies of the dead. Slowly and reluctantly they adopted the latter alternative. On the 27th they took the flesh from the bodies of the dead; and on that and the two following days they remained in camp drying the meat and preparing to pursue their journey . . .

Bartlett's voice breaks. For a while the room is silent. Into the silence Jim says hoarsely, "You mean they ate the flesh?"

"That's what's in the letter, Jim."

"Each other's flesh?"

"According to this fellow, Eddy."

"I know William Eddy."

"His word is all we have to go by," Bartlett says.

"And you say Uncle Billy Graves . . ."

"A Graves is mentioned, yes."

"Eaten?"

"Evidently, Jim. I know what it must be like . . ."

He can't listen to the rest. He rushes to the door, onto the hotel's verandah, where he stands in the wind gazing out across restless water toward the hills, the *contra costa,* his mind roaming farther east, across the wide valley, into the distant snow.

Charlie Stanton dead.

Uncle Billy, dead and eaten.

The man who would have hung him—gone. Consumed. His flesh jerked and dried for travel like a side of beef.

What savagery is this? And what else is there to know? By mid-December they were nearly out of food. What happened to the cattle? How could they run short of beef so soon? If eight of fifteen perished on the way, what then of the others? What hope is there for those they left behind?

He cannot think of it. Not now. He dares not think of it. The only questions he dares to ask himself are How to get there, What's the fastest way, and What to carry? He needs a plan. A sharper, cleaner, clearer plan.

At least he knows now where they are. Some have cabins. Some do not. From what the letter says, we'll need warmer clothing. More men. More food to cache along the way, and more to feed the stranded ones for the trek out. We'll need more of everything. Can one schooner carry it all? If we overload the schooner, it could take weeks to reach the fort, given the season and the rains and what he's heard about the currents during flood time. Suppose we split the expedition, then. Suppose we send all supplies by water, while the rest of us cross the bay and travel overland. Yes. Yes, two parties head north and east. One by water. One by land. In his mind it is like a battle campaign. A two-pronged assault. The enemy is altitude, and snow. Meanwhile, if it's true that a team is forming up at Sutter's, how much will they know about the high country? Will they wait for word of support from Yerba Buena? Or press on and hope for reinforcements? That is the essential part. Reinforcements . . .

At the edge of his vision a patch of blue is moving toward him. The Commandant strives against the wind, so skeletal and sticklike he can hardly stay upright. He staggers like a man who has been shot, but with a stoic determination. Miraculously he keeps his footing and arrives at the steps to the hotel. Holding to the banister as to the railing of a storm-tossed ship, he pulls himself up onto the verandah, where he stands apart from Jim until he gets his breath.

"You all right, sir?" says Jim.

"Fine, thank you, yes . . . very fine indeed. . . . Just on my way . . . to the gathering here."

Jim watches him breathe in long, asthmatic breaths, wondering what has sent him out into the wind, wondering what he can say to change the Commandant's mind. How can Jim get through to this frail and fearful man who holds the keys to the cash box and storage sheds?

As it turns out, the man needs no more persuading. For fifteen minutes he has been brooding at his desk. His breathing is steady now. Above scooped-out cheeks, the sunken eyes have filled with heat.

"That letter, Mr. Reed, I have to tell you . . . what those wretches have endured, it penetrates the very soul." His voice is low and guttural and muted by the wind. "Every exploring party comes back with horrendous tales, and I have heard them all. But when women and children are driven to such extremes . . . a daughter driven to eat of her own father's flesh . . . it is beyond imagining. By all the hosts of heaven, I swear that you men shall have whatever can be provided by this command, all necessary rations, clothing, any manner of pack equipment, whatever funds I have at my disposal . . ."

Jim grabs his hand. "Thank you, sir. That's splendid news!"

The phlegm-filled voice drops lower still, as if they stand here by design, the two of them alone upon the porch to share some confidence.

"No need to thank me, Reed. In times like this, what else is there for a man to do? We are not made of stone here in Yerba Buena. I have children of my own, you know. A grandchild, too, or so I'm told. Though I may be surrounded with louts and braggarts, the suffering of children is not lost on me. No. Not for a moment. I swear to you, this effort will be carried forward under the full authority of the Northern Department. In this particular matter, I have not consulted my counterpart, since he is secluded on board his ship. Do you see it there? Anchored farthest out? He claims to be indisposed and has sent word not to be disturbed until evening. Just between you and me, it's John Barleycorn he contends with, more than any of the hazards of the corporeal world the rest of us inhabit. This time he will have to live with my decision. Yes, and the Commodore too, wherever he may be. They can both be damned if they do not support me in this, though I believe they will. I do believe they will. Any man would, in such circumstances. Good God, Reed, what an insufferable situation for us all. Step inside with me now, while I transmit these thoughts to Bartlett and the others. And please rest assured. You have my word, as a man, and as a naval officer . . . you have my solemn word."

Homeward Bound

THE SKIES ABOVE the bay grow heavy, gray as lead. Hour by hour the moisture gathers, the impending rain. Another night passes. Another day.

In a silvery morning light two vessels sail out of Yerba Buena cove. Sutter's launch, the *Sacramento,* is loaded with tenting and beans, thick blankets and guernsey shirts, woolen stockings, frying pans, camp kettles, coils of line. Crates of rations have been transferred from the fleet's stores, enough to feed ten men for twenty days. Beside it a smaller schooner ferries Jim and a crew and three more volunteers who signed on once they knew the payroll was guaranteed. For a while they hold the same course, past White Island, sometimes called Alcatraz, for the pelicans that rest and hover, past Angel Island, on past the point called Tiburon, named for sharks seen cruising there.

They pass between jutting peninsulas and into the northern bulge of water called the Bay of San Pablo. The juttings seem to close behind them, as if they're on a landlocked lake, and the hills above Yerba Buena are out of sight. Here the cargo vessel heads east, toward the delta, while Jim and his crew bear due north toward the mouth of Sonoma Creek. It's drizzling now, a pelting drizzle that feels like sleet in the hard wind across the water.

An incoming tide helps them guide upstream, winding through marshland, miles of tule and grassy sloughs. At one edge of a puddle-dotted mudflat, gulls with folded wings hunker against the wind. On both sides of the creek, close-packed tule stalks lean like fields of wheat.

By the time they reach the little wharf, *el embarcadero,* they have left the wind behind. They hire two carts to haul their packs and weapons and foodstuffs, and in a spattering rain walk the last four miles to Sonoma, which sits at the base of a round and green-skinned mountain. Olive trees grow here. Grapevines hang from the balconies of well-kept adobes. There is another mission chapel, white and stark, though not as white as the heap of cattle bones and longhorn skulls in the plaza, made whiter by the downpour that now begins as the clouds release their burden, a straight-down rain that promises to fall for days.

Above the bones, the Stars and Stripes hangs damply from a high pole in the center of the plaza of the last town in Alta California. The adobe barracks were built to house the troops defending Mexico's most northerly frontier. Now they house the U.S. garrison. A lieutenant in charge is pleased to see an order from the Commandant instructing him to turn over ten horses with their saddles and all necessary gear. He is happy to have something to do. He wants to help. He too has heard the latest news. The story of the Snowshoe Party's fate has leapfrogged across the land, from rider to rider, from wagon to wagon, from ranch to ranch.

This lieutenant is friendly with Bill McCutcheon and believes he saw him an hour ago at a blacksmith's shop right down the road. "He's talked about you, Mr. Reed."

Jim finds him shoeing a horse, his huge frame hunched above the upturned hoof. With precise taps, firm but gentle, he drives the nail. Jim waits until Mac looks up, until the face opens in a broad and eager grin.

"My goodness, Jim! Why didn't you say something?"

"Always a pleasure to watch a talented man at work."

"You're about a month late, you know."

"I got here about as quick as I could. There's four men with me."

"Well, I got five."

His face has filled out. He has put on weight. His cheeks are pink, no longer from malaria but from a bursting health. Jim can see there is no fever in his body now, nor in his eyes, though the eyes are burdened in another way. No need to ask how much Mac knows, or if he knows his Amanda is among those who made it out. Nor is there any need to mention what they say she and others had to do to stay alive. All this is in his face. And yet whatever Mac knows has not defeated him. He has his health back now, his full strength. Jim can feel it in his arms when Mac takes him in a bear hug. Holding him like a long-lost brother, Jim remembers why he trusts this large and self-effacing man. Mac has a power of limb that takes on every task with relish and also with a sense of duty, a sense of honor. Since Jim left Valentine behind, honor has been on his mind, and what it means to ride with someone you can trust. The trouble with Valentine is not his posturing, it's his lack of honor. What a relief to be in Mac's company again. Jim realizes he would trust his life with this man.

When they set out the next morning, he feels on track at last, heading in the right direction. Jim is like the lonely sailor in a foreign port who runs into a fellow from his own hometown. With Mac at his side, some wide loop comes round upon itself. Though many show compassion for those caught in the mountains, no one truly knows what Jim left behind, no one but Mac, who also has a family waiting. It is odd. By the time they reached the Humboldt, Jim had come to loathe the wagon party and all its petty factions. Now, though he dreads what he may find, there is a sense of finally heading back to where he belongs.

MAC WAS THREE weeks at Sutter's, sweating through the fever one last time. Since crossing to Sonoma he has not rested, working for room and board with a local rancher and roaming all the valleys up this way, looking for recruits. Just a week ago a local citizens' committee set aside some cash to go toward wages. As Jim and Mac push north and east, the knowledge of their coming flies in front of them, like an invisible messenger.

In Napa there is a miller from Missouri who says he has dreamed of people waiting by a frozen lake. In this dream a tall woman is surrounded by her hungry children, and over them looms a perpendicular wall of rock. He has also dreamed of a man riding up to his ranch house on a mission to rescue these same stranded ones. The miller welcomes Jim with wonder and humility and offers him provisions already set aside and waiting.

"I told my wife you'd be here," says the miller, as if speaking to a saint. "And now you've come."

They pick up four men and some spare horses and move farther east, climbing through wooded foothills into a tangle of gulches and arroyos jagged with upthrust granite slabs. The trail is slippery, as it drops into a creek canyon, with damp oak groves where moss hangs in clumps from barren limbs otherwise stripped for winter. Rocky walls hold back the rain. For a while the clouds above are white as cotton shirts, and the riders pass through a luminous, dripping fog laced with shrouds and tendrils of toplit moss.

Where the creek widens, the canyon opens out to a valley puddled everywhere, slick with grassy mudflats. They find the outpost of another rancher, who also says he has been expecting them, though he won't say why. They spend the night and leave early with another mule, another horse. A day's ride north, in the next valley, they find a family Jim knew on the trail last summer huddled inside a new log cabin, caulking holes where the rain trickles in, watching their newly claimed acreage turn to muck. They've had no company in months. Jim brings them their first news of the southern campaign. Here more horses join the party and a couple of men who would like somehow to celebrate the conquest and would rather ride for pay than sit here soaking.

A swollen creek flows past the cabin, spilling into the valley of the Sacramento, sometimes called the Great Valley, where Jim and his party again bear north and east, riding hard to make the rendezvous. Their foe now is water, falling from the sky, filling up every low spot and marshy field in the wide, wet expanse before them. No hills to climb, no rises or promontories. What had looked to him like a sculpted park when he descended out of the Sierras last October, has become an endless slough. While it drenches them from above, the water is sometimes halfway up the legs of their horses, sometimes to the bellies. They splash through bogs and mudholes, seventeen men and forty animals, and come at last to the banks of the surging confluence of all the creeks and rivers that channel water from the mountain ranges east and west to make the broad stream that divides the valley.

Jungles of bare-limbed trees line both banks. Where the river bends to make a natural cove in the high embankment, an American rancher has cleared the brush back and built a dock. The cargo vessel was to meet them here and ferry them across. But no vessel is waiting. The dock is almost submerged. The river seems to be two hundred yards across, a brown flood slick with patches of chocolate sheen.

The river is so long and full there's no place to ford. Jim and Mac look out across the water. Half a day from Johnson's now, and they can't get to it.

"Lord have mercy," says Mac.

"What a mess. Worst mess I've ever seen."

"Now what?"

"I guess we wait."

"For how long?"

"They were supposed to be by here yesterday."

"You think they've come and gone?"

"They wouldn't do that."

"Damn, Jim, we have to get across."

"We'll send a couple of men down toward Sutter's to see if they've been heard from."

"We still have to get across."

"Hell, Mac, we all know that. Can you walk on water? Just go on out there and show us how."

"I can walk on water. If I take a mind to. It's all the rest of you will need the boats."

"That's right. If those boys don't show up, we might have to build ourselves some kind of boat."

"We built rafts a time or two, coming across the plains. I guess I could build a boat."

"There's fellas with us that have built hide boats."

"Damn that schooner for being late."

"It's no wonder," Jim says. "Look how that current moves."

He gazes downstream. In water like this the cargo vessel could still be fifty miles away. How long should they wait? Every day is crucial now. Every hour. Should they try to cross and keep on going? Suppose they made it to the other side? What then? Why press on without all that cargo so carefully assembled, the salt pork, the flour, the long underwear, the oilcloth . . . ?

Well back from the rising flow they make camp, giving thanks that the rain has stopped. From the rancher's shed they scavenge some dry wood to start a fire. In a marshy flat half a mile away a herd of elk stand grazing in the gray light of late afternoon. The hunters go out with rifles and bring back two, strip off the hides and butcher the carcasses. While they work, the sky begins to open for the first time in days, just a slit to let the sun through. Lifted entrails gleam in the unexpected light, and spirits rise at the prospect of fresh meat for dinner.

Watching their thick steaks turn and sizzle, they talk about building boats, how to take limbs off these trees along the bank and tie elk hides to the frame, whether or not you can pole across a river such as this, how to move the horses. They believe that they can do it, and their belief eases Jim's burden of decision.

"By God, boys," he says, "you are a breed apart. These deeds will not be forgotten."

"We ain't done 'er yet, cap'n," one fellow says. "Better wait to see who sinks and who swims out there."

A few men laugh. Jim reaches into his saddlebag and withdraws two quarts of aguardiente.

"Don't know about you, but I could use a snort. We been riding pretty hard."

"Why, cap'n," the fellow says, "you found those bottles just in time."

There's low laughter and muttered jokes as the bottles circulate. After a couple of sips Mac stands up, massive above the others, feeling the drink's first rush.

"I got to tell you boys something while it's on my mind. My woman is over there at Johnson's, hardly any ways at all now. But our baby girl, far as I know she's still up there at the lake. When we set out last spring she wasn't much past one year old. I figured we'd be settled in somewhere long before this, ya see. I always figured she'd have her second birthday out here in California. Now it's coming up again and I guess I want to make sure she gets this little geegaw I picked up at Sutter's some time back. That's why I got to get across this here river. And God's gonna help us do it, too. You hear me now?"

He takes in the circle of faces gathered by the fire, then reaches inside his coat and from its pocket draws the tiny wooden whistle made smaller and more childlike in his calloused hand. It dangles from a rawhide thong. The men regard it with a kind of awe, as if Mac is an illusionist who produced this curiosity out of thin air. They watch him lift the whistle to his lips and blow, and they listen to the high, plaintive penetrating call that drifts out across the puddled marshlands.

No one can speak. The men are embarrassed by this naked show of sentiment and the place inside each of them awakened by the lonesome note. It is dusk. High clouds to the west are edged with purple-pink that tints the river, the myriad ponds and water holes. It tints the bearded faces, adding to the spell.

Mac too seems embarrassed by the mood he has created. He puts away the whistle and looks around again. As if to ward off the whistle's call, he extends his hands, palms out, and tilts his head back, facing the sky.

In a loud and overly theatrical voice he intones, "I come not, friends, to steal away your hearts. I am no orator, as Brutus is . . ."

"Aw shit, Mac," one man calls out, "don't start that tonight."

The big voice rises. "But as you know me all, a plain, blunt man what loves my friend . . ."

"Plain and blunt," says someone else. "You got that part right."

He is bellowing now. "For I have neither wit nor words nor worth, action nor utterance, nor the power of speech . . ."

They are all grateful for this absurd display, for the chance to spend their feelings some other way. They throw their hats at him. They throw small sticks and tell him to sit down.

"Ol' Mac, he missed his calling."

"Yes, sir, he should've stayed in St. Louis, where they love his kind a talk."

"If he was a horse I'd shoot him."

"It's this rotgut done it to him. He can't have no more."

"Fie on thee," says Mac with a bashful grin, satisfied, reaching for the bottle. "Fie, fie, I say. A pox then on all your houses."

THAT NIGHT COLD stars are sprinkled across the heavens. Next morning the skies are blue again, and Mac's prediction has come true. A schooner is moored to the rancher's dock. To Jim, at first, it is an apparition, a dream boat, too good to be real. In brown eddies it sways, as if sent from heaven, or from wherever reside the powers watching over this journey. It is a cargo vessel, broad-decked, with a shallow draft, but not the one they expected. It belongs to a pilot who works the river between this ranch and the fort, or so he says.

He, too, could be an apparition, a river-spirit or a river-angel. He wears an oilcloth slicker, a skipper's cap. Strands of black hair fall below the cap to stripe his forehead and his cheeks. In the bright, dry light of morning he looks wet, as if he might have risen from underwater to take his place upon this empty deck. Jim feels compelled to test him.

"Where'd you come from?"

"Downriver."

"In the middle of the night?"

"I near quit trying. Then the wind turned. When the wind turns, you better take it. There was enough light left. I come on up."

Jim tells him they're waiting on the *Sacramento,* and the pilot nods. "Yesterday she was down below Sutter's. Been bucking that headwind for days and days."

"You think she'll come ahead?"

"I wouldn't if I didn't have to. With all you say they're hauling. I'd dock at Sutter's, unload there, and come ahead with animals."

"That's what I'd do, too," says Jim.

This pilot has heard of the seven who hiked out of the mountains in the dead of winter. He has heard of one fellow's solitary trek, hiking the last six miles by himself. With reverence he says, "The way the folks at Johnson's found all the others was by following his bloody tracks back up into the woods, six or seven miles of blood, they say. His boots had give out. He had rags wrapped around his feet, and the rags had rotted off. Imagine being frostbit and near starved to death and hiking six miles across the snow and the rocks, leaving bloody footprints every step of the way."

Plying up and down the river the pilot has heard of the rescue plans and of another party forming up. He's heard they left the fort two weeks ago. "I could of gone. Lord knows, I could use the money. But I don't like to leave the river. Some folks say the dampness can harm your lungs. I don't mind. I like things damp."

"How about taking us across, then?" says Jim. "What'd be your fee?"

"How many?"

"Two of us to start. With two horses."

The pilot smoothes the dark strands gleaming against his temples and looks at Jim with a cryptic grin. "I wouldn't charge you much. Probably nothing. I want to do my part."

"God bless you, friend."

In rocking backwaters his narrow, splintered gangplank scrapes the dock. The horses are skittish, climbing aboard. They don't like this at all. Jim and Mac have to tease them and talk them into it and rein them to the masts, where they pull their heads against the reins. Jim and Mac are crossing first and hope to be at Johnson's when the cargo team arrives. The others will kill a few more elk, build the hide boats, catch up when they can, some via the pilot's schooner, if he'll agree to come back and make this trip again. He won't say yes to this, and he won't say no.

Jim stands flat-footed on the deck, one hand on his horse's neck, his mouth close to the ear, murmuring, while he ponders how long it will take to move forty more animals across this flow and these fifteen men with packs and saddles. He wonders how you can pay them enough to do such things as they have done and have yet to do. Three dollars per day? Why would they do it at all? Jim could not blame them if they watched this vessel till it touched the farther side then turned around and rode on back to their wagons and their ranches.

Three Fathers

The sacramento flows on south to the delta, and the Feather River is a brown flood pouring into the Sacramento, and the Bear River dumps into the Feather, spilling down out of the foothills from a thousand rivulets and capillary trickles. As Jim and Mac follow the Bear eastward, all the fields and trails are made of mud. But the skies stay clear, rinsed clean by rain. It is warming up again, an improbable warmth, given what they can see in the far distance, the first smooth ridges and then, as from another world, as if rising from a continent unconnected to their own—snowcapped peaks against a sky of purest blue.

At Johnson's Ranch early grass has spread a gray-green skin across the slopes. A room has been added to the small adobe. Three naked Indian men are working on a new corral, lashing limbs to thick oak posts. They watch the riders pass but make no gesture and do not speak. Jim sees a couple of wagons standing under the trees, a few tents, some rough-hewn shacks that weren't here in November, half canvas, half logs. Drying clothes are spread upon the grass and hung from limbs. The shirts and trousers accentuate the quiet, as if they were hung out here and then abandoned.

Beyond the house they see a man sitting on the ground with his back against a felled tree, sitting very still. His hat is in his lap, his chin upon his chest. They dismount and walk over there and see that it is William Eddy with legs outstretched, sunning his bare feet. Streaked with scars and unhealed welts, they still look raw and mauled, as if Eddy had been kicking at an angry bear.

Jim says, "Hey, Bill."

The head lifts. He is instantly awake, blinking. "Where you boys been?" says Eddy, as if he last saw them yesterday instead of four months ago.

"Riding our tails off looking for you," Jim says.

"I been right here, just airing my feet."

"You could win a contest," Mac says, "with feet like that."

Eddy has lost a couple of teeth. The freezing nights he lived through still show in his cheeks. They look stiff, chiseled, rough as granite now, breaking into pieces when he smiles an oddly hopeful smile.

"They make a pretty sight, don't you think?"

Trying not to look at his mangled feet, Jim and Mac sit down on the trunk and watch the Indians lift a thick limb into place.

He's been expecting them, he says, though he wonders what they're trying to do. The rescue party is long gone. Two men alone shouldn't be going up in there.

"We're waiting for some others," Jim says, telling him then of the provisions and clothing coming from the fort, and of the men and animals now crossing the Sacramento.

"Once we get to the lake, we'll keep some to ride. We'll slaughter some for meat."

With a wistful grin Eddy shakes his head. "Horses can't make it through that snow, Jim. Rescue party had to send home every one."

"They're all on foot?"

"Yessir. I would be too. But I had to ride back with the horses. I guess I wasn't ready to walk that country one more time."

He wiggles his toes and winces and looks at them expectantly, seems about to continue, then falls silent.

Mac says, "We heard some of what happened."

"You haven't heard it all."

Again Eddy seems to have more to say. But he doesn't say it.

"How about the others," Mac says, "that come out when you did?"

"Some of 'em moved on down to Sutter's."

"My wife, Amanda . . ."

"All the women moved on down."

"But I guess she left Harriet at the lake," Mac says.

"The Graveses kept Harriet," says Eddy. "And it's a good thing too. Where we went, no baby could have lasted a week."

"Amanda, then . . . is she . . . all right?"

"None of us could walk nor stand up when we first come in. But we got some weight back, thanks to Johnson. She was one of 'em rode down to Sutter's. There's more beds, more women around. She's one hell of a woman, Mac, that's all I got to say." Eddy's voice catches. Sudden moisture glistens in his eyes. He turns away, blinking. "You're a lucky man, Mac . . . a mighty lucky man."

Lucky she's alive, he means. Lucky she's on this side of the summit now, out of harm's way. Eddy doesn't know what else to say, or how to say it, cannot bring himself to speak of his own wife, Eleanor, and their two young ones, still holed up at the lake camp, or speak of how he joined the rescue party when his feet burned and screamed with every step and wept when he had to turn around. None of them know what to say, or where to start describing what they've seen since Mac and Charlie Stanton left so long ago to ride across Nevada in search of food, since Jim left the party at the Humboldt with his scalp wounds seeping through the bandages. Each man has left a family and come through these mountains and tried to rejoin them and been turned back. Three husbands, three fathers, meet again at Johnson's Ranch and sit here thinking things they cannot speak, Mac yearning to ride down to Sutter's and join his wife and knowing he can't, not while Harriet is on the other side, and Jim envying Mac, wishing Margaret were now at Sutter's, yet how lucky would he feel knowing she too had eaten of another's flesh, had eaten Uncle Billy's flesh? Maybe it's a blessing that she stayed behind. He looks at Eddy's feet, thinking of the flesh he had to eat to stay alive, and wonders how a man can do that and then just sit here in the sun.

As if Jim has been speaking these thoughts aloud, Eddy says, "Margaret told me whenever I caught up with you to tell you not to worry, that they would make it through no matter what, but to come back as quick as you can. She said the children love you and pray for you every day . . ."

"Did they have enough to eat?"

"That's why we had to come out, Jim. It was gettin' skimpy."

"But they were warm?"

"They had a cabin. Charlie helped 'em raise it, and them redskins. Stayed there too, as far as I could tell. After we all left, I guess Margaret and your young'uns had it pretty much to themselves. You remember those two came up from Sutter's."

"I do."

"Salvador and Luis?"

"I met 'em on the trail."

"Well, now, by God, poor Charlie's gone. And them redskins too."

He stops and touches his chest, takes a deep breath as if his lungs are failing him, and expels the air. "I tell ya, boys, when we set out, I never once imagined it would end up this way . . ."

Again they wait for Eddy to continue. He breathes a while. Then one by one the stories come, the desert crossing, the glad arrival of Charlie and the Indians, how William Foster shot and killed his brother-in-law, how some cattle were picked off by the desert tribes and others were lost in the first storms by the lake, and how fifteen of the strongest left the lake in mid-December.

"After the summit it was twelve foot of snow, and we were doing all right, making five, six miles a day. But the sun come out, and up that high the snow's so bright it blinded every one of us for a day. Poor Charlie, he never did get his vision back. He stayed blind, and that's when we took the wrong route and had to leave Charlie behind. Pluckiest fella I ever knew, and he just gave out. He couldn't see. He couldn't walk. Rest of us, we could hardly keep ourselves from falling over. We had to leave him, Jim, it grieved me to do it. It grieves me still and will grieve me to my dying breath. We wandered up there for I don't know how long, days went by, everybody getting crazy from the hunger and the cold. There was blizzards that went on and on and we had nothing but our blankets. We ran clean out of food and did some awful things. We all did. But I swear, the worst was what Bill Foster did, toward the end, when we'd eat up our shoelaces and every last scrap of rawhide . . ."

Jim waits, finally says, "What was it? What did Foster do?"

"Well, Jim, he shot them redskins."

"Shot them how?"

"They must've stole something," Mac says. "Redskins'll steal you blind."

Eddy shakes his head. "There wasn't nothing any of us had worth stealing. I tried to talk him out of it. He was too far gone. For a while there I believe he just plumb lost his mind . . ."

"Was there any kind of fight?" Jim says.

"They were too weak to fight. Everybody was so weak I guess ol' Foster he figured we were all goners unless somebody could give up their life. It was ugly seeing what hunger will drive you to, watching each other day and night, wondering who will be the next to go. That's when he started yelling about shooting somebody for food. Any one of the women would have suited him fine. We talked him out of that. When the redskins got wind of what he had in mind they took off by themselves. I figured we'd never see them two again. But they couldn't get that far. Next day we come up on their trail, the bloody prints and all, and Foster went after 'em with his rifle."

"And you say he went alone," Jim says.

"That's right. He went after 'em. And then I heard the shots. I'll never forget that sound. Pretty soon he come back saying we had meat and come help him cut up the bodies. I couldn't do it. I could still hear them shots ringing through the woods. I'll always hear 'em . . ."

"Charlie spoke well of those fellows," Jim says.

"I never touched that flesh, boys, I swear to you. I am ashamed to say I ate off Uncle Billy, and I ate off Pat Dolan, after they had froze to death, God rest their souls. I'd have sooner starved than eat off them redskins who had stuck with us that far, when they had no reason to at all and could have lit out just about anytime they cared to and made it on their own. Weren't for them and Charlie, a whole lot more people would have fallen by the wayside a whole lot sooner . . ."

While Eddy talks, Jim imagines Charlie Stanton propped against a tree in a snowbank blinking at the glare. He sees Uncle Billy's burdened eyes, the last time they spoke, beside the blue and silent Humboldt. He sees Salvador and Luis as he saw them standing by their mules in Bear Valley, quiet, patient men, watching, watching in the bright autumn sun. If their people get word of this, he thinks, it might mean a whole other kind of trouble. Indian trouble is the last thing we need. He wags his head, heartsick, bewildered. How . . . how . . . how could things go so far wrong?

By the fallen tree they sit into the afternoon, waiting for the other men. Waiting for Johnson. Bill Eddy talks, and Jim sees again the day they stood together in the desert sand with weapons drawn, facing his accusers. He wishes he had that day back. He aches to have it back. He hears Margaret's voice again, telling him to ride away. He hears it loud and knows now that he should not have listened. He should have stayed. If he had stayed they could have made it through before the snows—this is what he imagines. Yes, he should have stood his ground. Those men who wanted to hang him, weren't they bluffing, after all? They are not killers, as Margaret feared, any more than he himself. Though he has killed a man, he is not a killer. Eddy here, he already knew the knife was drawn in self-defense. A few more days, the others would have come around. He should have stayed and waited them out. They would of course have talked about the stabbing, as Bill Eddy here has surely talked about it more than once, being a talker, a man who'll talk your arm off when he's in the mood. Jim has brooded over how their stories are going to sound, although by now the eyes that saw the stabbing have seen things far worse. Far, far worse. Take Uncle Billy, who cried so loud for vengeance—what did his eyes see before they closed forever?

That showdown by the Humboldt, it is an ancient drama from another land, so close, yet so far away. As he plays those days against the dark news Bill Eddy brings, the squabbles that divided them seem lacking in all substance. Out in the desert, men and women faulted Jim for veering south of Salt Lake, as if they themselves were held at gunpoint and forced to follow him. And there's another day he wishes he could live again, when they gathered at the Little Sandy to decide which route was best. He has met men with families who headed north that day, along the proven route, who made it through ahead of the snow, ahead of the rain. How he wishes he had joined them. He hears the voice of the Mountain Man from the Wyoming campfire last July.

I'd take the Fort Hall route and never leave it. That way you're sure to get there. And isn't getting there the main idea?

He's learned something none of them could have known back then. Lansford Hastings is no prophet, no one to lead you anywhere, just another enterprising rascal who got here earlier than most. Old-timers laugh at the mention of his book, wag their heads and say he ought to be ashamed, feeding people such extravagance. Everyone seems to know he has land along the Sacramento, with a town laid out where towns have never been. The more folks he can persuade to travel, the faster those lots will sell. That's why Hastings wrote his book, they say, and Jim berates himself for ever listening to such a charlatan, heading out across an untried route where wagons had never gone. He takes the blame for that day too and hears the truth of the accusing voices.

You're the one got us into this mess.
You've cast a shadow over the wagon party, Reed.
You're the one deserves a whipping . . .

What folly! He sees it now. And yet, why should he fault himself alone. Didn't the company take a vote? All agreed to share the risk. The Donners. The Breens. The Murphy clan. Keseberg. Eddy too. And Mac. And Charlie Stanton from Chicago with his derby hat and his burgher's paunch, now left in the snow to freeze and surely be devoured by wolves. . . . In times like these, who is to blame for what? Whose foolishness is more regrettable? Whose pride? Whose fear? Whose hunger? How do you weigh one grievous act against another and say this is worse than that, or more deserving of revenge?

AS THE SUN nears the treetops, the air cools fast. Eddy reaches for his boots. It pains him to pull them up around his welts and scars. It takes a long time, and he refuses help. With a broken grin he says, "I need me some moccasins."

His body has been shattered, but his spirit is intact. Jim wishes he had ten men like him for the trek back across the mountains, wishes Eddy could join them now, but knows he can't, not yet.

A Web-footed Caravan

JOHNSON THE RANCHER appears at dusk, riding with two Indian vaqueros. He is a bandy-legged horseman, uneasy in the saddle, glad to have a reason to dismount, to embrace these returning comrades. The ruined felt hat still looks as if his horse has been chewing on it. Tobacco has stained his red beard and moustache the color of mahogany. There is brandy on his breath and the aroma of a rotting tooth. But he is not the same. Something about these survivors who staggered out of the high country has shocked him and softened him.

"Toughest people I have ever personally known or heard of," he tells them, his eyes warm with pity and admiration.

The welfare of the stranded ones obsesses Johnson now. He says he wouldn't wait for whatever's coming up from the fort. Time has run out. He has cattle here. "As many as you boys need. You tell me. Flour, too. You got the guts to head back in there one more time, I'll give you anything you want."

When the first rescue party started out two weeks ago, he tells them, there were fourteen men on horseback and a string of pack animals. Next thing he knew, Billy Eddy and another fellow came back with all the horses. Two others stayed at Mule Springs, thirty miles in, with a cache of food. At Bear Valley three more turned around, just gave it up, Johnson says, lost their will when they found themselves on foot with fifty pounds to pack and the worst country still ahead.

"I guess they got rained on and hailed on and snowed on. Climbing in new snow with all that weight, it just wore 'em down. The leader upped their pay to five dollars a day, guaranteed by Captain Sutter and the good faith and credit of the United States Army, and that's a pretty damn good wage, you ask me, and even that wasn't enough to keep 'em going. I can't fault 'em, Jim. They are better men than me, just making it as far as they did."

The next morning his vaqueros bring in a small herd of longhorns. Jim and Mac shoot five of the fattest, which are skinned and gutted by the deft ranch hands, up to their elbows in the gore. The beef of five cattle is cut into strips and laid on racks to smoke above long beds of glowing coals. From his storeroom Johnson brings forth sacks of wheat to be ground into flour. His Indians pound it down with mortars. Ounce by ounce it is run through coffee grinders borrowed from the emigrant wagons. They all take turns cranking the little handles through the day and night, Jim and Mac and Johnson and Bill Eddy and the Indians wrapped in rabbitskin cloaks who do not yet know what happened in the mountains, who will not hear any version of Eddy's story for many weeks to come, who feel emergency in the night air and work side by side with the whites, lit by an orange glow from beneath the racks of smoking meat.

Two days later the rest of Jim's party rides up from the river, and still there has been no sign of the cargo team.

They move on, heading farther east along the Bear, seventeen men, their mules and horses laden now with bundles of jerked beef, hundreds of pounds of flour. By midmorning they're unbuttoning coats, unwrapping scarves. An eerie perspiring warmth raises their hopes a notch. An early spring might somehow ease the plight of those beyond the summit. Maybe these past two weeks have melted a track so that animals can make it after all.

They push into the foothills, where snow has receded some. But nor far enough. At Mule Springs it's three feet deep, and worse from there on in, according to the young fellows watching the cache of flour and beef. No one else from the first rescue has yet come back, they say. "You're the first ones we've seen hereabouts in twelve, fourteen days."

Jim leaves half the horses behind, some packets of food, along with three men to tend to the horses and raise some shelters for the emigrants he now expects to see at every turn and rise.

Below Bear Valley they hit chest-high drifts. The animals snort and strain in protest. Knowing it can only get worse, Jim sends all the horses back, with two more men. Later that day another man turns around when his eyes go bad. They are running with pus, and he can barely see. When yet another gives it up, from exhaustion and discouragement, two men sit down to rest, saying they ought to all head back to Mule Springs and wait there until the first rescue team comes out. But Jim and Mac can tolerate no more waiting. They have snowshoes this time. They can't let themselves be stopped by heavy drifts, or second thoughts.

"There's only seven of them ahead of us," Jim says, as he takes in each man with unblinking, urgent eyes, "and seven can't do it all. There could be sixty still waiting at the camps. That's a lot of people. No telling what shape they're in, since the strongest have already come ahead. It's mostly youngsters now, you see. And they'll need every hand. We have to stick it out. God will bless each man who sticks it out."

He lets this hang in the air. The two who sat down are standing again, hoisting their enormous loads.

"We're with you, Jim."

"Ain't no time to sit around the fire."

The party forms up again. After so much planning and purchasing and gathering of goods, they are eleven men without horses, a web-footed caravan, each packing as much food as he can bear. They have a base camp behind them and a hope that the *Sacramento*'s cargo of tenting and trousers and medicines and beans will find its way from the fort to the ranch and up to Mule Springs and be there waiting.

Through silent pines they plod along the same route Jim and Mac followed in November, and Jim listens as he did the first time for any sound ahead, for a hiss of creek water below the snowpack. It is like a dream of that other trip, same trail, same sloping stands of timber, same yearning to see a figure move against the white, though the snow is deeper. Charlie and his Indians came this way with their loaded mules, and it occurs to him that those three are riding again, right now. His neck hairs prickle at the thought that they are somewhere close by, watching his every move. He shakes his head and tells himself he has to get more sleep.

What Eddy Heard

Lying in the snow Salvador did not feel the snow. It could have been day. It could have been night. Lying on his back, he had no power in his arms or legs or hands.

He opened his eyes and saw the one called Foster, standing above them with the rifle and staring at Luis. His eyes were crazy. Foster's face looked like he was shouting, but his voice was small and cracked and faraway.

"Don't move!" he said, waving the barrel. "Don't try nothing! You're damn near dead anyhow, so what difference does it make? You two hear me now? You hear me?"

Salvador closed his eyes and waited and listened, and after a while he was a young man again, and he saw the face of his father on the day he told Salvador not to go back to the mission called St. Joseph. His father knew that place. He had worked for the padres. Then he had run away with his wife and sons, run back to the village by the river. Do not listen to them, his father had said. Do not listen to the padres.

Salvador had wanted the clothes. He wanted a buckle made of silver. He had seen the buckles on the belts of the vaqueros. He wanted jingling spurs to wear and a hat with a wide brim and a leather band.

"These things are very costly," his father had said. "You cannot trade for necklaces and robes of rabbit skin. The whites want more than that."

Salvador had waited, wondering what this meant.

"Much more," his father had said.

It was a grave warning, but Salvador did not hear the meaning of the words. Not then. His eagerness was too great. Now he heard, lying in the snow. Now he knew. "They want your life," his father was saying. "For all these things, they want your life."

He saw Jesus again on the cross above the altar in the mission church, in flickering candlelight, the pale skin, the pale and bleeding hands out wide. He saw shining robes and wings floating all around the hands, feathered wings. He saw the padre's fingers push a white wafer toward his mouth, said to be the flesh of the one who hung upon the cross. But how? Salvador did not have words to ask the padre how one man can eat the flesh of another man, even if he is a god in the shape of a man. Bread is bread. Flesh is flesh.

In the chapel of the Mission of St. Joseph he could not ask. Now he did not have to ask. Here in the mountains he had seen men eat flesh. White men ate white flesh. Into their bodies they took meat of another's body. And with the meat, the spirit. In his hunger Salvador ate flesh too. The hunger made him crazy, as crazy as the whites. Today they wanted his flesh. They wanted his spirit. Foster wanted it.

This is what the padre said. This is what his father tried to tell him. They wanted his life. You eat the bear, you eat the bear's life. You eat the elk, you eat the elk's life. And the bear is you. The elk is you . . .

He heard the first shot. He did not move. He could not move. He had no strength. His arms and legs lay still, and the snow was warm. As warm as a blanket. He listened for some sound from Luis. Nothing. Luis was gone. He heard only Foster, breathing. He felt the barrel upon his forehead. He felt its icy touch. At the far end of the rifle he saw the eyes small as a raccoon's eyes in firelight. He did not hear the second shot.

from *The Trail Notes of Patty Reed*

March 1921

And I heard the voice of many
angels round about the throne
and the beasts and the elders;
and the number of these was ten
thousand times ten thousand . . .

—Revelation 5:11

SOME *people say the darkest hour comes just before the dawn. Old sayings like that are easy to quote years later when you've had some time to think back over your life. You don't quote them when you're in the middle of that darkest hour and cannot see a flicker of dawn peeping through in any direction. Nobody was quoting it at the lake camp around about the middle of February, when every one of us was wasting away, some seeing things, others going blind. Keseberg's baby boy had died, and William Eddy's wife, Eleanor. In our family all that stood between us and starvation was three hides mama had conserved, and one morning Mrs. Graves showed up saying those hides belonged to her.*

She was claiming them, she said, until mama could settle her debt. She had worked herself into a fit. This time mama was not to be outshouted. They stood in the snow screaming at each other, pulling those smelly cattle hides this way and that. Mama finally tore two of them loose. Elizabeth still held on to one. She had brought along her seventeen-year-old son, who was as skinny as a stick, like the rest of us, but mama didn't have enough strength left to go after Elizabeth and her son too. They dragged that one hide back to their cabin, and mama set to work scraping at the two we had left.

After that I remember sitting still a lot. My mind would simply go away. I don't know how many days went by. It was about the time our last square of hide was boiled up that we heard a voice from somewhere far off, a voice we didn't recognize. We were down inside the Breens' cabin, with just the fireplace light. A little streak of late afternoon was leaking down the stairwell. I didn't say anything. I had been seeing angels in the darkness and hearing them sing beautiful songs. Sometimes they would call to me, and in my mind I would answer. I listened for this voice to come again. And it did.

"Halloww!" it called.

This time mama said, "Did you hear that?"

I looked around. I knew then everyone had heard it. Mama and Peggy Breen went scrambling for the ice stairs. I was right behind them. We came up into the light and saw men spread through the trees between us and the lake, big-bundled shaggy men, still calling, "Hallooww! Hallooww!" When they saw us they stopped and stared at what must have been a horrifying sight, witches and scarecrows rising out of the snow.

Mama's voice was just a scratchy quaver. "Are you . . . ?" She could hardly speak. "Are you men from California?"

"Yes, ma'am," one fellow shouted.

She fell onto her knees, weeping and laughing. "Thank the Lord," she said. "You've come at last."

Others were climbing out of the cabins now, my baby brothers, and Phillipine, the whole Breen clan. Patrick's prayers had been answered, it seemed, and Virginia's too. In our eyes these men were saints. Maybe they were the angels I'd been hearing in the dark, their voices floating toward me from beyond the mountains to the west. Maybe one of them was papa. I scanned their frosted eyes and craggy faces. He wasn't there. He wasn't there. I said, "Where's papa?" my voice so tiny in the hubbub of sobs and hallelujahs mama didn't hear me.

Once they slung down their loads, it didn't matter who they were or how they got there. They had packed in biscuits and jerked beef. We groveled and wept and gobbled up the morsels passed around to us, and begged for more, but they knew better than we did what can happen when you try to fill a shrunken belly.

The leader was a fellow named Glover. He had come across the plains and had camped with our party a time or two along the Platte.

Mama remembered him. That night he slept with us, while the other men divided up among the cabins. We didn't know it at the time, but they were almost as bad off as we were. Our pitiful shelters were the first warm spots they'd seen in three weeks of being wet and cold and worn down with the climbing.

Since that time I've heard it said that these men in the rescue party did it for the money. It's true that they were earning wages they couldn't have made any other way. This was two years before the Gold Rush. You could buy a pound of butchered beef for two cents and a whole chicken for fifty cents. Five dollars a day was a huge amount. But something else was driving them. It wasn't family. None of them had relatives to rescue. Maybe it was some sense of kinship for the big trek we would later call the Great Migration. They had all come across to California in the past six months. I happen to think it was more than that. From time to time in this life people actually do courageous things. In my view now, looking back, it was nothing but valiant, and I cannot fault any of them for what happened next.

Those seven men needed a lot more rest. They also knew the sooner we started out, the better. They'd come through two bad storms to reach us. Now the skies were clear. The big question was, Who to take? Counting our camp and Donner's camp there were over fifty still alive. Mr. Glover made promises. Rescue teams would be going back and forth, he said, until everyone was on the other side. Some folks were too weak to walk, or too sick. Uncle George Donner, for instance. The hand he cut trying to plane a new axle had festered and the infection had spread all through him. He couldn't travel, and his wife, Tamsen, she wouldn't leave without him. They sent two of their little girls and two of Jacob Donner's children. Lewis Keseberg was bedridden, but Phillipine was still healthy and not quite so loyal. She could hike out, she said, with their little girl, Ada. The Breens sent their two oldest boys, while the rest of the family stayed put a while longer, since they had some meat in reserve. As for us, mama had nothing left, not even a scrap of hide, so we all ended up among the two dozen who set out from the lake camp behind the rescue team.

Just before we left, Keseberg emerged from the hole leading down to his buried lean-to. No one had seen him for weeks. With his son dead and his wife and daughter leaving, he didn't want to live alone. He was hobbling down to widow Murphy's. He had cut a forked branch into a homemade crutch. His tangled beard was so greasy it looked gray instead of blond. The weeks of pain had lined his face. The way his tortured eyes blinked and squinted against the light, he was like a convict released from a dungeon. He didn't look at us. He just hobbled across the snow, wincing with each tiny step. I have to confess, I hoped then I would never see him again. What a relief it was to leave that man behind, to leave those dreadful cabins behind at last, the lice, the stink, the smoky darkness. I felt that I too had been imprisoned and was finally set free.

Up ahead, someone led the way in a pair of snowshoes. The rest of us were supposed to follow along, stepping where he stepped. If you had short legs like Tommy and me, it wasn't easy. We had to climb in and out of each deep step. Tommy was four, going on five. In the whole party he was the youngest one walking, and the smallest. I called back to him a few times, "C'mon, Tommy. Papa's gonna be here pretty soon." Then my breath gave out. I couldn't do both, call to him and climb in and out of those holes everyone ahead of us made deeper and mushier.

Mama urged us on, lifting us from time to time, but we fell farther behind with each step. The party had hiked about two miles, stretched out along the side of Truckee Lake, with me and Tommy right at the end, when Mr. Glover came back and told mama we were slowing everyone else down. If we couldn't make better time we'd have to go back to the cabins.

"I'm sorry, Mrs. Reed. I got to think about the welfare of the whole party and make it across while we got the weather on our side."

Mama said if we went back she'd go with us. The whole family would go back together and wait for another rescue team. Mr. Glover, he got real stern, said he couldn't let her do that. "Every person able to walk has to walk out of here. You go back with your children, you'll only eat the others' food. Everyone that goes helps them that stays behind."

Virginia and James Junior had started to cry. Mama begged Mr. Glover not to leave us. She said it wasn't fair, it wasn't right. He said he could tell by looking at us we were too weak to walk and we were too much to carry. Two of his men were already carrying infants, and there was still the summit trail to climb.

Mama couldn't stand what he was telling her to do. She looked *around at the four of us, and what I saw then was the most terrible look I've ever seen on any face before or since. It was the wild, stark, near-madness that comes into the eyes when you have eaten almost nothing for weeks and your flesh wastes away and leaves the bones and sockets showing. And it was something else. It was the mother's bottomless terror. She had already climbed the summit trail. She knew what awaited us up there. She now had to face the fact that Tommy and I would both perish if we kept on going the way we'd been going, spindly as we were, and down to nothing, with no meat on our bones. She also knew returning to the cabins was no better, maybe even worse.*

When Mr. Glover saw she could not speak, he said he would come back for us. Mama turned her anguished and accusing eyes on him. She made him promise that he himself would do this, and he said he would. When they got to Bear Valley, he told her, if no other rescue team had started in, he would turn right around and come back for the two of us.

Mama dropped to her knees in the snow and pulled Tommy close and told him to stay right with me, and she would be seeing us again in a few days. Poor Tommy was so numb and cold and hungry you couldn't tell if he had any idea what was being asked of him.

She hugged me close and looked into my eyes. "Never forget that I love you, Patty. And papa loves you too."

I still do not know what possessed me to say what I said just then. Something in me had shifted. I know enough now to give words to what it was. The little girl inside me went away, as surely as if a path had opened up through the trees. She just stepped out of my body and walked down that path and into the Sierra Nevada forest, never to return. I had already seen more than you ought to see by the time you are that age. I had seen my father stab another man in the chest and watched that man bleed to death. I had heard wounded animals screaming for water in the desert night, and heard the widow Murphy crying out from her cabin like a lone wolf howling in the woods. I had watched people starving and watched my own brothers shrivel up till there was nearly nothing left and watched my mother walk away from me, out across the snow and disappear. As she prepared to do this yet again I was able for the first time to imagine my own death and to imagine that I would not see her anymore. At moments like this you are supposed to cry. I wasn't able to cry. She was the one who cried. I was the one who stood there giving motherly advice. I know now my words cut through her as surely as if a sword of ice had dropped off one of the limbs above us and speared her heart. It makes me weep to think of it. Yes, seventy-five years later my own tears come dripping down to match those she wept that day.

"Well, mother," I said, "if you never see me again, you do the best you can."

Is that too hard-hearted for an eight-year-old? Somehow I was prepared for my death and for hers too. I told as much to Mr. Glover after we turned and started back. It disturbed him, I know. In my eyes then he seemed to be an executioner. Later I would see that he was a very decent man, though rough and rugged in his looks, red-eyed from the cold and from his monumental efforts.

"Don't you talk like that," he said to me. "I give your mama my word, and I mean to keep it."

He and his partner carried us, retracing the path of steps punched into the snow along the shore. Then we were standing again by the wide hole I thought we'd forever left behind. Mr. Glover called for someone to come up. I heard Patrick's piping voice, complaining about the steps. His legs were so stiff and weak it took him a while.

Patrick was still a puzzle to me. I could not then comprehend why he did the things he did. After he turned Milt Elliott away a second time I had come to hate him. Milt was like a brother and a father too, with papa gone. When he and mama and Virginia had tried to hike out in January, and Virginia had to be carried down from the summit, that trip was what broke Milt's health. When the rest of us had to move in with the Breens and Patrick turned Milt away, he went over to Alder Creek to stay with the Donners. But things got so bad he came back to the lake camp. He'd lost all his weight by that time and could hardly stand up. He begged Patrick to let him in. Mama begged too. Patrick said he didn't want his kids to have to watch someone die right there in his cabin. Mama had to drag Milt down to Murphy's and that's where he passed away, lying on the dirt floor with his head on a piece of kindling and mama feeding him snow water and melted rawhide.

I knew Patrick would not be glad to see me and Tommy coming back. When Mr. Glover told him what had happened, he just shook his John-the-Baptist head.

"Can't do it."

"These children need shelter," Mr. Glover said.

Patrick's face got pinched and angry. *"We don't have room."*

"It'd just be a few days."

"I got my own."

"You have more room now than you had yesterday, with Mrs. Reed gone, and your two boys . . ."

"I still got five mouths to feed. Plus the missus and me. That's seven to care for, Mr. Glover."

"There's no place else for these two to go."

"Widda Murphy has more room than anybody," Patrick said.

His wife had come up the ice steps. She was standing next to Patrick now, and her voice cut through the air.

"You know these children can't go down with widda Murphy!"

She spoke up so fast it took him by surprise. She was a tough one, Peggy Breen. She had a way of setting her face that there was no arguing with. I still remember how they looked at each other then, her eyes holding his, and Patrick's jaws working.

Mr. Glover said, *"We mean to leave some food behind."*

"How much?" said Patrick.

"Same as for everyone else. Seven days' rations. Ounce of beef a day, a spoonful of flour."

"For both these young'uns? Seven ounces?"

"It's what we can spare."

With a disgusted shake of his head Patrick said, *"God's will be done."*

He turned and headed down the ice stairs. Peggy nodded to us to follow him. Mr. Glover squatted next to me and said, *"I promised your mama, and I promise you, I'll be back as soon as I can. Or somebody will."*

Then he and his partner were gone, trudging off the way they'd come. I dreaded going back down those stairs. I was entering a tomb. My heart was empty. My body was like an empty bottle sitting on a dark shelf in an empty cupboard. A cold sun was shining. While we stood there the wind came up, rushing through the pines with a sound like surf, a gushing roar like water on the rise, as if an ocean of ice water had begun to pour across the world.

.   .   .

IT WAS LIKE *the first time mama left, but harder because Tommy didn't move much. Sometimes I had to hold a mirror to his lips to make sure he was breathing. Sometimes his eyes would open, and he would almost seem to speak. I would warm our slivers of meat and fry up some flour, then chew Tommy's portion to soften it and try to make him eat.*

I don't know who was worse off then—him, because he had no idea of what was going on around us, or me, because I did. I remember hearing Patrick and Peggy say things I didn't understand. Years later I came to see that they already knew what was happening at the other cabin, where someone had gone out and uncovered Milt's body, buried in the snow, and started cutting away parts of him for food. Whether it was the widow started it, or Keseberg, no one would ever be able to say for sure.

My heart went out to widow Murphy, and still does. She was called "widow" because her husband had died on her. The fact is, she wasn't much older than mama, not yet forty. You have to give her credit for trying something most single women wouldn't have dared in that day and age. She had started west on her own, with seven children. Two of her daughters had married young and had brought their children. For a while it had been quite a clan, three wagonloads. William Foster was her son-in-law. So was William Pike, the fellow Foster shot in the back. She'd lost a boy at the lake camp. Five more of her children had already hiked out, leaving her with one small son, a boy about my age. Little by little she'd been losing her eyesight and losing her mind. By the time Keseberg moved in, she'd probably forgotten who he was. In her sad hunger she'd probably forgotten who Milt was.

I thank the Lord I had lost the will to walk more than fifty feet at a time. After Mr. Glover left I never wandered far enough in her direction to see any sign of what was going on—though I think I must have known. Deep down I must have. I must have chosen not to understand the words Patrick and Peggy whispered on the other side of the blanket.

As I think back upon those weeks it seems as if the mountains themselves had revealed an appetite, as if somewhere among the snowy crevices and windblown granite slopes there were ancient and empty places that had to be filled, laying claim to what little energy and life force remained for us. It had a pull, and it had a voice, and you couldn't resist it. When the angels came to visit I could not tell if they were heavenly angels or mountain angels, and it didn't make much difference which, their music was so sweet. They would visit me at all times of the day and night, and before long I stopped hearing much of anything but their voices. They would come from far away like the flute notes of distant birds approaching, single notes I would hear before I saw the wings. Then they'd be all around, white-winged angels singing in a forest filled with silver light. Sometimes they wouldn't sing. They would float and beckon, and start to drift away, and I would call out, "Don't go! Don't go!" And back they'd come, as if they'd just been teasing me, flirting and teasing.

Late one afternoon, outside the cabin, I saw an angel walking toward me through the snow. The sun was low and sending dappled rays through the trees. A silver light rose off the snow. I watched and waited for the wings to lift and listened for the sweet voice to sing. This time there was no song, and I couldn't see the wings. The whiteness was a furry cloak. This was another kind of angel. Maybe it was an Indian angel. The face was brown. The hair was black. The cloak of white and gray was made of skins, and in his arms he carried some kind of bundle, like a gift. I knew then it was Salvador. Every day I had been wearing his abalone pendant to bring us luck, and here he was come back at last. When I called his name he stopped at the edge of the trees.

"Cómo está?" I said.

He didn't answer.

I started to run toward him but a hand stopped me, a hand gripping my shoulder. It was Patrick.

"Who are you?" he called out. "What do you want?"

The visitor held forth his bundle, then set it down in the snow and moved back into the trees. He didn't speak or make a sound. When he was gone Patrick went over there and found half a dozen roots shaped like onions. "Never knew there was an Injun within a hundred miles."

"It's Salvador," I said.

"Salvador," said Patrick with a snort. "What on earth would bring him clear back up here?"

I wanted to follow him, but the empty forest frightened me. I'd have to wait until he reappeared. I don't know how long I waited. The days and nights all ran together. On one of those days I turned nine, though it wasn't on my mind. All I thought about was food. We ate up the rations Mr. Glover left behind, then there was nothing. I sometimes chewed on bits of bark and pine twigs, hoping they might ward off the hunger pangs, which they never did. I was afraid to look at Tommy now. His face was like a skull. I know it snowed again and cleared up again. I noticed the weather less and less. Most of the time I sat by Tommy.

One day I felt compelled to get outside. Something was calling me up into the light, whether angels with wings or the white-robed visitor again, I did not know. Something was out there. I had to know what it was.

It took a lot of effort, climbing the snow stairs. I listened for the flute notes, the tender voices coming from the lake. I remember the sky was very blue when I stepped out onto the snow. The air was quiet. The figure coming toward me through the trees this time was dark and large. No wings. No furry robes. The arms were pumping, as if punching at the air, like someone running but in slow motion, fighting through the snow. And then a call came toward me.

"Patty!"

I knew this voice. It wasn't Salvador. It wasn't Mr. Glover. My heart stopped. I had been seeing so many things, hearing so many things, I closed my eyes. Again the voice called, "Patty?" like a question.

He was closer, his huge pack thrown down behind him, and his hat thrown down. I could see his face, his beard, as he lunged toward me, calling, "Patty! Patty! Is it you?"

I tried to run, sure he would disappear before I reached him. I tried to call out, "Papa!" My voice stuck in my throat. The snow had been melting. It was soft. I couldn't lift my legs high enough to run. I fell forward. Then he was over me, lifting me. I looked into his eyes. As he held me his face filled with fear at what he saw, and that made me afraid. I threw my arms around his neck. He hugged me close against his coat, against his chest.

"It's okay, darlin'," he said, "we're okay now," his voice soothing away my confusion, his voice sweeter than all those others I'd been hearing.

I still couldn't talk. With my face pushed into the thick, scratchy wool of his coat I sobbed and sobbed. He held me until I got my breath and found my voice.

"I'm so hungry, papa. I've never been so hungry."

"I know, darlin'. I have something for you that we baked last night."

He set me down and fetched his pack, where he had a little cloth bag. He brought out a tiny biscuit about the size of a thimble. I'd never seen anything so beautiful. "Here ya go, darlin'. Just bite off a little bit. Eat it real slow."

I ate that and he gave me another one. I could see the bag was full of these biscuit morsels. My heart swelled with new love for him.

"I knew you'd come back, papa."

"You knew I wouldn't leave my little girl behind."

"Did you see James Junior and Virginia?"

"Yes, we did. By now they're safe and sound in California."

"Have you been to California, papa?"

"I sure have, darlin'."

"Is it far away?"

"Hardly any ways at all. Where's Tommy now?"

"He's down below, papa. He's sleeping. He sleeps most all the time. I tried to feed him whenever I could. But after a while . . ." I started to cry again. "After a while there wasn't any more . . ."

The days and weeks of tears I hadn't been able to feel came gushing forth. Again he picked me up and held me close and I felt his body shaking next to mine, like the day by the Humboldt when we cut away his hair. Then he put me down and gave me another biscuit and told me to sit still while he went below.

I sat there nibbling, each crumb a precious gift, until papa climbed back up the stairs carrying Tommy, so small against his coat he looked like a doll. Papa had been crying again, and he was trying not to. He didn't have time to cry.

Patrick had followed him and stood at the top of the stairs. I don't know what had passed between them in the darkness. Maybe nothing. They watched each other for quite a while.

Papa said, "I thank you, Patrick, for giving shelter to my children."

"It hasn't been easy here."

"I can see that."

"We've got our own."

"I saw your boys up past the summit. They'll be all right. Glover's a good man."

"They're good boys too."

And there they stood, meeting again, two men from Ireland who never cared much for each other in the best of days. For the first time in all these months I felt sorry for Patrick. He looked so shrunken next to papa, who'd left the company in disgrace and had now returned, weary from the climbing but in good health and vigorous after five months of constant motion, while Patrick had been mostly waiting, stiff from sitting and from nursing his kidney stones. In his eyes there was a look I now understand. His fear was that he'd be left behind, that papa bore some grudge and would rescue us but no one else. Knowing Patrick, the way his mind worked in those days, this is probably what he himself would have done, if supplies were short and there were weaker ones to contend with. The night Milt Elliott starved to death, Patrick still had meat in his cabin. Maybe he was afraid papa would find out about that.

At last papa said, "Get your family ready. We're starting back right away, with everyone who can walk."

He had brought along a bundle of flannel wrappings. He broke off some pine boughs and spread these on the snow, wrapped Tommy in flannel, and laid him on the boughs in the sun, saying, "It'll be good for him."

I have met people who still imagine we spent every minute of those months up to our necks in drifts and blizzards while we scavenged for firewood and scraps of food. Well, we had our share of blizzards, and there were more to come, but we'd had our share of sunshine too. And this was such a day. Though thick clouds had gathered at the summit, right around us the daylight was bright and clean. You could see every needle on the pines. Faraway jagged ledges of granite looked so sharp you could cut your finger if you reached out to touch them.

Three more men had come through the trees in their thick coats and snowshoes. You couldn't tell by their hairy faces who they were, though one was so tall and broad he had to be Bill McCutcheon. The other men didn't linger. They headed off toward Alder Creek, where the Donners were. I waved to Mac, and he waved a little wave to me. He didn't move any closer. He stood back, waiting, while papa gave me two little biscuits to feed to Tommy and told me to stay right there and if the weather changed at all to wait for him down below. Then he joined Mac and they moved off toward Murphy's cabin.

Much later I learned that Mac already knew what had happened to his little girl. Maybe that's why he'd kept his distance. Maybe he was mourning so much he didn't want to look at me and Tommy. Up beyond the summit, when they ran into the first rescue, Mr. Glover had explained how the cabins were laid out and who was still alive. Mac learned then that Harriet had been dead a month. I have often wondered how he took this news. Did it shock him? Or had he known it all along? Had he known in his bones that such a young one couldn't last, and had he let her go long before he stood there with Mr. Glover and his men and the survivors, mama and Virginia among them, listening to the rushed accounts of what they'd find? I don't think the news would have stopped Mac in his tracks. But neither would he have let her go ahead of time. No. He wasn't that kind of man. His heart was too big. He might have bowed his head and thought about his wife waiting down at Sutter's. But he kept on coming. That is what strikes me, as I think back. With nothing up ahead but grief and hardship, Mac kept on coming. He was like a man possessed. By the time they started off toward Murphy's cabin he seemed to be bounding across the snow.

After a while Tommy said, "Who was that man?"

"The big tall man?"

"The man with the biscuits."

"It's papa, Tommy."

"You sure?"

"He told us he'd come back, and he did."

For I don't know how long Tommy's eyes had been so glazed over you couldn't tell if he was seeing anything at all. They lit up now with the faintest shine.

"He brought this for you." I held one of the biscuits to his mouth, and he took a small bite. I watched him swallow it. He took another bite.

"You sure it was papa?" Tommy's voice was as fragile as a dried leaf, his body as light as breath. "Is he really here?"

I told him yes and held the biscuit to his mouth, watching him bite. I ate another one myself, real slow, and watched the path they had cut, praying they would come right back. I had almost forgotten about leaving that place. With papa there my hope was born anew. It was hard watching him go away again. I didn't want to be left alone for long with Tommy. I didn't understand why they had to go to Murphy's, and I had no idea what awaited them. The fact is, many years would pass before it all came clear to me, what they found at the widow's and what they did.

Everything that happened during those weeks took years to find out *about, it seems. With the weather and the deep snow and the general fear and suspiciousness, you hardly ever knew what was going on anywhere but in your own cabin. Afterward it all depended on who you talked to and how much you thought you could believe, since they would always put themselves and their families in the best possible light, as people usually do. Some folks never talked at all, so stunned by what befell them, or so ashamed, they kept their silence to the grave. The men from papa's rescue party—the first ones to hike over to Alder Creek that day—they claimed they saw some of the Donner youngsters sitting on a log with blood running down their chins, eating Jacob Donner's heart and liver. As you might expect, when this got down to San Francisco Bay, the paper jumped on it and bugled it around the world, just as they would today if they had the chance. Sell as many papers as you can sell—that comes first. Along the way, if someone happens to get the story right, or one-third right, well, that is welcome icing on the cake. Yet those same youngsters, after they were old enough to tell their stories, they would say they couldn't remember any such thing. My friend Eliza Donner, who was four at the time, says the bodies of the ones who'd died at their camp were buried under so much snow no one had the strength to dig them out, even if they'd wanted to. They were like the cattle who'd been lost and covered, according to Eliza. That's why it took so many years to piece those weeks and months together. To this very day you will hear people arguing until they are blue in the face over things they themselves could not have seen and that none of us will ever know for sure.*

You take the Murphy cabin. We'll never know exactly how things looked or what had happened in the days before the second rescue came, though by all accounts it was worse than anyone had imagined. Papa found Milt Elliott's cut-up body outside in the snow. He could tell who it was by the face, which had not been touched. Other parts were gone. I'm glad I didn't have to watch what such a sight would do to him. How do you look at the face of your most trusted hand? How do you look at the faces of those who cooked his flesh? When Mac and papa appeared in the cabin, widow Murphy fled. She ran out into the snow, laughing like a madwoman.

Lewis Keseberg was in there, and William Eddy's boy, James, alongside Foster's son. They were both about Tommy's age, in about the same condition, or maybe worse. No one had been looking after them, even though the widow was little Georgie Foster's grandma. They hadn't been moved or been out of bed for days, both wrapped in filthy blankets, covered with lice, and calling out for food. If things had gone another way, that could have been me and Tommy. If the Breens had not taken us in the second time, this is where we would have ended up. Maybe papa knew that. Maybe he saw Tommy in the face of Bill Eddy's boy. Maybe Mac was seeing little Harriet.

Papa and Mac took off all their own clothes and piled them outside, so they wouldn't get infested with the things crawling around in the cabin. They filled a pot of snow and melted it down to warm water. They washed those boys, soaped their hair, rubbed them all over with kerosene from a bottle papa had brought along, and wrapped them in clean flannel so they'd be comfortable for a while.

Keseberg watched this in silence from his own miserable heap of bedding. I imagine he was like Patrick, with a headful of doubts and dreads, now that papa had returned. I have imagined him lying there with his thorn-punctured foot thick and purple from the swelling, the man who had tried to hang papa, had tied a gallows knot in the rope and in a blighted land where no trees grew had raised his wagon tongue, the same fellow who once stole buffalo robes from the funeral scaffold of a Sioux chief, filling our hearts with panic for days thereafter. Some have said this one selfish act brought on all the misfortunes that were to follow us clear across the continent. I don't believe that. I don't believe curses work that way. A man alone cannot bring down a whole wagon party, though certainly a man can darken the path of his own life. Was this perhaps on Keseberg's mind? Did he feel the doom upon his shoulders as he looked up fearfully, wondering what papa and Mac were going to do?

He always kept a rifle near at hand. Maybe he thought of using it, or brandishing it that day. He would have had no other way to defend himself. I have imagined the rescuers, white and naked in the firelight, looming over him. Mac was six foot six, big-boned and burly. Papa was not a muscular man, but he was lean and tough, and he'd been eating every day. If they'd wanted to, they could have lifted Keseberg and carried him outside and buried him up to his neck in the snow and left him there to freeze. I have imagined papa considering something along those lines, and Keseberg bracing himself.

Papa said, "Lewis, can you walk?"

The haunted eyes grew round. He couldn't speak.

"Just answer yes or no. Can you walk?"

"No."

"Then can you take your clothes off?"

"Look here, Mr. Reed..."

He tried to sit up, but fell back wincing.

"If you can't, we'll do it for you."

"Take off my clothes?"

"Can you stand at all?"

"Have mercy, please..."

"Which way can you move?"

"I can't. My leg."

"Have you a crutch?"

"A crutch?"

"Try sitting, then."

"I'm not sure. Just leave me be."

"We'll help you."

"I'm a frail man."

"We can see that. We're going to lift you now."

Together Mac and papa got their hands under his back and shoulders, raised him up and began to remove his clothing. He was almost as bad off as the boys had been, evidently lying there for days.

"Please. No," Keseberg begged.

"We're going to clean you up a bit."

"No! You can't!"

The grimy coat came off, the scarves, the trousers, the layering of shirts, the long underwear that hadn't been removed in weeks. I see them in that jumbled, fetid room, in the light of glowing logs, three pale men stripped of all their clothing. I see papa regarding Keseberg's nakedness and still marvel that he could reach out to such a man. Seeing his foot and leg, papa knew they'd have to leave him behind. Maybe he saw another father there, a man with wife and children gone and nothing remaining but his hunger and his pain. With warm water he began to soap the bony limbs, while Keseberg sat hunched on his mattress. Choking back phlegm and spittle he begged them not to do it.

"Please. Please. I cannot bear this."

"We need to clean you up."

"But not you, Reed. Anyone but you."

"*Be still.*"

"*How can you?*"

"*We would do it for anyone. We all need cleaning up.*"

Tears spread across Keseberg's cheeks while papa bathed him and Mac oiled him with kerosene, just as they had bathed and oiled the boys, the same tenderness, taking care with each limb, attending to every inch of skin, the lice-infested places and places fouled with feces.

"*Please, Mr. Reed. I cannot permit it.*"

"*Be still, man. We're almost done.*"

"*I do not deserve this.*"

Overcome, bewildered, he asked again and again, "How can you? How can you?" as they wrapped him in flannel and eased him back onto his bedding.

THEY LEFT SOME *food, as much as they could spare—a cup of flour, half a pound of beef—for Lewis and the bedridden boys and the widow hiding somewhere in the trees like a coyote waiting till these strangers went away. Papa left two men to help with the boys until another rescue party arrived. He expected them to show up at any moment, a contingent from the cargo team with more provisions brought up from the river.*

Over at Alder Creek George Donner was failing now and too far gone to travel. He had said his good-byes to his children. He was ready to say good-bye to his wife. But Tamsen still insisted she would never leave her husband alone. To this day I wish she had come with us. She was a woman with ambition. She wanted to open a school in California. She was smart and brave and still strong enough to make the crossing. George begged her to go. So did papa. But she said no, her duty was there by her husband's side. All papa could do was leave another man at Alder Creek.

On the morning we started out it hadn't snowed for quite some time. You could see old tracks through the forest and cut along the edge of the lake. This time I was not going to be sent back. I was going to make my own way or fall over dead trying. Papa carried Tommy in a sling and gave me a hand when he could. Other men had younger ones to carry. In our party there were fourteen children. The grown-ups, Patrick and Peggy and Mrs. Graves, were so feeble they could barely stagger along.

Papa hoped to be over the pass that first day. We only made two miles, about as far as Mr. Glover got before he split our family up.

The next day was a little better. We made four miles, which brought us to the end of the lake and the foot of the pass. But now we were a day behind, and food was already running low, after what they'd left at the camps. A cold south wind cut through us. Clouds were heaping high around the peaks. Papa knew what a risk it was, starting for the summit under such a sky. But there was nothing to go back to. The only hope lay ahead of us, hope that we'd meet the next rescue party before our supplies ran out, and that the darkening skies would get no darker.

Papa sent three men ahead to bring food back from one of the stashes higher up. That left four men from the rescue party and seventeen very weak survivors. I don't know how we climbed that pass. I thought I was already cold. It got colder as we climbed. Every step was agony for me. Whenever I fell someone would pick me up. "C'mon, little darlin'," papa would say, "we've almost got 'er licked."

I don't remember reaching the top, though we did, sometime after noon. I wish I'd looked back. I'd spent so much time watching that pass from down below, I deserved a moment to turn and see where we'd been for all those weeks. At the time I couldn't see anything but the next step and the next step and the next. . . . In my mind now I can pause and look out from that high promontory that had stopped us in November and nearly stopped us that day in early March. I gaze down from the summit at the icy ring of Truckee Lake, the one they now call Donner, and it's odd to think that neither George nor Jacob ever got anywhere near the lake that is named for them. For that matter, they never got within a day's ride of the famous pass that has made their name a household word—neither George nor Jacob nor Jacob's wife, Elizabeth, nor Tamsen, who nursed her husband to the end. It tells you something about the way things get remembered. Hundreds of others climbed out that year and got through the mountains in pretty good time. But the party they have named it for is the one that almost didn't get out at all. If they asked me, I would have named the pass for someone else. Maybe I would call it Charlie Stanton Pass. He and Mac were the first ones from our party to cross. Charlie crossed again to bring back those mule loads of provisions that got us out of the desert. He crossed it a third time before he lost his life trying to lead the Snowshoe Party to the other side. Isn't that the kind of grit you name some place in the mountains for? And by saying this I don't mean to take anything away from Uncle George, since he was a capable leader until his wagon broke down and he tore his hand open building a new axle. But it does make you stop and wonder about how things get named.

Our campsite was underneath some trees. The men spread pine boughs across the snow and got a fire blazing up from big logs they laid crisscross. I was too tired to eat. I fell asleep and slept until snowflakes and a howling wind woke me, and here it came, the storm we'd all been dreading, a ferocious blizzard that caught us totally exposed way up there at seven thousand feet with nothing but our blankets.

Everyone was yelling in the darkness, weeping and crying out and praying to God for mercy and salvation. The men rushed among the trees with their axes to gather more wood. If the fire went out we would surely perish.

They stayed up all night feeding the fire, papa and Mac and the others on the rescue team. They used pine limbs to build a kind of windbreak, where the snow piled up as the storm kept coming, all the next day and into the next night, sleet and pelting snow and a wind more terrible than all the wolves in the Sierras yowling right beside your cabin. We'd run out of food, and you could hardly move, it was so cold. The men were exhausted and knew they needed rest. The second night they set up a watch to keep the fire going. Papa took the first round. He was nearly blind from working all day in the wind, half frozen, and weak from exposure. He couldn't stay awake. He not only fell asleep, he fell into a coma. Mac must have been the one who found him. His voice woke me, shouting, "Jim! Jim!"

Mac was kneeling there, shaking papa hard. He slapped him in the face. "Jim, my God, man!" He slapped him again. "Wake up! Wake up!"

Papa didn't move. The fire was down to a few embers, with snow blowing so thick you couldn't see. Mac was frantic. He leaned his head back and cried to the heavens. "Goddam this wind! Goddam this cold!"

His voice scared me. I tried to sit up. I said, "Is papa sleeping?"

Mac put his head close to mine and shouted, "Stay under them blankets, Patty! Stay next to Tom! Don't move till I get back!"

He disappeared into the raging darkness, and I lay there shivering, praying for papa to roll over and get up. It had been bad enough watching him ride off into the desert. It was ten times worse huddling under that awful wind, not knowing if he was alive or dead, and the snow piling up around me. It was the worst night of my life, by far, with nothing to do but lie there and wait for Mac and the others to bring the fire back.

Later on I found out one of the men had split his hand trying to grip an axe. His fingers were so frostbit and swollen they just broke open. After that it was mostly up to Mac. He got the fire going again that night. Once it was roaring, he dragged papa in close to the heat and rubbed his face and arms until some circulation came back and his eyes blinked open. Then Mac was so tired and near frozen himself, he sat down by the fire and it burned through four layers of shirts before he felt the heat. His back was scorched and blistered, but it wasn't a time you could stop and worry for long about a blistered back.

The next morning, when the storm let up at last, they knew we had to push on, whichever way we could. Papa and Mac knew this. Patrick Breen, he saw it another way. All during the storm he had stayed beneath his blankets with his family, praying. Now he told papa he wasn't going to move ahead. They would stay right where they were until another rescue party came along. Papa said anybody else in these mountains would have been caught in the same weather and there was no telling how long a person might have to wait. But Patrick had his mind made up.

"We'll stick it out," he said. "We'll hold fast."

"We need to stay together, Patrick. You have no food. No shelter here."

"We'll hold fast."

Was Patrick crazy? Was he stubborn? Was he just tired of fighting the elements? Or tired of taking orders from papa? Or did he figure the next leg of this trip would be too hard on his younger children? Peggy had been carrying their one-year-old. One boy was three, another five. It was an awful decision to have to make. Every man was hurt, burnt, cut, limping from frostbite, weak from not eating. Papa still had trouble seeing. He blinked and squinted and rubbed a hand across his face like he was being assaulted by mosquitoes. Patrick too was nearly blind, his eyes half shut. He sat beneath his blanket like a mendicant monk, with his knees pulled up close, facing straight ahead, as if something out there reassured him.

"Yessir. We'll hold fast, that we will. Right here by these logs where it's warm."

One more time I see them, under lifting clouds, at the place that would come to be called Starved Camp. And I think of how they'd looked when this journey was still new, back in Kansas, after we had crossed the Missouri, their wagons loaded and pulled along by fat oxen and their herds of cattle strung across the plains. Here they were, two stubborn Irishmen, and nothing left but the clothes on their backs, frozen stiff, arguing again about who should stay and who should go. It makes you wonder about what causes one person to stay put and not budge, what drives another to plunge ahead, and why any of us keep on going at those times when your whole being says you ought to just roll on over and give it all up.

Papa knew we had no time to spare. He asked the others to bear witness that Patrick had decided to stay here with his family, out in the open, of his own free will. After he and Mac and the men had cut up three days' firewood, we started off again, hoping to reach Bear Valley or meet the ones papa had sent forward, or meet the cargo team, or at least get to a cache of food. Mac carried Tommy. Papa wanted to carry me, but I saw he couldn't stand up straight. He could barely walk. I told him I would be all right. Though I didn't know it at the time, none of them believed I would get very far. I didn't know how bad off I was.

As the men pushed through the heavy drifts they left tracks so deep I was climbing from one to the next. I must have decided to try and cut a track of my own. I remember being in the middle of a wide white field that had no borders, and suddenly it was warm, instead of cold. The air around me was filled with light, and the light was warm, and my angels were coming back. I saw them floating across this field of white, tiny in the distance, far across the field of white, floating toward me. This time the music came from a chorus of voices, thousands of tiny angel voices filling the air while the angels surrounded me. They were the same color as the snow. They were pure white. It was a blinding white, with a pure light that shone through as they floated. This time I was floating among them. I felt like I too was an angel in the snow. I danced with them and sang with them, my voice joined theirs, as I sang out their names. They were all familiar to me. We were angels together. I knew all their names.

I was dancing in the whiteness, whirling my arms, floating on a blanket of white angel wings. I felt no weight. It was pure light. I too had wings. When I felt strange arms wrap around me, I tried to pull *away. These were not the arms I wanted, human arms bulging with cloth. I reached for the snowbright angels, but papa's voice was saying, "Patty. Patty. Get up now, darlin'. Get up. It's me. It's papa. C'mon. C'mon now."*

If I'd had the strength to cry I would have. I wanted to go with them. I could have. I was ready to. The cold came creeping in again, so cold it hurt all through my body, hurt my feet, my hands. I watched my angels float away and disappear. It was papa brought me back. He rubbed my hands and feet and neck and arms and found the last scrap of food that could be found for twenty miles in any direction. It was just crumbs, this pitiful thimbleful of crumbs and specks of leftover bread crust he had scraped from the bottom of a sack sometime before we set out. It reminds me now of things you hear people say to exaggerate how much food was consumed at a holiday dinner. "Ol' Walter, he scraped up every last crumb on his plate and he hollered out for more." Well, that is literally what it had come to. That's how close we were to starving.

Papa had stuffed a mash of crumbs about the size of a large pecan down into the end of one finger of his glove, saving it for the direst moment, which, in his view, now had come. In the hope that he could call me back toward the living he put these crumbs onto his own lips to soften and moisten and warm them. Then he placed them on my lips so I could draw them in. I swear to you I can still recall the taste, for I had not had a morsel to swallow in forty-eight hours. It was the sweet clear taste of grain. If you know the taste of biscuits made from wheat flour without much salt and left standing a day or two—it was just a dusty whisper of that taste. I guess it reminded my body it was still alive and still had things to do.

I opened my eyes and saw his face very close, his skin burned bright red and blistered white by the wind, his eyes bloodshot and raw and cold and strained with the fear that I would die right there in front of him. Then his eyes squeezed shut a little, toward a painful, broken smile.

"That's my Patty. C'mon now, darlin', we're going to make it now. We're all going to make it through."

From then on he carried me. I was half dreaming, dozing in and out. I don't remember much about the next few days. The men were so feeble from lack of food they moved along like cripples and often had to stop and rest. I knew we passed some others going in with another res-

cue team. Much later I would learn that they found the Breens at the bottom of a deep pit the fire had melted down through twenty-five feet of snow. They'd spent a week up there with no shelter and nothing to eat but the wasted bodies of Betsy Graves and her young son and one of the Donner children who'd died on the worst night of the storm.

Poor Betsy, who'd given mama so much grief over those two pitiful cattle, she too had stayed behind, afraid to move on. She died from exposure the day after we left, then she kept the Breens alive until the third rescue got there. And who can judge them for the taking of such flesh? Surely not I.

If things had gone another way, that could have been us at Starved Camp. That could well have been us. Another blizzard, another couple of nights like the ones we'd had—who knows what our little party would have resorted to? Who knows how close any one of us might have come to ending up like the Breens?

Luckily papa spied some food hanging from a pine limb, left by the men he'd sent forward before we started the summit climb. More should have been stashed along the way, but bears and martens had broken into the packages. The men themselves, they were caught in the same storm that stopped the rest of us and barely got out with their lives. It was one mishap piled upon the next. All those well-laid plans had been broken into pieces by the weather and hungry animals and the awful distances you had to cover on foot and the slow pace of ema-ciated children, along with the unexplainable absence of the cargo team—which was not all that unexplainable once you found out what a task they'd had fighting the Sacramento River in flood time.

Somewhere above Bear Valley we finally ran into their advance party, and from that day onward there was enough for all of us to eat. At Mule Springs animals were waiting, and relief crews. Pretty soon we were low enough on the western slope you could see patches of good green earth again. Another day brought us out to Johnson's Ranch.

Papa had rigged another sling to carry me on his back, and I clung to him the way I'd held to Salvador when we followed the Truckee west out of the desert. I was wishing we could ride on like that forever. We would ride to the ocean and plant vegetables and live off the land. We would take Tommy with us, of course. But mainly we would just keep on riding. I didn't think about mama. I realize now I wasn't letting myself think about her. In my mind I could see Virginia and James

Junior somewhere up ahead, looking just as they'd looked before we left Springfield. I did not see mama.

It was forty miles from Johnson's to the ranch where they were staying. I didn't see her until we reached the gate. She'd been waiting there for days, and her eyes were brimming over with relief and love and pain and heartache. Some ranch hands lifted me out of the sling. She scooped me up. It wasn't forgiveness I felt. There was nothing to forgive. I guess I was wiser than I had been. In that instant I knew her. I knew all she had endured. A great warmth poured through me, sadness and gratitude all swelling together.

While mama held me, a cloud of ducks flew past. It was the middle of March. Weak as I was, it made the spirit soar to see all that green, flat country, so well watered, right on the edge of bursting forth, with living creatures everywhere you looked, or so it seemed to me. It could have been the first day of creation, and that flock of ducks had just been born among the tules. In the whole history of the world they were the first ducks to swarm up from the banks of the wide river and try their wings.

SOONER OR LATER we all straggled down out of the snow, the families who'd survived, and the pieces of families. Six months earlier there'd been eighty-seven in our wagon party. All told, forty-eight had come through the winter, among them Patrick and Peggy and their seven kids. After the third rescue team helped them get to Sutter's, they sat still again, while they built up enough strength to move. There'd been days when I hated Patrick, but I see now I'd already left my hatred back in the mountains that had set so many demons loose. Everyone knew the grim details of how they'd fed themselves at Starved Camp. It was another story the reporters could not leave alone. Around the fort people would watch them with covert eyes or sometimes stare with shameless and undisguised fascination. "It's awful to think about," you'd hear someone mutter. "Still, you got to give 'em credit. They brought every last one of their young'uns through, they surely did." Before long the Breens were heading south, away from so many questioning eyes, to a warm valley where a Franciscan padre befriended them, gave them a sheltered place to camp and heal.

The last one to leave the cabins was Lewis Keseberg. When the fourth and final rescue team reached Truckee Lake, they found him alone, still nursing his infected foot, surviving on the remains of those who'd died around him, various children, the widow Murphy, and Tamsen Donner too, who'd stayed with her husband to the end. The fellows who brought Keseberg out described detestable sights inside his den, kettles where flesh was cooking, arm and leg bones strewn indoors and out. During his weeks of solitude, they said, his humanity had slipped away, he had become a monster, addicted to his ghastly diet. Once they all got back to Sutter's, Keseberg disputed these charges, claiming his only other choice was death by starvation. But few listened. He became an outcast. Boys threw rocks and called him "cannibal." He felt safer on the river, for a while working as a schooner pilot, thanks to Captain Sutter, who took pity on him, perhaps because they both spoke German and had relatives back in Europe.

It was a season for pity. Everyone, it seems, found a benefactor. The rancher who took us in said we could stay through the summer if need be, and for a month or so it looked like we would. The trek out had nearly broken papa's health. For two weeks he was laid up, his toes frostbitten, his hands bent like claws. He'd lost some sight in one eye. For that matter we were all laid up. Tommy almost died. He was like a campfire that dwindles down to the last dim glow of the final ember. Little by little, mama brought him back, though for months he couldn't walk more than fifteen or twenty minutes before he'd lose his breath.

About the time we all got to where we could hobble around and take short hikes across the field, a wagon appeared in the yard one afternoon. It was something like the wagons we'd left in the Salt Desert, a mule-drawn Conestoga with canvas curving over high hoops. The driver said he'd come to carry us to Napa Valley, where a friend of papa's awaited our arrival. He referred to the miller who'd helped papa put his rescue team together, the one who'd dreamed in advance of people held captive by the mountain snow. Though he had never been near those mountains, he had dreamed this vivid dream three nights in a row and forever after felt bound to papa and to our family, since he knew without a doubt that we were the very ones revealed to him in his vision.

The miller had got word of our whereabouts. He wanted to help out any way he could. He too was inviting us to stay as long as we needed, and papa took him up on it. With so much coming and going right there around the fort, drifters and refugees and other families like ours wondering what was going to happen next, papa figured there'd be more room at the miller's ranch, as well as more peace and quiet.

The next morning we were pioneers again, riding along in a covered wagon, almost like when we'd started out from Springfield, rolling across the Sacramento Valley toward another mountain range, on one more leg of our trip to California, except this time it wasn't papa's wagon or papa's mules, and we didn't have anything to load but our bodies and the clothes we wore and a few odds and ends brought from the lake camp and one big canvas tent papa bought on credit from Captain Sutter.

Just like he promised, we had made it through at last, our whole family. I owed my life to him, and it was heaven to be together again, though I can't forget, as I think back, that if it weren't for papa we would never have found ourselves split apart in the first place and in such a dire fix. And saying that doesn't mean I love him any less. I don't love him any less. I don't. You couldn't have stopped him. Or stopped them. Or stopped any of it. Not with an army division and a long row of cannon on the banks of the Missouri River telling everybody to turn right around and go back home. It was his own desire and refusal to be thwarted that had put us on the trail and led us up to that high altitude and also brought him back into the mountains to carry on the journey, and right in there somewhere is the very nub and mystery of it all.

Springtime 1847

In the coastal valleys sheets of color spread across the grass and climb the slopes, blue-purple lupin, poppies, goldfield, paintbrush, fiddleneck, white and yellow daisies. Here and there owl's clover lays a broad magenta stripe. Up and down the land, swarms of color charm the eye, while the rivers carry barges once again. Between the port and Sutter's, cargo schooners ply the Sacramento. Floodwaters have receded, though the rivers run full, as snow melts in the high country to feed the many creeks and trickling tributaries and flow to sea level, surrounding the delta islands, merging with the salty tides that fill the bay.

Ships of war that held the north have sailed away, heading back around Cape Horn for Boston and Long Island, or making stops at Mazatlán, Acapulco, closer to the battlegrounds where the war with Mexico will continue through the summer. As a show of force a thousand new troops have landed at Monterey, rowdy, restless Army volunteers. Other ships have come with new commanders to oversee the transfer of power. New American alcaldes are appointed. Edicts spill forth in English and in Spanish, pages full of words to govern actions in this far-off and barely governed corner of the world.

The Californians—the vaqueros, the politicians, the men and women of the ranching families—are still divided among themselves. Some refuse to hear these pages, mistrusting foreigners and their promises. Others welcome the words and welcome the Americans, now that the fighting is done, glad to be free of Mexico's corruption and indifference, and believing they will soon have an equal place in the new democracy they've heard so much about.

The emigrants are divided too. Some listen to the edicts, some ignore them, figuring they did not travel all this way to be ruled by captains and commodores. They fan out among the towns and fertile valleys. Twelve hundred came across last fall. Some say it was closer to fifteen hundred. Already more are on their way, more wagons, more oxen, more wanderers and renegades, more families with their heirlooms and their guidebooks, though not as many as set out last spring, since the news of what befell those trapped through the winter has reached the eastern papers. Lurid, bloodthirsty tales have made some would-be travelers cautious. First the war, they think, and now this? Maybe they'll wait a year and weigh the wisdom of a continental crossing. They haven't heard much from the wagon trains that made it through in good time. They only hear about the one that didn't. And so it is in Alta California, where neighbors and drinking pals do not trade stories about travelers who arrived intact. They vie with one another to embellish the dark story from the mountains. Like the snowmelt with its many sources, the story trickles down to sea level. Everyone wants to talk about it, everyone but the survivors, who only wish to get on with their lives.

In the valley called Napa, north of San Francisco Bay, Jim and Margaret have pitched their tent downstream from the ranch house of the miller. They have watched the bodies of their children bloat with unfamiliar nourishment, then watched the bloating subside. The children are looking normal again, normal youngsters who romp and scamper as the springtime juices rise into limbs reborn. The mother and the father need an hour to themselves, and so one sunny afternoon they set out hand in hand across the meadow.

The air is balmy. The sky is clear. Jim carries his coat. He wears his wide-brim Spanish hat at an angle. Margaret doesn't wear a hat. Her hair is bunched loosely in a knot. The miller's house is far behind them, under oaks, in the lee of a sheltering hump of a hill. His mill stands beside the creek. Beyond the house, outside their tent, Patty sits upon a stool with her brothers at her feet. She is the teacher, they the pupils. Underneath the burly, twisted limbs the boys take turns reading, spelling out words they do not know.

As soon as Jim and Margaret walked away, Virginia passed the reader to her little sister and slipped behind the tree to peek into a thin volume of stories taken from *The Lives of the Saints*. She steals this chance to read in secret, knowing how papa would disapprove. Virginia is true to her mountain vow, inspired by Patrick's incantations. She believes his praying saved them, and she still repeats the prayers learned in the wintry cabin. Before long she will marry an Irish Catholic, a handsome fellow ten years her senior, and Jim, the outraged father, will take down his shotgun and threaten to shoot him on sight for robbing the cradle. The bride and groom will have to flee on horseback and hide until his Irish temper cools. But that is many moons away.

Today, while Virginia relishes the persecutions of thirteen-year-old Saint Agnes, Virgin and Martyr, Jim and Margaret walk through a meadow quilted with flowers. The miller's house is out of sight. Underfoot the earth is spongy, so fecund you can almost hear the grasses growing blade by blade and tiny blossoms opening wider to the sun.

As if to gather in a bushel of the fragrant air, Margaret throws her arms out wide.

"Is there a lovelier place in all the world?"

"There can't be many," says Jim.

"We ought to stay right here, you know."

"Perhaps we will."

"We ought to settle here and never leave."

"First I want you to see another valley, down the bay."

"Can it possibly have flowers as magnificent as these?"

"I guarantee it. I have a spot picked out, right beside an orchard, with a view to take your breath away. We'll take the children there. You'll fall in love with that place too."

"On such a day as this, James, the mountains are nothing but an awful dream."

"Well, that is all behind us now."

"Yes. On such a day there is no need to speak of it. I don't ever want to speak of it."

"On this very day," Jim says, "our lives begin anew."

While they walk he slips an arm around her waist and tugs to pull her closer. She resists the tug but lets his hand linger. Through the cloth he feels the flesh that has filled out around her ribs and hips. He savors it. With wonder he presses it, explores the flesh, grateful for this fullness that has finally returned. He would rather not remember what he felt there when they met in the snow. But her waist reminds him and will always remind him of her frail voice calling as he ran to her and how she stumbled and collapsed and could not rise. She had to wait until he raised her, and how light she was, with no body there, it seemed, nothing but the skeleton. If he held too tightly he could break her into pieces. His arms around her back could feel sharp ribs and spine, as if underneath her cloak the skin and muscle had dissolved. Something passed from her to him, like an electric current, and he knew then what had been done and what it cost. In her fleshless ribs he felt it, and in her eyes he saw it. Protruding bones gave them a mad, unearthly look. Horror and grief filled him with nausea, and he, too, nearly lost the power to stand. He wanted nothing more than to keep her in his arms and carry her down the mountain to Bear Valley and on down the canyons to warmth and food and safety. He could have carried her all the way, without a stop. But she pushed him back, saying Patty and Tommy were still waiting at the lake, saying this with a terrible warning in her voice, as if the children spoke through her, with that call of frantic emergency that is different from every other cry and can never be ignored. He had to leave her, and leave Virginia, with what provisions could be spared, trusting Glover to lead them out.

Three weeks later, when they met again at the ranch across from Sutter's, Jim was the shrunken one, the bent and nearly broken one, with Patty on his back, her spindly legs hanging past the sling—his knees swollen, his fingers throbbing, his body burned and bruised and cut and suddenly overwhelmed with a deeper weariness than he'd ever known. For a month he had not slept three hours in a night. But only then, as he saw Margaret standing by the fence gate, with Virginia and James Junior, did he allow himself to feel it. The whole five months caught up with him as he surrendered to this bottomless fatigue. He looked then as she had looked when he met her in the mountains. In the eyes that wanted to welcome him and welcome Patty, he saw the mirror of what they had all endured. He couldn't speak. Somehow he climbed off the horse. For twenty-four hours he slept.

Since that day, little by little, he has recounted to her his pilgrimage through Alta California. And Margaret has listened, but has yet to tell him much at all. Glover has told him that taking Patty and Tommy back to the lake camp was his idea and that Margaret wept afterward for two full days. She is like someone badly wounded in a war, who cannot begin to tell you how it was. Her eyes are sometimes bright with tears about to spill, sometimes as hard as steel, aimed at him as if they would slice him into strips. He can't read these eyes, what form of pain they carry, or anger, or bitterness, or shame. He watches her handle each piece of bacon, each scoop of flour as if it is the last, to be treasured and honored and defended. Twice she has appeared to him in dreams, looking as she looked when they met in the mountains, her shrunken face, while his hands feel the ribs protruding. Twice in the darkness his eyes have sprung open, and he has reached out to touch her, to test the thickness of her flesh.

This afternoon the flesh across her waist is soft. Beneath it her back is tight. Inside the stand of redwoods, fallen leaves and tiny russet needles are softly layered. Many seasons have made a brown cushion here. Bars of sunlight fall through higher branches to dapple the ground. Jim lays out his coat, and they sit side by side, not talking. So long since they've been alone, a thousand things to talk about, and Jim does not know what to say. As he looks up into the mote-filled dome, he feels fingers easing through his dark hair, where sun rays light the scalp.

She touches half-hidden scars, probing for the place she last saw on the day it was torn open, the day his blood spilled. The welts are hard and smooth. Her touch is careful. Her brows squeeze with worry. He doesn't want to speak. He wants to sit very still, with her hand upon his scalp. If her fingers remain there long enough the scars will recede and disappear.

"Such a blow you took that day," she says.

"And so did you. He knocked you to the ground."

"Mine was just a bruise. This must have been a long time healing."

"It's come around. I don't feel it anymore."

She pulls the hand away and locks her arms around drawn-up knees, as if waiting for something. But for what? For me, he thinks. She is waiting for me to justify myself.

"Margaret . . ." he begins.

She looks straight ahead. "You mustn't apologize, James."

"If I could have that one day back . . ."

"What you did there, you had to do."

In the shady grove her voice is soft, almost a whisper. Somehow her voice releases him.

"I'll make it up to you," he says.

She shakes her head, her voice hoarse, and lower still, as if rising from somewhere else, from subsoil waters where the trees are drinking.

"Each one did what they had to do. And that is all I am ever going to say. I have thought about this. It is all anyone can say. Do you understand me? You saw our cabins, what we were reduced to. You saw the winter in those mountains. We are not the ones to judge. Only God can judge such times. If we spend our days judging one another we will never be able to continue with our lives."

She waits a while, as if waiting for him to speak. But he cannot. His throat has closed, his chest is filled with heat. His eyes are brimming. So are hers, when she eventually turns to face him.

In a lighter voice she says, "Do you believe in miracles, James?"

Now something glints through her tears. A flicker of some younger Margaret?

"Perhaps I do," he says.

"Then touch my head."

"Where?"

"Wherever you feel like touching. Tell me what you find."

She leans toward him, lets him draw her head in close, while he presses his hands against her hair, here, then there. Each touch for him is a gift, a little ecstasy. He feels like laughing.

"Is anything different?" she says at last.

"The hair and head of my same sweet Margaret."

"It must be true, then."

"What must be true?"

"What they say about the climate."

"What who says?"

"My headaches have gone away."

"Just now?"

"Entirely."

"You mean this minute?"

"Sometime back, I think. I can't say just when. Only this moment did I realize . . . we've been so occupied . . . but it has been days, perhaps a few weeks!"

"My dear, this is wonderful news."

He watches her mouth twist and open. Her mouth wants to laugh. She tries not to, as if she does not deserve to laugh. But she can't repress it. Like brook water it ripples forth, almost a reckless laugh. He laughs with her, remembering a picnic long ago in Illinois on a springtime riverbank, just the two of them, before Patty came along.

"Can you believe it, James?"

"Of course I can believe it. And I tell you what. We should announce that a marvelous cure has now been found . . ."

"Don't make a joke of this."

"I'm not joking."

"It's a blessing. A great blessing."

"Of course it is. All I'm saying is that we must advertise and follow the example of the infamous Lansford Hastings. Three months in the Sierras and your headaches will be forever cured . . ."

She pretends to be insulted, starts to rise up from their loamy couch. Jim grabs her wrist and pulls her closer still. In the shaded grove they laugh again, old lovers with a secret.

She says, "We must be quiet."

"No one will find us here."

"The children scurry everywhere. They are like forest creatures."

"I have watched them. They never roam this far from the ranch house."

"So you have planned this out ahead of time."

"I simply share with you what I have observed."

Her eyes begin to glow. In her cheeks high color rises, as if she runs a fever. He kisses her forehead, her eyes, her crimson cheeks.

"Softly, James."

His hand slides across the skirt, bunching it against her leg.

"Be gentle," she says.

"Such a long time . . ."

"I know."

"So very long."

"I know. But please . . ."

"My heart's so full."

"And mine too. But I beg of you . . ."

"My love . . ."

"Gently. Please."

"Love. My love. Is your heart as full as mine?"

"Yes, oh, yes. But please, James, please . . . remember."

from The Trail Notes of Patty Reed

One More Entry

California is like a pretty girl.
Everybody wants her.

—*Lt. Francisco Arce (1846)*

For some people a desert is the magic place. For some, it is the mountains. For some, the sea. It's good for the soul, they say, to live within view of one or the other of these great sources of inspiration. In all these years I've only been back to the mountains once, and I didn't like it, for reasons anyone could understand. As for the desert, one look in that direction, my eyes begin to sting with sunburned salt, my throat goes dry as an empty riverbed. So I have ended up here in a seacoast town right next to the ocean, which thus far has never hurt me.

I told that to my son when he bought this house and insisted I move in with him. There are many rooms, mother, he said, a garden, a wide front porch. You won't have a single thing in the world to do, he said, but enjoy the view, and you won't have to lift a finger. Though I was comfortable where I'd been, I knew coming here would bring me that much closer to the sea. And so I came. And each day now it gives me something. I never know quite what to expect. You have to wait. You have to watch.

This afternoon a storm moves toward us across Monterey Bay. You can see slate clouds gathering, edging out the puffy white ones that have hovered since dawn. The water takes its color from the sky, gray as metal now, but not a gloomy gray. The surface has a grain, like tree bark. Each scoop and ripple catches light, a thousand specks of light thrown across the water from a patch of silver way out there past the point.

Somewhere behind the cloud cover, bright sun is shining down to make that one stretch molten. There are no downward rays, as you might expect. Under a dark sky, at the far edge of the metal-colored bay, this silvery patch has its own special life. And in the very midst of it I see a wave lift, like a huge fish coming to the surface, as if drawn up into this one bright region of the water. It rises, it peaks, the white foam leaps forth, and it occurs to me that certain moments in your life can be like this wave, singled out and fully lit. A year later, or five years later, or seventy-five, you regard them as if they are still happening. I think in particular of the day I saw Salvador again, in the mission orchard, or thought I did, wondering why he had followed us such a long, long way; and I think also of the day, a few weeks earlier, when we left Napa Valley and started south for San Jose.

To make such a journey you could take horses clear around the bay and skirt the delta, going by way of the San Joaquin and Livermore valleys, which might mean a week or more, depending on the weather and the width of the streams. Or you could take one of the ferrying vessels.

We had crossed many streams and creeks and rivers. But I had never been on open water. From Sonoma landing we took a cutter down through the curving creek, past the marshland, out onto the broad blue bay. For the first time I felt the tidal pulse, the flowing in and flowing out of waters pushed by oceans I had yet to see. The briny smell was like perfume. I can smell it now, from my front porch, and it lifts my spirits still. Off to the right of us Tamalpais humped against the morning sky, holding back a cotton wall of fog. The mountain seemed to cast a shadow across the water. But it wasn't a shadow. The sun was overhead. It was a swarm of seals as closely packed as kelp. A world of seals had darkened one whole corner of the bay.

I remember a lone gray gull with a white beak, hanging on the wind as if suspended from an invisible cord. We moved along, but the gull didn't move. It hovered, watching us pass, and it seemed wondrous to me. I studied it for as long as I could, amazed by how it used the wind to hold its place in the air.

As I look back, each moment of the sailing was like that. By age nine I had come to see that each hour of my life was a wonder. Life itself was a precious gift. And simply being warm. I was still a long way from taking warmth for granted, or sitting in the sunshine, or having a dress to wear that was not wet and stiff with ice, and having food before us whenever we were hungry. Any form of food filled me with gratitude. To this day I will not waste a morsel if I can help it. Each morning I give thanks for the gift of my life.

That afternoon we anchored at Yerba Buena cove. The fellow who rowed us in was a Mormon. It seemed like half the people there were Mormons. With a challenging eye he asked papa what he thought about the town's new name. Papa said he couldn't say unless he knew what it was. He'd run into the fellow once before, the first time he crossed the bay to take care of some business at the port. He already knew the name but acted like a newcomer, just leading the fellow on.

We all got a lecture then. We heard this boatman scoff at Washington Bartlett, formerly the mayor. Before he sailed back to New England with the fleet, he had renamed the town San Francisco. To match the name of the bay, Bartlett said. According to the boatman, a lot of people didn't like it, and some never would.

"Every town on this whole blamed coast is named after a Catholic," he complained, "from San Diego clear on up!"

We stayed overnight in a rooming house papa knew about. He showed us the hall where they held the meeting to raise money for the rescue and told us who all was there. The changes in the town amazed him. In just eight months the population had doubled, he said. It still wasn't much to look at, by today's standards, but it was the biggest town I'd seen in over a year. There must have been fifteen ships offshore. Two years later, of course, the bay would be filled with ships from every port on earth, and the town spreading every which way, up the hills and out toward what they call North Beach, and clear over to Mission Dolores. Wharves would poke into the bay like the fingers of a giant hand, as crowds poured in looking for the nuggets that would make them rich.

I've heard people say the Gold Rush made California the kind of place it is today. Why do you think it's called the Golden State, they will say. I suppose they're right. But as I look back, the towns were already filling up with dreamers and schemers, my papa, James Frazier Reed, among them. The day we stopped in San Francisco was still four months before James Marshall came into Sutter's Fort with the little sack of shiny flakes and flecks and pebbles he had taken out of the American River. It was September 1847, and already there was a current in the air. I can't help thinking if it hadn't been the Gold Rush it *would have been some other kind of rush. There was a look in the eye of every person you saw of something on the verge and about to burst forth. You could see it in papa's eye after we had climbed the hill from the beach, as he stood in Portsmouth Square counting the buildings he hadn't seen before. He'd lost a hundred animals and three loaded wagons and most of his money. He'd lost a lot of his pride too and his stubbornness. But he had not lost his drive or his will. He was not too old to start over. The fact is, there were no two ways about it. In those days you could not take out much time to lick your wounds. It was start over or die.*

THE NEXT MORNING *we were on the water gain, tacking against a steady wind out of the south and west. As we neared the lower end of the bay I could see a green fringe ahead, with mountains swelling on both sides. Far away to the south the ranges seemed to meet. It looked like we were sailing into a flat-bottomed bowl. The fringe turned out to be a border of tule fields. Guadalupe Creek came out of the coastal mountains and flowed across Santa Clara Valley from south to north and wound through these tules for six or seven miles, among the sloughs and muddy islands. The wind was out of the north now. It ruffled the blue-green water and eased us along a twisting channel lined with stalks and tassels rustling in the wind.*

As I imagine how we must have looked that day, coming up to the wharf, I am reminded of men we would see years later when there were streets in San Jose and San Francisco, men we'd known in the mountains. You would never be able to tell, from the tailored cut of their coats and fancy hats, the unspeakable things they had done to one another. As we stood on the deck, you would never have known what mama's eyes had seen, or my eyes, or papa's, or Virginia's. We were just one more load of emigrants like those who'd been rolling and riding and sailing in for all these months, glad to be there and looking for a new place to set down roots.

A wagon carried us into the pueblo. We stopped long enough to pick up some provisions and three horses papa had bought and kept boarded at a livery stable. Then we rode on around the southern shore of the bay and up to the Mission of St. Joseph and pitched our tent underneath an old fig tree with limbs so thick and layered we almost could have got along without the tent. The ground smelled like figs and grass and sweet jam, though the trees had been picked clean. Papa had ferried down from Napa twice to get the fruit harvested, those acres of pears and apples and figs and quince. He had found his first nest egg hanging from those limbs. He got the fruit dried and sacked and hauled to the port and shipped clear across to the Hawaiian Islands to trade for sugar and coffee and coconut oil. Captain Sutter told him how to do it. He'd been out to Honolulu and knew half the people there, or so he claimed.

Once we had our camp set up, papa started mending walls and fences, puttering around the trees, clearing a place where he believed he would build a house once he had an uncontested title. Every couple of days he would ride into the pueblo, where he had been elected to the new town council. He was that kind of go-getter. They already had big plans for Alta California, which in those days stretched clear across to Utah. It could all be one big state of the Union, they told one another, with the capital right there in San Jose de Guadalupe.

At age nine, of course, I didn't know all this. I was busy savoring each day. I think of it as the high point of our gypsy period, a golden time that came to a sudden and unforeseeable end.

I had started keeping a diary, as I'd seen Virginia do. There was a bulky apple trunk I liked to hide behind while I wrote out my little entry for the day. One afternoon, deep in concentration, I heard a scrape and peeked around the side of my tree and saw an Indian about fifty feet away, sitting on a horse. There were still Indians all through that country but we had not seen any close to the mission. It was odd for him to be there alone, like a man staring through a window who doesn't think anyone can see him.

The air was still. The leaves around him hung in silence, the only sound a distant <u>chuck</u> of papa's axe where he was cutting wood. A low adobe wall ran along one side of the old garden compound, with the orchard starting behind this wall, and that's where he was, back in among the trees, studying our tent. He looked familiar to me, the way he sat so straight, the shape of his head and face, the black hair hanging beneath his hat, though the hat was different and the clothes too, high boots, a Spanish jacket. But the buttery light of late afternoon gave his brown skin a softness I remembered.

Nine months had passed since the Snowshoe Party left Truckee Lake. I still didn't know all that happened on that trip. While we were at the fort I'd seen the wounded eyes of Bill Eddy. I'd seen Mary Graves, who once would glare at me but now looked like a prisoner released from solitary confinement. When I asked mama about Salvador and Luis she shook her head and looked away and said they'd been lost in the mountains. I knew "lost" could mean dead. I guess I also wanted it to mean they might still be "found."

So I observed this fellow carefully, while he observed our tent and around it the dormitories and remnants of the mission garden and beyond that the old sheds and abandoned warehouses and mud-walled chapel with its deep-set window frames, and roof caved in, as if he'd been sitting on his horse for centuries watching things appear and disappear.

When I could bear it no longer I stepped out from behind my tree. Like a little test of my voice in the orchard quiet, I said, softly, "Cuidado, señor."

His body jerked, and this startled the horse. His features changed so quickly, I cried out. The smoothness turned hard and angry. It was a stranger's face. I ran to the wall and through the gateway, calling to papa, just then bringing an armload of kindling up to the fire pit behind the tent, where mama cooked. Beside him James Junior and Tommy came dragging branches.

I said, "There's a man here, papa."

"Looks like two men, darlin'."

I turned and saw another rider, leading a string of horses along the far side of the orchard. He was a white man with a black chin beard, in a fancy riding jacket and buckskin pants. He carried a pistol at his waist, a rifle, a powder horn, and a Bowie knife. The Indian had a rifle too and a big knife in his belt, and he wore the kind of cap I'd seen marines in San Francisco wearing, flat and blue with a narrow bill. Everyone carried weapons, of course. It was the white man's voice that fed my apprehension, mocking, insinuating. As he came up beside the wall he said, "Good evening, Reed."

"I told you not to bother me out here."

"We're only passing through."

"You thought I was joking."

"Not you, Reed," he said with a high laugh, too loud, it seemed to me. "You wouldn't joke about that."

"Then be on your way."

"If I refuse, will you bring my name before the council?"

"Don't provoke me."

His horse was restless, snuffing and jerking, pawing through mulch as if it wanted to leap the wall. Both riders were straining at their reins.

"You and the Alcalde are plotting the future," he said. "Large plans are afoot, or so I hear."

"These days," papa said, "everyone has plans."

"Yet I am not part of them."

"Is this what you came to tell me?"

The commotion brought mama round from where she'd been cutting up some meat.

"Is this Mrs. Reed?"

Mama nodded.

"Abner Valentine," he said with a bow over his pommel and a smile of excessive courtesy. "It is my great pleasure and honor. Your husband and I rode together on the plain of Santa Clara . . ."

"Yes. I've heard about that."

I'd heard about it too. I'd heard papa talk with other men about the battle and heard the way they spoke of one called Valentine. He had become a notorious figure who roamed the hills and valleys, a man who hated Mexicans and possessed vast horse herds somewhere inland. They made it sound as if he'd rounded up every animal west of the Mississippi. No one claimed him as a friend, but you could tell they reveled in the stories of his exploits and his treachery. As is the case with most notorious figures I have happened to run into, he was a disappointment up close, smaller than I expected him to be and something of a dandy.

He sat in his saddle with an expectant smile, as if waiting for mama to say more about what she'd heard, or perhaps invite him to come sit with us, which is what she would have said to almost anyone else who rode up out of nowhere this close to dinnertime. She just watched him, the way papa did.

As if he had some claim on all this property, Valentine looked around and said to mama, like a landlord, "I congratulate you, ma'am, you've made quite a pleasant campsite." Then he said to papa, "I need a brief word with you. Is there a place where we can talk?"

"Tomorrow will be fine. In San Jose."

Valentine shook his head with a bitter smile, almost a sneer. "I'm finished with the pueblo."

Now papa's face was tight. "What's your business, then? Get to it, and be on your way."

"You disappoint me, Reed. I was hoping you'd be in a more sociable mood. Under the circumstances I can make a long story short. You remember my friend Carlos . . ."

"Indeed I do," said papa. "Buenas tardes."

With a curt nod the Indian muttered, "Buenas tardes." He wasn't looking at papa. He seemed to be looking right at me.

Valentine said, "Carlos has come to collect his money."

I could feel papa bristle. He took pride in never owing any man for long. "And what money is that?"

Valentine spoke to mama, as if enlisting her support, but with an edge of syrupy sarcasm. "It's a matter of history. I once told your husband all these trees were for the taking. But I was wrong, and I apologize. Carlos asks me to remind you that his father was an orchard man for the padres. All these trees were planted by his father, who tended them, nurtured them as he nurtured his own sons. Now Carlos would like some compensation, that's all. It's not a lot to ask."

Mama looked at papa. With the color rising through his beard, papa looked at Valentine. Whether or not Carlos understood what had been said on his behalf, you couldn't tell. He still looked at me, his lips parted, as if he'd seen a ghost.

Papa said, "You're making this up."

"Isn't it true that fruit was harvested . . . ?"

"I have petitions. I have papers . . ."

"Surely some respect and recognition is due for those who brought these trees to life . . ."

He was so smug I knew papa wanted to take him by the neck. Valentine seemed on the verge of laughter, as if playing with us, as if he'd made this stop to stir up papa, pester him for having a family and landing a seat on the council, and if he could scare some money out of him along the way, well, that would be a bonus. Maybe he'd been drinking. It had the feel of an ugly prank. But something happened he didn't expect, judging by the look that now replaced his smirk.

Carlos was talking in Spanish, talking fast, pointing with one hand at me, holding the other against his throat.

Not so cocky, Valentine said, "That pendant your daughter wears . . ."

My hand reached up to touch the smoothness of the shell. Papa glanced down at me. My head felt light.

He said, "Keep my children out of this!"

"Where did it come from?"

"Do you hear me, Valentine?"

"Carlos is telling me it belonged to his brother."

"His brother?"

"He wants to have a closer look."

"What brother? Patty," papa said, "I told you not to wear that thing."

As Carlos once again filled the air with Spanish words none of us could follow, papa's anger boiled up.

"You sonofabitch! Get off this property, both of you! Margaret, go get the rifles!"

"My God, James!"

"Get them," he said, not looking at her. His eyes stayed on Valentine. "Make sure they're loaded."

"Hold on, Reed. There's no need for firearms."

"That's right. As long as you are on your way."

Mama came out of the tent with two rifles, passing one to papa, holding the other to her chest like a sentry. Right behind her came Virginia, pale and hunched a bit. She'd been down all day with stomach cramps but could not bear to remain inside the tent. Carlos looked at Virginia, and looked at the rifles. You can imagine what was going through his mind, one Indian and all of us whites, and he probably didn't trust Valentine any more than papa did.

"He says his brother rides for John Sutter."

"We've finished talking, Valentine."

"Wait!" said mama. Straight to Carlos she said, "What is your brother's name?"

I think he understood this. But he wouldn't answer. In Spanish Valentine repeated it. Still he wouldn't answer, as if he did not want to say the name.

"Was it Salvador?" said mama.

Carlos nodded, then, very agitated, spoke again to Valentine, whose voice took on a new urgency.

"When did you see his brother?"

"Many months ago," said mama.

"Is it true he was killed in the mountains?"

Papa said, "That was none of our doing."

"Carlos believes his brother was killed by whites."

Now mama spoke up, worry and compassion in her eyes. "Tell him his brother traveled in our party. Before he went away he left this orna-ment . . . as a gift."

As Valentine relayed all this, Carlos became very still in his saddle. His horse was still, and he was like a statue. Not a muscle moved. But his eyes were wild. It was like the moment before an earthquake hits, when the air is charged with a power you cannot name. You could see he wanted to do something and was going to do something. Who knew what he was thinking, seeing his dead brother's pendant around the neck of a white girl.

I think their words had hit him hard. I know they hit me, confirming what I'd feared but couldn't look at. I'm still glad I did not yet know the rest of Salvador's story. Years would have to pass, while the shreds and versions of the many stories came to me, of how lives were lost or saved that winter, before I saw that our guides were the only ones shot for food, the way you'd shoot a deer or a buffalo. A lifetime later it can still make me sick with rage. But on that day I only knew that they were dead. I felt no rage. I felt a huge grief. It filled my chest like a stone. I lifted the cord of woven fiber over my head and took a step toward Carlos.

"Patty!" mama cried. "You get inside the tent!"

I didn't look at her. I stood with the pendant on my outstretched palm. In amazement Carlos regarded it, and Valentine too. Neither of them knew what to do.

I said, "Para usted, señor." For you.

He seemed transfixed by the pendant. It had some features anyone would be able to recognize, a slight curve from the shape of the shell, and five sides, each one cut smooth. In certain light its pearly colors made a looping line like a distant river gleaming in the sun.

I said, "Salvador es mi hermano también." He is my brother too.

Carlos lifted his gaze and looked at me for a long time, right into my eyes. He blinked once. Twice. I saw Salvador then, inside his eyes. I knew with certainty that they were brothers, and that all of them had once lived here where we were standing, the sons, the father, the mother too, a family much like ours, living in one of the shacks now falling to pieces, while the father laid out the orchards.

At last he said quietly, "Si. Es un regalo. Es la suya." It is a gift, it belongs to you.

Something rose out of his throat then that was not Spanish, and it was not English, nor any language you could name, unless it be the most basic language we can utter. His head tipped back and a low groan came forth that swelled to a howling wail. My arm hairs prickled and the hairs on the back of my neck stood out. I'd heard this same sound once before, on the morning we woke just below the summit, covered with snow. I looked at papa. His eyes were wide in a way I saw only that day and never again, his whole face naked.

The long, lamenting call became a word, the first word of a chant, as the voice itself began to crack and weep, and what I heard was Salvador coming through his brother. It was the same mournful and piercing voice, filling the orchard and all the air around the mission, as over and over the words were chanted, and we knew something then we did not know before. We knew something about what had been harvested from those rows of trees, though no one mentioned it, on that day or any later day. Papa knew then, though he never said so out loud, that we would not remain any longer on the mission grounds, as he had envisioned. Someone else would have to take over the orchards, someone who had not heard the voice of Carlos wailing for his brother.

His chant finally dwindled and fell off into silence. Abruptly he turned his horse and began to trot away.

Valentine called, "Donde va?"

He waited for an answer, then shouted, "Carlos! Donde va!"

Carlos stopped and turned in the saddle, his dark face again a mask. "Voy a buscar mi padre." I'm going to look for my father.

He pulled off his vaquero's jacket and threw it on the ground. He threw down his marine's cap, so that his black hair swung loose. As he moved off through the trees his horse broke into a gallop and he was gone.

I heard Valentine murmur, "Cabrón."

Papa said, "Will he be back?"

"No telling what he'll do. A dangerous fellow in the best of times."

"Will you see him again?"

"I don't know."

"*You tell him the man who killed his brother is way up north. I couldn't begin to say where. It was none of our doing.*"

"*You need some protection here. Perhaps you'll invite me to stay the night.*"

With a nervous, incredulous laugh papa said, "You think we'd feel safer with you around?"

Valentine looked wounded by this remark. Then he revived his cocky smirk. "If you need me I won't be far away. The Indians are a vengeful people, but different from the Mexicans, who lack patience. Give me a thousand dollars to split with Carlos, and we'll call it square."

Papa raised his rifle and cocked it. "Good-bye, Valentine."

"*Forget about Carlos. Forget about the Indians. With them or without them we'll do quite well. But don't forget my offer. It's always open. Why fritter away your talents on the council when there's so much more to be had for the taking? Ride with me, Reed."*

Papa didn't speak. They looked at each other until Valentine turned and trotted over to his string of horses. He led them back the way he'd come, past the trees, toward the hills beyond the mission.

That evening at dinner nobody said much because papa was so pensive. Next morning two of his horses were gone. He figured it was Valentine, something he'd do for his own amusement, hoping we'd read it as an Indian warning and Carlos would get the blame.

Papa didn't go after him that day, said he'd catch up with him sooner or later, though to my knowledge he never did. Papa was not a vengeful man. He did not feel compelled to settle every score. If he never saw Valentine again, I heard him tell mama, it might be worth two horses. The fact was, papa didn't have much time just then for getting even. After he'd finishing cursing Valentine and his devious ways and the day they'd met, he said we were going to leave the mission grounds and move closer to town.

"*We're too exposed," he said. "Anything could happen."*

Mama didn't disagree. Overnight we'd had a heavy rain. It was the first of October. The tent was soaked through and all our bedding.

"*The children will be better off," he said, "where there's more folks to help us keep an eye on things. We're sitting ducks out here."*

He didn't say the name of Carlos or of Salvador that day or on any later day, nor did mama, nor did we ever see Carlos again or hear any word of him. It was as if he and his brother and Luis had never existed, as if they had been added to all the names and places and trials and tribulations mama and papa hoped to leave behind.

"Let us never speak of those months," mama told us all, soon after we'd come out of the mountains. "Talking cannot change the past. What's done is done, and life goes on." While that is surely true, it is also true that the places you have been stay with you, whether you talk of them or not.

BEFORE THE RAINS *came again, he rented us an adobe cottage across from the pueblo church, on what is now Market Street. It wasn't much, one room with a dirt floor and a hole in the ceiling to let smoke out, and one door made of stiff cowhide like the door William Johnson had at the edge of his wilderness. The Alcalde put papa in touch with an old-time ranching family like his wife's, and papa paid them cash for a sizable tract of pueblo land. Come spring he took off for the goldfields along with all the other men in San Jose. By the end of summer he was back with enough to build a big adobe ranch house, close to what was soon to be the southern edge of town, where he thrived until the squatters moved in.*

I guess you could say the squatters shared Valentine's view of life out west. A lot of forty-niners and disgruntled argonauts, once they learned there wasn't near enough gold to go around, went out looking for land, any parcel that appealed to them, whether claimed by some-one else or not. It rankled them that some folks had got here early and made a stake. Squatters and drifters broke John Sutter, when they over-ran his fort, then burned down his country house. Some others took a dislike to Abner Valentine, who had become a wealthy man. When he tried to run them off, they set fire to his barn and stables, and he was trampled to death by his own horses, trying to put the fire out.

Squatters nearly broke papa too, setting up tents, refusing to budge. One morning he looked out our kitchen window and saw a man he'd never seen before plowing the field right beside the house, getting ready to put in his own crop of wheat. It took papa years to drive off such fel-lows, cost him thousands, with many trips to court.

When I met my husband and got married, we lived there at the ranch, bringing up our children. It was after mama and papa and my husband had all passed away that we lost it, in a crooked deal engi-

neered by a lawyer papa thought we could rely on. One day we had a house and land we'd occupied for thirty years, the next day it was gone. It makes you wonder if we were supposed to own any land at all in that valley. I was widowed by then and had to move my family into a smaller place. Like mama starting west in the middle of her life, I had to begin again. But that is another story, one I'll save for another time.

Suffice to say, having raised my children and left those Santa Clara Valley years behind, I have been the one to complete this last little leg of our long passage, over the final ridge of the Coast Range, and end up perched here at the farthest edge. I watch surf splash upon the sand beyond the rail line that carries all the shoppers and travelers and beachgoers back and forth along the busy shore, and I think of the pouch papa used to carry. I have it here inside my son's house, on a shelf in a closet, with the papers still intact. It's about all we have left to show for the mark he made—his name on a street sign in downtown San Jose, and this pouch full of letters and deeds and agreements, some in English, some in Spanish, the pieces of paper large and small he collected along the way.

I think of mama and papa buried in San Jose, and grandma buried in Kansas beside the emigrant trail, and the generations of my forebears buried here and there across the land, Illinois, Virginia, North Carolina, as well as overseas in Ireland and Scotland and Poland and who knows where else. For a century my people moved, and I have stayed put longer than most. Still a newcomer, of course, compared with those who used to live around the borders of this lagoon taking shellfish from these beaches. Yet seventy-five years is long enough to feel connected to a place. The way a plant will suck up water from the soil to quench its own thirst, we nomad humans suck up something from wherever we decide to stop, and it feeds us. It feeds us. If only we could find a way to inhabit a place without having to possess it. It's possession that divides us, fills the squatter with resentment, sets a man against his neighbor, turns lawyers into millionaires.

Around our shoreside lagoon, flocks of waterfowl still congregate, geese and ducks and cormorants, reminding me that a hundred years ago there would have been a tribal gathering place around here somewhere, with so much wild game flying in, and all the clams and mussels and abalone to be collected too. So many lives were lived here before we arrived, and surely their spirits are among us, along the shore, in the mud of the lagoon, hovering above the water, perhaps the very spirit of whoever found this luminous piece of shell I hold. It could have come from our bay out there, where shellfish cling to rocky ledges, gathered up who knows when. It is like an old photograph of some long-gone time, of how the world looked years and years ago, though it is better than a photograph. It moves. It has its life. I move my hand just slightly, and the pearly colors move. The tiny curve of light shifts across the surface like a river finding its way to the sea.

A NOTE ABOUT THE AUTHOR

James D. Houston is the author of *Continental Drift, Love Life,* and *The Last Paradise,* honored with a 1999 American Book Award from the Before Columbus Foundation. Among his several nonfiction works is *Farewell to Manzanar,* coauthored with his wife, Jeanne Wakatsuki Houston, based upon her family's experience during and after the World War II internment. A former Wallace Stegner Fellow at Stanford, he has received the Humanitas Prize, an NEA writing grant, and a Rockefeller Foundation residency. He lives in Santa Cruz, California.

A NOTE ON THE TYPE

Pierre Simon Fournier *le jeune*, who designed the type used in this book, was both an originator and a collector of types. His services to the art of printing were his design of letters, his creation of ornaments and initials, and his standardization of type sizes. His types are old style in character and sharply cut. In 1764 and 1766 he published his *Manuel typographique*, a treatise on the history of French types and printing, on type-founding in all its details, and on what many consider his most important contribution to typography—the measurement of type by the point system.

Composed by Creative Graphics, Allentown, Pennsylvania
Printed and bound by Quebecor Printing, Fairfield, Pennsylvania
Designed by Robert C. Olsson

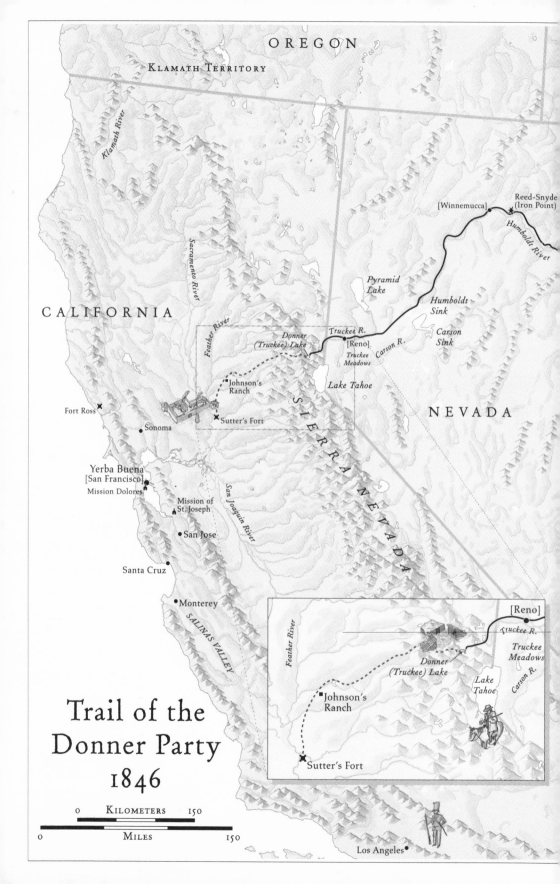

OREGON

KLAMATH TERRITORY

Klamath River

Sacramento River

CALIFORNIA

Feather River

Fort Ross ✕

Sonoma ●

Yerba Buena
[San Francisco] ●
Mission Dolores ♦

Mission of
St. Joseph ♦

● San Jose

San Joaquin River

Santa Cruz ●

● Monterey

SALINAS VALLEY

Reed-Snyde
(Iron Point) ✴

[Winnemucca] ●

Humboldt River

Pyramid
Lake

Humboldt
Sink

Carson
Sink

Truckee R.

Donner
(Truckee) Lake

[Reno] ●

*Truckee
Meadows*

Carson R.

Lake Tahoe

■ Johnson's
Ranch

✕ Sutter's Fort

SIERRA NEVADA

NEVADA

Trail of the
Donner Party
1846

[Reno] ●

Truckee R.

*Truckee
Meadows*

Feather River

Donner
(Truckee) Lake

Lake
Tahoe

Carson R.

■ Johnson's
Ranch

✕ Sutter's Fort

Los Angeles ●